THE DETECTIVE'S DAUGHTER

ERICA SPINDLER

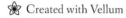

ONE

Rourke Conners

1994

4:05 P.M.

The Hudson Mansion, New Orleans, Louisiana

The first officers had already set up an outer perimeter, closing off one lane of St. Charles Avenue for a half a block in either direction of the scene. Traffic had slowed to a snarl and drivers were pissed. Sorry someone was dead, but damn, it *was* Friday afternoon, places to go, people to see.

Detective Rourke Conners held up his shield and the patrol cop waved him through the entrance gate. He parked in front of the stone mansion—arguably the most unique residence on The Avenue—but didn't cut the engine. In the drive around the side of the house, he saw several work vehicles—a painters' van, a landscape company truck, a couple battered looking pick-ups and an ADT security systems van.

Rourke drew in a deep breath, then took a quick glance in the rearview. He looked like shit. Red eyes. Dark circles under them. Lines around his mouth that hadn't been there a month ago.

He tightened his hands on the wheel, willing them not to shake. *Pull yourself the fuck together, man. It's go time.*

He cut the engine, then swung out of the car, mustering a confident swagger from memory. His partner had arrived right behind him, and Rourke met him halfway. Mikey Bruzeau was ninth ward, all the way. Or as Mikey would say, the 'nint' ward.

"Good to have you back, partner," Mikey said, slapping him on the back.

"Good to be back." They fell into step together. "Cleared for duty an hour ago."

"Just in time to make the party."

"Lucky me," Rourke muttered. "What do you know?"

"Not much. Vic's name is Cynthia Hudson, wife of Bill Hudson, the son of Charles Hudson."

"The oil and gas, real estate magnate Hudsons?"

"The very ones."

"Damn. That's one hell of a welcome-back party."

"I expect the chief will be making an appearance any moment."

Rourke inclined his head. "Makes sense. I'm surprised the press isn't all over this already."

As the words passed his lips, the first news outlet arrived—the FOX affiliate. A reporter jumped out before the van had completely come to a stop.

She ran to the gate. "Detectives! Any information you can share at this point?"

Ignoring her, they made their way up the azalea-lined walkway. All in bloom, the path was a riot of brilliant pink.

Rourke couldn't quite look at them. They reminded him too much of Maggie. She'd loved spring. Loved when the azaleas burst forth, covering the city in pink and white blossoms.

Fuck. He felt like he was drowning.

"How's Quinn?"

"Cries for her mother every night."

The words came out thick. Revealing.

"Damn, man, I'm sorry—"

"No." Rourke cleared his throat. "Don't be. Thanks for asking."

"If there's anything Betsy and I can do, we're here."

"Appreciate it."

They reached the palatial home's front entrance. Crime scene tape stretched across the door. At the sight of it, Rourke's heartbeat quickened, his palms began to sweat.

A fight or flight response. Considering his line of work, it was probably slowly killing him, but it gave him an edge on the job, too. The same response that made his adrenaline spike, heightened his senses. All of them.

They ducked under the tape, stepped inside. Cavernous. Ornate. The whoosh of a tomb—or of monied silence. The fireplace in the open seating area dead ahead was massive. As big as Quinn's nursery.

Rourke wandered toward it. The lemony scent of furniture polish stung his nose, mixing with the perfume wafting from the huge spray of blossoms in the entryway. A clock ticking, somewhere close.

He shifted his gaze; it landed on the couch. A magazine tossed carelessly aside. He crossed to it. *New Orleans Magazine,* open to a piece on the innovative, female chefs taking the city's restaurant scene by storm. A cigarette butt in an ashtray. Beside it, a rocks glass. Mostly empty save for melting ice. Rourke bent, sniffed. Whiskey.

From behind him, Mikey greeted the officer at the bottom of the staircase. "Yo, Peanut. What do we have?"

The small, fastidious man didn't seem to mind the moniker. "Dead female. Looks like a blow to the back of her head killed her."

"Who called it in?"

"Vic's father-in-law. He's pretty shaken up. He's waiting on the patio. The household staff is with him. Officer Pratt is keeping them all company."

"Don't let him go anywhere. Where is she?"

"Upstairs, then left."

Rourke rejoined his partner, nodded at Peanut. They started up the stairs. A huge tapestry occupied the wall to the left. Seemed a bit overblown, even for this place. But what did he know? He'd grown up in a small shotgun house in the Marigny neighborhood—way before the Marigny had become cool.

They reached the top floor and went left, heading toward the officer stationed outside an open door. He looked bored.

"Vic's in the ensuite," he said.

They entered the bedroom, then split up, Mikey heading toward the ensuite bathroom, Rourke hanging back. Rourke preferred to take in a scene solo. Put his own thoughts together before they were contaminated by those of others.

Rourke moved his gaze over the room. Cynthia Hudson had put up a hell of a fight. Drapes pulled from the rod. Bedside lamp shattered. Dresser drawers open, clothing strewn about.

The drawers gave the impression of a robbery, maybe interrupted in process. He drew his eyebrows together. If so, what had the perp been looking for?

He turned back to the bored sentinel. "Has a complete search of the home been done?"

"It has, Detective."

"Any of the other rooms disturbed?"

"Not that I saw, no."

Rourke nodded, turned back to the scene, gaze settling on the four-poster bed. The rumpled spread lay half on, half off. Like somebody had been trying to crawl over the bed and was dragged back. Rourke lowered his gaze. Something peeked out from under the bedskirt.

He fitted on scene gloves, squatted down, noting the carpet was wet. He slid his gaze. Flowers, purple and pretty, strew across the floor. Where was the vase? Making a mental note to look for it, he lifted the bedskirt and peered under. An open suitcase. He slid it out. It was empty save for a few T-shirts and a half a dozen pairs of panties.

"Find something?"

He looked over his shoulder at Mikey, standing in the doorway of the ensuite. "Maybe. Take a look."

He joined Rourke, then met his eyes. "Interesting."

"Yeah. I wonder where she was going?"

"Or maybe she was returning?"

Rourke frowned. "Maybe."

He stood, made his way into the master bathroom. Beauty products spread across the vanity counter, spilling over onto the floor. Cynthia Hudson, face down in front of the vanity. The back of her head was bashed in, blonde hair matted with blood. Spatter on the adjacent cabinetry. Low, close to the floor.

Rourke picked his way around the body. Location and trajectory of the blood spray indicated the perp hit her when she was already down.

He glanced over his shoulder, to the bedroom. The carpet had been wet. Flowers strewn across the thick pile.

He took in the area, visually sifting through the disarray. Whatever the perp used to kill her, he'd taken it with him.

He moved on, squatting beside her. One hand lay flat, fingers splayed. Like she had tried to break her fall. Nails, he noted, looked clean. No help there.

The other hand was curved into a fist. Rourke leaned closer to get a better look. No, not a fist. Something shiny peeking out from between her curved thumb and forefinger.

The tip of cuticle scissors. She had gone for something to protect herself. She'd never gotten the chance to use them.

Mikey appeared at the door. "Come check this out."

"You saw the scissors?"

"I did."

He started to stand, then stopped, noticing bruising on the victim's neck. He inched aside her shirt collar. More bruises, in a ring. Two that looked like thumbprints.

"Holy shit," Mikey muttered, "I missed that."

Rourke stood, stepped back from the victim. "The perp attacked her in the bedroom. She fought hard. My guess is, he got his hands around her neck, but she managed to get free. She runs in here, looking for something to defend herself with—"

"The scissors."

"Right, but she doesn't get the chance to use them. He follows her into the bathroom, knocks her down and whacks her on the back head, killing her."

"We may have a bigger problem," Mikey murmured.

Rourke frowned and followed him into the hallway, to the next room on the right. The door stood ajar.

Mikey nudged it the rest of the way open. Rourke's gaze travelled past Mikey, into the room. A nursery, outfitted in pink and white ruffles.

He crossed to the crib, took in the soft, pink blanket and stuffed toys. The abandoned pacifier. He pictured Quinn.

His blood went cold. He met his partner's gaze. "Where's the kid?"

TWO

Rourke felt sick to his stomach. There was no reason to expect the child was in danger. Nothing about the bed or room suggested violence had befallen her. The grandfather hadn't sounded the alarm.

Yet, something felt wrong here, something that caused his skin to crawl.

He turned in a slow circle, taking in every detail: rocking chair, changing table, more plush toys than any child could love, dresser topped with a Mother Goose lamp, framed photos and a sterling brush and comb set.

He crossed to the photos, examined each. All babies were beautiful, but this one seemed particularly so. In each photo, rosy cheeked and cherubic, with blue eyes and a head full of blonde curls. In another picture, a young and beautiful Cynthia Hudson, before someone had stolen her life from her. In another, the happy mother, child and father.

He picked up the sterling brush. It was engraved with an ornate *GAH.*

He set it down and turned to find Mikey watching him. "What?"

"You okay?"

"Why wouldn't I be?"

He shrugged. "I don't know, too close to home maybe?"

He bristled. "I can have a kid and be a cop."

Mikey held his gaze a moment, then nodded. "Life can be pretty messed up, that's all I'm saying."

He had that right. "I think it's time to have a chat with Mr. Charles Hudson."

CHARLES HUDSON SAT ALONE, shoulders bent, head in his hands. On the other end of the massive patio, a clutch of household staff huddled together, whispering.

Hudson looked up as they approached, then stood. Rourke saw he was tall and thin, with sharp, hawkish features and eyes that missed nothing. Despite the situation, he emanated strength.

Rourke wasn't surprised. You didn't control an empire like Hudson's by being weak or sloppy.

"You're going to get the animal who did this," he said fiercely. "You will make him pay."

"That's why we're here, Mr. Hudson." Rourke held out his hand. "I'm Detective Conners; this is Detective Bruzeau, and I promise you, we'll do our best."

"I don't accept that. Not good enough."

"Excuse me?"

"You heard me. I want this animal caught, drawn and quartered."

Mikey stepped in. "We understand that, Mr. Hudson. So I'm sure you'll do anything in your power to help us—"

Rourke cut him off. "The baby, where is she?"

He swung his gaze back to Rourke. "Grace? With the nanny."

"Her name?"

"Lucy Praxton."

"You're certain Grace is with her?"

Alarm flickered in his eyes. "Where else would she—" He turned, strode toward the group of household staff. "Mrs. Thompson," he called. "A word. Now."

The body language of everyone in the group changed. A woman with graying hair separated herself from the others and hurried to meet the older man, smoothing her skirt and jacket as she did.

She stopped before him; her lips trembled slightly. "Sir?"

"Is Grace with Miss Praxton?"

She looked terrified. "I don't know."

"Have you seen her today?"

"Grace or Miss Prax—"

"For God's sake! Miss Praxton!"

Rourke stepped in. "The child is not in her nursery. Mr. Hudson thought she might be with her nanny."

"She could be, of course. I did see Miss Praxton this morning. I'll page her immediately."

She hurried off and Rourke looked back at Charles Hudson. "Perhaps your granddaughter is with your wife?"

"Simone is in Paris, visiting family."

"When did she leave the country?"

"A week ago." He grimaced. "I don't know how I'll break this to her. She'll insist on returning immediately, of course."

"What about your son, Grace's father? Could she be with him?"

"That would be unusual, but not impossible. I sent my man Shaw to find him."

"To 'find' him?"

"He and Cynthia are building a house in Lake Vista. He went to check on progress there."

"When was that?"

"Sometime after lunch."

Now it was nearly dinnertime. "You haven't seen him since?"

"That's right."

"Have you spoken with him?"

"No, but there's no reason I should have—"

The housekeeper hurried back. "Lucy isn't responding."

"Keep trying."

Another staff member, this one male, approached with a phone. He held out the cordless handset. "Mr. Shaw on line one, sir."

Hudson took the phone. "Is Bill with you?" He paused then asked, "You told him about Cynthia?"

Rourke watched the man closely. Something about his reactions seemed off. Too composed, almost mechanical. It could be shock. Or maybe ice water ran through his veins.

"Is Grace with him?" he asked.

Hudson looked at them and shook his head.

Rourke swore softly, met his partner's concerned gaze. He knew Mikey's thoughts mirrored his: this could be a murder, kidnapping situation. Mikey tapped his radio, then jerked his head in the direction of the patio doors.

Time to call in the cavalry.

Rourke held out a hand. "Mr. Hudson, the phone."

He passed it over. "Mr. Shaw, this is Detective Conners, NOPD. Are you with Mr. Hudson now?"

"I am. He's—"

"Put him on the phone, please."

"He's in no condition—"

"Now."

The man expelled a sharp breath. Rourke suspected he wanted to argue, that he was accustomed to taking orders from no one but Hudson senior. He obviously thought better of it, because a moment later another man came on the phone; his voice choked.

"This is Bill Hudson."

"Detective Rourke Conners here. We're concerned for the safety of your infant daughter. Do you know where she is?"

"With the nanny. At least I think . . . Cynthia—" his voice cracked "—said something about a wellness visit with the pediatrician—"

He started to cry. The sound rang in Rourke's head as his own, deep sobs as he clung to Maggie's lifeless hand.

He cleared his throat, hanging on to his composure by a thread. "We're sending a cruiser for you. Stay put. Put Shaw back on."

A moment later, Shaw was on the line, voice rock solid. Rourke got the two men's location, then called for a cruiser.

"Was that really necessary?" Hudson asked, taking the phone.

"Was what necessary?"

"The cruiser. My man could have brought him here."

My man. Not associate. Not employee or assistant.

Distaste for Charles Hudson rippled over him. "Why would I want your son here?"

"Excuse me?"

"My partner and I need to question your son as soon as possible. The best place to do that is at police headquarters."

Two bright spots of color bloomed in the man's cheeks. "This is outrageous."

"I'm sorry you feel that way, Mr. Hudson, but this is the way it's going to be. You, on the other hand, we'll give a choice. Would you prefer to be questioned here? Or downtown?"

THREE

Charles Hudson chose to be questioned in his study, a large, luxuriously appointed room, complete with a sitting area, fireplace and bar. Hudson headed straight for a drink.

Rourke watched Hudson drop two cubes of ice into a rocks glass, then add whiskey. He noticed his hands shook.

"You don't mind if I partake?" he asked.

"Of course not. This is your home."

As Rourke expected, Hudson sat at his massive desk, no doubt for the psychological advantage it gave him.

Mikey began, tone conversational. "Mr. Hudson, I want to assure you we are taking every step we can to apprehend the individual who did this. A BOLO has been issued for your granddaughter's nanny and her vehicle. Major Crimes has been notified and will be on scene any moment, and additional detectives have been called in to question the staff. The crime scene investigators are here, as well as the coroner's investigator."

Rourke took over. "I understand you're the one who discovered your daughter-in-law?"

"That's right."

"What time was that?"

"I'd been out. I'd had several meetings today as well as lunch with my son. Mid-afternoon."

"Could you be more specific?"

"I cannot."

"I would have thought a man of your responsibilities would always be aware of the time."

"It's Friday. Frankly, my mind was on a cocktail and a few minutes of quiet before dressing for dinner."

"You had plans?"

"Dinner at the club with friends."

"When you arrived home, did you notice anything unusual?"

"When I pulled in, I saw Cynthia's car in the garage. That surprised me."

While he spoke, Hudson tipped his rocks glass ever so slightly from side to side. The light caught the ice's movement in the amber liquid. Rourke found his gaze drawn to it. "Why's that?"

"She and Bill were going away for the weekend."

The suitcase. Explained.

"Where were they headed?"

"We have a place in Destin. Nothing fancy, just a nice getaway."

Again, he fiddled with his glass, this time making the ice clink against the sides. Rourke realized that Hudson had not yet taken a sip.

"They were under a lot of pressure," he murmured. "An infant, building a house . . . business pressures."

"How was their marriage?"

"Excuse me?"

Rourke looked down at his notebook, then back up at Hudson. "Like you said, that's a lot of pressure to be under. Less can tear a young couple apart."

"Their marriage was solid, Detective."

"Then nobody was having an affair?"

He stiffened. Angry spots of color stained his cheeks. "They were very much in love."

Mikey spoke up. "How long were they married?"

"Three years next month."

Mikey nodded, expression amicable. "Practically newlyweds."

That's how he and Mikey worked best. Rourke asked the hard questions; Mikey kept it easy breezy. Sometimes he got tired of being the asshole, but most of the time he liked being able to say what he thought.

"Exactly." He glared at Rourke. "I resent the insinuation."

"Just doing my job."

Mikey smiled, gestured to a photo on the desk. "How old is little Grace? She sure is a cutie."

"Six months."

Rourke stepped back in. "A lot of work trucks were here when we arrived. What are you having done?"

"A property the size and age of this one always has something being updated or repaired. I'd have to speak to the housekeeper about the specific—"

He stopped, eyes widening. "Oh my God. You don't think one of the workmen . . . that they . . ." His voice trailed off helplessly.

"It's a possibility. We'll have a full list of everyone who was on the property by the end of the day. You have a security system, Mr. Hudson?"

"Of course. Alarm, motion detectors, closed circuit surveillance cameras at the front and back."

"Does someone monitor them?"

"At night. Intermittently during the day."

"The system records and stores the footage?"

"It does. I'll make it available to you immediately." He reached for his phone, then stopped. He looked at Mikey, then Rourke, his expression horrified.

"Have you remembered something, Mr. Hudson?"

"We were having the entire system updated today." He ran a

hand through his hair, a movement that seemed uncharacteristic for the man. "It was off. The entire system was down. Dammit!"

He pushed violently back from the desk and launched to his feet, strode to the window, stared out. "Son of a bitch!"

Rourke gazed at the man's ramrod-straight back. If someone had a plan, today would have been the day to execute it. "Who knew the update was happening today?"

"The family. The entire staff. The security company." He looked over his shoulder at them. "This is bad, isn't it?"

"It's not good," Mikey agreed, "but it doesn't mean we won't catch the guy. It'll just slow us down."

"Mr. Hudson, how did you happen to go find your daughter-in-law's body?"

"Like I said, I knew she was here, figured she was running late, finishing packing. I didn't think much more about it, and fixed a cocktail."

"What prompted you to go upstairs and look for her?"

"The quiet and the fact that quite a bit of time passed with no sign of her. I decided to go check on her, say hello. Truthfully, I thought—" He cleared his throat "—that I was wrong, that she and Bill had left for the beach."

"What happened next, Mr. Hudson?"

"I tapped on the door. It wasn't shut tight, and it opened . . . As soon as I saw, I knew—"

His eyes filled with tears. He blinked against them, looking furious with himself for the show of emotion.

Rourke waited. After several moments, Hudson pulled himself together and started again. I made my way in . . . She was there, on the floor." He flexed his fingers. "My poor son . . . he didn't deserve this."

"What about her?" Rourke asked softly. "Did she deserve it?"

His mouth thinned. "What the hell kind of question is that?"

"What did you think of your daughter-in-law?"

"I resent what you're insinuating."

"I'm not insinuating anything. It's a simple question."

"She was a lovely girl. I was very happy with Bill's choice."

At his hip, Rourke's pager vibrated. He checked it. *Dispatch.*

"Could I use your phone?"

"Of course." Hudson motioned it.

Rourke dialed. "This is Conners." He listened to the dispatcher, a feeling of anticipation coming over him. "We'll be there as soon as possible."

He replaced the receiver, turned to Hudson. "Mr. Hudson, we have to cut this short. Thank you for your time."

"I'm done?"

"I'm certain that we or one of our associates will need to question you further, but for now, yes."

Hudson stood, came around the desk. "That call, was it about Cynthia? What's happened?"

"I'm sorry but I can't discuss it."

Hudson grabbed his arm. "Is it about my granddaughter?"

Rourke looked the man dead in the eyes. "Sir, take your hand off me."

He did but didn't move back or break eye contact. "I have a right to know."

"You do. But until I have information that I've personally verified, it would be irresponsible of me to share it."

"Just so you know, I'm friends with the mayor. Hell, I was at the governor's daughter's wedding. If I want something, I get it."

"I'm sure you do. We'll be in touch, Mr. Hudson."

As soon as they exited the house, Mikey glanced his way. "What's happened?"

"Bill Hudson and his lawyer have arrived and are waiting for us."

"You couldn't have told Hudson that?"

"Sure, I could have. I chose not to." They made their way down the flower-lined walk. "Wanted to see how the old man reacted. Besides, that's not the only thing I learned on that call."

"Has Lucy Praxton been located?"

"Nope. But a judge approved a search warrant for her residence, and it's in the hands of the officer on scene. I say we head that way and let Hudson junior and his attorney cool their heels for a bit."

Mikey smiled. "I like the way you think."

They reached the end of the walkway; Mikey lowered his voice. "Hudson senior, you think he might be our guy?"

Rourke thought a moment, letting the question settle in hard. "It's possible but in my opinion, doubtful."

"How come?"

They ducked under the outer perimeter tape and passed through the iron gate to the sidewalk. "Way too much emotion involved in that murder. Charles Hudson is one cold customer."

Mikey made a sound of agreement. "It'd be more likely he'd hire someone to do it for him. Wouldn't want blood on his hands."

"Right," Rourke said. "At least not that people could see."

FOUR

5:35 *P.M.*

Rourke pulled up in front of Lucy Praxton's Uptown double, parked and cut the engine. Mikey parked right behind him. He climbed out, collected his partner and together they crossed to the unmarked squad car directly across from them.

The officer lowered the window as they approached. "Any sign of her?" Rourke asked, stooping to meet the man's eyes.

"None." He handed Rourke the warrant. "Praxton's landlord lives in the unit on the left. He's home and said he'd let you in when you arrived. Name's Chris Phillips."

Rourke nodded, took the warrant and slid it into his inside jacket pocket. "Keep a close watch, in case she shows."

"You got it."

A couple minutes later the nervous-looking landlord unlocked the door. "Is Lucy in some sort of trouble?" he asked, swinging the door wide.

"That's what we're trying to figure out. We'll need to ask you a few questions later, do you mind hanging around?"

"I'm grading papers, so I won't be going anywhere. Just knock."

They thanked him and entered the residence. "I'll start in back," Mikey offered and headed that way.

Rourke turned in a slow circle, taking the space in, looking for the thing that was wrong to jump out at him. The way he figured it, they were working with a couple possible scenarios here. Either Praxton was in on it—or she was dead. After all, she had left with the child that morning and hadn't been heard from since.

Of course, there was always the chance that she had been involved in it but was now dead. As the old saying went, there was no honor among thieves.

He moved his gaze over the interior. Her style was feminine and neat, with cozy-looking furniture in soft fabrics and soothing colors. A vase of fading flowers sat on the coffee table. He fitted on scene gloves and crossed to it, plucked the card out of its clip.

For everything.
L, JP

What was 'everything,' he wondered. Love? Forgiveness? Hot sex? Or could it be referring to something darker? Like cooperation in a crime?

Rourke made his way to the bookshelves, scanned the titles. Everything from romance novels to childrearing to relationship self-help; some texts appeared brand new, others were dog-eared. Not the library one expected of a hardened criminal or wannabe kidnapper.

He pulled out each book, flipped through their pages, finding nothing tucked into those pages but a year-old birthday horoscope clipped from the newspaper and a bookmark from the Garden District Bookshop.

After checking drawers, decorative boxes and under couch cushions, he headed for the kitchen. Three photos were fixed to the refrigerator, held by magnets in the shape of flowers: a peony, a daisy and a sunflower. Two of the photos were of her and baby Grace, the third of her and a bearded man in an LSU ball cap.

Rourke studied the photo of her and the man. Between the beard and ball cap he couldn't get a clear view of his face, but from what he could see he looked to be a similar age to Praxton, somewhere in his early thirties. The two were obviously romantically involved, judging by the intimate way they were posed, cheek-to-cheek and smiling broadly at the camera.

Was this the JP of the flowers? Most probably. A woman wouldn't have one man's flowers on the table and another man's photo on the fridge.

He shifted his gaze to the photos of her and Grace. Judging by her loving expression, if he didn't know better, he would think them photos of a mother with her own child.

Rourke felt the frown forming between his eyebrows, the tickle of unease that went with it. How attached did nannies become to their charges? Sometimes so attached they couldn't let go? That they would do anything to make the child theirs? Even commit murder?

"What'd you find?"

Rourke looked over his shoulder at Mikey. "Flowers from someone named J.P. A photograph here of her and a guy, most probably J.P., and a couple more of her and Grace Hudson."

Mikey sauntered over. "There were a couple of her and the kid on her bed table, too."

"Maybe Praxton got too close to the baby?" Rourke murmured. "Started thinking she was hers, you know?"

Mikey nodded. "Maybe she and Cynthia had words. Could be she threatened to fire her, something like that?"

"Praxton snaps. Could happen." Rourke circled back to the photos. "Any pictures of her and the guy in the bedroom?"

"Not that I saw. There was a post-it on the bathroom mirror—Dinner with John Paul. 7:00."

"No date?"

He shook his head.

"I'm going to take a look." Rourke indicated the rear of the home and headed in that direction. Two bedrooms, he saw. One and a half baths. He checked out the powder room first, then the main bathroom. Compared to Cynthia Hudson, Lucy Praxton appeared to be a simple, no-frills kind of girl. A couple lipsticks, a small clutch of cosmetics, one perfume.

The guest bedroom came next. Obviously, she didn't host often—the room had no bed and a dozen sealed moving boxes took up a third of the space.

Was she planning a move, he wondered? Or were these still unopened from her move to this address?

Her bedroom reinforced his initial assessment of her style preferences. No glamour or frou-frou; of her six pair of shoes, there wasn't a high heel in the bunch. A pearl necklace was the flashiest item in her jewelry box.

As Mikey had already indicated, there were two framed photos of her and baby Grace by the bed, but also what looked like a family portrait on the dresser—pictured with what he assumed was her mom, dad, brother and a sister.

He slid out the bed table's small drawer. Condoms. A small notebook and a pen. He flipped through it, hoping for diary type entries—or a detailed kidnapping plan—but finding to-do lists, phone numbers, and daily menu plans instead.

As he went to put it away, he noticed the edge of a photo peeking out from under a Chinese take-out menu.

He slid it out, caught his breath. It was a picture of Bill Hudson.

"Rourke?"

He looked at his partner, standing in the doorway, held the photo out. "Look what I found."

Mikey came closer, whistled under his breath. "Bill Hudson? I did not see that coming."

"Me either." Rourke tucked it back into the drawer, placing it exactly as he'd found it.

"You think the two are having an affair?"

"Let's have a quick chat with the landlord, then we can ask Mr. Hudson that ourselves."

FIVE

Lucy Praxton's landlord invited them in. "Can I get you a coffee or anything?" he asked.

"We're good," Mikey said. "Thanks."

Rourke followed his partner across the threshold. "We won't take a lot of your time." He motioned the stack of papers. "You look busy."

"Always." He pushed his tortoise shell rim glasses up to the bridge of his nose. "I'm an associate professor at Tulane."

"What subject?" Mikey asked.

"Anthropology."

"Bones and stuff?"

The hint of a smile tugged at the corners of the man's mouth. "The study of human societal and cultural development and adaptations."

Mikey mock-grimaced. "That's a mouthful."

Rourke stepped in. "Have you been at the university long?"

"Five years."

"You live alone?"

He frowned slightly. "I do, but I don't know why that should matter to you."

Rourke ignored the comment. "How long has Lucy Praxton rented from you?"

"About a year and a half." He shifted his gaze from Rourke to Mikey and back. "What's going on? She's okay, right?"

"We hope so, Mr. Phillips. How well do you know her?"

"Not very well. She keeps to herself, a quality I appreciate in a tenant. She pays her rent on time and doesn't bother me unless it's an emergency."

"Do you know who her employer is?"

He looked surprised by the question. "I don't. I know she's a nanny. She used to work for the public school system but gave it . . ." His voice trailed off; his eyes widened. "Does she work for that family . . . the one in the news today?"

"The Hudson family. Yes, she does."

He suddenly looked uncomfortable. "Like I said, I hardly knew her."

"Did she ever talk with you about the child she cared for?"

"We really never spoke other than a 'good morning' or if there was something she needed me to take care of." He paused. "She had a baby with her at her place a few times, I figured she was babysitting or something."

"Notice anything else?"

His brow furrowed in thought. "Yeah, that she seemed to light up when the kid was there. Kind of made her come out of her shell."

An image of Maggie with Quinn popped into his head. The two of them on the floor, a stack of brightly colored blocks between them, Maggie looking up when he walked in, her eyes shining with love and happiness.

Phillips folded his arms across his chest. "Look, I've got a lot of grading to finish tonight—"

"When she was here with the baby, did they stay awhile?"

"I think they hung out. I heard her singing."

"Singing?"

"Yeah. Old McDonald, stuff like that."

"Sweet." Rourke made a note. "Is there anything else you can share?"

"Other than her taste in men, she seems like a really nice woman."

Rourke met his eyes. "What about her taste in men?"

He shrugged. "The guy she was dating . . . he was kind of a hard ass."

"Hard ass, what do you mean by that?"

"You know those guys, a bit of a bully, more swagger than substance. They had an argument a week or so ago. I heard them through the walls and didn't like the way he spoke to her."

Rourke resisted the urge to look at Mikey. "Did the argument turn violent?"

He shook his head. "If that had happened, I would have called you guys."

"Did you catch what they were arguing about?"

He shook his head. "I heard a word here and there, all from him. I'm pretty sure he called her stupid and weak."

"Sounds like a hell of a guy," Mikey muttered.

"That's what I thought."

"Had they been seeing each other long?" Rourke asked, redirecting to the interview.

"Several months, but that's a guess."

"You wouldn't happen to know his name?"

"Actually, I do. He owns a car repair place and gave me his card. I'll get it."

A moment later the man returned with the card:

Russo's Automotive Repair
Owner John Paul Russo

Rourke handed the card to Mikey, who tucked it into his pocket. "Thank you, Mr. Phillips, we may be back in touch."

It wasn't until they'd reached their vehicles that Rourke spoke. "Let's locate Mr. Russo and send a car to pick him up. Who knows, maybe Praxton and the baby are with him?"

SIX

Second District Station

Rourke paused outside the interview room door, taking a moment to mentally prepare himself for whatever came at him. In that room was a man whose wife was dead. A man who may or may not have been the one who killed her. Either way, he needed to be on top of his game.

He felt far from that. Like a million, fucking miles.

He breathed deeply through his nose, pushing aside thoughts of Maggie and Quinn, of the dark chasm his life had become. He focused on the questions he needed to ask, ticking through them in his head. Reminding himself of the things he needed to look for in the man's answers to those questions. His body language. His eyes. How they moved. When. The sound of his breathing. It all mattered. It all told the real story.

He glanced at Mikey, who nodded slightly, then opened the door. They stepped inside.

"Gentlemen," Mikey said, "thank you for waiting."

Both men stood, turned toward him and Mikey. They looked

hopping mad.

Rourke took the lead. "I'm Detective Conners, this is my partner, Detective Bruzeau."

The one in a suit spoke first. "I'm Daniel Shaw, the Hudson family attorney. Is this your idea of a sick joke?"

Rourke arched his eyebrows. "Excuse me?"

"We've been waiting two *hours*, Detective. My client has suffered an inconceivable loss and you treat him like some common *criminal*? It's outrageous."

"I'm sorry if our timing is inconvenient to you, Mr. Shaw. Active investigations aren't polite. Besides, I'm sure your client would prefer us to be out hunting for his wife's killer than here making certain he's comfortable." Rourke turned his gaze to the younger man. "Isn't that right, Mr. Hudson?"

Physically, Bill Hudson couldn't have been more different than his father. Where Charles Hudson was tall, trim, and narrow-shouldered, Bill Hudson was built like a block. Not overweight, just square from his neck down. The kind of guy you definitely wanted on your tackle football team.

The dissimilarity didn't stop there. The younger Hudson was an emotional wreck. His eyes were bloodshot, his face blotchy. His hair was a mess, and his white Oxford cloth shirt was untucked—and stained with something that might be vomit.

"I'm sorry for your loss, Mr. Hudson."

He nodded, then looked away, not speaking.

Overcome with emotion? Rourke wondered. Or under orders from his lawyer?

Shaw drew him aside, spoke low. "Is this really necessary right now, Detective? As you can see, my client is devastated."

"Understandably. But as you know, it is essential. I promise, we'll make this as quick and painless as possible."

"We appreciate that, but at the very least, couldn't we change venue? Doing this at his home would be so much less traumatic."

"We're here now, Mr. Shaw. How about we get this over with?"

Rourke turned back to Bill Hudson. "For your protection and ours, Mr. Hudson, we're taping this interview."

On cue, Mikey crossed to the camera mounted in the corner and switched it on. Hudson turned to the lawyer, expression alarmed. "Daniel?"

"It's okay, Bill. He's right, it's for everybody's protection. Plus, you have nothing to hide."

He nodded, took his seat. Shaw positioned himself to his left, within close earshot.

Mikey stepped in. "Can I get anybody anything? Coffee? Soft drink? Water?"

Always the comfort engineer. He and Mikey joked about that and the fact that he was the *dis*comfort engineer.

They both declined, and Rourke took the seat directly across from Hudson. Mikey hung back, leaning against the door, positioning himself for a clear view of Bill Hudson's face.

Rourke began. "Mr. Hudson, you are aware of what occurred this afternoon at your St. Charles Avenue home?"

He moved his head in agreement, eyes downcast, throat working. "Cynthia is . . . dead. Someone . . . killed her."

Shaw laid a hand on his shoulder, squeezed. Made a sound of sympathy.

Everyone playing their part, Rourke thought, including him. "When was the last time you saw your wife?"

"This morning."

"What did you talk about?"

Hudson's leg jerked. "Our trip to the beach."

"That's all?"

"Baby Grace and how much we would—" He dropped his head into his hands.

"Detectives," Shaw said, "I really have to protest. This man is clearly in no state to continue."

Rourke ignored the lawyer and resumed. "Take your time, Mr. Hudson. We know how difficult this must be. You were talking with your wife about your daughter?"

"How much we were going to miss her. It was. . . the . . . first time we were going to leave her for the weekend."

Maggie, fussing over Quinn. Anxious. "A whole weekend, Rourke? I don't know if I can bear it."

Rourke dragged his thoughts back to Mr. Hudson, his line of questioning. "You and your wife were going away for the weekend and leaving your baby behind?"

He didn't meet Rourke's eyes. Guilt over leaving his child for the weekend? Or something else?

"With Lucy and my dad," he said.

"Lucy?"

"Miss Praxton," Shaw offered. "Has she been located?"

Mikey stepped in. "If she hasn't been yet, she will be soon. Every patrol car in the city is looking for her."

"How well did you know her?" Rourke asked.

"I'm sorry—" He dragged a hand through his rumpled hair. "—what?"

"Lucy," Rourke said, deliberately using the nanny's given name. "How well did you know her?"

Shaw answered. "She was thoroughly vetted, Detective. I took care of it myself."

"I wasn't asking you, Mr. Shaw. Please allow your client to answer the questions. Mr. Hudson?"

"Like he said, he would have taken care of that."

"Were you intimately involved with her?"

"Detective!" Shaw exclaimed. "That was out of line."

"Was it?" He opened the folder on his desk, to a photo of Lucy Praxton, a pretty blonde with pert features and an infectious smile. "We're all grown-ups here. Things happen."

"I loved my wife, Detective. Period."

"What would you say if I told you we found a photo of you in Miss Praxton's bedroom?"

Hudson's face went bread dough white. "That's . . . impossible."

"Why's that?"

"I hardly knew the woman."

"Yet you allowed her to care for your daughter."

"Because she was thoroughly vetted!"

"Detective, I hardly see how a photograph of my client found at the home of one of his employees is relevant to this line of questioning."

"Really?" Rourke arched his eyebrows in exaggerated disbelief. "The employee who cared for his child? The same employee who is the last known person to be with that child, the one who is currently missing?"

Rourke leaned forward. "Could it be that Lucy Praxton had feelings for you, Mr. Hudson? Feelings she thought were returned? Maybe when she learned they weren't, she took matters into her own hands? Killed your wife and kidnapped your child?"

"If she did, I had nothing to do with it! I didn't sleep with her!"

"My apologies," Rourke said, tone mild. "I hope you understand we have to explore every possible lead?"

"Of course." Hudson's voice shook. He glanced at Shaw as if for approval. "Do you . . . think that's what happened? That Lucy killed Cynthia and has Grace?"

"We don't know yet. Like I said, we're exploring every angle." Rourke shuffled through his notes. "How was your wife's relationship with Miss Praxton?"

"Good."

"Were the two close? Did your wife confide in her?"

"I . . . don't . . . about Grace, of course. Otherwise . . . she was an employee, Detective."

"She was happy with Miss Praxton's service?"

"Yes."

"As far as you know, they hadn't argued?"

"No."

"She hadn't mentioned any issues?"

"No . . . I—" He brought a hand to his head. "Right now, I . . . This is too much. I can't think straight."

"Are we done here, Detectives? As you can see, my client—"

"Not quite." Rourke shifted his gaze back to Bill Hudson. "Where were you this afternoon?"

"I had lunch with Dad."

"What time was that?"

"Early. Eleven-thirty or so."

"Is that a Rolex you're wearing?"

He glanced at his wrist. "Yeah. A Submariner."

"Beautiful watch. If I had one of those, I'd always know what time it was."

He flushed. "Around eleven-thirty. That's the best I can do."

"You and your father had lunch. Where did you eat?"

"Our club."

"Which is?"

"The Boston Club."

It figured. The Boston was the oldest private club in the city. Secretive, elite, and men-only, thank you very much.

"What did you eat?"

"A club sandwich."

"Did you have an alcoholic beverage with lunch?"

"Why does it matter?"

"Answer the question, Mr. Hudson."

"A gin and tonic."

"Just one?"

"A couple." Rourke made a note. "What next?"

"I went to check on our new house. We're building in the Lake Vista area."

"What time did you leave the club?"

"Again, this isn't exact. One, one-thirty."

"It takes that long to eat a club sandwich?"

"Dad and I had business to discuss."

He let that pass. The club would have records to confirm or contradict his timeline. "After lunch you headed for Lake Vista?"

"Yes."

"Any stops?"

"None."

"Not even to fuel up, make a call, nothing like that?"

"No, no stops."

"From downtown, with no stops, you're in Lake Vista about a half hour later, give or take a few minutes." He inclined his head; Rourke went on. "Your contractor can corroborate?"

He glanced at Shaw. Nervously, Rourke thought.

"No. I was alone."

"Alone?"

"We're so close to completion." He unclasped his hands, dropped them to his lap. "It's mostly finishing work now. Getting the subs out there has been a big problem. You know how it is."

Hudson seemed to be hitting his stride, his speech and story falling into a practiced rhythm.

"No, actually I don't." Rourke looked over his shoulder at his partner. "You know how that is, Mikey?"

"Nope."

Hudson frowned. "Well, it is."

"We'll take your word for it. You're out there all alone. You walk through the place, then what?"

"Shaw shows up."

Rourke arched his eyebrows. "How long were you there?"

"A while."

"A while," he repeated, reviewing the timeline in his head. "Alone the whole time? What, you take a nap or something?"

He bristled. "I made notes for the contractor . . . things left to do and others that had been done in an unsatisfactory manner. That takes time."

"You have that list?"

"We do," Shaw said, taking a folded piece of paper from his pocket. He handed it to Rourke.

Rourke scanned it. The paper had been ripped out of a spiral notebook. The sheet wasn't crisp or clean, but slightly battered, coated with builder's dust. The notations had been made in black ink. "I'll need to keep this."

"Of course." Shaw glanced at his watch. "Do you have any other questions for us?"

"I want to go over this timeline again, make certain I have it right." Rourke looked over his shoulder at Mikey. "Yo, Mikey, did you write any of this down?"

"Course I did, Partner."

"The timeline, read it back. We've got to make certain we've got this right."

Mikey complied. "You met your father for lunch, eleven-thirty or so. Left The Boston Club at one, one-thirty and drove directly to Lake Vista. A half hour, give or take. You take notes, then Shaw arrives."

Rourke turned his gaze on to the lawyer. "What time would that have been, Mr. Shaw?"

"Four-thirty."

"You're certain about that time?"

"Of course."

Rourke turned back to Hudson. "You were alone in your unfinished, unfurnished home for two, two and a half hours? That's what you want to go with?"

"It's the truth!"

"How was your marriage, Mr. Hudson?"

Hudson's eyes flooded with tears, his Adam's apple worked. "My marriage was perfect. Cynthia . . . was perfect. I don't know what—" He struggled to find the right words. "—how I'm going to . . . go on without her."

Rourke understood. God, he understood. He'd felt the same way every day since losing Maggie.

Then why didn't he feel an ounce of compassion for this man?

"May I see your hands, Mr. Hudson?"

"My hands? I don't—"

"Your wife was brutally murdered in her bedroom. It may sound shocking to you, but more often than not a crime like this is perpetrated by a family member."

"My God—" He recoiled. "—you're not suggesting that I . . . could hurt my wife?"

Of course he was, and everyone in the room knew it, including Bill Hudson. "Of course not, Mr. Hudson. We're eliminating suspects. That's what we do. We eliminate those closest to the victim, then we widen the net."

"Go ahead, Bill. You've got nothing to hide."

He nodded, held them out. They trembled. Rourke inspected the fronts, then the backs. They were clean.

"Satisfied?"

"Not quite. One last thing, Mr. Hudson. Could you remove your shirt?"

"This is too much!" Shaw said. "You want my client to remove his shirt? Charge him with a crime."

Rourke ignored the attorney's posturing, his gaze not wavering from the younger man's. "Your wife put up quite a fight, I imagine she got a few licks in. Perp's most probably sporting a few bruises."

"Whatever it takes, Detective. I didn't kill my wife."

He stood, removed his shirt and handed it to the lawyer.

"Arms out, please."

He complied. Rourke took his time, inspecting every inch of his torso, front and back. He was clean.

This didn't feel right. None of it.

"You can put your shirt back on."

"That was humiliating." Hudson snatched his shirt from Shaw's hands. "Happy now?"

"Happy, Mr. Hudson? A woman is dead, viciously murdered in her own bedroom. I won't be happy until I find out who did it."

SEVEN

Rourke turned into the driveway of his small, Lakeview neighborhood home. He'd bought the single story, brick ranch with part of Maggie's life insurance payout. They'd taken out policies after Quinn was born. He'd argued with her about the need for one to cover her. Insure him, sure. He was the breadwinner.

She'd argued the opposite. How was he going to take care of Quinn if something happened to her? In the end he'd agreed, more to appease her than the thought that anything could happen to her.

He couldn't help wondering: if he hadn't acquiesced, would she still be alive? As if they had somehow tempted fate by taking out that policy. Or had she known, on some deep, instinctual level that something was wrong with her?

Weary to his bones, he climbed out of the car. A hot shower, he thought. A shot of whiskey, then bed and, hopefully, a few hours of sleep before he had to get back at it.

They'd been unable to locate John Paul Russo. His home and business had both been dark. They had located an employee who said that Russo had been in the shop early that morning, then had taken the rest of the day off, no explanation.

Rourke massaged the bridge of his nose, the knot of tension there. The guy had a record, one that included sexual assault. He feared this case was going to get worse before it got better.

He unlocked the front door, stepped into the small entryway. His mom, he saw, was asleep on the couch. He gazed at her, affection and gratitude swamping him. He didn't know what he'd have done without her and his dad. In fact, he'd chosen this house for two reasons, its excellent public schools and the fact that it was located down the street from them.

As if she felt his presence, she opened her eyes.

"Hey Mom."

"What time is it?"

"Not too bad. About eleven-thirty."

She frowned slightly. "You're working that big case, aren't you? The Hudson murder."

Although no ransom request had come in, but because neither the nanny nor baby had been found, internally they were calling it a kidnapping investigation as well.

She sat up, automatically smoothing her hair, the way he had seen her do hundreds of times before. "You have any leads yet?"

"You know I can't discuss an active investigation." He watched as she refolded the quilt. "You might as well stay. I'll have to be out of here really early."

She looked over her shoulder at him. "How early?"

"Seven or so. Unless I get called in earlier."

"Quinn needs to see you in the morning."

"I'll do my best, Mom. You know that."

"I do." Her tone turned cautious. "But I'm not sure you . . . understand how much she needs you, Rourke. Her mommy is gone and—"

"You don't think I understand that? Seriously? It's my job, Mom. What would you have me do?"

"Quit. Find another one. A nine-to-five. Quinn's going to need a stable home life."

She was right. He shouldn't be angry; she only had Quinn's best interests at heart, but he was. Not only at her, but at the whole fucked-up world as well. "And do what, Mom? Be a security guard somewhere? Be a mall cop?"

"Why not?" she challenged. "It's honest work. "Your dad's done honest work all his life."

"What about my pension? Gone. How about insurance? Gone. How much do you think a security gig pays? In this economy, not enough to raise a child—" his voice thickened "—alone."

She crossed to him, laid a hand on his arm. "You're not alone, Rourke. We'll make do. We'll get through this."

He shook off her hand. "There's no 'we'll get through this.' It's me and Quinn. We were a 'we' with Maggie but she's gone."

She looked as if he'd struck her; tears sparkled in her eyes.

He regretted the words, lashing out at her that way, but he couldn't take them back. "I'm sorry, Mom. I appreciate everything you and Dad are doing. Quinn loves you a lot."

"I love her, too. You know that." She took a deep breath. "You dreamed of opening a restaurant once, maybe—"

"With Maggie."

"I think she'd like that. She'd—"

"Mom! Enough. We've talked about this before. I'm done with this conversation."

Breathe, Rourke. Deep and even. She's not the enemy.

"Look, it was an intense day; I'm dead on my feet."

She nodded. "I'm going to head home."

"It's so late, stay. I promise not to bark at you anymore."

"Your dad likes me home." She patted his arm, the way she had done since he was a kid. "I'll be up early. Call me."

He walked her to the door, watched her climb into her Toyota Corolla and back down the drive. He could see her driveway from his front door; he didn't return inside until her saw her in it.

He shut the door, then headed for the kitchen, retrieved his bottle of Jameson and poured himself a stiff shot. He downed it and poured a second. He lingered over it, thoughts churning, fatigue gnawing.

Could he have been any more of a dick to his mother? Jesus, help him. Maybe he *should* quit. Get hired by one of the local universities.

The thought of it made him squirm. He threw back the second shot. It burned going down, the same way the idea of giving up a job he was good at and loved.

Quinn was more important. The most important.

Rourke stood, weaving slightly; more the effect of exhaustion than the booze. He rinsed his glass, then put the bottle back in the pantry, the third shelf up, away from little hands.

He made his way to the back of the house, turning off lights as he went. He stopped at Quinn's door. The glow from the Minnie Mouse night light fell over his daughter's sleeping face. She was so tiny in her first big-girl bed, a twin with guard rails so she wouldn't roll off in the middle of the night.

She was so beautiful. Just looking at her brought a surge of protectiveness. It rose up in him, pressing at his chest. Making him ache.

He tiptoed across the room, knelt beside the bed, tenderly brushing a red curl back from her forehead. She'd gotten Maggie's strawberry hair and hazel eyes; another reason that every time he looked at her, he thought of Maggie.

Tears stung, and he blinked furiously against them. A man's job was to protect his family. To take care of and provide for them. Lead.

He hadn't been able to do that for Maggie.

He would for Quinn. Nothing else mattered.

―――――――

THE PHONE DRAGGED Rourke out of a deep sleep. "Maggie?" he answered.

"Wake up, partner. It's me."

The image of Maggie disappeared, leaving behind a gaping loss. "What time is it?"

"Six." He paused. "They found the nanny's car."

Rourke sat up, struggling to shake off the cobwebs but hold onto the sweetness of his dream. In it, he and Maggie were together—and it'd been the cancer that hadn't been real. He couldn't do both—and a part of him wanted to die, too.

"She's dead," Mikey went on. "Single gunshot to the head."

Fully awake now, Rourke swung his legs over the side bed and stood. "What about the kid?"

"Gone."

The worst-case scenario. "Fuck."

"You got that right. The Feds, Major Crimes, everybody's in it now."

"Where?"

"Tangipahoa Parish."

"Pick me up?"

"On my way already."

EIGHT

7:40 A.M.

Mikey rolled to a stop behind a Tangipahoa Parish cruiser, its blue lights flashing. The crime scene van had also arrived, and it looked like the Major Crime guys were already inspecting the abandoned Buick Skylark, pulled off to the side of this deserted stretch of bayou near the fishing village of Manchac.

Rourke glanced at his watch, thinking of Quinn. Afraid he wouldn't make it home again before her bedtime, he'd quickly dressed then awakened her. They'd sat in the rocker, her snuggling against him as he sang "Old MacDonald Had a Farm." She always giggled wildly when he made the pig sounds.

It had been perfect until he'd had to go. She'd clung to him, crying and asking for her mommy. His mother had had to pry her arms from around his neck.

It had re-broken his heart, all over again.

Mikey glanced at Rourke. "You ready?"

Rourke blinked and came crashing back to the moment. He nodded and they simultaneously opened their doors and stepped out.

The sun struggled to penetrate the heavy canopy of trees, and near the water's edge a pelican screeched its disapproval as their feet crunched against the gravel.

"Yo, Partner, time to suit up."

Mikey held out a package containing a Tyvek coverall. Rourke took it and slipped it on.

"Booties, too." Mikey motioned to a box outside the inner perimeter, delineated by scene tape.

Outdoor crimes were particularly difficult to process because of the uncontrollable aspects of the weather and the nature of the surrounding area. It was often like finding a needle in a haystack, and the last thing they wanted to do was bring additional debris to the scene. Especially hair or fiber.

Rourke nodded and collected a pair. A moment later he ducked under the yellow tape and made his way to the Buick.

The closer he came, the more the scene took on the quality of a carnival midway. The warm, sticky air. The flashing, swirling lights and bursts of sudden, unreal laughter. He felt lightheaded, unsteady on his feet, as if he was making his way through a fun house.

He didn't want to be here. He wanted to be with Quinn, sweet and sleepy, head nestled against his chest.

Not here, paying a call on death.

He'd had enough death to last a lifetime.

Get your shit together, Man. This is your job.

Rourke squeezed his eyes shut, shoving aside his grief and regret, his longing for his daughter. When he reopened them, he was again fully present, the scene before him starkly, unavoidably real.

His gaze landed on the car. It was parked at an angle, half on the road, half off. He wondered at Lucy Praxton's emotional state at the time. Had she been frightened? Anxious? Or simply inattentive?

What the hell had she been doing way out here?

Mikey greeted the guys from Major Crimes. Rourke knew their names but couldn't recall them. He heard the three talking but didn't listen. He made his way around the sedan, inspecting the vehicle, the ground around it. Something shiny caught his eye.

He squatted down to get a better look. A small scrap of pink fabric? Satin? Ribbon?

He motioned to one of the crime scene techs, pointed it out. "Make certain you collect this."

Mikey ambled over. "What did you find?"

Rourke showed him, then stood. "You look inside yet?"

He shook his head. "Rick and Perry did. It's pretty grisly."

That's right, their names were Rick Humphrey and Perry Price. Who the hell gave their kid the initials P.P.?

Rourke went around to the driver's side door. The window was down. Flies swarmed around pretty Miss Praxton's head. She'd been shot in the temple; her forehead rested against the steering wheel; the dash and passenger side door were splattered with blood and brain matter; the window was intact.

"Looks like the bullet lodged in her brain," Rourke said.

Rourke peered around her. Keys were in the ignition. Passenger side door was unlocked, window up. Her purse was on the floor, not the seat. He shifted his attention to the backseat and the empty car seat.

His heart began to thump against his chest. Sweat beaded his upper lip and trickled down his spine. Feeling sick, he stepped away from the vehicle, sucked in a deep breath.

"You okay, Partner?" Mikey kept his voice low.

"Yeah, fine. Just needed some air."

Moving deliberately, putting one foot in front of the other, he went around to the passenger side of the vehicle. Opened the back door. Car seat with a pink, ruffled cover. Colorful toys hanging from the handle. He tugged the seat, found it securely fastened in.

He dropped his gaze. On the floor in front of the car seat, lay a tiny shoe. A slipper, with a shiny pink bow. He felt sick. The sausage biscuit he'd wolfed down on the way here rose in his throat.

Don't lose it now, Rourke. Whatever you do, you cannot lose it.

He forced it back, moved his gaze again. Clean back seat. Nothing else on the seat or floor, not even a gum wrapper.

He straightened, looked at Mikey. "Perp took the diaper bag."

"Yeah, so?"

"Grace Hudson's alive. Why take the bag if you mean to kill the kid? No doubt, we've got a kidnapping on our hands."

NINE

Quinn Conners
  Present day

2:10 P.M.

Sunlight streamed around the edges of the blinds, creating brilliant patches on the rumpled bed. Detective Quinn Conners
stretched languorously, enjoying the warmth of Rick's body against
hers as her heart slowed and her flesh cooled.

"I'm glad you could get away," she said, propping herself up on
an elbow to gaze down at him.

"Are you kidding? The bar could be burning down right now for
all I care."

She smiled with pleasure, although they both knew it was just sex
talk. Pour, his wine bar on Magazine Street, was his baby. Like her
rank and badge were hers.

"I love your hair." He coiled one of the fiery curls around his
finger.

She and her mass of wild, red curls had a complicated relationship. Less adversarial since she'd finally learned it was useless to fight what nature had given her, but still complicated.

"Bane of my existence," she said.

"Liar. You love it too."

"Only because it makes me look like a crazy, bad ass bitch. Throw in the badge and gun, and my job's half done."

A smile tugged at his mouth. "What does that say about me that I find that sexy as hell?"

She playfully nipped his shoulder. "Poor judgement skills?"

He laughed. "Maybe so, but that doesn't change the fact that I'm crazy about you."

"Again with the questionable judgement."

He leaned away to look at her. A frown marred his brow. "Why do you do that?"

"What?"

"I say I'm crazy about you, and you make a joke."

A knot of tension formed at the base of her skull; she resisted the urge to massage it. "I'm just having fun." She walked her fingers across his damp chest. "Aren't you?"

He was quiet for a moment, then untangled himself. "I need to get back to the bar."

"Wait." She caught his hand, lowered her voice to a seductive purr. "Don't go."

He made a sound of frustration. "Just having fun, Quinn? We've finished with *this*, haven't we? Why should I stay, fun's over."

"Don't be like that."

He pushed away her hand and sat up. "What way is that? Offended that you think of me as a middle of the day booty call?"

"That's not what I meant. Besides, would being the best booty call *ever* be so bad?"

Judging by the way he yanked on his jeans, it wouldn't be great. He zipped and fastened them, then met her eyes once more. The blue of his looked cold.

"How long have we been seeing each other?"

"Rick—"

"Do you even know?"

She didn't. Not exactly. "Several months."

"Nice copout. It's been eight months, Quinn."

She sat up and the sun fell across her face, leaving no place to hide.

He grabbed his shirt off the bedpost and pulled it over his head. "What are we doing here, Quinn?"

Her mouth went dry. She wasn't ready for this conversation. She didn't want to have it.

"I'm a cop," she said. "Cops suck at relationships."

"That's such lame bullshit, and you know it. You're afraid, that's what I think."

"Of what? Being *hurt*? Please."

"Well, let's see . . . your mom died when you were a baby and the person you loved most in the world offed himself without so much as leaving a note."

She never should have shared that with him. Never should have given him that glimpse into her heart.

She plucked her panties off the floor, shimmied them on, then retrieved her shirt and slipped it over her head. She felt exposed enough right now without being naked.

"Last I checked you ran a wine bar. When'd you earn the psych degree?"

"It's so obvious, I don't need a degree."

Shit. What could she say to that? She grabbed the scrunchie from the nightstand and gathered her hair into a ponytail.

Silence fell between them. He sighed. "I really like you, Quinn. You're smart and strong. Sexy. The question is, do you *really* like me?"

"You know I like you—"

"You can't even say it."

"That's not true." She shook her head. "You're an amazing guy, we enjoy being together, and the sex is great. No, better than great. I don't understand what's wrong with that."

"That sounds a lot like 'just having fun' or a friend with benefits."

Quinn felt like she couldn't breathe. "You're being ridiculous."

He dragged a hand through his surfer-boy blond hair, then let out a long breath. "Is it ridiculous to want to take this to the next level? To want something more? We're not kids. You're twenty-nine. I'm thirty-two."

Breathe in, Quinn. Breathe out. The elephant that had been in the middle of the room between them for weeks was now sitting squarely on her chest.

"What do you want from me? Marriage? Kids?"

"That's not what I'm talking about."

She fisted her fingers. "Then what?"

"More than this! More than phenomenal sex with a woman who holds me at arm's length."

"That makes a lot of sense."

"Now who's taking the chickenshit way out? You know what I want. More of you. More than this."

"I don't have any more to give, Rick." She threw her arms out wide. "This is it. You've got it all."

"Right."

Her cell phone, parked on the bedside table, sounded. Her partner, she saw. On a Saturday afternoon that could only mean one thing. She reached for it.

"Of course you're going to answer."

"It's my job, Rick. I'm a cop. Hey Dobby, hold a sec—"

"Take your call, Quinn." Rick snatched his jacket from the arm of the chair, shrugged into it. "This is over. Don't text or call, and don't come by the bar. By the way, I was going to suggest we move in together. Stupid, huh?"

She didn't deny it or go after him, and the next sound she heard was the front door slamming shut.

TEN

Dobby beat her to the scene—a Mid-City crawfish boil that had turned deadly. In front of the small, frame house a *Congratulations Graduate* banner fluttered in the breeze. Dobby stood at the outer perimeter, in conversation with an officer named Creed. No doubt getting the particulars.

Detective Ron Dobson. Nicknamed Dobby after the house elf from the Harry Potter series because, among other things, of his slight build and oversized ears. Apparently, unique looking as he was, before he'd met his wife Cherie, he'd been popular with the ladies. Really popular. The guys around the Second liked to joke his appeal had to do with the correlation between the size of those ears and the size of other parts of his body. Which could be true, but Quinn figured it more likely women loved him because he was a hell of a nice guy.

She climbed out of her car and hurried to join him. "Sorry I'm late."

"Just got here myself, Partner. Lunch at my mother-in-law's. What's your excuse?"

"It took a minute to get out of the house, that's all."

He nodded and grinned. "I thought I heard Rick's voice."

"You did."

"Seems like you two are getting serious."

"We're not."

If he heard the edge in her voice, he ignored it. "You've been dating awhile. It'd be natural."

"Not you, too?"

He caught the edge. It'd been impossible to miss that time. "What's that supposed to mean?"

She stopped, looked up at the cloudless sky a moment, then back at him. "You have any idea how long he and I have been seeing each other?"

He thought a moment. "Yeah, about seven or eight months. Why?"

Figured. Shit. "Nothing. Forget it."

"Fine by me."

"I didn't know, okay? He doesn't get that me and relationships don't mix."

"I take it he knows now?"

"Yup, it's over."

"Oh, crap. I'm sorry, Quinn."

He actually looked disappointed for her. Why did every man think she needed a man to complete her? "How about we focus on what happened *here*. What do we know so far?"

"The basics. Too much sun, too much booze and one drunk, dumb fuck steps on another drunk, dumb fuck's toes and war breaks out. Now we've got three dead and eight wounded."

"Seriously?" She rolled her eyes. "Who brings a gun to a kid's graduation party?"

"Obviously, you forget we live in Louisiana."

They ducked under the tape delineating the inner perimeter, then went around the side of the house to the back yard.

Quinn took in the scene: the smell of crawfish boil mingling with the sound of weeping; blood-spattered celebration cake; crime scene tape fluttering in the breeze. Somebody's graduation. Yeah, it had gotten messed up.

She thought of her dad, could hear his voice in her head. *"Slow down, Quinnie. Deep breath, that's right. Take your time. Don't miss anything because the truth is in the details."*

She took that deep breath, mentally prepared herself. The thing about a scene like this was the sheer size of it. No mystery to be solved here. No hunting for a suspect.

It still had to be documented. Evidence collected. Witnesses interviewed and stories sorted. Emotions to be soothed, truths coaxed out and lies exposed. Grueling. An exercise in both stamina and self-control.

They stopped beside the first victim. Guy in his forties. Dressed in an LSU T-shirt and shorts. Blood. Lots of it. Looked like he'd taken the bullet in the neck. Hit the carotid.

"Damn," Dobby muttered.

"Poor bastard probably bled out before the ambulance even arrived."

They moved to the next: a woman, young and pretty, her whole life in front of her. Shot in the back. Twice. The third was a kid. Just a boy. Maybe twelve. Made her hurt, deep down, in a place that stored this kind of shit.

Quinn glanced at Dobby. He stared at the kid, mouth set in a grim line, a muscle in his jaw twitched.

"Focus on the good news," she said low, as much to herself as to him. "We got the assholes. They're gonna pay. No weaseling out of this one."

"Creed indicated they were both in custody," he said, voice tight. "Get this, one doesn't have a scratch on him, and the other's injury is minor."

"It fucking figures." She squinted against the sun. "How about I start with the Hatfields." She indicated the group of shell-shocked partygoers huddled together on the home's back porch, then motioned toward another group clutched together at the other end of the property. "You take the McCoys. We compare notes later."

HOURS LATER, Quinn and Dobby exited the Second District station. The hot, humid day had become a still, swampy night. Quinn breathed it in, admitting exhaustion. Running on bad coffee and vending machine crap wasn't what it was cracked up to be.

The dead-to-rights perpetrators were locked up and had lawyered up. One of the party guests had been videoing the celebration and caught the moment the clash began, leaving no doubt which one of the two idiots had drawn his weapon first. Now they waited on ballistics to determine which gun—or guns—had delivered the fatal shots.

She glanced at Dobby. "You want to grab a beer and a burger?"

"Nah. Cherie will have something for me. Besides, Jimmy's got a T-ball game in the morning." He grinned. "Come watch him play. He'll be the one in the outfield chasing butterflies."

"Mmm, sounds enticing but I think I'll have to pass."

He laughed. "You don't know what you're missing. Have a good rest of your weekend. See you Monday!"

They'd parked in opposite directions and started for their cars. She stopped, looked back.

"Hey, Dobbs?"

"Yeah?"

"Give Jimmy a kiss from his Aunty Quinn."

"Give him one yourself. Game is at nine."

He gave her a thumbs-up and jogged to his vehicle.

She watched him a moment, then turned and headed towards hers. She really *didn't* know what she was missing. She hadn't played team sports. Nor had she taken dance or music classes. Her childhood extracurricular activities had included crime scenes, evidence collection, and visual acuity competitions. When she was old enough, the shooting range and mixed martial arts.

Yeah, a little unconventional. Some might even call it creepy. Those folks could kiss her ass. It'd been her and her dad's thing and until five years ago when he'd decided to eat a bullet, it had sustained them.

Fucking coward. She shook her head, jammed her hands into her pockets. Checking out that way. The truth was, he'd left her years before putting the gun to his head. That was the part that hurt.

Quinn reached her SUV. Someone had left a flyer under her windshield wiper. She plucked it out, then climbed into her vehicle and started it up. Shifting into reverse, she backed out of the parking spot and moments later was heading down Carrollton Avenue.

As she drove, maneuvering the streets from memory, her thoughts lingered on her father. No goodbye. He'd decided it was time to go and left her to carry the emotional baggage. Regret. Guilt. Anger and resentment.

Good stuff, pops. Thanks a bunch.

Quinn tightened her fingers on the steering wheel, pissed at herself for her thoughts. She made the turn onto Canal Boulevard, heading toward Lakeview. She had to let this shit go. He was gone and that was that. Time to move on.

Maybe she needed a distraction? Like a boyfriend. Oh, that's right. She'd had one. He'd dumped her today.

She shoved aside thoughts of that lovely moment. Perhaps a vacation? How long had it been since she'd taken any real time off?

Not since she'd been forced to after her dad's funeral. Captain said it'd give her a chance to get her head right.

That hadn't gone well. She wasn't her favorite person to be around, and by the end of the two weeks she'd been crawling the walls.

Fact was, she liked the job. Besides being part of her DNA, it took her mind off her own messed-up life.

She smiled grimly to herself. Maybe she was more like her old man than she wanted to admit.

ELEVEN

9:20 P.M.

Beignet, her one-eyed tomcat, was waiting at the door for her. The cat, the color of a perfectly fried beignet sprinkled with powdered sugar, had adopted her. Just shown up on her porch one night, bloodied and hungry, and never left.

He was both a lover and a fighter, and he mewed and rubbed himself against her ankles as she unlocked the door.

"Hello, big boy," she said and scooped him up. She pushed the door open with her hip. His motor was running, and she smiled and rubbed her forehead against his.

"Hungry?"

His purring grew louder, and he jumped out of her arms and ran to the kitchen. She kept a bowl of water and kibble on the back porch for him, but at night she fed him a can of the good stuff. Tuna or chicken, even salmon every once and awhile.

It was her way of ensuring he'd return every night.

Quinn didn't examine what that said about her and followed him inside. She opened the can, dumped it in his bowl, then went to the pantry for her bottle of Jameson Irish whiskey. She kept the bottle on the very top shelf, so she had to work for it. She poured herself three fingers, added a splash of water, and sipped.

The smoky taste, its burn, was familiar. And calming. Like the presence of an old friend.

Her dad used to joke that Conners came out of the womb with a taste for whiskey. It had been funny. Until it hadn't been anymore. Until he had turned to that old friend more than any flesh and blood one.

She sipped again, understanding how that could happen. How one could turn to artificial numbing to escape the shit life threw at you, day in and out.

Taking another sip, Quinn opened the refrigerator. Not much to choose from, she saw. Leftover pizza. She lifted the lid. One slice. It would do.

Not bothering with a plate or even heating it up, she took a bite. Not exactly a culinary delight, but it was already taking the edge off. Her gaze drifted to the flyer she'd snatched off the windshield and stuffed into her bag.

Taking another bite of the pie, she plucked it out and flipped the paper over. Not an advertisement. A message, written in bold, black marker.

The pizza stuck in her throat. For a moment she forgot how to breathe.

Your father didn't kill himself

Quinn stared at the words. Her father . . . not a suicide?
But if not suicide . . .
Homicide.
Quinn gave herself a shake. Not possible. She'd found him. She'd examined the scene. The evidence. She pictured it. His eyes wide, rolled back. The death mask. The blood. Horrible.
Oh, Daddy. No, please no.
Quinn crossed to the table, pulled out a chair and sat. Path report

had confirmed what the nearly empty bottle of Jameson told her it would, a sky-high blood alcohol level.

He'd been dead two days when she found him. That still cut deep, an oozing swath of guilt. At least neither of her grandparents had been alive to see what had become of their son. If for nothing else, she was thankful for that.

Quinn downed the whiskey, went for the bottle, poured another. He'd called that night. Drunk, slurring his words. Rambling about having finally found it. He didn't have to say what the 'it' was—she knew, the same one 'it' always was—who killed Cynthia Hudson and what happened to baby Grace.

Quinn brought the glass to her lips. She'd hung up on him. Tough love, she'd told herself. Keeping her promise: if he wanted to have a relationship with her, he had to clean up his act.

Dammit! Rourke Conners had been a lot of things, but she hadn't counted a coward among them.

She returned her focus to the anonymous message. Somebody knew where her buttons were and how to push them; that was exactly what they had been attempting to do when they left this message.

One of the guys, she thought. Their idea of funny. Harmless retribution for her having stepped on their toes. Evans, maybe. Or Marco. Funny guys and not-so-secret sexists. They hadn't appreciated Captain Franks turning one of their investigations over to her and Dobby.

The area around the station was wired to the hilt. Whoever'd slipped this under her wiper would have been caught on surveillance tape. She'd take a little peek, confirm her suspicions, then take care of the perpetrators herself. If she brought it to the captain, they'd know they'd gotten her goat.

No effin' way. She would not give them the satisfaction.

TWELVE

8:15 A.M. Monday.

Second District Station

Quinn studied the video image. She'd arrived early to access the department's visual evidence platform before the day heated up. A kid, she saw. Ten, maybe twelve, years old. Trotting nonchalantly across the lot to her car, pausing beside it to tuck the flyer under the driver's side wiper, then trotting off.

She looked from the monitor to the video technician. "Can you blow this up and get me a still of the kid?"

"Sure thing, Detective. It'll be in your inbox in a few minutes."

"Thanks, Peg."

"What's that all about?"

She glanced over her shoulder at her partner. Typical Dobby, cleaned, pressed and looking like Captain America, elf-style. Also unlike her, he'd obviously gotten some rest since she'd seen him last.

She handed him the flyer. "This was left on my windshield Saturday night."

His eyebrows shot up. "Shit, Quinn. Somebody's trying to push your buttons."

She angled the monitor toward him. "Thought I might be able to catch the asshole in the act."

"A kid?"

"My money's on Evans and Marco. They knew I'd check the footage, so they paid some neighborhood kid to do it."

"You going to confront them?"

"Hell no. It'd give them too much satisfaction."

He seemed to consider that a moment, then nodded in agreement. "Ballistic report is in. I got the call as I was leaving the house. They emailed it."

"Hot damn. Let's take a look."

She followed him to his desk. He accessed his email program, located the document, then opened it. Quinn read it over his shoulder. Then read it again.

"This can't be right." She looked at him in disbelief. "A third weapon?"

He shook his head, expression as stunned as hers must be. "How can that be? Not one witness reported a third shooter."

She closed her eyes, recalling the scene. "The first shots are fired. Pandemonium ensues and no one notices when a third shooter enters the melée? I don't buy it."

"Agreed. Why didn't anybody talk?"

"Because it wasn't in their best interest. Maybe it was their family or loved one."

He inclined is head. "Or someone they were afraid of."

She balled her hands into fist. "Dammit!"

"This makes us look like schmucks," he muttered. "I never asked about another shooter. Did you?"

"Like two wasn't enough for one Saturday afternoon crawfish boil? Captain's gonna be pissed."

"When do you want to talk to him?"

"My preference is never, but since that's not an option—"

"Just rip off the Band-Aid."

"Exactly."

Captain Anton Franks was old school, from his clean-shaven face and closely cropped dark hair, to the way he carried himself, like the marine he had been for ten years. He did not suffer fools.

Unfortunately, at that moment she and Dobby were lining up, jester hats in hand. "There's been a hiccup, Captain," she said.

His eyebrows shot up. "What kind of a hiccup, Detectives?"

"Ballistics indicated the presence of a third shooter."

A dull, red flush climbed her superior officer's cheeks. "I thought we'd put this one to bed Saturday night?"

"We did as well, Captain. The initial report indicated there were two shooters. No one we interviewed mentioned a third."

"We have a video," Dobby said. "Clear as day, two shooters."

The man glowered at them. "Clear as day?"

"Let me rephrase—"

He cut Dobby off. "What are your jobs, Detectives?"

She and Dobby exchanged glances; she lost the stare-off and answered. "To investigate crimes, ascertain the sequence of events, pinpoint and arrest the guilty party."

"That's right. It's an active role. You're not there to simply takes notes and have answers handed to you on a smart phone."

"No sir."

"Think it through!" His voice rose. "You're not rookies, dammit! First glance rarely tells the whole tale."

She felt herself flush. Dobby stepped in. "Yes, sir. It . . . this one seemed obvious, sir."

Quinn jumped in before their Captain exploded. "This morning we plan to re-interview the party guests, focusing on the presence of a third shooter and also make sure we've identified all video of the incident that exists. Seems to us, somebody else must have pulled out their cell phone."

"You think?"

Quinn winced at the sarcasm. "Yes, sir. Before that, we'll contact the lab about an audio enhancement of the recording we already have."

"Get to it and keep me informed." He waved them out. "That's all."

They exited the office. Dobby grinned. "Well, that wasn't so bad."

The eternal optimist. Nauseating. "My God, how did I get you as a partner?"

"Because everyone else passed?" When she all but growled at him, he laughed lightly. "Shake it off, Partner. Nobody's perfect."

Maybe not, but he didn't have her family history to overcome.

By noon Quinn had a headache, one of those blinding, make-you-want-to-kill-somebody brain-bashers. Not a single interview had gone well, and not one person admitted possession of a video of the melée.

And the guy standing squarely in his Mid-City doorway glaring at them wasn't going to ease her pain. Ray Russell, fiancé of victim Karlee Painter and, judging by his attitude and demeanor, all-around tough guy.

"What do you want?"

"Like I said, Mr. Russell, a few follow-up questions."

"You questioned me Saturday, there's nothing more I have to say."

She silently counted to ten. "It's hot, Mr. Russell, and it's been a long morning. Could we come inside?"

He hesitated a moment, then grudgingly stepped aside and allowed them to enter. The home was one half of a traditional New Orleans shotgun double, and the entrance dumped them directly into the front living area.

The place's vibe was boy meets girl. The girl part evidenced by pretty floral throw pillows, framed photos and artfully arranged this and thats—a vase with dried flowers; a grouping of candles, a wedding planner. The boy part was represented by everything else.

"Could we sit down?" she asked.

"Sure."

She and Dobby took seats on the couch; Russell the chair opposite them. "New information has come to light," she began.

He moved his gaze between the two of them. "What kind of information?"

She cut to the chase. "The presence of a third shooter."

He frowned. "No way. I was there."

He wasn't the first this morning to respond that way. "Ballistics don't lie."

"What's that supposed to mean?"

Quinn ignored his question, countering with one of her own. "If you don't mind, could you paint the scene for us once more?"

"I do fucking mind! I already told you everything." He leaned forward. "Karlee and I were planning our wedding. Now I'm planning a funeral. How do you think that feels?"

Dobby took over, ever the good cop. "I can't imagine, Mr. Russell. If I lost my wife that way, I can't imagine how I'd react. I do know, I'd want justice. And that's what we want, too. For you and Karlee.

The muscles in his face and neck seemed to soften. "Like I told you Saturday, it all happened so fast. There were shots. Then screams. Then—" He brought his hands to his face. "I saw Karlee go down." He looked up. His eyes were dry, his expression stricken.

"I ran to her. I knew . . . the blood . . ." His voice cracked. "She was wearing a white sundress . . ." His voice trailed off. He looked away.

Quinn remembered it. The delicate white marred by ugly red. Obscene. The best in life juxtaposed with the worst.

She found her voice. "We have a schematic of the scene." She nodded at Dobby; he unfolded it and laid it on the coffee table in front of Russell. The simple drawing diagrammed the backyard. "The porch and house," she said, tapping them, then moving on. "The tented area with the cake and food. The fence and row of bushes."

"Karlee was here." She indicated one of the three Xs on the diagram. "Where were you, Mr. Russell?"

He was staring at the drawing; his face had turned ashen.

"Mr. Russell? Are you all right?"

He nodded but didn't speak.

"Approximately, where were you at the time the gunfire commenced?"

He pointed. His hand trembled.

"Are you certain?"

He nodded again, throat working.

Dobby reached over, pen in hand. "Here?"

"Yes." The word came out raspy, raw with emotion.

Dobby carefully penned RR on the spot, then refolded and pocketed it. "Mr. Russell," he asked, "can we get you a glass of water?"

When he shook his head, Quinn pressed on. "By any chance, did you take any photos at the party?"

He appeared confused by the question. "Photos?"

"Yes, before the gunfire broke out. Or any video."

"Karlee was the picture taker. Not me. Check her phone."

"We'll do that. One last thing, do you own a gun?"

"Me?" He shifted his gaze between them. "Why do you want to know that?"

"We're asking everyone who was at the party. Even the host's seventy-five-year-old grandmother."

"No." The word came out hard.

"What about Karlee?"

His eyes filled with tears. "Seriously?" He looked away, then back. "No, Karlee hated guns."

Quinn looked at Dobby; he shook his head, indicating he didn't have any other questions. They both stood. "Thank you for your time, Mr. Russell. Again, we're so sorry for your loss."

"Wait."

They stopped, turned back.

"Those bastards better pay. Karlee—" He choked the last back, as if overcome with emotion. "Make them pay."

"We will, Mr. Russell. I can promise you that."

They exited the home. Neither spoke until they were in Quinn's Ford.

She buckled her safety belt, then looked at Dobby. "What did you think?"

"About Russell? Besides feeling bad for him?"

She nodded. "Yeah."

"He seemed legit."

She started the car. "I suppose."

"You think he was lying?"

"I don't know." She eased away from the curb. "There was something . . . off about him."

"Like maybe his fiancé was just killed in a spray of bullets? For me, everything hit all the right notes. His responses, voice, body language. Everyone responds differently to grief."

She turned onto Carrollton Avenue, heading uptown. "Yeah, I guess you're right."

"I am. Your headache is probably skewing your point of view."

The headache. "Holy shit."

"What?"

She met his eyes. "It's gone. My headache's gone."

THIRTEEN

8:05 A.M. Wednesday.

The Blue Dot Donut line stretched out the door and around the side of the bakeshop's bright blue, wood-framed cottage. The line inched forward, and Quinn checked her watch. If she left now, she'd be lucky to clock in on time. Which sure as hell wasn't happening, because she was not starting her day without a maple bacon donut. Period. End of story.

In her pocket, her cell went off. She answered it, voice a warning growl. "This is Conners."

"Whoa, somebody woke up on the wrong side of the bed."

Dobby. "I'm on a mission and the universe isn't cooperating."

"Let me guess. The mission is coffee, donuts or both, and the problem is traffic."

The man did know what motivated her. "Close. My need for a maple bacon donut has run headlong into everyone else's in the city's need for one. I've been in this God-awful line ten minutes already, so don't tell me somebody was murdered."

The young couple ahead of her sent worried glances over their shoulders, then scooted forward as if to put a bit more distance between them and her.

He laughed. "Keep you from a mission like that? Never. Especially since you're going to bring me two of the chocolate-iced, with rainbow sprinkles."

Rainbow sprinkles? She smiled. "Not every grown man is confident enough to eat donuts with sprinkles."

He laughed again. "I've got nobody to impress."

A group of four girls in their Catholic school uniforms exited the store, and the line moved forward again, landing Quinn inches from the door. The smell of the pastries made her mouth water. "What's up?"

"Heard from the Medical Examiner's office. Doc Jillian wants us down there."

"Any hint to the context?"

"The triple, but that's all I know. I'll meet you there."

Seventeen minutes later Quinn arrived, her donuts consumed, and her mood improved. Dobby was waiting for her, leaning against the back of his car, face lifted to the sun, the picture of chill. How did he do that? she wondered. Being so relaxed was contrary to her nature.

He didn't move even when she reached him. "It's supposed to rain later. Figured I'd better enjoy the sunshine while I can." He turned his head, cracked open one eye. "A life philosophy you could try?"

"Sure, if I had time." She held out the Blue Dot bag. "Sprinkles delivered."

Grinning, he took the bag and fished out one of the pastries. He took a big bite, and they fell into step, crossing the parking lot. The building that housed the coroner's office was state-of-the-art. Well-deserved after making due for seven years post-Katrina in cramped, temporary facilities—including refrigerated cargo containers to house bodies.

Dr. Jillian Krantz was small, efficient and fiercely dedicated to her job. She'd overseen the completion of the new autopsy suite and had fought for the items she felt she and her fellow forensic pathologists needed to do their jobs as precisely as possible.

Quinn thought of her as a tiny dynamo and believed the rumors that the woman needed only a couple hours of sleep a night.

"Jillian," she said and held out her hand. "It's good to see you again."

"You, too." She nodded in Dobby's direction. "You as well, Detective Dobson." An amused twinkle in her eyes, she tapped the corner of her mouth. "You missed a couple sprinkles, Detective."

She led them to her office, then motioned them to take a seat. "Thanks for coming in," she said, retrieving a file from a stack. She opened it, extracted a photograph and slid it across the desk to them. "Karlee Painter."

It was the pre-autopsy photograph of the young woman's back and the two adjacent, closely spaced bullet wounds. The woman's skin was pale and waxy gray; the wounds, bloodless now, seemed too small to have caused the death of this vital young woman.

Krantz slid over a second item, Painter's wound chart. A simple outline of a female, front and back, with entry and exit wounds marked. Dashed lines indicated the path each bullet had travelled, with Krantz' handwritten notes detailing the internal damages.

"Somebody was a good shot," she said.

Quinn frowned. "Excuse me?"

"The bullets collectively perforated her heart, left lung, and diaphragm, causing her simultaneously to bleed to death and drown in her own blood." Krantz tapped the photograph. "If you're going to be shot in the back, this is pretty much the deadliest place to take that bullet. She took two in essentially the same spot."

"You're saying she wasn't caught in the spray of gunfire?"

Dobby sounded disbelieving. Quinn felt him look her way, but she couldn't take her eyes off the photograph of Karlee Painter's back and those two, neatly placed holes.

Quinn nodded. "Somebody wanted her dead. Gunfire broke out and they saw their chance. That's what you're saying, isn't it?"

"It's my job to document what I observe, not to establish intent. That said, I wanted to make certain you were aware of this particular observation."

"The third shooter," Dobby said. "Son of a bitch."

Quinn stepped in. "Thank you, Dr. Krantz. May we keep these?"

"Absolutely. I made those copies for you."

They started for the door; Krantz stopped them. "I almost forgot. Karlee Painter was pregnant. Eight weeks."

FOURTEEN

Ten minutes later Quinn was behind the wheel, tailing Dobby as he maneuvered traffic on his way to the I-10 on-ramp. Karlee Painter had been deliberately targeted. She'd also been eight weeks pregnant. The possible ramifications of the information reverberated through Quinn. Dead was still dead, but intent changed everything.

Murder in the first degree. Maybe.

Her phone went off. Not surprisingly, it was Dobby. She thanked God for Bluetooth and answered, greeting him with a question. "What're you thinking?"

"That we need to apprise Captain Franks, ASAP."

"Agreed, but not without a plan. Franks will tear us a new one if we don't present next steps."

Up ahead Dobby angled onto the I-10 ramp. Moments later, she made the ramp. "I think we start with Russell," she said. "He wouldn't be the first guy to find out his lady is pregnant and decide he wants out."

"My thought, too. I've got to say, he didn't strike me that way. Seemed pretty torn up."

"He did but you know as well as I do, folks can lie their asses off—"

"When they're trying to save their ass? True, but why kill her? Why not just break it off?"

"Because he'd still be the kid's dad—and financially beholden. Forever."

"Besides questioning Russell again," Dobby said, "let's follow up on his and Painter's wedding plans, find out if they'd set a date and booked a place, how many non-refundable deposits were made and whose bank account they came out of."

"While we're at it, let's check Russell's financials. Maybe they took out life insurance policies on each other? Odd for a young couple to be thinking that way, but it happens."

"Or maybe Russell took one out on her—after he learned about the pregnancy— Hey, Cherie's calling. Let me grab it then I'll call you right back."

He hung up and Quinn flexed her fingers on the steering wheel, thoughts racing. If not Russell, who? They hadn't delved into any of the victims' situations, not their families, friends or work lives. That's not the kind of crime this was.

Not the kind of crime they'd *thought* this was. Dammit.

She exited I-10 onto Carrollton Avenue, and hit gridlock. An accident, she saw. Cruiser and tow truck were already on scene, so it shouldn't be long. She refocused on the road, on inching forward. Finally, the tow truck exited the scene, smushed vehicle in tow.

As she rolled past, her cell sounded. Dobby calling back, she saw. "Everything all right with Cherie?" she asked.

"She's fine, but the school called. Jimmy has a fever and threw up. She was on her way to get him."

"Gotcha." She paused. "I was thinking, shy of a full confession—"

"Which won't happen."

"—we're starting all over. We'll need to interview their families and friends. It's going to be grueling—"

"Crap," he said, "it's Cherie again. Hold on while I see what's—"

"Take your time. I'll see you at the station."

FIFTEEN

Second District Station

Quinn closed the war room door behind her and, notebook and scene folder in hand, crossed to the dry erase board mounted on the back wall. She stared at the expanse of white, visualizing the backyard where the triple had occurred. She heard her dad's deep voice in her head: "*Document, document, document. It's your job to put the pieces together and make sense of what you see. One way to do that is by sketching the scene.*"

How old had she been? Twelve? No, she remembered, she'd been ten. In the fourth grade. He'd proceeded to show her some of his sketches, explain bird's eye view, then let her give it a try.

She remembered it now, a smile tugging at the corners of her mouth. He'd set up a mock crime scene. A break-in, a missing pair of Nikes, clues aplenty.

No wonder she'd had so few friends, who wanted to hang out with a kid who did *that* for fun?

Quinn, shifted her thoughts back to the present, to the triple homicide and Karlee Painter's death. She laid the folder and notebook on the table, then carefully removed her original sketch. She affixed it to the white board with a magnet.

Using it as a reference, she delineated the scene's perimeter, a six-foot, wooden fence. She'd liked drawing as a kid, and it had carried over to this part of the job. Not that she had any great skill, but at least her figures looked human. The one sketch she'd let Dobby handle—she'd thought she was being magnanimous—his victims had looked oddly like porpoises. Luckily, he enjoyed taking measurements, which she loathed, so it worked out well.

Using his measurements, she carefully added the reference points: the gate out to the driveway where the host had been boiling crawfish, the deck, the big oak tree center-left, and the shed in the far-right corner.

"Hey."

Quinn looked over her shoulder at Dobby. "Hey. What's happening with Jimmy?"

"Cherie's taking him straight to the pediatrician. In the few minutes between her first and second calls to me, the school contacted her again because Jimmy's temperature jumped to 102."

"What are you doing here? Go. I've got this."

"We decided we'll make that call after the pediatrician sees him." He joined her, moved his gaze over the board. "What're you doing here?"

"Recreating my sketch from the scene of the triple."

"How can I help?"

"In the folder there are photos of the three victims, as well as the one Krantz gave us today. Could you grab them for me?"

He didn't ask what she wanted him to do with them; he already knew. He hung them alongside the sketch.

She studied them a moment, then began. "Okay, the gunfire erupted over a game of horseshoes." She penned in the spot, then noted perpetrator 'A' and 'B'.

"Now for the victims." She placed each, saving Karlee Painter for last, then stepped back. That was the beauty of these bird's-eye view line drawings—their perspective and simplicity. With all the extraneous distractions of a photograph eliminated, you had a clear visual of the action, allowing a piece to fall into place.

Like now.

"The first shooters are here." She tapped the board. "They get crosswise with one another, it gets physical. Partygoers pull the two apart, which is when perpetrator 'A' pulls a gun and fires. According to witnesses, pandemonium ensues. Perpetrator 'B' then brandishes his weapon and begins firing."

Dobby nodded. "That all transpires between the deck and the oak tree."

"Exactly." Quinn indicated the spot on the drawing. "Karlee Painter is here, between the oak and the shed. Could she have been hit by random bullet? Yes. Could she have been struck in the back, not once but twice, in nearly the same spot?"

"No effing way."

"The third shooter," she said. "He—or she—joined the melee for one reason."

"To take out Karlee Painter."

"Who happened to be eight weeks pregnant."

Dobby narrowed his eyes. "It's gotta be Russell. Right?"

"That's what I'm thinking." Quinn looked at the sketch, then back at Dobby. "All we have to do is figure out how to prove it."

SIXTEEN

Quinn flexed her fingers on the steering wheel. Captain Franks had agreed that Russell was their most likely suspect—but hadn't agreed with her instinct to haul him into the station for a proper interrogation. Pay him a visit at his job? It seemed like a half measure to her, but she was a balls-out kind of girl.

She felt Dobby's gaze on her. "You still pissed at the Captain?"

"I think it's the wrong call. Russell's the one. We're wasting time."

"What if he's not?"

Then he was a guy who had lost the love of his life *and* his unborn child.

From the corner of her eye, she saw Dobby check his phone yet again. "You're worried about Jimmy," she said. "Clock out, partner. I'll take you back to the Second. You head home; I'll grab one of the other guys to assist."

"Nah, I got this."

She figured he didn't, but let it go anyway. "You ever see one of those Russian nesting dolls?"

"Yeah, sure. Why?"

"That's what we've got here. A crime in a crime. Get it?"

She didn't look at him, but knew she'd gotten a quick grin out of him. "It's like whole new case. How were we supposed to anticipate that?"

"No way we could," he said.

"Right. Different perp. Different motive. Different crime."

He let out a weary-sounding breath. "I wish she'd call," he said. "Why hasn't she called?"

As Quinn opened her mouth to try to reassure him, his cell went off.

He had it to his ear in a flash. "Cherie, what's happening?"

Quinn tuned him out, both to give him his privacy and mentally prepare for the interview ahead. She needed to shake Russell up but do it with kid gloves. Keeping him unbalanced would make it more difficult for him to lie convincingly. The truth was automatic. Lying— for everyone but the true psychopath—wasn't.

They'd called Russell's employer, learned they could find him at the site of the new hotel going up downtown. Quinn navigated the construction gridlock—nothing like taking an already congested roadway down to one-lane to cause the blood to boil—eyed an illegal parking spot cater-corner to the site and grabbed it.

"Jimmy has strep," Dobby said, pocketing his phone, the relief in his voice palpable. "Doc gave him a fever reducer right there; his temp's already down." He let out a long breath. "Prescribed antibiotics and rest. He's going to be okay."

"Never doubted it, partner."

"That makes one of us."

Quinn flipped down her visor to display her NOPD credentials and climbed out. Dobby came around the car and together they crossed to the construction zone barricade and made their way through.

He nudged her with his elbow. "Thanks for being so understanding."

"No thanks necessary, Dobbs. I get it."

The site manager met them at the door to his trailer. "Detectives Conners and Dobson?" They nodded and he opened the door wider. "I'm Ned Ford. The boss called, said you needed to speak with Ray Russell."

"That's right," Dobby said. "We appreciate your cooperation."

"No problem. Hell of a thing to happen. I honestly don't know what the world's coming to." He waved them toward a couple folding chairs. "Have a seat, I'll make that call."

Quinn preferred to stand and moved her gaze over the trailer's interior. Except for the framed, full-color artist's rendering of the future, completed building, the place was industrial basic. Desk and chair, desktop piled with papers, including blueprints. The two folding chairs. A window unit to keep the place cold or warm, depending on the season.

Dobby made his way to the easel to get a closer look.

"It's going to be a beauty," Ford said, joining him. "All suites. Every detail, top of the line."

Dobby whistled low, under his breath. "I wonder how much a night here would set me back?"

"That's not up to us, but I'm sure it won't be cheap."

Quinn stepped back in. "Is Mr. Russell on his way?"

"He is. It should only be a couple of minutes." He motioned toward the chairs again. "You sure you don't want to sit?"

"We're sure," they answered in unison.

An awkward silence settled over them and Ford cleared his throat. "The company offered Russell the week off, but he insisted on coming back. Said he needed to be busy. Can't say I'd be any different, under the circumstances."

"How well do you know, Mr. Russell?"

"He's a good worker. Well-liked. Never given me—or the company—any trouble."

The trailer door opened; Russell stepped through. He stiffened when he saw them.

"Hello, Ray," Quinn said.

His eyes narrowed slightly at her use of his given name. "Hey."

"The trailer is yours," Ford said, making his way to the door. "No rush. Make yourselves comfortable."

Russell shuffled his feet. Quinn indicated the chairs. "Have a seat."

He suddenly looked apprehensive. "I get paid by the hour. I hope this won't take too long?"

"It shouldn't."

He sat, hard hat cradled in his hands. "Has there been a development in the case?"

"You could say that."

He moved his gaze between the two of them.

"Were you aware that Karlee was pregnant?"

He stared blankly at her, the only indication he had heard her was a muscle twitching in his jaw.

"Mr. Russell?"

He blinked. The hard hat slipped from his grasp, making a soft thud as it hit the floor. "What did you say?"

"Your fiancé was pregnant. Eight weeks."

He dropped his head into his hands. Gave it a shake.

"She didn't tell you?"

"No." He looked up. There were tears in his eyes. "We . . . talked about having kids . . . someday."

"You wanted children?"

"We both did."

"But you didn't want them yet, is that right?"

"What do you mean?"

"You weren't ready?"

"*We* decided to wait. Until we were more financially stable."

"Why do think she didn't tell you?"

"I don't know."

"Could it be she was scared of your reaction?"

His forehead wrinkled. "My reaction? No. Why would she be?"

"Because she knew you weren't ready."

"You're putting words in my mouth. We planned to wait, but that doesn't mean if an accident happened, I'd be angry. I loved her." The words came out choked, strangled by tears. "I would have loved our baby."

"I still don't get it. Why didn't she tell you?"

"Maybe she was going to surprise me?"

"Maybe, but she was eight weeks along. That seems like a long time to wait to me." She paused. "Does it seem like a long time to you?"

He shifted in his seat. "I don't . . . not really."

"It is," Dobby offered. "I'm a dad. When a woman's pregnant, it's the biggest thing in her life, probably ever. Hard to keep that a secret."

Quinn jumped on the opening. "Did you two keep secrets from each other?"

"No, of course not."

"Clearly, she kept them from you," Quinn said.

Dobby made a sympathetic sound. "Eight weeks. Wow, man. I'm so sorry."

"She must have wanted to surprise me." Russell covered his face with his hands again. "We loved each other. We were happy."

Real anguish in his voice. Despair. Quinn fought the pinch of guilt. Like Dobby had said, instead of a villain, he could be a guy who, in one tragic moment, lost the love of his life and his unborn child.

As if sensing her internal struggle, Dobby stepped in. "We need your help, Mr. Russell. We need to determine which shooter killed your fiancé."

Russell turned his gaze to Dobby. "What can I do?"

Quinn took the copy of the preliminary crime scene sketch from her jacket pocket, unfolded it and held it in front of him.

"Can you reconfirm where you were standing at the time gunfire erupted?"

He tapped the mark from the other day.

"You're certain?"

"About there. It's hard to be exact."

"Approximately, then. About here?"

He nodded. "Yes."

Quinn held out her pen. "Could you initial and date next the spot, please."

"What?" He looked from her to Dobby, then back. "Why do you need that?"

"Since we're reconstructing details of the scene after the fact, we have to follow a special departmental procedure. This insures neither we, nor the NOPD, will be accused of falsifying information."

He hesitated a moment, then took the pen and paper, and using his leg as a support, initialed and dated it, then handed it back.

She pretended to study it a moment. "Just for clarity, you were here, and she was walking away from you."

"No, she was walking toward me."

"Are you sure? I seem to remember you telling us the opposite the day of the incident." It was a fib, but worth a try.

"No. She was walking towards me."

She tilted her head, feigning confusion. "I was sure you told me that as she walked away, she looked back at you and smiled."

"Yeah," Dobby spoke up, "I think I remember that, too."

He suddenly looked pasty. "That couldn't have happened."

"Why not?"

"Because she was coming towards me!"

"From where?" She held out the drawing.

He tapped the spot, hand shaking.

"She wasn't with you?"

"She was at the party with me, but she had gone to talk to someone."

"Who?"

"I don't know . . . I don't remember." He shook his head. "It was a party, that's what people do. It could have been anyone there."

"Who were you standing with when the shooting began?"

He blinked. "What?"

"Like you said, it was a party. People visit with each other. Who were you visiting with?"

His brow furrowed. "No one."

"No one?" She said, hoping to infuse the question with the right combination of surprise and sympathy.

"I was watching Karlee."

"A moment ago you said you didn't know who she was talking to?"

"I mean I was waiting for her," he corrected. "So we could go."

"You weren't having a good time?"

"They were her friends, not mine."

"I didn't realize she'd dragged you to the party."

"No, not dragged." He looked at Dobby as if for help. "You know how it is. I knew most everybody, but through her."

Dobby nodded. "I get it. It's part of being a couple."

Quinn jumped back in. "To be clear, you were standing there alone, waiting for her so you could leave?"

"Right."

"When the first shots were fired, where was she?"

"Walking back to me."

Quinn paused, pretending to study her notes and compare them to the sketch, deliberately letting several moments tick past. He shifted uncomfortably in his seat.

"I should probably get back to work."

"It's so strange," she murmured.

"What?"

"The direction of her body on the ground confuses me."

A fine sheen of sweat had broken out on his upper lip. "I don't know anything about that."

"Your fiancé was shot in the back, Mr. Russell. Twice."

"I want the bastard who did it to pay."

"We want that, too, Ray. Believe me, that's all we're after."

He snatched up his hard hat and stood. "I really have to get back to work."

"Please sit down, Mr. Russell."

"I've told you everything I know!"

"Unfortunately, we haven't told you everything *we* know."

His face dropped. "What do you mean?"

"Sit down, Mr. Russell." He did. "Karlee was not killed by random gunfire."

His gaze darted between her and Dobby. "I don't understand."

"The third gunman we told you about, he killed Karlee. He shot her the back with deadly precision. With such precision in fact, that there's no way it could have been an accident. What do you have to say about that?"

"That's not possible," he managed after a moment, voice choked. "I was there."

"Exactly, Ray."

"What does that mean?"

She didn't blink. "You tell us."

He dropped his head. Seconds ticked past like heavy heartbeats. Finally, he lifted his gaze. When he met hers, she saw resentment smoldering in his. "I'm not saying another word until I have a lawyer."

SEVENTEEN

7:10 P.M. *Friday.*

Quinn stood in front of her open refrigerator, perusing the meager contents. She really had to make the time to go grocery shopping. Tomorrow, she promised herself, reaching for the carton of eggs. Two left, she saw, then checked the expiration date. Past their prime, but only by a day. It was either chance it or wait for a take-out delivery—she was going to take her chances.

Eggs, toast and a stiff whiskey. How many times did she and her dad have that very same dinner—substitute milk for the booze, for her anyway—while she was growing up? Too many to count. Same went for grilled cheese sandwiches, chicken noodle soup from the can, and PB&Js.

While she pulled together the meal, she mentally shuffled through the week. It'd flown by. The triple had dominated her and Dobby's days, although new cases had demanded their attention as well.

They'd searched the Department of Public Safety's database, hoping to find proof that Russell owned a gun. Problem was,

Louisiana gun laws were some of the most lenient in the country—neither registration nor background check was required to own, purchase, or openly carry a handgun. However, a permit was required to carry a concealed weapon—but that search came up empty.

She poured the whipped eggs into the hot skillet, then quickly dropped the bread into the toaster.

Painter's obstetrician had agreed to speak with them between patients, but they'd had to wait. Dobby seemed to find himself right at home in the crowded waiting room, even chatting with the very pregnant woman across from him about Lamaze classes and the perils of assembling a crib.

Quinn, on the other hand, found herself uncomfortably flipping through the only two non-house-home-baby magazines: *Field and Stream* and *Golf Digest*.

The wait had proved a waste of time—the doctor had never met Ray Russell and couldn't recall Karlee ever mentioning him in any way other than "the baby's father."

Quinn finished scrambling the eggs and scooped them onto the plate, then buttered her nearly scorched toast. She carried it to the table and sat, absently consuming her dinner and sipping the Jameson, thoughts miles away from the food. The toughest moments of the week had been when they questioned Karlee's mother. She hadn't known about the baby and had become hysterical. Her husband had held her up to keep her from collapsing. The conversation with Karlee's sister hadn't been much easier. She'd taken the news of the pregnancy with disbelief, accused them of lying. Apparently the two had shared everything—or so she'd believed.

Quinn pushed away the plate and sat back, bringing the whiskey to her lips. She and Dobby had ended the week tracking down Karlee's friends and co-workers, figuring she might have shared the news she was pregnant with someone, and to also inquire if Karlee had spoken of any problems with Russell.

Besides some outright hostility, they'd gotten nothing. She had to admit, it was starting to look like they were wrong about Russell, and they were going to have to look in another direction.

What direction she didn't know.

Her cell phone sounded, and she answered without looking at the display. "This is Conners."

"Quinn, it's Uncle Mikey."

Lieutenant Mike Bruzeau, her dad's former partner and best friend, served in the Third District. He also happened to be her godfather.

"Uncle Mikey," she said, pleased. "It's so good to hear from you. It's been awhile."

"I've been falling down on my Godfather duties. How you doing, kiddo?"

"Can't complain."

"You still dating that fella who owned that fancy-pants wine bar Uptown, what was his name?"

"Rick," she said, ignoring the pinch in her chest. "Nope, we broke up."

"Then he obviously wasn't good enough for you."

"You know how it is, Uncle Mikey. Cops can be tough to love."

"That they can be. Hey, I hear you pulled the Mid-City triple homicide. How's it going?"

"Not the slam-dunk we thought it was, but it's progressing."

"The surprise third shooter."

"News travels fast and far."

"That it does. You ever need anything, bounce a theory around, I'm available."

"I appreciate that, Uncle Mikey. I may take you up on it." She took a sip of the Jameson. "I suspect, however, you didn't call to discuss my love life or case load, am I right?"

"You are. I wanted to give you a heads-up. A woman was in to see me about the Hudson case. Asked me a bunch of questions about it and about your dad."

Quinn frowned. "About Dad? What kind of questions?"

"Why he never gave up, what were some of his theories, why he killed himself. She wondered if his suicide had something to do with the case."

She reached for her whiskey. "What the hell? That's none of her damn business."

"That's what I told her, too. She said she's writing a book about it. Plans to call you too, she said. Her name's Eden Riley."

The name didn't ring any bells. "Me? Why?"

"Thinks you might be able to give her a glimpse into your dad's thoughts."

"Help her write a book and drag his name through the mud? Fat chance of that."

"She was persistent, I'll give her that. Personally, I don't think she has any idea who she's up against or what kind of pushback the Hudsons can deliver."

"You have any info on her?"

"A little. She says she's from Dekalb, Illinois and teaches English at the community college there. She did mention that her mom passed away in early March. She's been in town about a month."

"She left you her contact information?"

"Of course. You want it?"

"I do. I might play offense and give her a call."

"I'll text you what I have. Let me know how it turns out."

"I will. I—" She thought of the flyer and changed tack. "Hey, Mikey?"

"Yeah?"

"I've been thinking about dad a lot lately and I was wondering . . . why do you think he killed himself?"

He hesitated before answering, as if her question had caught him off guard. "You've got me there; other than the drinking, I don't know."

"You saw the scene . . . any question in your mind that he . . . didn't do it?"

He was quiet for a long moment. When he finally answered, his voice was low and vibrated with sympathy. "Sorry, kiddo. I know how much it hurts."

It did hurt. More than if it he'd been murdered. Because the way it stood, he chose to go. He chose to leave her. "Why didn't he leave me a note?"

"Maybe he was a selfish son-of-a bitch. Or maybe it had grown so dark in his own head that he couldn't see another way out. Between that, the booze and his fixation on the Hudson case . . . I don't know," he said again. "I didn't see it coming. Maybe I should have, but I didn't."

"Yeah," she said, fighting the lump of tears that settled in her throat. "Maybe I should have, too."

"Let's get together soon, okay?"

"I'd like that." She paused, then asked, "Uncle Mikey?"

"Yeah?"

"What was the last straw? For you, I mean. You and Dad were so close . . . then you weren't."

He was silent for a long moment. "There were so many last straws—"

"Then the beginning of the end? When you first thought he'd changed, that he would never be the same as before?"

She heard him breathe deeply, then exhale slowly. "The baby clothes," he said. "His thinking altered, became . . . I don't know, not irrational but . . . irrationally adamant."

She drew her eyebrows together. "I don't understand."

"After those clothes arrived, he refused to accept that Grace Hudson was dead."

EIGHTEEN

Rourke Conners
1996

2:20 P.M.
Second District Station

Rourke propped the phone to his ear with his shoulder. "This is Conners."

"Detective, it's Daniel Shaw."

The unit buzzed with activity, and Rourke turned his back to the room and pressed the receiver tight to his ear. "I'm sorry, who is this?"

"Daniel Shaw, the Hudson family attorney."

The name, what this call might mean, affected him like a jolt of caffeine. He had been waiting for a break in the case; waiting, somehow certain that eventually it would come.

Rourke worked to tamp down his excitement. "How can I help you, Mr. Shaw?"

"Mr. Hudson received a package this morning. He needs you to come to the St. Charles Avenue residence immediately."

"Which Mr. Hudson?"

"Hudson senior. He was adamant it had to be you."

Rourke checked his watch. Nearly 2:30. He'd promised his mom he'd relieve her of Quinn by six. "What kind of package?"

"I wasn't fully informed."

Bullshit. "I don't have time for games, Mr. Shaw. What kind of package?"

"He said it was urgent. That's all I can tell you."

The entitlement of the request got his back up and Rourke tried a bluff of his own. "I'm sorry, I have conflict this afternoon. If it can't wait until tomorrow morning then my partner will be happy to—"

"It can't wait, and he won't do."

"Then maybe Mr. Hudson should have called me himself. I'm not going to miss an important family event for another something that's nothing."

"Mr. Hudson thinks it's . . ." The attorney's voice turned rough. He cleared his throat and tried again. "He believes the package contains the clothes that Grace . . . that she was wearing . . . that day."

For a moment, Rourke couldn't find his breath, let alone his voice. He processed, fought for equilibrium.

"Detective? Did you hear—"

"I'll be there as soon as I can." He hung up and looked over his shoulder at Mikey. "That was Daniel Shaw. There may be a break in the case."

Mikey stood, grabbed his jacket off the back of his chair. "What kind of break?"

"A package came to the St. Charles Avenue mansion; it looks like the clothes baby Grace was wearing the day she was taken."

Mikey whistled. "After two years?"

"*If* it's for real. They want us there ASAP. Hold tight, I need to let Mom know I might be late."

She picked up on the first ring, sounding rushed.

"Mom, it's me."

"Your dad and I on our way out the door to pick Quinn up from pre-school," she said. "Is everything all right?"

"I wanted to let you know I may be late."

"Again?"

"There's been a break in a case."

"It's *that* case isn't it."

She sounded the way she used to, when he was a kid and she caught him doing something he knew he wasn't supposed to. Disappointed. Chiding. "Mom—"

"Isn't it?"

"Yes. Something big has happened—"

"Something big is always happening." She let out a frustrated sounding breath. "It's almost like you'll do anything to stay away from home."

Her words, like a high-velocity bullet, tore through him. "That's not fair, Mom."

"Isn't it? Do you realize how little time you actually spend with your daughter?"

"For God's sake, it's a couple hours."

"The hours add up and lost time is lost forever. Losing Maggie the way you did, I would have thought you'd learned that lesson."

"Now Maggie's death was a lesson?"

The words came out choked; she made a sound of regret. "Your dad and I planned to go out to dinner. The Peterson's are going to meet us."

"Damn, Mom, I'm sorry. I'll try to make it by six, I promise."

She sighed. "If you don't, we'll bring her with us."

He hung up and joined Mikey. They didn't speak until they were both buckled into Mikey's Chevy. "You okay?" Mikey asked, backing out of the parking space.

"Yeah, I'm fine," he muttered, though he wasn't. He was a world away from fine.

"Was she guilt-tripping you?"

"Nah." Rourke let out a long breath and leaned his head against the rest. "I wouldn't blame her if she had been. She and Dad wanted to travel during retirement, now they're saddled with raising my kid. They can't even meet friends for dinner."

His partner didn't comment, and Rourke went on. "You know what really sucks?"

"Besides the whole situation?"

He looked away, then back. "It's that she knows Quinn so much better than I do. I'm like the babysitter. I provide the caretaker relief. Fuck." He dragged a hand through his dark, wavy hair. "I've got nothing in common with my own kid."

Mikey made the light at Jackson Avenue. "We're partners, right? I can be brutally honest?"

Rourke grimaced. "I don't know if I can take brutal right now."

"Tough, you're getting it anyway. You've got to have balance, man. When you're cleared for personal hours, take 'em. If you need to punch out, punch the fuck out. This could have waited. Or I could have gone without you."

"This feels important."

"It could be." Mikey turned onto St. Charles Avenue, crossing the neutral ground ahead of a streetcar. "So what? This is a two-year-old case. The clock's not ticking, and the contents of that box will still be there in the morning."

Rourke pinched the bridge of his nose. "You're right. It's just I . . ."

"What?"

He shifted uncomfortably in his seat. "I felt like I had to be there," he said.

"I get it, man. I really do." He paused, then added, "My kids are older, I see how fast time goes by. Quinn's five now, and it sounds corny as hell, but you're going to blink your eyes and she'll be ten. Then you'll blink again and she'll be graduating from high school. Think about that."

NINETEEN

The Hudson Mansion

Charles Hudson himself opened the door. He looked hollow-eyed and drawn, as if his flesh had begun to sink into his skull. "I let everyone go for the day," he said, swinging the door wide and stepping aside so they could enter the cavernous foyer. "I didn't want this news to leak before we're ready."

"That was wise," Rourke said. "We don't even know if what you're dealing with is legitimate."

He didn't comment on that and indicated for them to follow. "My son and Shaw are waiting in my office."

Moments later they entered the room. Bill sat on the couch, gazing vacantly at the floor. He briefly glanced up when they entered but didn't speak. Shaw, standing at the window and looking out, turned to greet them, expression grim. "Thank you for coming, Detectives."

"Of course." Rourke indicated the open cardboard box sitting on the desk. "Is that the item in question?"

Charles Hudson took over. "It is. Have a look."

Rourke fitted on a pair of gloves. Mikey did the same. "Who else knows about this?"

"Just three of us," Senior replied.

"Not your wife?"

"No. I didn't want her to see it. Simone, she—" He paused, seeming to collect himself. "—she bought Grace that outfit. I remember it."

"This outfit, she was wearing it the day she was abducted?"

Bill spoke up. "Yes. She was wearing it when I kissed her good—"

He couldn't finish. The word hung heavily in the room anyway. Goodbye. He had kissed her goodbye.

Rourke felt sick. He supposed that intellectually he'd known Grace must be dead. If not, why no ransom demand? Still, his heart had still held out hope.

He and Mikey crossed to the desk. Rourke scanned the outside of the box. Plain brown cardboard shipping box. No company logo. No remnants of a previous shipping label or tape.

It had been purchased specifically for this purpose, most probably at a pack and ship type store or an office supply.

Rourke shifted his focus to the top of the box and its open flaps. Hudson or one of his people had ripped away the packing tape. The sender had used a lot of tape, opening it had torn away a layer of the cardboard, taking much of the cardboard flap with it. From what remained, he saw it had been addressed by hand in black ink— marker, judging by the blackness and width of the line—no return address had been included. The printing was precise but slightly lopsided. Self-applied postage, he saw from what was left after the destruction caused by the removal of the tape.

Rourke nudged the flap down, peered inside. Tissue paper. White. Crinkled now that it had been shoved back into the box. He carefully inched it aside. Fabric below. Pink and white stripes with appliquéd daisies and bumble bees.

Charles Hudson spoke. "That's as far as I got. I saw the fabric and I knew."

Rourke glanced up at Mikey. His partner nodded, understanding. They needed to document what they were looking at.

"While Detective Bruzeau retrieves his camera, I need to establish chain of custody for the box. You received it when, Mr. Hudson?"

"Yesterday. My PA delivered it to me here."

"Your PA?"

"I have all mail routed through the office. For both safety purposes and convenience."

Rourke nodded. "What's the process after being delivered to the business?"

"Mail is sorted then delivered to the various floors. My PA separates my personal and business mail, then delivers both."

"Personal mail here?"

"Yes."

"He delivered this box himself, yesterday?"

"Patrick, yes. I believe you met him the day of the . . . incident."

Hudson couldn't say it even after two years—murder, kidnapping. Instead, he sanitized it by calling it an incident. Because it was too painful? Or something else?

"Had he opened it?"

"Yes. However, he wouldn't have inspected the contents."

"Exactly, what does that mean?"

"He opens everything for my convenience, but if something is obviously personal—"

"Did he or did he not, see the contents?"

Hudson looked uncharacteristically hesitant. "I don't know." He glanced at Shaw. "If he had seen what I did, surely he would have . . . brought it to my attention."

Mikey returned with the camera. Rourke didn't take his gaze from Hudson.

"Were you home when he delivered it?"

"No, Mrs. Thompson would have let him in, and he would bring it here, to my desk."

"Typically, does he open packages here or at the office?"

"I've never specified one over the other."

Rourke made a note to contact the PA. The packing tape had either been disposed of here or at The Hudson Group's headquarters; he needed to get his hands on it before it landed in the dump.

"Let's move on," he said. "So, you didn't get around to any of your mail until today?"

"That's right."

"Was anyone with you?"

"No. I was alone."

Rourke's mouth went dry imagining the moment. "What happened then?"

"I called both Daniel and Bill."

"In that order?"

His brow creased. "Pardon me?"

"Who did you call first?"

"Why does it matter?"

"Maybe it doesn't. I'm painting the picture, creating the timeline."

"Daniel. Then Bill."

He'd called the fixer first. Interesting. It said something about the man, about what and who he valued.

Rourke slid his gaze to the younger Hudson. He hadn't known that, he saw by his expression, and it didn't sit well.

"What then?" Mikey asked, slinging the camera strap around his neck.

"I had Daniel call Detective Conners."

"Why me?" Rourke asked.

"Because you're the only one who hasn't given up."

It was true, he hadn't been able to let go. As time allowed, he reviewed the case for something that had been missed. Checked in with witnesses, tried to jog their memories, see if they had recalled something new. Sometimes the smallest things made the biggest difference.

He glanced at Mikey. "We're ready?" He nodded and they returned to the box. Rourke gazed at it a moment, the crinkled tissue.

How the contents had been packed meant something. Why the tissue? You wrapped a gift in tissue. Some retailers wrapped tissue around an item before bagging it. A sign of quality, and respect for that quality. Maybe even reverence.

His thoughts caught on that. *Reverence*. As if something precious was wrapped in here. In the eyes of the sender, worthy of care.

An iron taste filled his mouth. The hairs at the back of his neck prickled. Important, he thought. This was important.

Paper peeled away, Rourke carefully drew out the garment, held it up. A strangled cry came from Hudson senior; a low moan from junior. From Shaw, nothing. He stared, expression blank, face bloodless.

A stain on the sweet, flowery top. Dried and vile. An atrocity against innocence. Rourke recognized the substance, its deep reddish-brown color. Blood. Old. Oxidized.

Neatly folded underneath the tunic top was the rest of the outfit. Carefully, Mikey removed the other items: matching bottoms, pink socks, and one achingly tiny shoe, also stained.

A match for the one left behind in Ms. Praxton's Buick. A detail that had been kept from everyone.

Rourke swallowed hard. This was the real deal—the clothes baby Grace had been wearing the day she was taken.

"That stain, what is it?" The choked question came from senior. "That's not, tell me it's not—"

"We won't know for sure until we have it tested—"

"For God's sake, Dad!" Junior launched to his feet, visibly shaking. "You know what it is! It's over . . . it's over now!"

As abruptly as he had stood, he went down. Hard. Head to hands, shoulders hunched and shaking. Silent.

Quinn had had a similar outfit. Soft cotton and pastel colors. Sweet. Like a little girl.

Breathe, Rourke. This isn't Quinn.

Someone else's tragedy. Not yours.

Mikey stepped in, as if understanding Rourke couldn't. "Let's not jump to conclusions. We only know what we see. The lab will test the substance—"

"You think it's blood, don't you?"

That from Shaw. Directed at him, not Mikey. Rourke met his gaze, working to maintain a deadpan expression. "I do. That doesn't mean it's hers."

"A sick joke," Senior said, voice steely. "A business rival, maybe. A former employee. Someone with an axe to grind."

He didn't voice his doubts. That tiny shoe. Left behind. No one could know that; it hadn't been publicized.

"I'll crucify them," Senior said. "They'll have nothing left when I'm done with them."

Rourke didn't doubt the man meant it. What that would look like he didn't know, but it wouldn't be pretty.

"Let us deal with this, Mr. Hudson. My partner is going to call it in. Get the evidence team involved. Considering how important this might be, I want to ensure its chain of custody from this moment on and preserve any trace material that might still be available to us."

Shaw had collected himself. "Anything we can do to help. Consider me to be at your disposal, twenty-four seven."

"Thank you."

While they waited for CSI team to arrive, Rourke contacted the PA. The man believed he had opened the package at the office, adding the caveat that he opened a lot of packages for Mr. Hudson so there was a small chance he was confusing them. In an abundance of caution, Rourke and Mikey donned Hazmat suits and assisted a crime scene tech with the dirty work of sifting through the Hudson's trash—but came up empty. Picking through the Hudson Group's trash was not going to be nearly so easy. Or quick.

No way he'd make it home by 6:00. He'd be lucky to make it by 10:00.

Shaw escorted them out. "I've made arrangements for Ned Stahl, the Hudson Group's office manager, to meet you. He has the trash collection schedule and will direct you to the bins. You both have my personal number?" he asked.

"We do."

"Good."

Without another word, the fixer went back into the home. Odd and final. As if it was done, over now. The question mark erased, replaced with a period.

No more hope.

That stuck in Rourke's throat, resisted being swallowed. Who gave up that way? He imagined Quinn taken, missing. Without proof he would never lose hope. Never.

They climbed into Mikey's Chevy. Rourke fastened his safety belt, looked at his partner. "There's something about this I don't like."

"There's nothing I like about it. I feel like I need a bath."

Rourke understood. The image of those ugly stains on that petite garment would haunt him. Unfortunately, no amount of soap and water could wash them away. Whiskey would, he'd learned. For a short time anyway.

"It's blood," Mikey said.

"Oh, yeah it is."

"Maybe it's not human?"

It was. He knew it in his gut. Judging by Mikey's expression, he knew it, too. "Maybe. That's an easy test. We'll have that quick."

"DNA will take longer." Mikey pulled away from the curb. "What's not sitting right? You think somebody's messing with the Hudsons?"

That wasn't it, but he couldn't put his finger on exactly what *was* it. Or maybe it was him. He wasn't ready. He couldn't let go.

Mikey didn't seem bothered by his silence. "No doubt the Hudsons have made a lot of enemies over the years. You heard Hudson senior in there?"

Mikey glanced at him, then back at the road. "Crucify," he said. "He meant it. Dude's got ice water running through his veins."

"Did you pick up that Senior called Shaw before he called his son?"

"Yeah."

"That's odd, don't you think? He called his fixer before his son, Grace's daddy?"

"I don't know, people like that . . . they think differently than us regular folk do."

"About something like this?" Rourke turned his gaze to the window. The streetcar passed, a blur of faces at the windows. "What about that thing Junior said— It's over. What did he mean by that? It felt weird to me."

Mikey thought a moment, then shook his head. "Not so much to me."

"What did he mean?"

"That it was literally over. He couldn't hope anymore."

Rourke's hands turned to fists; he voiced his earlier thought. "I'd never stop hoping. Not until—"

He choked on the words, turned his gaze to the window once more.

"Think of what they're going through. What they've been going through for two years now. It's about closure, man. There's relief in *knowing*. We see that all the time."

They did. But this was a kid.

The light ahead turned red. Mikey stopped, turned to Rourke, his expression concerned. "There's something you're not saying."

There was, but it was out of focus, slightly beyond his reach. "It's hard, man. Once we have the lab results, we'll have our next move."

TWENTY

Rourke sat at his desk, Jameson within reach, Hudson case photos spread out in front of him. Photos of all the players involved, of the scene and now, the box with its disturbing contents.

Thoughts of the day jumbled together, creating a chaotic, sleep-stealing mix. His mother's —*"It's almost like you don't want to come home."* — cut him to the quick. He couldn't stop the words from replaying in his head.

Because there was truth in them.

There, he'd admitted it to himself. He didn't look forward to coming home at night, would rather stay at the Second in the company of criminals, victims and his colleagues. How messed up was that?

He sipped the whiskey. The pain he encountered there wasn't his own. Not like here. Every time he looked at Quinn, he thought of Maggie—and of what he had lost.

He tipped the glass side-to-side, staring at the amber liquid, the way it caught the light. The Hudsons had lost their precious girl and here he was, avoiding his. What kind of a father was he? What kind of a man? Maggie would be so disappointed in him.

His eyes burned and Rourke threw back the drink. He was failing Quinn. What did he know of young daughters and their needs? That was to be Maggie's area, her job. How did he turn this ship around?

He refocused on the crime photos. He had to be missing something. Every suspect, every new lead, dead-ended. Was it him? Was it the fog of grief that never left him? Was it clouding his vision, his ability to see the truth?

"Daddy?"

Rourke dragged his gaze away from the photos fanned across his desk and looked over his shoulder at four-year-old Quinn. She stood in the doorway to his office, rubbing her eyes, red hair sticking out in every direction.

"Quinnie, baby, why aren't you asleep?"

Her chin trembled. "I woke up."

Rourke checked the time, noted it was nearly midnight, and swiveled his chair around and held out his arms. "Come here, sweetheart."

She scurried over and he lifted her onto his lap, his heart melting as she snuggled into him. "Did you have a bad dream?"

She shook her head no, but her next words told him she had. "Tell me again 'bout Mommy."

"She loved you so, so much, Quinnie. You were her very favorite person in the whole, wide world."

Her little face wrinkled in thought. "Why'd she go away?"

Tears burned his eyes and he blinked against them. They had been through this many times before, but each time it hurt more than the last. And each time he felt like a fraud. Because every word from his tongue felt false—what did he know of calming a little girl's fears or healing her broken heart?

He turned back to the desk to reach for his whiskey, then remembered he had finished it. "She didn't want to go. Remember, baby? She got really sick."

He felt her sigh. "Grandma says she's an angel now."

A knot formed in his throat. His mother always knew the right thing to say, same as Maggie had. "Grandma's a smart lady." The words came out choked but she didn't seem to notice. Apparently, the photos spread out on the desk had caught her attention. With a sense of horror, he realized that one of them was a photo of the bloody crime scene and Cynthia Hudson. He quickly turned the photo over, praying she hadn't noticed it.

His prayer appeared to be answered as she pointed to the photo of baby Grace. "Who's that?"

"Her name is Grace Hudson."

She nodded and indicated one of Bill Hudson. "Who's he?"

"Grace's daddy. And that—" He tapped the one of a very much alive Cynthia Hudson. "—is her mommy."

One by one, Quinn asked him to name each person pictured. When he'd finished, she asked, "They friends of yours?"

"No, baby, this is for my work."

She smiled up at him. "Police work."

"That's right. I'm a detective."

"De-tec-tive," she repeated, carefully sounding out the word. She'd heard it before and sounded it out before. In fact, he wasn't quite sure why, but she sounded it out every time.

"They do something bad?" she asked.

"Something bad happened," he corrected. "It's my job to figure out what."

She frowned slightly and he explained. "Policemen—detectives, like me—solve crimes."

She looked from the photos to him. "How you do that?"

He thought a moment. "You like puzzles, right?" She nodded and he indicated the photos. "Think of all these photographs as puzzle pieces. Somehow, they all fit together. I need to figure out how."

She looked up at him again, frowning. Obviously, she didn't understand.

He tried to explain in a way she could grasp. "You know how, with a puzzle, you can't see the whole picture until you—" Realizing what he was trying to explain was still too abstract for her barely four-year-old mind to grasp without a visual, he changed tack. "I'll show you what I mean, okay?"

"'kay."

She slid off his lap and held out her hand. He took it and they walked to her bedroom. From her toy shelf he retrieved one of her wooden puzzles, then dumped it on the bed and scrambled all the pieces.

"Now, let's turn them over." They did, then he asked, "Do you know which one of your puzzles this is?"

She studied the pieces a moment. "Sesame Street."

"Good. You have three different Sesame Street puzzles. Do you know which one this is? Elmo, Burt and Ernie, or Big Bird?"

She screwed up her face in thought. He could all but see her comparing the pieces, trying to decide. Watching, her eyes flicked from one piece to another, as if visually assessing the amount of red versus that of yellow, looking for the telltale stripes of Bert and Ernie's sweaters or Big Bird's familiar feathers.

He'd always seen Maggie in her but at that moment, he saw himself. Pride swelled up in him.

"Not sure," she said.

"That's okay. I'm not sure either. How can we find out?"

"Put it together!"

"Right. Let's do it."

Together, they began placing the pieces around the edges of the board; while they did, he spoke.

"As a detective, Daddy tries to figure out the truth of what happened. It's like I have all these pieces that make up the whole picture."

He paused. "First, I examine the pieces, which I call clues. There are twenty here, look at all of them carefully." He gave her a minute. "Study the colors and shapes and patterns. Did you do that?"

She nodded and he smiled at her in approval. "Next, let's start placing the pieces."

With him mostly watching her work, they did. It wasn't the first time she'd put this one together, but still she went about it methodically, starting with the outside, then moving on to the interior pieces.

He liked doing this with her, he realized. Like seeing the way her mind worked, the way she drew her eyebrows together into a serious little frown.

"It's the Elmo one!" she squealed. "Look!" She pointed to Elmo's face. "I'm a detective, too!"

"Not so fast, Quinnie. Sometimes it *looks* like you have the answer, but you don't, not yet. You have to take it all the way to completion because when you're a detective, you don't guess."

She nodded, expression intent. She placed the rest of the pieces, one-by-one, occasionally misjudging and refocusing herself. She never seemed to get frustrated, never got bored or gave up.

When she set the last piece, she looked up triumphantly. "I was right, it *is* the Elmo!"

"You *were* right. I'm proud of you!"

She giggled. "This puzzle is easy, Daddy. I've had it since I was a baby."

Since this past Christmas. He supposed when you were four, three seemed like a lifetime ago. He ruffled her hair. "I'm proud of you because of the *way* you did it. Just like a detective would."

She yawned and he set aside the puzzle. "C'mon, baby, let's get you tucked in."

Back in her room, she crawled under the covers. "Daddy, are all your cases like that?"

He sat on the edge of the bed, nudging one of her riotous red curls off her forehead. "Sometimes my cases are simple puzzles, like that one was. Other times they're really complicated with lots and lots of pieces."

She smiled sleepily. "That was fun. Maybe I can help you 'vestigate again?"

Her eyelids drooped and he bent and pressed a kiss to her fore-head. "I'd like that, Quinnie. I'd like it a lot."

TWENTY-ONE

Quinn Conners
  Present Day

8:00 P.M.
  Lakeview

After saying goodbye to Uncle Mikey, Quinn poured herself a second whiskey. She'd forgotten about the baby clothes. How, after two years of nothing new emerging, the Hudsons had received a package containing bloodstained baby clothes, the items identical to the ones Grace had last been seen in.

She sipped the alcohol, lost in thought. The blood had been analyzed; DNA had proved the blood was Grace Hudson's. Even so, her dad had refused to accept she was dead.

Why? There must have been a reason, something her father picked up on.

Whiskey in hand, Quinn made her way to her small dining room. She flipped on the overhead light. A small, oak table sat in the middle of the room, all four chairs were pushed up against the walls, her puzzle-in-progress spread across the top. This one—an image of endless donuts in all manner of colors, flavors and sprinkles—had been a gift from Dobby, a lighthearted poke at her being a donut-loving cop. Her mouth watered every time she worked on the damn thing.

She took a sip of the whiskey and moved her gaze over the puzzle. She worked blindly, the reference image studied once and tucked away. It was a game she and her dad played as a way to improve their visual acuity. Colors registered. Patterns. Textures. Shapes. She shifted her focus to the pieces, scanning. One jumped out. Then another. Still another. She collected them, snapped them together, the image emerging—hot pink sugared crystals dusted over light pink icing.

She pictured her dad, his dark gaze intently on hers, his expression serious as he said: *"Quinnie, that piece doesn't fit in this puzzle, not the one I'm putting together."*

"Why, Daddy?"

"Because it doesn't make sense."

Of course, that was it, the reason: the arrival of the baby clothes hadn't made sense to him.

Her phone pinged the arrival of a text. From Uncle Mikey, she saw. Eden Riley's contact information. She smiled to herself, checked the time, then tapped the number.

The woman answered on the third ring. "Hello?"

She sounded slightly out of breath; Quinn heard music in the background. She was obviously out enjoying her Friday night. "Is this Eden Riley?"

"Yes, it is."

"This is Detective Quinn Conners, I understand you want to talk to me."

The moment of silence that followed told Quinn she'd caught her off guard. Which, of course, had been her intention.

"Ms. Riley?"

"Yes. Yes, absolutely. Can you hold for a moment while I move someplace a bit quieter?"

"Of course."

A minute later she returned to the call. "Thank you so much for contacting me."

She didn't sound out of breath, Quinn realized. She sounded young. Really young. "How can I help you?"

"I'm writing a book on the—"

"Hudson case. Yes, that's what I was told. How can *I* help you?"

"Oh, um . . . I wanted to ask you some questions about the case."

"You do know I was two-years-old at the time?"

"Of course, but your father was lead detective, over the years he must have discussed the case. Any insights or recollections—"

"I'm afraid not, Ms. Riley."

"Call me Eden, please."

"Where are you from, Eden?"

"Me? Dekalb, Illinois. At least that's where I've lived the past thirteen years. My mom and I moved around a lot when I was young."

"How old are you now?"

"Twenty-eight—"

Not so young, after all. "Where in Illinois is Dekalb?"

"About an hour west of Chicago. We're known for our sweet corn."

"You're a long way from home, Ms. Riley."

"I am. New Orleans always fascinated me, so I'm—"

Quinn cut her off again. "You say you're a writer?"

"Yes."

"You don't sound convinced."

"I don't?"

"No, you don't."

She laughed nervously. "Probably because this is my first book."

"You're unpublished?"

"No. I've published a few short stories, some academic essays."

"That pays the bills?"

"I also teach English and creative writing at the community college."

"The community college? There, in Dekalb?"

"Yes. Some people turn their noses up at community colleges but—"

"I understand you've been in town a month."

"A little more, actually."

"In that time, you must have connected with the principals in the case."

"Some, yes."

"By now you must have acquired a good amount of information?"

"Actually, not that much." The woman was silent a moment. "The folks I need to interview—"

"Are resistant, maybe even hostile, towards you?"

"Yes," she said.

"I'm going to give you a bit of advice because you seem like a nice person—way too nice and way too trusting for what you're setting out to do. I suggest you go back to your corn fields and comfortable little community. It's safe there."

"Have I offended you?" she asked stiffly. "Why are you saying this to me?"

"Because you're out of your depth here. People like Charles and William Hudson don't place nice. Their team of lawyers are sharks in suits who will do anything necessary to make their clients happy, and the Hudsons are a very important client. Take it from me, there are some bears you don't want to poke."

"Why would they stand in the way of me writing this book? Don't they want to know what happened to baby Grace? Don't they want justice for Cynthia? Don't you?"

"Those questions show how out of your depth you are." She paused to let it sink in. "Do you think you're the first?"

"Pardon me?"

"The first writer to come along determined to write the Hudson story? You're not. Writers with a lot more chops than you have tried, and been shut down. *That* I did learn from my father."

"You have no idea what kind of chops I have."

"Sorry, Eden, but I can't help you."

"I know your dad had a special interest in the case. You might even call it obsessive."

Quinn's felt angry heat stain her cheeks. "Excuse me?"

"I heard it from several sources. In fact, they described him as fanatical about the case."

"What sources?"

"Reliable ones." She paused. "I also learned from those same sources that your dad took his own life. By the way, I'm sorry for your loss. I know how hard that is."

Quinn pictured the flyer left under her windshield wiper. The hair at the back of her neck prickled. "What does my dad's suicide have to do with you?"

"Meet with me and we'll talk about it."

Quinn didn't hesitate. If people were talking about her father's involvement with the case, she meant to find out who they were and what they were saying. "Unless I get called in, tomorrow's good. 10:00 A.M.?"

"Perfect. How about my place?"

Quinn agreed and after the woman rattled off her address, she hung up and went in search of her computer. She intended to meet with Eden Riley armed with as much information about her as possible.

Three hours later, growing blurry-eyed and with the beginnings of a headache throbbing at the base of her skull, Quinn stared at her computer screen. Everything Eden Riley had told her about herself and where she lived had been true. She did, indeed, teach English and creative writing at the community college there.

She'd also learned she had done both her undergraduate and graduate work right there in Dekalb at Northern Illinois University. She had published three essays and four short stories; the essays had been writing related, and all four short stories women-in-jeopardy type suspense.

She'd taken the time to read them and had to admit they had been entertaining, with interesting characters and good twists at the end. Her favorite had been the one with the unreliable narrator; as she read, she'd found herself uncertain who or what to believe.

Quinn stretched her arms to the ceiling and rolled her shoulders. Interesting that Eden taught creative writing and had published fiction yet had decided on true crime for her first book.

She tipped her head and drew her eyebrows together in thought. Why choose *this* crime? Yes, it had gotten national press, but never gained the notoriety of renowned cases like Jon Benét Ramsey.

Maybe that was *why* she'd chosen the Hudson case, lesser known meant less exposure already but with all the elements of a bestseller.

Quinn refocused on the screen. First, explore her family, starting with her claim that her mother had recently died. A few clicks later, she sat back in surprise. Eden's mother hadn't just died in the spring, she'd been murdered. In her own home, in the bright light of day. The police believed the perpetrators were addicts looking for drugs. The case was yet unsolved.

Eden Riley had found her mother's body.

Why was she here, only a few months later and far from home, investigating another murder? To write a kind of book she had no experience in writing?

Quinn drummed her fingers on the desktop. For the most part, human beings acted and reacted in ways that could be predicted, that made a certain kind of emotional sense.

There were exceptions, of course. Sociopathy. Mental illness. Extreme physical or emotional trauma.

Excluding those, when circumstances were studied, decisions followed an expected norm. This did not.

Something about Eden Riley being in New Orleans flat made her itch. She had until ten in the morning to find out why.

TWENTY-TWO

9:15 A.M. *Saturday.*

When her cell phone rang, Quinn leapt for the device. She'd placed a call to the Dekalb police department first thing and had been waiting for the detective in charge of the Angela Riley murder investigation to call her back.

"This is Conners," she answered.

"Detective, this Detective Rhea, Dekalb PD. I'm returning your call."

"Thank you, Detective Rhea. I'm sorry to bother you on a Saturday."

"No problem, there's no such thing as a day off in law enforcement."

"Don't I know it."

"How can I help you?"

"I'm calling for information about one of your cases. The Angela Riley murder."

"You're with the New Orleans PD, correct?"

"That's right."

He was silent for a moment. "By any chance does this have something to do with her daughter, Eden Riley?"

Bingo. "It does. How did you know?"

"Because she came to me with this wild theory about her father being the killer."

"It's a wild idea, why?"

"Let me count the ways. First, Angela Riley hadn't had contact with the man in twenty-some years. In fact, Miss Riley has never even met him and doesn't know his name."

Quinn made a note. "That's a stretch, for sure."

"Yet she wanted me to somehow hunt down this ghost."

"She must have had some sort of reasoning to support the idea of him appearing from the past to kill her mother?"

"Oh, she did. Apparently, her mother told her he was bad man and she never wanted them to meet. Ms. Riley speculated that's why her mom took a gig as a traveling nurse."

"Because she was on the run from him."

"Yes. Which, along with everything else she proposed, didn't square for me."

"Why not?"

"She'd been living here in Dekalb for thirteen years. If he'd been after her, why wait thirteen years to exact revenge?"

He had a point. A good one. "That was the whole basis for her argument?"

"There was more. Riley was born in New Orleans. Her mom left with her when she was still a baby."

"Running from the father."

"Presumably. In the weeks before the murder, her mother received two calls from New Orleans."

"Which Ms. Riley believes her father made."

"Yes. Her mother responded by telephoning the NOPD."

"She didn't make a complaint to us," Quinn said, taking a stab, knowing it made it sound like Eden had already shared this information. "There's no record."

"Exactly," he said. "What was I supposed to do?"

"Nothing you could do."

"I get it," he said. "We all grieve differently. It's hard to accept when someone you love is killed like this. You know, somebody looking for a few painkillers. It's senseless and sad."

"No arrest yet?"

"Nope. We had a couple suspects but nothing to link them to the scene. "It sucks."

"Yeah," she agreed. "I feel bad for her, but I've got a job to do."

"Don't we all? It never lets up."

"To be clear, it's one hundred percent your position this whole scenario of hers is fiction? Not one grain of truth in it?"

"In my opinion this is a cut and dry case of a burglary gone bad. Riley should have been at work at the time of the break-in, but came home unexpectedly, startled the perpetrators, they panicked and shot her. We've had six other, nearly identical break-ins in the last six months."

"Thanks for your help. If you think of anything else, I'd appreciate you passing it along."

"I will. You have a good one, Detective."

She told him to do the same and hung up. That was it, the why she was in New Orleans, what her connection to the city was. Quinn drummed her fingers on her thigh. Why the Hudson case?

She didn't know, but she intended to find out.

TWENTY-THREE

Freret Street.

Quinn parked across the street from Eden Riley's apartment. She lived above The Kolache Kitchen bakery and across the street from Mojo coffeehouse. As far as Quinn was concerned, throw in the bar and Dat Dog down the block and life's most important necessities were within walking distance.

Quinn climbed out of her car and crossed to Riley's door. She pressed the call button.

"Is that you, Detective Conners?"

"It is."

"Coming down."

Moments later, the door swung open. The woman on the other side had shoulder-length brown hair and perfect bangs that framed her stunning, wide-set hazel eyes. Her gaze was earnest, her smile welcoming.

"Hey, come on up."

Quinn followed her up the flight of stairs and into the apartment.

She moved her gaze over the interior, with its crown molding and ceiling medallions. "Great place. I love these old buildings."

"I got really lucky," she said, closing and locking the door behind them. "I found a Tulane graduate student subletting for the summer." She motioned Quinn further inside. "He'd had someone lined up who fell through at the last minute, thank goodness for me."

Quinn saw that she'd set out a small plate of breakfast pastries. "You know this isn't a social visit?"

"But it's not official business, and I really appreciate you agreeing to meet me this morning."

Quinn wondered if she would be as appreciative after they talked.

"Would you like an orange juice or coffee?"

"I'm good. Thanks."

She looked disappointed. "Oh, okay. I'm going to grab a juice for myself, sit wherever you like."

The grad student lived well, Quinn thought, taking the single chair instead of the couch. Better than she did, with her old, mis-matched furniture. This place looked like it had been recently outfitted with straight-from-the-showroom IKEA. Even the knick-knacks looked new.

Riley returned to the living room with two glasses. "I brought you a water anyway, in case."

"Of what? I got parched in the next fifteen minutes?"

"In case you changed our mind," she answered, cheeks turning pink.

Quinn admitted to herself that she could be a little nicer. She wasn't going to be, but she could.

Eden handed her the water; Quinn set it on the side table. "I had a conversation with a friend of yours this morning."

She looked surprised. "A friend of mine?"

"Mmm hmm, Detective Rhea, from the Dekalb P.D."

Her face fell. "What did he tell you?"

"Quite a lot. Everything he knew about you and—" She paused for effect. "—your mom's murder."

Eden wet her lips. Set down her juice.

"You weren't honest with me."

"Yes, I was." Her voice trembled slightly. "I said my mother passed away, and she did."

"He believes she interrupted a burglary in progress, the perpetrators panicked and shot her."

She nodded. "Addicts looking for pharmies."

"You don't believe that do you?"

She shook her head, chin angling up. "No."

"According to Rhea, you think your father killed her."

"You know that's what I think because that's what *he* told you. Of course he didn't believe me. He refused to even consider anything but his own theory."

"You don't think much of him, do you?"

"No, I don't.

"He had his reasons."

"Oh, I'm sure he did. He's like a teacher who only wants to teach the easy kids, the gifted ones, the ones who don't step out of line. Then they're great at their jobs. It makes me so mad."

She stood, obviously agitated, and walked to the window that overlooked the street and coffeehouse. She gazed out a moment, then turned back to Quinn. "Did he tell you I was born here, in New Orleans?"

She didn't wait for an answer. "We left when I was eleven months old, and we moved constantly until I was fifteen."

"Your mom was a nurse."

"Yes. During those years, a traveling nurse. She took short-term gigs. Six months, a year. Rarely two years. She was a single mom and it paid really well. The increased pay provided stability for us."

Financial stability, Quinn thought. Instability in every other way. Funny how life did that. "That must have been really hard on you."

"We had each other. We were really close."

Quinn could imagine. She thought of her own life, her single parent. They had never moved. Hell, she still lived in the house she'd grown up in. But they, too, had been very close. Until they hadn't been.

By then it had been too late.

"When I was old enough, I asked about him, my dad. She wouldn't talk about him. The only thing she would say was that he wasn't a good person and she never wanted me to meet him.

"I saw how upset it made her when I brought him up, so I didn't. Somewhere along the line, I realized—" As if becoming aware she was clasping and unclasping her hands, Eden tucked them into her pockets and began again. "It wasn't only that she didn't want him to find us, but that she was *afraid* of him finding us."

She let out a long breath. "That's what I think happened. He found her, and he killed her."

"It's a compelling story, but I see some huge leaps in logic. Being a creative writing teacher, you must see them, too."

"I do know how to plot, Detective. I just haven't shared the whole story yet." She crossed back to the couch, sat and reached for her orange juice. She held it but didn't sip.

"The day she died, she called me. I was in class and didn't get the message until I was leaving. She was home, not at the hospital. Which was very odd. She never missed work.

"She asked me to come by as soon as I could. There was something she had to tell me. Something important, that couldn't wait. I went, and I found her. Bleeding out."

"She wasn't dead?"

She shook her head. "She tried to tell me something . . . it was garbled, pieces of words, disjointed and . . . so soft I had to strain to hear." She looked down at her juice as if surprised to see it in her hands. "It was only later I realized what she was saying. *He found us.* That was it. That was what she was trying to tell me.

"Detective Rhea blew off all of it. Mom's call, her trying to tell me something. He said that when people are close to death, they oftentimes try to speak. They have this instinctual need to reach out to a loved one . . . or anyone, really, one last time."

"That's true, Eden. I see that a lot."

"I know it's what she said!"

"I'm not suggesting she didn't," Quinn said gently, "only that it's easy, after the fact, to put two-and-two together. Or to believe you have."

"Great," she muttered. "Apparently, all you cops are the same."

"Whoa. You're the creative writing expert. Think of me as the editor. I'm here to poke holes in the story. Look—" She leaned toward her. "A crime occurs. Everything about it tells a story. As an investigator, it's my job to figure out the plot. What happened, how it happened, and why it happened."

"Not the 'who done it?'"

"If you figure out the why, you figure out the who." She paused. "Some crimes are simple. Some are not. That's when the 'why' becomes really important. What else do you have?"

"Days before her murder, there were some calls on her cell phone, to and from New Orleans."

"One of them to the New Orleans police, correct?"

"Yes. Why would my mother have called the New Orleans police? And what about the coincidence that she called the them the day before she was murdered?"

Quinn turned the questions over in her mind. This is what she did. It's what her dad taught her to love about police work. Weigh the options. Try out the various pieces of the puzzle, see how they fit.

"Break down the order of the New Orleans calls she received and made."

"She received a call from a 504-area code five days before her murder. It registered as a missed call. The caller did not leave a message, at least that I saw. Two days later, she returned that call.

The call's duration was four minutes, so she obviously reached someone, but the call was short."

"Did you try calling the number?"

"I did. It was no longer in service."

Quinn frowned slightly. It was a red flag Rhea would have noted. "To confirm, there was only one call to and from that 504-area number. No more?"

"Yes, only those two. Then, two days later Mom called the NOPD *and* The Hudson Hotel. She was on with the police six minutes and the hotel for three."

Quinn felt herself coming fully to attention, as if all her senses had turned on at once. "She called The Hudson?"

Riley must have seen the change in her in her demeanor because she got excited. "You think it means something, too."

Quinn ignored the comment. "Was she planning a trip?"

"No."

"Could she have been thinking of taking one, but hadn't discussed it with you?"

"Not to New Orleans, not ever. She never shared memories from her time living here. In fact, she refused to discuss it. She never mentioned favorite places, her job, or friends from New Orleans. Besides, she would have told me. We discussed everything."

"Not everything. Obviously."

Color stained her cheeks. "This is what she wanted to tell me, why she wanted me home that day. That he, my dad, had found us."

"Your guess. You can't know for certain."

Eden opened her mouth as if to argue, then shut it, looked away.

"Why do you think she called The Hudson Hotel?"

"Looking for my dad, maybe. I think he worked there—at least maybe he did twenty-eight years ago."

"Okay, you're in New Orleans because you think your dad is here and that he killed your mom."

"Yes, but also to write a book about the Hudson kidnapping and murder."

"That last part, bullshit."

"It's not! The Hudson case is a fascinating mystery. It has everything: the rich and beautiful, a lovely, young mother murdered, a child taken. This book would have an audience."

The words trotted off her tongue with practiced ease. Quinn leaned forward. "Why are *you* writing it?"

She bristled. "I told you. Plus, I always promised myself I'd write a book, so I took this opportunity to do it."

"This opportunity? You mean your mom being murdered?"

"That's . . . awful. No. She wanted me to write. I'm doing it for me . . . and her."

"You're lying."

"I'm not!"

"None of this makes sense. You think your dad killed your mom, but she tried to call him? You say you're writing about the Hudson case because it 'has all the elements of a bestseller' and will make a great book, but you think, maybe, your dad used to work at a Hudson property? You teach creative writing and have published fiction, but you've come to New Orleans to research and write non-fiction?"

"Yes!"

"You're either lying to me or hiding a private agenda, or both." Quinn stood. "I've got to go. I get few days off and don't want to waste anymore of this one."

"You're leaving?" Riley sounded incredulous. "Please, I need your help."

"Finding your dad? Hire a PI." She started for the door.

"With research," Eden called after her. "Your dad knew this case and all the players better than anyone else."

Quinn looked back. "I'm sure he'd help you if he was alive. He was always ready to jump at the next 'break' in the case, no matter how far-fetched it was."

"You're being unreasonable!"

"What's your connection to the Hudson case?"

"I told you, my mom called the hotel and I figure my dad—"

"I call bullshit, Eden. I wish you luck with whatever you're up to here."

"Wait! You're right, there's more. I'll tell you everything."

TWENTY-FOUR

10:50 A.M.

They sat side by side on the couch, the coffee table pulled close, a large, over-filled manila envelope in front of them.

Eden started to speak, then stopped and took a deep breath—as if for fortification—then began. "I found these things when I was going through my mom's stuff, cleaning out her home. I didn't discover them in one sitting, but I'll share the how and why as we go along. Okay?"

"It's your party."

She nodded, tucked her hair behind her ear, then carefully, almost reverently, it seemed to Quinn, opened the envelope and drew out the first item.

A baby's memory book, its pink and white cover embossed in gold with *The Story of You*. A cut-out picture frame in the center contained a picture of the squished face of a newborn, eyes barely open. Peach fuzz for hair. Rosy, pursed lips, hands curled into wee fists.

Eden looked at Quinn, eyes bright with tears. "Go ahead, flip through it. Then tell me what jumps out at you."

Quinn took the book, laid it in her lap, opened it. The first page included details about Angela Riley's pregnancy, a sonogram of baby Eden, as well as an attached envelope that included a copy of Eden's birth certificate. Next came the birth: a tiny footprint, carefully taped to the page. Eden's mother had neatly penned her baby's weight: six pounds, six ounces; her length, fifteen and a half inches.

Then her name. Eden Rose Riley.

Eden, she'd written. (*paradise, perfect garden*). Rose (*beautiful flower*). *Riley* (*Mine*). She'd underlined the last, as if for emphasis.

Quinn drew her eyebrows together, curious about that emphasis, about the 'why' of it. Because she'd been feeling possessive? Or because she was parenting alone, without a baby-daddy? It made sense, especially considering the adjacent section, designated 'Daddy,' was conspicuously blank.

As if reading along with her, Eden suddenly spoke. "I wondered how she was feeling when she wrote that. I tried to put myself in her place, you know? Fiercely protective? Determined, maybe. Beating back fear, telling herself she could do this alone, without *him*?"

Quinn nodded, wondering about her own father. How he must have felt, suddenly raising her without his partner. Only he hadn't been alone. In many ways he'd abdicated his role, letting her grandparents do the day-to-day heavy lifting of raising her. She'd always figured she'd gotten the best, most interesting, part of him.

Quinn skimmed the next page with its series of names and places, then moved on to Eden's many firsts: first smile, first tooth, first time she'd rolled over, when she'd first begun to crawl, toddle, then—

Nothing. Quinn flipped to the next page, then the next, and next. All blank. After lovingly filling in each blank, not even one quick notation.

Angela Riley had stopped writing in the book at Eden's eleventh month.

Eden spoke. "Weird, huh? The way she stopped."

"My mother did the same thing, but she died."

"I'm so sorry."

Quinn glanced at Eden, annoyed with the empty condolence and with herself for sharing a piece of her personal history. "It's not a big deal. I was two, I don't remember it. Or her."

"What happened?"

She shook her head. "This is about you, not me. Let's move on."

"I want to know. What happened to her?"

Quinn felt the other woman's gaze on her, questioning. Sympathetic. She let out a short, resigned breath.

"Breast cancer," she said matter-of-factly. "She was so busy caring for me, she ignored symptoms, putting them off as something associated with having recently given birth. The cancer was an aggressive strain and by the time she was diagnosed, it was everywhere."

"That must have been so difficult on you and your dad."

"Like I said, I don't remember." She pushed on before Eden could comment again. "This is what you wanted me to see, right? The thing that jumped out at you?"

Eden nodded. "Writing in the pages was obviously a daily ritual for her. Stopping cold turkey, like this? That's not the way human nature works. Human beings are creatures of habit."

She was right. Most folks didn't stop a habit abruptly, but let it fall away, little by little until they forgot it was ever part of their lives. This abrupt *nothing* felt unnatural.

Something in her life had changed.

"Maybe she went back to work?" Quinn offered. "Or went back to work full-time?"

"I wondered that, too. I thought it was odd, but at the time it didn't ring any alarm bells."

Quinn reached for her glass of water. "Then, what did?"

"I couldn't stop thinking about it, her death, the things she'd said about my dad. As time passed without the police making an arrest, I started to wonder if they were on the wrong track. I mean, how hard could it be to find the person, or persons, who'd killed her? It happened in broad daylight, for heaven's sake!"

She looked at Quinn, expression almost pleading. "Do you see what I'm saying? The perpetrators Detective Rhea described didn't sound like criminal masterminds. They either used drugs and were desperate for them or sold them and were desperate for money."

"I get you," Quinn said, "but sometimes the ones that look easy turn out not to be."

"No. Not this time." She shook her head for emphasis. "Hear me out. Remember when you were in school, and you had to write a thesis paper?"

Quinn made a face. "I didn't like school so much, and I *really* didn't like writing papers."

Eden's lips twitched. "Most people don't. I was one of the weird ones. The definition of a thesis is: a short statement that summarizes the main point or *claim* of a paper, which is developed, supported and explained using examples and *evidence*."

Quinn held up her glass. "You sound like a couple teachers I had."

"Don't zone out. Relate this to what you do. In this case, Detective Rhea's thesis maintained that my mother was killed in a botched burglary, one in which the perpetrators were looking for drugs. He set out to prove his thesis by finding the *evidence* to support it."

"Okay. So?"

"What if his premise was wrong? He'd be looking for evidence to support a faulty thesis. Naturally, he wouldn't find it because that's not the way the crime went down.

"He wouldn't listen. He was one hundred percent convinced of what happened and kept telling me to be patient and to trust him."

"Said those same words myself, many a time."

"I tried, but when I found those calls on Mom's phone, I knew something was up. He reassured me again, but I knew he was looking in the wrong direction."

She took a deep breath, then released it in a whoosh. "I couldn't sleep, couldn't concentrate. I kept hearing her in my head, those garbled sounds, the urgency of—"

She paused, calm seeming to come over her. "Then I realized what she'd been trying to say. That he'd found us. After all those years, he'd tracked her down and killed her."

Eden reached into the manila envelope, drew out a plain white, legal-size envelope. "What could I do? Detective Rhea had already discounted that she was trying to tell me anything at all. Death babble, he said. A final need to connect, an instinctual, animal response. Then this came." She handed her the envelope. "Open it carefully."

Quinn examined the outside first, saw it was addressed to Eden Riley, care of Dekalb Community College. Stamped and sent from New Orleans, according to the postmark. As she extracted the envelope's contents, a white, granular material spilled out.

Her heart leapt to her throat. "What the hell!"

"Don't freak out. They're only breadcrumbs."

Breadcrumbs. Quinn studied the stuff a moment. Not a powder. Grainy. Irregular in color, not pure white. She cautiously collected some of it and rubbed it between her fingers. The texture confirmed her visual inspection.

She looked at Eden. "For a minute there, I wondered if you were some kind of nut job who meant to kill us both."

"Sorry about that. I actually thought the same thing when I first opened it."

Quinn unfolded the sheet of paper. A piece of stationery from The Hudson Hotel. Not a mark on it, front or back.

"When did you get this?"

"In May. Check the postmark."

Quinn did. May 10. Someone was playing games with Eden Riley. Or was Eden Riley playing a game with her?

"Don't you get it? Follow the breadcrumbs. Whoever sent this wants me to follow the breadcrumbs."

"Did you take this to Detective Rhea?"

"Are you kidding me? No. Do you really think he would have done anything about it? He would have blown it off, like he blew everything else off. Who knows, maybe he would have suggested I'd somehow manufactured this myself."

She looked at her. "Did you?"

Angry color flooded her face. "No! God, what is it with you cops?"

"Calm down."

"You know what he said to me the last time I approached him? That 'this was real life, not fiction.' Like I was making it all up. Conjuring it somehow. Asshole."

Quinn didn't defend the other detective. It had been a dick thing to say. Although, in the same circumstance, she might have said something similar. "Who do you think sent this?"

"My first thought was my dad, but that doesn't hold water."

"Because you're convinced he killed your mom."

"Yes." She stood and moved restlessly around the room, twisting her fingers together as she did, appearing lost in thought. Quinn watched her, intrigued by the woman, acknowledging she was smarter than she'd first given her credit for—and a whole lot less naive.

She acknowledged she was being drawn into Eden's story.

Eden finally stopped wandering and returned to the couch. "If my dad did kill my mother, as I'm convinced he did, why would he send me this? As a nudge to follow the clues to find what? Him? Hardly.

"However, someone in New Orleans *did* contact my mother. Someone with a connection to the The Hudson Hotel. Obviously, they had a reason to contact her. They wanted something, and now they've reached out to me, most probably for the same reason. They seem to be suggesting I follow the breadcrumbs."

"Clever. What conclusion did you come to?"

"That I needed more breadcrumbs."

A smile tugged at the corners of Quinn's mouth. "You're thinking like a cop, Ms. Riley."

She grinned. "Or a writer."

"I'm guessing there are more 'breadcrumbs' in there?" Quinn said, indicating the large, manila envelope.

"There are." She picked up the envelope; the paper crackled as she did. "At first I didn't know where to turn. Then I remembered the boxes of mom's paperwork I found while cleaning out her house. I hadn't taken the time to really go through them; it'd looked like mostly old bills, bank statements, stuff like that. I'd even thought about tossing it all, but that didn't feel right so I'd boxed it all up and brought it to my place."

She set the envelope on her lap, then drew out a clutch of bound papers and a folded map. A red marker was clipped to the map. She released the bull clamp and handed her the first item.

A newspaper clipping. Quinn held her breath as she gently unfolded the yellowed, brittle clipping; when she read the headline her breath released in a hiss.

Search for Cynthia Hudson's Killer Continues

Quinn scanned the piece, already knowing the information by heart, then moved on to the paper itself. Not a clipping in the traditional sense. This had been torn from the newspaper. In a hurry, it looked like.

She shifted her gaze. The piece was dated April 12, 1994. Two days after the crime occurred. It hadn't been ripped from The Times Picayune, but a newspaper from Memphis, Tennessee, a city six hours north of New Orleans.

Without speaking, Eden opened the map and laid it out on the coffee table. It was a map of the U.S. She took the marker, made an 'X' on the map.

"McComb, Mississippi. April 12 at 4:00 in the morning."

She handed Quinn a receipt from a gas station.

"Jackson, Mississippi," she said next, making a second 'X' on the map. "One and a half hours later."

A McDonald's drive-thru, Quinn saw when she handed her the receipt.

Then came another 'X.' "Memphis, Tennessee. A trip to Walmart for diapers and baby food."

She handed her the corresponding paperwork. "St. Louis, Missouri. Food, more gas and a room for the night."

She continued; expression set. "Chicago, Illinois. Madison, Wisconsin." She marked the two 'Xs.' "And finally, Grand Forks, North Dakota."

She laid the receipts in front of Quinn, then took the red marker and connected the Xs.

Quinn looked at that damning red line, mouth going dry. A coincidence? Maybe.

What if it wasn't?

Eden started to speak; Quinn held up a hand, stopping her. "I need to think. Give me a minute."

Her mind raced. What could Eden's mother have had to do with the Hudson crime? How could she have known this family?

Her mother had been a nurse. A single mom. Not a socialite. Not a woman of means. Eden had been eleven months old at the time, Grace Hudson six months. A daycare? A mother and child play group?

No. Grace Hudson had had a nanny.

Quinn stood. Went to the window, gazed at the street beyond, the flow of vehicles, foot traffic in and out of the coffeeshop. A hospital, the great equalizer. The maternity ward. Possible. Quinn massaged the spot between her eyebrows and the headache forming there. Maybe the kidnapper had connected with her there. Made her an offer she couldn't refuse?

Problem: baby Grace hadn't been taken from a maternity ward.

She caught her thoughts and reined them in. Is this what had happened with her dad? One question had led to another and another . . . like a puzzle he couldn't complete but couldn't let go of? Until the case had become a tormenting siren song, quieted only by whiskey?

Stop it, Quinn, this isn't about him. It has nothing to do with him.

But it did, dammit. It was the case that killed him.

She forced herself to focus. Just because Angela Riley had a clipping of a story about the crime didn't mean she was involved in it. Maybe she'd worked the maternity ward where Grace was born. That would be enough of a reason to keep the news story. To see it and be affected personally, on a visceral level. She ripped it out of the paper; tucked it into her purse or a pocket. Meaning to look at it later or maybe to remind her to call and ask a friend back in New Orleans about it.

Yes. Quinn nodded to herself. That made sense.

Except she'd been on the run when she saw it.

No, Quinn, back up. There was no proof here that the woman had been on the run. On a cross-country trip, yes.

Alone. With her eleven-month-old child.

What new mother would choose to take that trip?

Not any that she'd known.

"Please, say something."

She met Eden's anxious gaze. "This is compelling."

Eden sucked in a sharp breath. Nodded.

"It doesn't mean she was involved with the murder or kidnapping."

Eden released the breath, brought a hand to her chest. "Of course, she wasn't! There's no way she could have had any part in that."

Eden Riley was a smart woman. Every scenario she'd played out in her own head, no doubt Eden had played out in hers as well.

"What do you think this means?" Quinn asked.

"She was on the run, yes. Because she was afraid for her life. And mine. I think . . . I think she knew something, or saw something—"

"Why didn't she go to the police?"

She brought her chin up a notch. "Whoever killed Cynthia Hudson and snatched her baby, they were seriously dangerous people."

"Obviously."

She flushed. "My father was involved in the crime. That's what I think. That's why she ran. She left in the middle of the night and only stopped to sleep and buy provisions. She went north, as far as she could without leaving the United States. Five days in the car with an infant. Why make such a grueling trip unless she was terrified and thought she had no other choice?"

"Like I said, it's compelling, but I can't help you."

Eden looked crestfallen. "I don't understand. You said . . . you called it compelling."

"It could lead to something. Or it could lead to another dead end."

"Reopen the case. Go to your boss with this and—"

"That's not the way it works."

"You could make it work that way."

"I'm not the right cop."

"You're exactly the right cop. Your father—"

"It's *because* of my father that I can't. He was a good cop, a great detective, until this case. With this case he crossed lines and stepped on toes." She paused a beat. "It ruined him, ruined his reputation. In the end, essentially, it took his life."

"You could solve it." She curled her hands into tight fists. "Redeem him, you know? Don't you want that?"

"Eden," she said softly but with steel in her voice, "when I found him, brains splattered on the walls, he was surrounded by his Hudson case notes. On the desk. On the floor. On wall mounted display boards."

Eden leaned forward, expression pleading. "Because he knew the whole story hadn't been told! He wanted justice for Cynthia and Grace Hudson—"

"Stop! Don't you get it? I *hate* this case. I hate it for what it did to him. I hate it because of what it stole from me, and I'm sure as hell not going to risk my reputation by being its champion."

"Just take it to your superior officer—"

"I'm sorry." Quinn stood. "I can't be the one to help you."

Eden reached out a hand, pleading. "Share your dad's notes with me. I might see something. Maybe my mom is—"

"When he died, I destroyed them. I wanted them gone."

Eden's eyes filled with tears. "Someone murdered my mom. It had something to do with this case."

"You don't know that."

"I do!" She pressed her fist to her belly. "I know it, in my gut. My mother travelled across country, alone with a baby, without stopping. It would have been horrendous trip. Why?"

Eden didn't expect an answer pressed on. "Because she knew something. Something that put her—and me—in danger."

"You don't know—"

"Don't say that again. I do!" She pulled herself together. "Why else would she make that trip?"

"A new job with a tight start date."

"You don't believe that."

"I believe it's a possibility. A strong one."

"Then why did she call The Hudson Hotel?"

The case, its questions, pulled at her, a seductress, beckoning. The other woman's desperation tugged too.

Quinn stiffened her resolve and took a step back.

She couldn't get pulled in. She wouldn't. "Take this to Lieutenant Tillerson in the Major Crimes division. They're responsible for re-opening cold cases. If he thinks it has merit, he'll champion it."

Eden's eyes flooded with tears. "Please, what did your dad find that kept him searching?"

"I'm sorry, I've got to go." Quinn gathered her things, headed to the door and down the stairs.

This time, Eden Riley didn't try to stop her.

TWENTY-FIVE

2:00 P.M.

Quinn spent the next few hours taking care of the necessities she didn't have time for during the work week. Like grocery shopping, which she despised. She was getting low on both peanut butter and toilet paper, and when that happened, she knew she was in trouble. From the grocery store, she headed to the drugstore to pick up the refill of her birth control pills and anti-depressants—also must haves. Then the liquor store for Jameson and cleaners to pick up her laundered and pressed shirts.

The entire time, she pictured those receipts, one after the other, pictured that damning red line on the map. She had wrestled with Eden's question as well: "What did your dad find that kept him searching?"

She'd come to the conclusion it had never been just one thing. It had been anything and everything. New evidence emerging. New witnesses coming forward. A whisper overheard, a theory shared.

Always something.

The last of the groceries put away, Quinn grabbed the four-pack of toilet tissue and carried it to the bathroom, tucked it into the cabinet under the sink, then started back down the hall.

As she neared the attic hatch door and the string that dangled from it, she reached up to bat it, the same as she had since she was a kid and had to jump to make it. Only this time she stopped and instead of batting it, grasped it and lowered the attic ladder. She hit the light switch, saw that the bulb had burned out and went for her flashlight.

A minute later she climbed the attic stairs, penlight stuck in the waistband of her pants. She reached the top, snapped on the light and pointed it at the cluster of six plastic tubs.

Her father's life's work filled those tubs. Case notes. Interviews. Copies of photos. Schematics of crime scenes. From all his big cases, although there was more of the Hudson case than any other. In a weird way, the contents of those tubs represented her childhood. She could look at a case and remember how old she'd been when he introduced her to it. Explained the unfolding of the investigation, the surprises and revelations, the disappointments.

The best parts of her had come from him.

She pictured the receipts, the map, the red line. What if this was it? The break in the case her dad believed would come? That he had spent his life looking for?

Her dad taught her to consider every lead, to divorce herself from preconceived judgments, to value minutia and to never, ever be lazy. Sometimes, he said, you have to sift through shit to find evidentiary gold.

What if? As wild and unlikely as Eden's story was, what if? Didn't she owe it to him to at least give it look?

She snapped off the penlight and backed down the ladder. As the hatch clicked back into place, she called up Eden's number, hit send.

The woman answered. "Hello?"

"It's Quinn Conners. I'll give you the rest of the weekend. Meet me at my place as soon as you're able to. Consider yourself on the clock."

TWENTY-SIX

Quinn and Eden stood side-by-side, surveying the line of plastic bins on the living room floor. Of the six bins in the attic, three contained her dad's Hudson case information—a visual commentary on how much of himself he had devoted to the case.

Eden looked at her. "I can't believe you lied to me about having destroyed all this."

At Eden's incredulous tone, Quinn's lips lifted in amusement. "Sorry."

She wasn't, of course, a fact that wasn't lost on Eden. "But you're a cop."

Quinn dragged her gaze from the dusty bins. "Your point is?"

"I didn't think cops could lie." As if realizing how silly that sounded, she rolled her eyes. "Okay. Why'd you lie?"

"I didn't want anything to do with this case. It took over his life and ultimately, destroyed him."

"Why'd you change your mind?"

Quinn was silent a moment, deciding what, how much, she wanted to say. "Because it was so important to him. Because he jeopardized everything for it." She lifted a shoulder in a lopsided shrug. "I figured I owed him this much."

"Not quite the reason I was hoping for, but I'll take what I can get."

"Let's do it then."

They decided on a methodical approach, starting with the day of the crime, with each reviewing every page and item. Their thinking was, Quinn would be coming at the material as a cop—looking for lapses, things missed, faulty logic. Eden would be looking for the familiar, that something that jumped out at her by ringing a bell.

Knowing the order of the bins was easy—her dad had written dates on each bin in bold, black marker. The last bin was also marked with *Notebooks*.

Quinn removed the lid off box number one, thumbed through the first file. Her dad had basically recreated the case file, not exactly an NOPD approved practice. Some pages were photocopies—from the days before digital file keeping—others dot matrix printouts, and still others rewritten in her father's precise hand.

"You start," she said to Eden and handed her that first file. "I'm going to take a look at his notebooks."

Quinn pried off the tub's lid and set it aside. Her dad had preferred a top bound spiral in the slightly larger, 4 X 6 format with a black cover. She gazed down at the neatly organized stacks of them. He had been as methodical in his approach to those as he had the case files. He'd labeled each with the case name and date and lined them up in chronological order.

Then she saw them, outliers. Different sizes, a side spiral, a blue cover, a red one, a yellow.

A lump formed in her throat. Her first notebooks. He'd kept them. She didn't know why that made her want to cry, but it did. She had labeled them, exactly as he had instructed her, same as he labeled his; and Quinn took the top one from the bin. She trailed a finger over her childish handwriting.

She flipped it open. There, at the top of the first page, she had penned the date 9-12-2001. She'd been nine. That was when her training to be a cop had begun in earnest.

As she stared at that date, her mind tumbled back to that September afternoon.

"Grandma," Quinn called, dumping her backpack on the entryway floor. "I'm home!"

"I'm in here, Quinnie."

Dad? She frowned slightly, wondering why he was home on a Friday afternoon. "I'm gonna grab a snack," she called back.

She darted into the kitchen, pausing a moment to study the puzzle-in-progress spread across the table before heading to the refrigerator. The image, New York City's Times Square at night, beginning to emerge. They worked without benefit of the box for reference, allowing themselves only five minutes to study the image before putting it away. To train her to see, he'd explained. To notice the tiniest details and put them together.

All her friends thought they were weirdos. Maybe they were, but they were weirdos together.

She went to the fridge and grabbed a slice of the previous evening's pizza dinner. Munching on it she headed for his office. He sat at his desk, back to her. She caught a whiff of whiskey.

He looked over his shoulder. "How was school today?"

"Boring."

"That bad, huh?"

She took another bite of the pizza and crossed to stand beside him. "Worse."

"Can't say I was crazy about fourth grade either," he said. "Of course, I wasn't crazy about any of the grades. Your mother, on the other hand, loved school."

"I guess I take after you."

He grinned. "Sorry about that."

"I'm not." She took the last bite of pizza, then talked around it. "What are you doing home?"

"I took the afternoon off to spend time with you."

That was a first. "Me?"

"Yeah, you. I have something for you."

He slid open one of the desk drawers, extracted an Office Depot shopping bag and held it out.

"What is it?" she asked, frowning.

"So suspicious. Open it and find out."

She did and discovered three spiral bound notebooks of varying sizes and three writing implements: a ballpoint pen, a fine tip felt marker and a mechanical pencil.

"Okay . . ." she dragged the word out in question.

"Every investigator carries a notebook. In it he—or she—notes their observations about the scene and suspects. It's a place to record, orga-nize and legitimize your thoughts. I figured it was time you had one."

"You got me three, Dad."

He laughed. "Every cop learns what they prefer. Some like a side spiral, some like a top. Some prefer a bigger format, some a smaller. There are pros and cons to each and many more than these to choose from."

She'd asked him about his notebooks before, and he had allowed her to flip through one of his. "How do I decide what I like better?"

"You experiment. Trial and error, like everything else in life."

She laid the three out on the desk, silently studying them. "You always use the same one."

"Yup, exactly the same. Four by six inches, top spiral, black cover. I like how orderly that is." He pulled out his bottom desk drawer, revealing a neat stack of notebooks. All top spirals with black covers.

He'd bought her one like his, and she knew in her gut that was the one she was going to like using the best.

He pushed away from the desk and stood. "C'mon, kiddo. I've got another surprise. Bring your notebooks and pens."

Excited, she followed him down the hall to her bedroom. The door was closed, which was weird, and she looked up at him in question.

He grinned and opened the door slowly. "You've been called to the scene of a crime. A burglary. The homeowner, a devastatingly hand-

some man, was awakened from a nap by a loud thump, followed by a crash. When he went to investigate, he realized his antique gold watch was missing. He's given his preliminary statement and is the living room awaiting further questioning. You will interview him after carefully inspecting the scene."

He started to go; she stopped him, panicked. "Wait! I don't know what to do or where to start."

"Sure you do. The scene is a puzzle. Carefully examine it. Don't rush. Don't be so distracted by the obvious that you miss the obscure."

"Quinn?"

Quinn blinked, startled back into the present moment. Eden was looking at her, forehead wrinkled in question. "What?"

"Did you find something? You look like you saw a ghost."

A ghost from her past, she thought. "Just remembering something about my dad, that's all."

"Want to talk about it?"

"Nope."

Eden didn't press and returned her attention to the files. Quinn flipped through the notebook, reading her notes, her observations. The open window and toppled lamp. The partial shoe print on the windowsill, the cracked open dresser drawer and displaced socks. She recalled being confused that no other drawers had been opened, no other clothes displaced, recalled making a notation in her spiral. Only the framed photos on the dresser and night table had been disturbed—suggesting the thief had taken time to stop and look at them.

She had written herself the question: Could the homeowner himself have stolen his watch? Why?

Quinn smiled to herself. In the end, that was exactly what had "happened." The "suspect" had confessed and she had handcuffed him and read him his rights. It was the first of many times her father had created crimes for her to solve. As she'd grown older, they become more complex. For her thirteenth birthday, she'd investigated her first murder. He had based it on one of his actual cases and after she'd "solved" it he'd allowed her to look at his notes and even the crime scene photos.

Her grandma had found out and been furious. After that, the two of them had decided that her crime scene investigation lessons would be 'their little secret.'

Quinn closed the notebook, tucked it back into the bin and reached for her dad's initial Hudson case spiral and began to read, immediately pulled in. As she read, the words became his voice. She pictured her dad, tall and lanky, dark-haired, and so very serious. She visualized him arriving at the Hudson mansion, his keen gaze taking in the scene: the sights and smells, Friday traffic, the brilliant blue sky and flowers lining the walkway, the Romanesque style structure at the end of it.

Eden gasped. "Oh, my God!"

Quinn started, looked at Eden. She was staring at a photocopy, eyes wide, skin ashen. Her hands shook; a tear rolled down her cheek.

One of the crime scene photos, Quinn realized. "Eden," she said softly, "you don't need to look at that."

"Yes, I do. It's so—" She cleared her throat. "—horrible. I saw my mom, but this—"

Quinn reached for the page; Eden jerked her hand away.

"No, please. I'm okay. I need a minute." She stood. "I'm going to get some air."

When she returned, she seemed steadier and the next several hours passed without incident. They'd barely spoken, each took notes, only stopping for bathroom breaks and to eat a grilled cheese sandwich.

As the hours passed Quinn had to admit she'd been wrong—she wasn't approaching the material like a cop, she was approaching it as a daughter.

She struggled to focus on the material, the facts being presented, the investigative logic and protocol. Her mind kept wandering. With each turn in the case she remembered her dad, how it had affected him, what had been going on in their lives.

"I have a question about the baby clothes."

Wrenched back to the present, Quinn looked at Eden and blinked. "I'm sorry, what?"

"There was no return address on the box the baby clothes arrived in, correct?"

"Correct."

"There would have been a postmark, but I didn't see a mention of it. I could have missed it, but I don't think so."

"I don't remember mention of it either." Quinn crossed to the appropriate bin, retrieved the file and scanned the material. "It's weird that it's not here. No way the investigators would have missed that."

"Could your dad have deliberately left it out?"

Quinn rolled her shoulders. "Anything's possible, but given my dad's detail-oriented nature, it's very unlikely." She stood and stretched. "I know who I can call and ask. He'll know."

"Mike Bruzeau?"

"Yeah. How about we call it quits for today? Pick it up tomorrow? I've got nothing left."

"Sounds like a plan." Eden stood, checked the time. "Besides, I have a date. He's gorgeous, by the way."

"Lucky you." Quinn walked her to the door. "Have a good time but be careful. You have pepper spray, right?"

Eden rolled her eyes. "Seriously?"

"What do you think?"

Eden sighed. "Okay. I won't forget pepper spray. You'll call Detective Bruzeau? About the postmark?"

"The minute you leave."

"Keep me posted."

True to her word, Quinn dialed Mikey. He answered before it rang a second time. "Hey, kiddo. This is a surprise."

"Hey, Uncle Mikey. I hope it's okay that I called you on a Saturday?"

"Are you serious? Of course, it is. C'mon, this is your Uncle Mikey you're talking to."

"I have a question about the Hudson case."

"Wow, I didn't expect that."

She laughed. "I don't know how you could have. That writer, Eden Riley, I met with her. Agreed to look over the case. The baby clothes sent to the Hudsons, where were they sent from?"

He didn't even have to think about it, answering without pause. "There was no return address and the postmark was missing."

"Missing," she repeated, frowning. "I don't understand, what do you mean?"

"The box was sent to The Hudson Group corporate offices. The staff member who opened it ripped the packing tape away, removing the postmark with it."

"The tape was discarded."

It wasn't a question; he answered in the affirmative anyway. "Yes. There was some confusion about the date the package came in, but we did a thorough search of the company's trash receptacle but came up empty. We deduced the box had arrived the day before trash pick-up."

"You decided to let it go?"

"Not us. It was Major Crime's call. Your dad was furious, got in a full-out argument with the Captain over it."

"I'm surprised dad made no mention of it in his notes. He was always so meticulous."

"You have his case notes?"

She wondered if she should have kept that to herself and back-tracked. "You know how Dad was, he saved his notebooks. Kept mine, too."

He chuckled. "Most parents save their kid's artwork. He was so proud of the way you took to crime scene investigation."

Quinn smiled. "Remember how, when I was thirteen, he let me see photos from a murder scene?"

"How could I forget? Your grandma threatened to take you away from him. She even saw a lawyer about it."

Quinn couldn't have heard correctly. "Wait, what?"

"She threatened to sue for custody. Said he was unfit. You didn't know that?"

Quinn struggled to catch her breath. She couldn't believe her grandma would have done that. "No. I'm . . . stunned."

"He promised to change and as far as I know, that was the last of it."

Quinn heard Mikey's wife calling to him. "You've got to go," she said.

"Dinner plans with the kids and the grands. Pizza. No surprise there."

She laughed. "No, I suppose not. Tell everybody I said hi."

"Will do, kiddo. Let's get together soon."

"I'd like that. Hey, could you do me a favor? Don't mention to anyone that I was looking into this."

"No problem, although I can't imagine anyone would care."

"You're probably right, but considering Dad's history with the case . . . I don't want to go there."

TWENTY-SEVEN

9:50 A.M. *Sunday.*

Quinn was on her third cup of coffee when the doorbell sounded. Eden, she thought, and started for the door. She glanced in the hall mirror on her way past, noting her curls were even more out-of-control than usual. She really needed to take the time for a haircut.

She opened the door, one greeting dying on her lips, another forming.

"Dobby?"

"Hey."

Jimmy was with him, grinning up at her from under the rim of his baseball cap. "'Lo, Auntie Quinn!"

"This is a surprise." She smiled at him. "Something tells me you have a baseball game this morning."

"Nope. Played yesterday." He beamed. "I even had a hit!"

"Wow, that's awesome! Congratulations."

"Can I play with Beanie?"

She said yes and he tore into the house, calling for Beignet. She turned her attention to Dobby, and saw pride radiating from his expression. "Was it a home run?"

"In the T-ball universe it was. Knocked it right off the tee."

She laughed. "C'mon in." He stepped inside; she closed the door behind him. "What's up?"

"Cherie sent me over to give you this." He held up a grocery bag. "It's some of her lasagna. She remembered how much you loved it."

Quinn took the bag, stomach rumbling at the thought of the layers of cheese, sauce and spicy Italian sausage. "You married a saint. I've got coffee made, you want a cup?"

"Thanks, but I've had my limit." He glanced toward the living room and the row of bins. "What's all that?"

She pursed her lips, wondering how he would take what she had to say. "All my dad's personal notes on the Hudson case."

"The Hudson case?" He headed into the living room, stopping at the bins. He popped off the lid of the first and slid a file folder out. "What's going on?"

"Long story, but the upshot is my Uncle Mikey called, said he'd been contacted by a woman writing a book about the investigation. She asked a lot of personal questions about my dad and said she wanted to talk to me. I decided to contact her first, see what she was all about."

"And?"

"I learned her interest in the Hudson case is personal. She believes her mother knew who killed Cynthia and kidnapped baby Grace, and that she ran from New Orleans to escape him. She believes that man was her father."

"She has evidence of that?"

"Not really. What she had is more of a compelling story backed up by coincidences."

He didn't comment on that, his attention drawn to the file he was thumbing through. "This is really thorough."

"It is."

"Thorough enough to be a copy." He met her eyes. "You're okay with this?"

She folded her arms across her chest. "Why wouldn't I be? It was his case, it never closed, and he worked on it until the day he died. You know that."

"You should have turned this over to the department."

"I disagree."

He shook his head, brow furrowed. "I'm not comfortable with this."

Always the Boy Scout. "It was his life's work, Dobby. The department has all the files, they've all been digitized. What would they need with this?"

"What would you need with it, Quinn? Nothing."

Jimmy darted out of the back bedroom, distraught. "Beanie won't come out from under the bed! I just wanna pet him!"

His question still hanging in the air between them, she turned to the boy. "Come on, buddy, I'll coax him out."

Just then, Beignet made an appearance, saw Jimmy and turned tail and ran. The boy took off after him, leaving her, Dobby, and the heavy silence between them.

Quinn broke it. "You don't understand me and my Dad, what we had. This—" she made a sweeping motion at the bins "—was such a big part of it."

"The Hudson case?"

"No, his work. Being an investigator. We shared that."

His stance softened. "I know how close you were to your Dad and how much it hurt when he went off the rails. He was a good cop—"

The doorbell sounded. Quinn's stomach sank at the timing. Forcing a smile, she opened the door.

Eden all but bounced in. "Good morning! I'm glad you're up, I was worried that—"

She saw Dobby and bit the last off. "Oh. Hello."

"Eden, this is my partner, Detective Ron Dobson. Dobby, this is the writer I was telling you about, Eden Riley."

"Nice to meet you," Eden said, holding out her hand, smiling widely.

Quinn saw him hesitate and frowned. Dobby was pretty much the nicest guy on the planet, but he seemed to have taken an instant dislike to Eden.

"Good to meet you." He turned to Quinn. "I'm going to collect Jimmy and get out of your hair. Don't forget to put the lasagna in the fridge."

Moments later, Quinn accompanied him and the protesting four-year-old to his car. He got Jimmy buckled into his car seat and went back around to the driver's side.

Quinn followed him. "Dobby, wait. My dad *was* a good cop, and he died thinking there was something amiss with the Hudson case. He taught me everything he knew, including to think like him. How could I ignore this lead? Maybe I'm the only one who can figure out what he saw?"

His expression softened. "Quinn—"

"He called me that night. He said he'd figured it out—"

"He was drunk, Quinn. Totally inebriated. That's why you hung up on him. Remember?"

Tough love. Wasn't that what she'd told him? That she loved him but until he sought treatment for his alcoholism, she wouldn't be a part of his life?

Grief and self-doubt formed a tight ball in her chest. She fought past it. "What if . . . what if I'd listened—"

Dobby laid his hands on her shoulders and looked her in the eyes. "Don't do this to yourself, Quinn. Your dad made his choices. Yeah, he *was* a good cop. Until he wasn't. Don't let that happen to you."

He climbed into his vehicle and drove off. She watched him go, feeling as if something had shifted under her feet. Something that had kept her steady and on a straight path forward for a very long time.

TWENTY-EIGHT

8:25 A.M.

Monday morning, Quinn arrived at the Second, feeling unusually unsettled. She and Eden had spent the rest of Sunday going through the bins. Eden had brought with her a list of her mother's New Orleans connections, all of which she'd compiled from scouring various sources, including her baby book: names of her mom's friends and colleagues, her employer, Eden's pediatrician, the address where they'd lived, the hospital where Eden was born.

Cross referencing that information to information found in the case files they got one hit: Angela Riley had been a nurse at the then Mercy-Baptist Medical Center on Napoleon Avenue, the hospital where Grace Hudson had been born.

It was something, but not the slam dunk they had hoped for. A medical facility as large as Mercy-Baptist would have employed hundreds of nurses spread across its huge campus; as far as Eden knew, her mother had never been a maternity ward nurse.

After reviewing the entire case, Quinn had to acknowledge that from what she'd read, protocol had been followed, every thread pulled, then tied off.

The single unanswered question had been the unrecoverable postmark.

Eden had taken that bit of news hard. She'd taken Quinn's decision to bow out even harder. There was nothing more she could do for her, she'd said, then urged her to contact Lieutenant Tillerson in Major Crimes.

She greeted the desk sergeant, punched in and headed for her desk. In addition, she'd been unable to shake what Dobby said to her before he'd driven away on Sunday:

"Your dad was a good cop. Until he wasn't.

"Don't let it happen to you, Quinn."

He was right. It could happen to any cop, one too many steps over the line, failing to see the cliff ahead of the abyss below. Ruined relationships, career in tatters, physical or mental health destroyed. With the work they did, the shit they saw, even the most grounded of them was vulnerable.

Cops like her, with the kind of history and family *situation* she had, were even more susceptible.

"Morning," she said, crossing to Dobby's desk. She set a bag that contained the emptied and washed Tupperware container on his desk. "Tell Cherie I said she's the indisputable Queen of Lasagna, hands down."

Dobby grinned. "I will."

"I owe you some thanks, as well," she said and plopped down onto the folding chair in front of his desk.

"Yeah? What for?"

"The comment about my Dad being a good cop until he wasn't. Thanks for always having my back."

"You'd do the same for me." He closed his laptop. "You and Riley come up with anything?"

"Nada."

"You said she had a 'compelling story supported by coincidences.' What was that all about?"

"I told you she believes her mother had inside information about the Hudson murder and kidnapping?"

"You did."

Quinn crossed her legs. "Here are the details. A day after the Hudson murder and kidnapping, Angela Riley packed up her eleven-month-old daughter and drove from New Orleans to Grand Forks, North Dakota."

Dobby frowned. "Straight through? Without stopping?"

"Quick stops and overnights. She made it in five days."

"With a baby on board?" He whistled. "Brutal."

"Exactly. Riley found an envelope with her mother's papers, in it were receipts from stops along the way."

He lifted a shoulder dismissively. "She took a new job and they wanted her to start ASAP. It happens. She kept the receipts for income tax purposes or for reimbursement by her new employer."

"I considered that, but in addition to the receipts, Riley found a clipping from a Memphis newspaper about Cynthia's murder and baby Grace's disappearance."

His silence told Quinn he was processing. After a few moments, he said, "What else did she have?"

"Riley's mother was murdered in March. She's the one who found her."

"That's a tough thing. I feel for her."

"There's more. When Riley found her mother, she was still alive. Before she died, she told Riley that 'he found them,' although it was so garbled, she only put it together after the fact."

Quinn saw by his expression he wasn't impressed. "Going through her mom's phone, she learned that days before before her murder, her mom received and made several calls to New Orleans, including one to the NOPD and one to The Hudson Hotel."

"A second physical link to the Hudsons," he murmured. "That's good. Is there more?"

"Yes." Quinn leaned slightly forward. "An anonymous piece of mail from The Hudson Hotel. The envelope contained two things: a blank sheet of hotel stationery and breadcrumbs."

That one surprised him. "Breadcrumbs? Like real crumbs?"

"Yup. Riley figures somebody wants her to follow the breadcrumbs."

He took a moment to digest the information. "Her theory? She must have one."

"She has two. That her mother left New Orleans because she knew something about the kidnapping and was afraid for her and her child's safety, or because her baby's father was somehow involved in the crime and she was running from him."

"Extrapolating, she believes this 'ghost from the past' finally caught up with her and killed her?"

"Yes."

He tapped his index finger against the desktop, something he often did while weighing his thoughts or options. "Then why the breadcrumbs? Why lead Riley to New Orleans?"

"Your guess is as good as mine."

"It sounds like the plot of a Hollywood thriller."

"Meaning you think she's making it up?"

"It's worth considering."

Quinn turned the idea over in her mind. "She does teach creative writing. However, she didn't make up her mom's murder. I called the Dekalb PD and talked to the detective in charge of the murder investigation. Additionally, she didn't make up the receipts, I looked at each one, even checked the dates. Besides, why would she?"

"Why do most perps make up a bunch of crazy shit?"

"She's not a perp."

"True, but why do they do it?"

"To get away with—" Quinn bit the last back because it wasn't quite right. "To get what they want."

"Bingo. What does she want?"

The question left her with an uneasy feeling in the pit of her stomach. Was it possible that the young woman had made up pieces of the story? Manipulated what she had in an attempt to intrigue her?

"Just what she got, I suppose. My time, access to the case, but that's over."

He pursed his lips, expression skeptical.

"Seriously, it is. The only thing we found was that her mother was a nurse at the hospital where Grace Hudson was born, but so were hundreds of other women from the metro area. I recommended she take it all to Tillerson, because this is what his guys do."

Before he could respond, she got a call from the front desk. "Detective Conners, this is Officer Williams. There's a woman here who says she needs to see you and Detective Dobson. Says her name's Joy Rudd."

"Did she say what it's in reference to?"

"She won't say, and she looks like she might bolt. What do you want me to do?"

"Don't let her leave. I'm on my way to collect her now."

TWENTY-NINE

Quinn spotted the woman immediately. Short dark hair, almost a boy cut save for the tendrils around her face and at her neck. She wore a shift-style dress in a springy print; she stood with her arms wrapped around her waif-like figure.

She did, indeed, look like she wanted to bolt.

The desk officer confirmed the young woman was Joy Rudd and Quinn crossed to her. "Ms. Rudd? I'm Detective Conners. You needed to see me?"

She nodded. "Can we . . . go someplace . . . I don't want anyone else to hear what I have to say."

"Of course. Come with me." She led her to the interview room. Dobby was waiting outside for them. "This is my Partner, Detective Dobson."

After greeting one another, they entered the room. Dobby closed the door behind them; Joy Rudd went white.

Quinn smiled reassuringly at the young woman. "Don't let the setup spook you. This is as private as we can get in this building, there's no chance you'll be overheard in here."

Rudd pointed to the video camera. "You don't have to record this, do you?"

"I don't even know what 'this' is, Ms. Rudd. As far as we're concerned, we're simply having a private chat."

Looking somewhat calmer, Rudd nodded and sat. Quinn took the seat directly across the table. "Can I get you anything to drink. Water, Coke—"

"No, nothing. Thank you."

"Why are you here, Ms. Rudd?"

"You're the ones investigating the murder of Karlee Painter, right?"

"Right," Quinn said, keeping her gaze fixed on the other woman's. "Do you have some information about that?"

"Maybe" She wrung her hands. "I promised I wouldn't tell."

Quinn glanced at Dobby, then back at Rudd. This was it. The break they'd been waiting for. Quinn worked to keep her expression neutral. "Sounds to me like a promise you shouldn't keep. You know it, that's why you're here."

She bit her bottom lip, nodded again. "I can't stop thinking about the fact that she's dead." She brought a hand to her mouth, used the moment to pull herself together, then began again. "Since she's . . . gone, the promise doesn't count, right?"

"Right," Quinn agreed. "What did you promise to keep a secret?"

"That she was having an affair. Karlee was having an affair."

Quinn was so surprised it took a moment for her to fully comprehend what she'd said. Russell wasn't cheating on Karlee.

Karlee was cheating on Russell.

She glanced at Dobby. Judging by his expression, he was as stunned as she.

Quinn cleared her throat. "I need you to back up a little bit, okay?"

She twisted her fingers together. "Okay."

"How did you know Karlee Painter?"

"I'm her hair stylist."

"How long have you been doing her hair?"

"Years. Maybe five."

"You work out of a salon?"

"I used to. Too much drama, so I opened my own place."

"How long ago was that?"

"About two years ago. Karlee and Ray had just started dating."

"What's the name of your shop?"

"Hair Joy."

Quinn made a note of it. "Cute name."

A ghost of a smile touched her mouth. "Thanks."

"How long had she been having an affair?"

"I've known for three months." She paused. "I was shocked when she told me."

"What's his name?"

"She didn't tell me that."

Quinn frowned. "She must have called him something, when she talked about him."

"That's the thing. She told me about the affair, then clammed up. Said she felt awful and was going to end it. Said she loved Ray."

"Did she ever talk about the affair again?"

"When she came in for her next appointment."

"How much time had passed?"

"Six weeks. She was an every six weeks client."

Quinn nodded. "What did she say?"

"That she was still seeing the guy. She was upset with herself and didn't know what to do."

"Anything else?"

"Not that time. She came in the Saturday before she was shot."

"How was she?"

"Anxious." Rudd's voice shook. "She told me she was going to break off her engagement. That she was trying to find the courage."

"Did she talk at all about how she thought Russell would react?"

"She was scared about it. She said Ray was a really intense guy."

"Those exact words?"

"Yes."

"She give you any example of behavior that illustrated the description?"

Rudd took a moment, seeming to search her memory. "He had a temper, and was . . . controlling."

Quinn made a note. "Did she tell you she was pregnant?"

Rudd eyes widened and she brought a hand to her mouth. "Oh my God . . . no."

Quinn leaned forward. "Joy, why did you feel it was important to come in here today and tell us this?"

She moved her gaze between them, her eyes bright with tears. "Because . . . I think Ray . . . I think he found out and killed her."

THIRTY

4:00 P.M.

"What are you saying?" Karlee's sister, Tiffany, moved her gaze between Quinn and Dobby. "That Karlee was cheating on Ray?"

"That is what we're saying," Quinn said.

"That's ridiculous. She wasn't."

"This source—"

"Was lying! Karlee loved Ray. They were getting married, for God's sake! I should I know; I was going to be her maid of honor."

Quinn gave the other woman a moment to compose herself, then began again. "We have a strong reason to believe this source is telling the truth."

"Over me? Her sister?" She brought a hand to her chest. "We told each other everything!"

Dobby stepped in. "Ms. Painter, we understand that you're upset—"

"Do you? She's been stolen from me once, now you're doing it again!"

Recognizing that the woman was on the verge of falling apart, Quinn gentled her approach. "It very well may not be true, but we still have to explore the possibility. We wouldn't be doing our jobs if we didn't, and we wouldn't be doing right by Karlee."

She twisted her fingers together. "The two shooters are in jail, so why does this even matter?"

"Because there was a third shooter. He killed your sister, and only your sister."

Quinn could see the woman was having difficulty fully comprehending what she was saying and how it impacted the investigation. She spelled it out for her. "If your sister was having an affair, and I said if, we have to locate him. Maybe he was at that party. Maybe she broke it off with him and he was angry. Maybe, when the gunfire erupted, he saw the opportunity and shot her?"

Painter's throat worked. For a moment, Quinn wondered if she was going to throw-up and she really, really hoped she didn't.

Dobby stepped in. "It offers us another scenario as well. That Ray found out and—"

"No." She shook her head vehemently. "He couldn't have. He'd never hurt Karlee."

"Personally, I agree with you," Quinn said. A small lie, one of many required by the job. "Help me prove it."

"I'll vouch for him. I wouldn't have introduced them in the first place, if I didn't think he was a good guy."

"Of course you wouldn't have. Let me ask you, Tiffany, does Ray even own a gun?"

She wrung her hands. "These days it seems like everybody does."

"True." Quinn nodded. "So Ray, like pretty much everyone else, owns a gun."

"I don't think he carries it with him or anything. It was for self-protection at home, in case someone broke in."

Russell lied about owning a gun.

Quinn struggled to keep her excitement from showing. "Do you know what kind of gun it is? We might be able to eliminate him right now."

She thought a moment, then shook her head. "I never saw it.

Karlee mentioned it, though. He wanted her to learn how to use it and took her to the range a few times."

"Some sort of handgun? Not a rifle or shotgun."

"Right."

Quinn looked at Dobby. "Detective Dobson, any further questions?"

He shook his head, and Quinn stood. "Thank you for coming in today, Tiffany. You've been a lot of help."

She handed Painter her card. "If you think of anything else, call me. Anytime, day or night."

Painter took it, started for the door, then stopped and looked back. "There was no way Karlee was having an affair. Take a look at her planner. She put everything she did and everywhere she went in it. It was almost like a scrapbook for her. If this 'affair' isn't in her planner, it wasn't in her life."

No sooner had Tiffany Painter cleared from earshot than Dobby turned to her. "Holy shit."

"You got that right, partner. I think we have him. Why would he lie about owning a gun if he wasn't guilty?"

THIRTY-ONE

8:45 *P.M.*

Quinn let herself into the house and headed straight for the kitchen, Beignet mewing and rubbing against her ankles the whole way. She'd stopped at her favorite pizza joint and visited with the owners, two women she had known since high school.

The restaurant had been quiet, so she'd eaten there at the bar. It'd been nice to catch up, a pleasant distraction from a hectic day and the waiting game they were playing now. They'd submitted a request for a search warrant for Russell's residence; at this point she was hoping they'd have it in the morning.

Beignet meowed plaintively—he was hungry, and she was obviously moving too slowly for his liking. While she was taking care of his needs, her cell phone sounded, and she answered without looking at the display. "Detective Conners."

"Kiddo, it's Uncle Mikey. How's it going?"

"Can't complain. We finally got a break in the triple homicide."

"Good for you."

"Thanks." She finished serving Beignet, gave him a scratch

behind the ears and started toward her bedroom to change into a pair of yoga pants and T-shirt. "Caught the prime suspect in a lie."

"The fiancé?"

"That's the one." Using her shoulder to prop her phone to her ear, she opened her dresser drawer and collected the items. "Don't have enough to charge but we're on our way now. Waiting on a search warrant."

"I'll be keeping my fingers crossed."

"I didn't expect to hear from you so soon. What's going on?"

"I got a call today, I thought I should share it with you."

Something in his tone caused her to straighten. "What kind of call?"

"Someone high up in the department food chain, they know Eden Riley has been in contact with me, and they warned me not to talk to her about the case."

"What?" She frowned, not believing what she was hearing. "Why not?"

"Since it was never closed, it's considered ongoing."

"That's ridiculous, Uncle Mikey. It's a twenty-eight-year-old case."

"Don't shoot the messenger. Like I said, the warning came from somebody high up on the department food chain."

"High enough you're not going to tell me who."

"Bingo." He paused a moment. "I think she's asking a lot of questions and upsetting some important people."

"The Hudsons."

"Don't know that for a fact, but considering history, that'd be my guess." He paused a moment before adding, "I don't think they know you've spoken with her and I certainly didn't tell them. I think you should be careful, Quinn."

That the department would do the bidding of a private citizen and pressure a sworn officer, rankled. Not a little bit, a lot. "Thanks, Uncle Mikey. I appreciate the warning."

"You bet. And Quinn?"

"Yeah?"

"You don't have your dad's notes on the case, do you?"

The hair at the back of her neck prickled. "Why would I?"

"When you called me about the postmark, you said something that made me think you did."

He left it hanging, forcing her to either admit she had the files or lie. He was her Godfather; she'd trust him with her life. But for some reason, not with this.

"I cleaned out his office right after he died, Uncle Mikey."

"I thought you said you had his notebooks."

She narrowed her eyes. Where was all this coming from? she wondered. Surely not a simple warning call from a higher up? Could there be something in her dad's files that Mikey didn't want her to see?

"Some personal notebooks," she said, steel in her voice. "They're special, and they're mine."

"Of course," he said quickly, tone once again easy. "I don't think it would be smart for you to have them, that's all."

"You worry too much, Uncle Mikey. I'm a big girl now, it's going to be okay."

As she ended the call, Quinn couldn't quell the uneasy feeling that things wouldn't be okay, that perhaps she had stepped into something that would cost her everything.

Just the way it had her father.

THIRTY-TWO

Rourke

2004

9:10 A.M. SATURDAY.

The phone caught Rourke elbow-deep in dishwater. From the living room he heard the pings and pops of Quinn's video game. No help there. He grabbed the dishtowel and got himself dried enough to answer.

"This is Conners."

"Is this Detective Rourke Conners?"

"It is."

"This is Lynette Green."

He recognized the name, but it couldn't be who he thought it was; it had been ten years. "Who did you say you were?"

"Lynette Green. Cynthia's aunt."

Cynthia Hudson's only close-living relative, a maternal aunt. She'd lived across the Mississippi River Bridge in Terrytown, at least she had back in the day.

"You gave me your card, back then . . . I saved it all these years and—"

She stopped, and he gently prodded. "What Mrs. Green? Why are you calling me?"

"I miss her so much," she whispered, voice thick. "I can't keep quiet any longer."

He pulled one of the kitchen chairs out from the table, sat heavily. The Hudson case wasn't his any longer, it hadn't been in a long time. The Chief himself had turned it over to Major Crimes for the Cold Case crew to keep an eye on. He should refer her to them. He should but . . .

It had taken her all these years to reveal whatever was eating at her and she had contacted *him*. It was a trust issue. The comfort of a familiar name and face. If what she told him was credible, he would personally bring it to the appropriate bureau.

"Where can I meet you?"

"I'm still in Terrytown, but I've moved . . . got my own trailer now."

Located across the MRB on New Orleans' Westbank, it was a twenty-minute drive, give or take depending on traffic. He and Quinn had their regular Saturday appointment at the gun range near the airport. He checked his watch. It was going to be tight.

"Give me thirty minutes."

Ten minutes later, he and Quinn climbed into the car. He glanced at her. She hadn't been thrilled about being dragged away from her video game. "Sorry to hurry you out that way, but a lead came in that I had to check out right away. We'll hit the range after."

Beside him, Quinn fastened her safety belt. "The call you took?"

"Yup."

"What case?"

"The Hudson case."

She whistled under her breath. "No shit?"

He sent her a sharp glance. "Language."

She rolled her eyes. "I'm going to be a cop, cops curse. A lot."

"You're not a cop yet. You're a kid."

"I'm almost thirteen. Besides, it's not that bad a word."

It wasn't, and no doubt she heard worse at school. But he knew Maggie wouldn't want her to talk that way, and he figured he should at least try to honor her wishes.

He sighed. "Don't give me a load of crap about this, kiddo. Just watch your language. Okay?"

She shrugged. "Okay."

"Thank you."

She angled in her seat. "Tell me about this lead that came in."

"Don't get too excited, it could be nothing."

"It has to do with the Hudson case, so *of course* it could be nothing." She gave him that almost-thirteen-*duh, Dad* look. "I think you're the one who's getting too excited."

He chuckled; gaze fixed on the steep rise of the bridge ahead. "Stop being such a little know-it-all."

She laughed. "Takes one to know one."

He mock-glowered at her. "The call was from Cynthia Hudson's aunt. She said there was something she's been holding back but she's ready to talk."

She seemed to digest that, brow furrowed. "Why not take her information over the phone?"

"Good question. Because it's too easy for an informant to give in to second thoughts and—"

"Chicken out?"

"Right. Or backtrack later, deny they ever said anything." He glanced at her, then back at the road. "Looking someone in the eyes is a commitment. You can't hang up on a person sitting directly across from you. Plus, physical notes are hard to deny later. One-on-one is always a better way to go. Remember that, Quinnie."

They fell silent while he navigated heavy traffic. Once they crested the bridge and started down the other side, she broke the silence with a question. "How come you didn't call Uncle Mikey? Two sets of eyes and ears are always better than one."

Another thing he'd taught her, he acknowledged, proud. She was like a sponge, the way she sucked up and stored information. "It's Saturday, kiddo. It's not an active case, so why screw up his day off?"

"Then I'm your backup. Cool, Dad."

She smiled and sat back, busying herself with her Gameboy while he navigated the Westbank streets that led him to Shadow Pines, Lynette Green's trailer park.

He turned in and rolled slowly down the lane until he found her number, then pulled into the parking spot in front of her shiny doublewide. He cut the engine, looked at Quinn. "Keep the doors locked. If you need me, lay on the horn."

"Can't I come in?"

"Sorry, kiddo. Truth is, it's sketchy I'm even here."

She frowned and opened her mouth as if to question him; he didn't give her a chance. "Stay put, doors locked. Understood?"

She gave him a thumbs-up and after locking her in, he crossed to the mobile home and tapped on the door.

Lynette Green came to the door and peered through the screen. He held up his shield. "Mrs. Green?"

She nodded, pushed open the door and he stepped inside. The interior was neat; it smelled of cigarette smoke and bacon. He noticed her hands were shaking. Badly.

"Can I get you anything?" she asked. "A coffee or Coke?"

"I'm good, thank you."

They sat. She clasped her shaking hands together. The last ten years hadn't been kind to her, he thought. They were etched on her thin face; in the way her bony shoulders drooped.

He gave her a moment, when she still didn't speak, he broke the ice. "Thank you for calling me." She nodded; her throat worked. "Are you nervous, Mrs. Green."

"A little," she admitted twisting those hands together.

"You have nothing to be nervous about, not with me." He worked to keep his voice even, soothing. "We're going to have a conversation, nothing more."

She cleared her throat. "It's not you I'm worried about. It's those people."

"Those people?"

"The Hudsons."

"Do they frighten you?"

She held up a pack of cigarettes. "Do you mind if I smoke?"

"It's your home."

She opened the nearest window and lit up. She took a long drag, then blew the smoke out the window. "There isn't a day that goes by that I don't think about my Cyndi or her sweet baby."

He understood. There wasn't a day that passed that he didn't think of Maggie, and long for what he lost.

"I'm sorry."

Her eyes teared up. "I wish she'd never gotten involved with that family. He never liked her."

"He?"

"Old man Hudson. Thought she was beneath them."

Hardly a startling revelation, but he went with it. "Did she tell you that?"

"Didn't have to. I saw it in the way he looked at her."

"Was Cynthia happy in her marriage?"

She didn't reply, instead taking another long, anxious drag on the cigarette.

"Mrs. Green? When you called, you said you couldn't stay silent any longer. About what?"

"He was cheating on her," she said bitterly. "From day one. I don't know how they kept it under wraps. I kept waiting for someone to step forward, but no one ever did."

He had wondered about Bill Hudson's fidelity himself, but had been unable to find evidence of anything other than a strip club habit. A big one.

"Are you saying he was having an affair?"

"An affair? More like he was screwing around." She tamped out the smoke. "My Cyndi, she was a beautiful girl. A good girl. She gave him a beautiful daughter. She didn't deserve that."

"You're saying he was a serial cheater?"

"Yeah, I am. He even slept with the nanny."

He recalled the photo of Bill Hudson, tucked into the woman's night table drawer. "Lucy Praxton? You're certain of that?"

"Positive. Cyndi came to me, heartbroken. She'd looked the other way with the others, but Lucy . . . she felt so betrayed. She trusted her."

"Did she talk about firing her?"

Green nodded. "She would have, but she was so good with Grace." She paused. "They had a huge fight."

"Cynthia and Ms. Praxton?"

"No, Cynthia and Bill."

He drew his eyebrows together in thought. "How much before the murder did this fight occur?"

She thought a moment. "Weeks, I guess. A month. I don't remember for sure."

"This fight occurred at the mansion?"

"That's where they were living."

"Did anyone overhear them? No one I interviewed ever mentioned a big argument between them."

"Then they were covering for him."

"Why did she stay in the marriage?"

"Grace, of course."

"You sure it wasn't the money?"

She flushed. "She was no gold digger, Detective. She told me Bill threatened her. Said if she left him, he'd take Grace away from her. That his lawyers would make sure of it."

He had no doubt of that. Rourke leaned slightly forward. "Why are you telling me this, Mrs. Green?"

"Because the truth needs to come out about him."

"That's not what I'm asking. What do *you* want to accomplish?"

She shifted in her seat. "I don't know what you mean."

"Do you think Bill Hudson killed Cynthia?"

She recoiled. "I'm not saying that! Why would he?"

Rourke lifted a shoulder. "Because he wanted his freedom?"

"He had it, the way he screwed around." She reached for the cigarettes, lit one. "Whatever happened with that freak the nanny was dating? The sex offender."

John Paul Russo. A record for sexual assault. Bizarre behavior the morning of the crime, being unable to locate him for twenty-four hours. Turns out he had been in Mississippi, defending himself in a civil trial. "He had a rock-solid alibi."

"I don't believe it."

He hadn't wanted to believe it. "I understand you feeling that way, but I promise you John Paul Russo had nothing to do with your niece's murder or baby Grace's kidnapping."

He glanced at his watch, folded his hands in his lap. "You still haven't answered my question, Mrs. Green. What do you hope to accomplish by telling me this today?"

"I want everyone to know what a lying sack he is."

Rourke muffled a sigh, put away his notebook. "Mrs. Green, I certainly understand the way you feel. You lost someone very important to you, two someones actually, and I want to help you, but I have to be honest, from an investigative standpoint I don't think there's anything here—"

"You have to do something!" She jumped to her feet. "What about that security guy? Cyndi said he gave her the creeps, always following her around, but Bill wouldn't do anything about him. She told me she figured he had something on Bill. A tape or something."

"She thought he was blackmailing Bill?"

"She didn't use that word, but that's what she meant."

Rourke worked to keep his excitement from showing. "Why didn't you mention this back at the time of the incident?"

"You didn't ask me about him and with everything . . . I didn't think about him."

He plucked his notebook back out of his jacket pocket. "Which security person was it, Mrs. Green?"

"I don't remember his name." She took a drag on the smoke, hand shaking badly. "Oh my God, could he be the one?"

"Let's not jump the gun here. Can you tell me exactly what Cynthia said about this man and how he made her feel?"

Green set her burning cigarette in the ashtray, the acrid smoke curling toward the ceiling. "I'll try . . . it's been such a long time . . ."

She sank back against her seat and curved her arms around her middle. "She was telling me about Bill's cheating, and she mentioned it. What was his name? Tony, Teddy—"

"Toby?" Rourke offered. Toby Bannon?"

"That's it, yes! She said she felt like he was always watching her, and she'd even caught him staring at her."

The head of security both at the mansion and the Hudson Group headquarters. He had been in and out of the mansion that day; it was he who had scheduled the security system upgrade that disabled it for that day and time.

"Did he ever touch Cynthia inappropriately?"

She shook her head. "Not that she told me."

"How about inappropriate comments, something sexual in nature?"

She pressed her lips together, obviously searching her memory. "Yeah, I mean he didn't come right on and hit on her, but it wasn't right."

"Do you have an example?"

"He would comment on how she looked . . . like 'you look sexy in that skirt,' or 'that dress makes your body look good enough to eat.' Things like that."

Rourke made a note. Yeah, he'd call that crossing the line. Big time. "She shared her feeling about Mr. Bannon with her husband?"

She nodded. "He blew her off. Said something like, she should take his attention as a compliment. She was pissed about it."

Rourke recalled interviewing the man. Slick. Composed. An explanation for his every action.

But he'd had a tic. The smallest twitch at the corner of his right eye. Between the tic and his involvement in the video surveillance being down, Rourke had been suspicious enough to request he take a lie detector test.

He'd passed with flying colors.

Between that and witnesses who verified his timeline that day, he'd been cleared from suspicion early on.

"Why did she think Bannon had something he could use against her husband?"

"She'd seen Bill fire people for lots less."

A couple minutes later, Rourke climbed back into the car. Quinn looked up from her Gameboy. "That took a lot longer than you thought it would."

"Sorry about that, kiddo."

She tipped her head and studied him, gaze narrowed. "You look excited. What did she have to say?"

Rourke fastened his seat belt. "Something I wish she'd told us a long time ago." He shifted the SUV into drive. "It's a solid lead."

"Why didn't she tell you before?"

"She'd forgotten about it."

"She forgot it?" Quinn screwed her face up. "I don't think so, Dad."

"In an investigation, sometimes it's the littlest things that become the biggest things."

She seemed to ponder that a moment. "Like what?"

"In this case, an offhand comment wrapped up in something that appeared bigger and more important."

"Like what?" she asked again.

"Bill was cheating on Cynthia."

She made a face. "Pig."

"I agree."

Quinn pursed her lips. "What's your next step?"

"I haven't decided yet. What do you think it should be?"

"Take it to your captain. That's what you're supposed to do."

He smiled slightly. Spoken like a by-the-books cop. The kind of cop he had been training her to be. "True. Usually anyway."

She frowned in the way that she did, all serious consternation. "Maybe talk to Uncle Mikey about it. Ask him what he thinks. That's what partners are for."

"Again, usually true."

"Not this time? It's *Uncle Mikey,* Dad."

"I know, kiddo. That's what makes it so hard."

"I don't get it. Why wouldn't you talk to him?"

"Because I'm not sure he's on my side anymore."

She reached across the seat, curled her hand around his. "You'll never have to worry about me, Dad. I'll always be on your side."

Tears pricked his eyes. Not wanting her to see them, he kept his gaze trained on the road ahead. "Thank you, baby. That means everything to me."

THIRTY-THREE

4:10 P.M.

Rourke knocked on Mikey's front door. His oldest daughter, Sara, answered, looking way too grown up to be the pig-tailed girl he'd carried on his shoulders during Mardi Gras parades. She was a high school senior this year and preparing to head off to LSU in Baton Rouge in the fall.

"Hey, Uncle Rourke!"

He gave her a quick hug. "It's good to see you. How's school?"

"Great." She flashed him the thousand-watt smile that had cost Mikey five grand in braces. "Seniors don't take finals, so I'm done in three weeks."

"Congratulations. I'm proud of you."

"Thanks. I'm late for work, so I've got to go. Dad's out back, you know the way. See ya!"

He watched her head to her car, a corner of his mouth lifting in amusement. Before long, that would be Quinn. Off to work. Off to school. Just always . . . off someplace. He had to admit, the thought made him anxious.

He made his way through the small, chaotic family room to the sliders that opened to the back patio. He wondered where Betsy was today and acknowledged that being a high school teacher with four kids of her own, she could be anywhere from the grocery store to a debate team competition several states away.

Rourke found Mikey performing home surgery on his lawn mower. Owen, their youngest, and a couple of his buddies, were in the tree fort, engrossed in some sort of card game.

"Hey, Partner."

Mikey looked over his shoulder at him and grinned. "Well look what the cat dragged in." He straightened, reached for his work rag to wipe the oil off his hands. "What brings you over?"

"Something came up I wanted to get your opinion on."

Mikey's brows shot up. "A phone call wouldn't do?"

"Maybe I missed your pretty face."

Mikey laughed. "Want a beer?"

"Sure."

"Owen!" he called, "I'll be inside with your Uncle Rourke if you need me."

The boy signaled he'd heard with a thumbs-up, called hello to Rourke, then returned to his game.

"Where's Bets?"

"Chaperoning at a Girl Scout Campout with the twins." He took two Dixies out of the fridge and popped the tops. He handed one to Rourke. "Come on, let's sit. I'm beat and I've got a long night ahead." Mikey took a swallow of the brew. "Man, that hits the spot."

Rourke followed his lead, admitting the crisp, cold lager really did hit the spot. "What's up tonight?"

"Since the twins are at a campout, I promised Owen and his friends a campout in the back yard, complete with tent, roasted weenies and s'mores. They're pretty fired up."

Rourke held up his bottle in a salute. "I don't know how you do it all."

They conversed another couple moments, then Mikey turned the conversation to the elephant in the middle of the room. "You said there was something you wanted to kick around with me?"

"Yeah." Rourke rolled the sweating can between his palms. "I got a call this morning from Cynthia Hudson's aunt."

Mikey's demeanor seemed to alter slightly, the way an animal's might at the scent of a predator. "And?"

"I went out and took her statement."

"Jesus, Rourke—"

"It's not our case anymore, I know."

"Then what the hell were you thinking?"

"Just hear me out, okay?"

Mikey didn't look thrilled about it but sat back in his seat and waited. Rourke proceeded to share what Green said about Bill Hudson being a serial cheater, that he had slept with Lucy Praxton and that he and Cynthia had a huge fight over it.

"We suspected the guy was a scumbag," Mikey said, splaying his fingers, "and he is. It'd be salacious news, it'd make him look bad in the community, but—"

"There's more. While she's recounting all this, she remembers Cynthia telling her how the head of security for the Hudsons gave her the creeps."

Mikey waited, expression intent. "Apparently, she felt like he was always watching her and he made some inappropriate comments. She went to Bill with it and he did nothing."

"I can't recall his name—"

"Toby Bannon."

"That's right. He took a polygraph, and passed."

"We both know they can be beaten, and he would have known that as well, his business being security."

Mikey nodded. "This could be something."

"I agree." He let out a pent-up breath. "What's our next move?"

"Your next move," Mikey corrected him. "I had nothing to do with this."

"If this leads to the guy—"

"I'll cheer for you. I don't need the recognition, Rourke. It'll be enough to know we finally got justice for Cynthia and Grace."

Mikey didn't want his name associated with this in case it blew up on him. It wasn't going to, not this time. "If you're sure—"

"Positive."

"Do I take it to the captain or Major Crimes?"

"It's your call. Do you want to hand it off or have the opportunity to see it through?"

"I think you know the answer to that."

"That I do." Mikey drained his beer and stood. "I need to get back to that lawn mower."

"It's not going to fix itself," Rourke agreed and followed him to his feet. "Thanks for the beer and the ear."

Mikey grinned. "Anytime, brother. You know that."

THIRTY-FOUR

2:45 P.M. *Friday.*

Rourke gazed at his captain, Antoine Arceneaux, certain he must have misheard. "What did you say?"

"Lynnette Green recanted."

He felt the words like a blow to the chest. It took him a moment to catch his breath and speak. "That's not possible."

"I'm afraid it's true. I got the information from Lieutenant Tillerson himself. Green called him a little bit ago, admitted she made it all up."

Rourke's mind raced. He recalled her halting speech, her expression as she spoke. "Bullshit. I was there, I took her statement."

"I know how much you have invested in this case and I sympathize but—"

"I'll call her. She was skittish . . . I should have been the one dealing with her instead of those two clowns from Major Crimes. They said something that frightened her, they must have—"

"Detective, it's done."

He shot a glance at Mikey. No help coming from that direction, he saw. "If you'd let me talk to—"

"I said it's done, Detective."

"You're wrong. If you would—"

Captain Arceneaux rose slowly to his feet. Palms on his desk, eyes narrowed, he leaned forward. "What did you say to me?"

"Partner. . . ."

That came from Mikey, low, a warning.

Rourke wanted to tell him he was wrong, that it wasn't over, not by a long shot. Instead, he thought of Quinn, of the things he was trying to teach her about responsibility and respect, about chain of command; he stifled the urge.

"Yes, Sir. Understood, Sir."

"That's what I thought you said." He motioned to the door. "Take the weekend to cool off and get your head straight. Don't come in Monday unless that's happened. Detective Bruzeau, you stay."

Rourke stormed out the captain's office. He went to his desk, collected his stuff, then strode out of the station house, aware of his colleagues' eyes on his back. Screw 'em all, he thought angrily. He didn't need their affirmations—or their pity. He was right about this— the Hudsons had gotten to Lynette Green and convinced her to change her story. Privileged assholes.

"Rourke! Hold up!"

He didn't stop, didn't look back. Mikey caught up with him at his car, slightly out of breath.

Rourke turned on him. "You didn't back me up. Not one fucking word."

"What was I supposed to say? Captain was right, Green recanted. It's over."

"The Hudsons, they got to her. They either threatened her or paid her off, and you know it."

"I know no such thing." He jammed his hands into his pockets. "You can't go around saying shit like that, Rourke. You're not right, man. You haven't been in a long time."

"What's *that* supposed to mean?"

"Forget it."

He turned to walk away; Rourke grabbed his arm. "Bullshit. You started it, finish it."

"This is about Maggie."

Rourke looked at him in disbelief. "Maggie? What the hell are you talking about?"

"The Hudson case was your first one back after her death. Losing her was so fresh and this crime hit too close. That's why you can't let it go. It's why it's so personal to you."

"You're a shrink now? It isn't enough to be my partner? My best friend?"

"I wouldn't be either if I didn't tell you the truth. You've never gotten over her loss, I get it, but you have to move on."

"Move on? Get over it? What do you know about loss? You didn't lose *your* wife. You don't wake up alone every morning. You don't have to wonder why her and not you every single, fucking day."

"You're right, I don't know what that's like and it isn't fair. You've got to start living again, man. Maybe get out there, try dating—"

"I'm out of here!" Rourke unlocked the car door, yanked it open and climbed in.

Mikey grabbed the door before he could slam it shut. "You don't think I haven't smelled the booze on your breath? You don't think I've covered for you? I shouldn't have, I see that now. You need help."

"Is that why Arceneaux held you back? To ask you to 'talk some sense' into me?"

"Maybe he did. You're a good cop and he doesn't want to see you—"

"Let go of the damn door."

"You're blowing it, Rourke! Your career. Your relationship with Quinn—"

"Leave Quinn out of this!" He started the car, gunned the engine. "We're fine. In fact, we're *great*."

He grabbed the door handle and yanked. Mikey let go and stepped back. Rourke roared out of the parking area, betrayal fueling his bitterness. He'd been right to doubt Mikey. To doubt the depth of his friendship, his allegiance to their partnership.

How many times over the years had he stepped up for Mikey? Defended his actions? Covered his ass? The time he and Betsy split came to mind. Also after the twins were born, when Mikey had been so sleep-deprived he'd made mistakes, some of them dangerous.

Who'd protected him? He had.

Now he gets a "you need help" from his friend. Really? He throws drinking in his face? Yeah, sometimes he needed a little bump to face the day. Didn't mean he had a problem, and sure as hell didn't merit his *partner* calling him out. Psychoanalyzing him, for God's sake.

Rourke flexed his fingers on the wheel, barely aware of traffic. Registering red lights and green ones, the blur of commercial developments becoming mixed-use residential, becoming oak-lined boulevards and large, single family homes.

His indignation turned bitter. Who was Mikey to judge his and Quinn's relationship? To judge *his* parenting? He and Quinn were closer to each other than Mikey was to any of his kids. Through the years, how many times did Mikey have to talk to a teacher or school principal? A lot. How about the time he caught Sara drinking at thirteen, or when the twins were picked up for shoplifting?

Quinn had never done any of that. She'd never required him to attend even one teacher meeting, let alone sneaking beers at thirteen. Truly, who was the one "blowing" it?

The light ahead had turned red, and Rourke jammed on the brakes. The safety belt snapped tight against his chest; and he became acutely aware of his surroundings. St. Charles Avenue. Heading uptown.

Two blocks from the Hudson mansion.

He checked the time. Just after five on Friday. Happy hour.

Very happy hour at the Hudson's. They'd successfully silenced Lynette Green by either threatening her or bribing her.

Nobody saw it but him.

The blood began to pound in his head, louder and louder. With the drumbeat came a thought. No, an urge. To act.

Don't let them get away with it.

He passed the mansion. He glanced that way. He imagined himself barging in, demanding to know what they done to shut Lynette Green up.

There would be consequences. Big ones.

He couldn't let them get away with it. He couldn't. If he didn't stand up for what was right, who would? Just like he was teaching Quinn.

He told himself to keep driving but changed lanes instead, taking the first available U-turn, crossing the streetcar tracks, then repeating the move six blocks up.

Rourke squeezed the steering wheel, at war with himself. He wouldn't lose, not if he did the right thing while still working within the system. Be smarter. More persistent. Never give up.

That's what he was teaching Quinn.

He took a right on the street that bordered the mansion, maneuvered into a parking spot directly across the Hudson's side drive and the ornate iron gate that protected entry. He shifted his gaze first to the keypad with card reader and call button, then to the collection of luxury vehicles parked beyond the gate.

He would recognize the opportunity when it arrived. The minutes ticked past. He slouched deeper in his seat.

Finally, a sign of life. A young man emerged. Tall, dark haired, strong features that didn't quite fit his face. On his heels came Daniel Shaw. He hugged the kid, then clapped him on the back. His son Logan, Rourke realized. The teary-eyed and traumatized eight-year-old he'd interview would be eighteen now.

That's who he needed to talk to.

Shaw the elder went back inside, the younger crossed to a BMW coupe and climbed inside. A moment later, the gate slowly opened, and he exited. Rourke started his engine, eased out of his parking spot and followed.

The kid stayed on St. Charles Avenue, heading Uptown. He only went as far as Fat Harry's on St. Charles and Napoleon Avenues, found a parking spot and hopped out.

Rourke caught up with him steps outside the bar. "Logan Shaw?"

The kid stopped, looked back. His gaze slid over him in question. "Yeah?"

Rourke held up his shield. "Detective Conners, NOPD."

The kid's expression transformed from easy to guarded. "What's up?"

"Do you remember me?"

"I do." He stuck his hands in his pockets. "There's not much I don't remember from that time."

"That's kind of what I was hoping."

His eyes narrowed slightly. "I'm not sure I like the sound of that."

"You have a minute?"

He glanced at his watch. "Not really."

"The question was rhetorical."

He blew out an annoyed sounding breath. "Figured."

By unspoken agreement, they moved out of the flow of patrons going in and out of the bar.

"Did you ever meet a woman named Lynette Green?"

"Not that I recall. Who is she?"

"Cynthia's aunt."

"Cynthia Hudson?"

"Yes. You ever hear her name mentioned?"

"Maybe. I don't recall." He shifted from one foot to the other. "I'm meeting someone, so—"

"Sure, of course. Just a couple more questions. How about the name Toby Bannon?"

"Yeah, I remember him. He worked for Charles. Security. I remember because he carried a gun."

"What did you think of him?"

"Why does it matter?"

He lifted a shoulder. "Just curious."

"I didn't like him."

"Why's that?"

"Because he didn't like kids and didn't make a secret of it."

"You remember Cynthia, right?"

He folded his arms across his chest. "Of course."

"Did she like him?"

He frowned. "How should I know?"

"Kids pick up on things, oftentimes better than adults do."

He seemed to think a moment, then shook his head. "I couldn't say."

"Did you ever happen to see them together?"

"Oh, I get it now."

"What's that?"

"What this is about. Lynette Green, Toby Bannon, Cynthia . . . You want to know if I ever saw him behave inappropriately with her."

"Yes. Did you?"

He shook his head. "No. Besides, I thought all this was settled."

"All what?"

"The aunt's crazy-ass story about Toby Bannon stalking Cynthia. I thought it had been debunked."

"Is that what you heard?"

"Yeah. What's the big deal?"

"The *big deal* is it was a lead. Now it's dead."

"Can't help you." He turned and started for the door.

"Logan." He stopped, glanced over his shoulder. "I remember you begging me to bring Grace home. Do you remember that?"

Something like animus flickered behind his eyes. "You know what I recall, Detective? That you said you would bring her home to me, but you didn't."

THIRTY-FIVE

Quinn
Present day

2:40 A.M.

The shriek of her cell phone yanked Quinn from a deep sleep. She fumbled for the device and got it to her ear. "This is Conners."

"Someone was in my apartment!"

A woman's voice. She sounded a hairsbreadth shy of hysterical. "Who is this?"

"Eden." Her voice broke on a sob. "I don't know what to do!"

"Are you hurt? Do you need medical attention?"

"No, thank God!"

"Hang up and call 911 immediately."

"He warned me not to. He said—"

"He's gone?"

"Yes."

"Are you certain?"

"Yes. I heard the door shut, then I ran and locked it."

Quinn hesitated. Getting involved would be a mistake. She should be understanding but firm, insist she call 911 and offer to stay on the line until officers arrived. Which could be an hour. Maybe more for a non-emergency like this one.

Son of a bitch, Quinn, you're doing this, aren't you?

"Stay put," she said. "I'm on my way."

EDEN'S TEETH were chattering despite the warm night and the heavy sweatshirt she was wearing. She sat on the worn couch, a throw pillow clutched tightly to her chest and her legs curled up under her.

"It's going to be okay," Quinn said softly. "Deep, slow breaths. In through your nose and out through your mouth."

She did as Quinn instructed and little by little her shaking stopped and her grip on the throw pillow eased.

"Can you talk about it?" Quinn asked.

When she nodded, Quinn opened her spiral notebook. "I'm going to take some notes, to make certain I get all the details right. Start whenever you're ready."

She swallowed hard, then began. "I was sleeping and I . . . woke up. You know how that is? You're suddenly completely awake and alert?"

"I do."

"I knew something wasn't right." She rubbed her arms as if chilled. "I thought I heard something, like the floor creaking and I—"

She stopped. Pressed her lips together.

"I'm here," Quinn coaxed. "You're safe. Tell me what happened so I can help you."

She cleared her throat, then began again, seeming to force the words out. "I started to get up but before I could he was on top of me."

Her chin quivered and her eyes filled with tears.

"Take your time, Eden. We're not in a hurry."

She nodded, began again. "He came out of nowhere. He—" She breathed in and out, calming herself. "He covered my mouth with his hand."

"Was he wearing gloves?"

She didn't hesitate. "Yes."

"Did you see his face?"

She pressed her trembling lips together. "No. He was wearing a ski mask."

"What color eyes did he have?"

For a split second, her expression went blank, then she said, "Blue. I thought he was going to rape me."

"Did you fight him?"

"I was too scared. It was like I was frozen." She teared up. "I took a self-defense class; some good it did me."

"You were terrified," Quinn said. "What you're describing is a common reaction, don't beat yourself up about it. You're alive and unhurt, focus on that."

She hugged the pillow tighter.

"On the phone, you told me he warned you not to call 911. Did he say anything else?"

"To go home. That if I didn't . . . he wouldn't be so nice next time."

Quinn processed that. An implied threat of future bodily harm. "Then he left?"

"Uh-huh. When I heard the door click shut, I hurried and locked it, then barricaded it with the loveseat."

She had. It was still by the door, now shoved aside to allow Quinn to slip through. "Do you have any idea how he got in?"

"I always lock the door when I . . . especially after Mom . . ." Her words trailed off.

Quinn went to examine the door. A deadbolt lock, standard pin and tumbler. No chain. She looked back at Eden. "What about the downstairs entry door? What kind of locking system does it have?"

"I don't know."

"What about a security camera?"

"I never noticed."

"I'm going to take a look. I'll be right back."

Quinn trotted down the flight of stairs. No security camera, she saw. Similar deadbolt to the apartment's.

Good for keeping out common criminals and street thugs, but not someone who knew what they were doing. Not someone focused on a single target with one objective.

Frighten Eden Riley. Send her back to where she came from.

Quinn paused at the bottom of the stairs, thoughts racing. Riley had been asking questions. She'd stepped on toes. The wrong ones.

Eden appeared at her door at the top of the stairs, peered down at her. "Are you okay?"

She'd been worried about her. Silly but sort of sweet. "Of course." A corner of her mouth lifted in a half grin and she started back up. "Thanks for checking on me."

"What did you find?" Eden closed and locked the door behind them.

"Not much. No security camera, no special locking system, and no sign of a forced entry."

"Then how'd he get in?"

"I hate to break this to you, but it's incredibly easy to pick a lock, you need nothing more than a lock pick set and practice."

She went white. Crossed to the couch and sank onto it. "He could come back. Anytime."

"He told you to go home. Maybe you should."

"I can't." She curled her hands into fists. "I won't."

Quinn sat across from her, looked her dead in the eyes. "I don't think this was an idle threat. I believe that man—or the person who sent him—meant business. You're in real danger."

"I'm not going. Whoever's behind this killed my mother—"

"You don't know that."

"Yes, I do." She tipped up her chin. "I'm not going to let them get away with it."

"Is it worth dying for?"

She didn't hesitate. "Yes."

Quinn chose not to argue. Instead, she refocused on the break-in, and the reason for it.

"Who do you think is behind what happened tonight?"

"The person who killed my mom. Which may, or may not, be my father. I'm certain that before she died, she said 'he found us.' She was referring to the person she was running from when she left New Orleans. Whether that was my dad or someone else, I don't know, but it definitely has something to do with the Hudson murder and kidnapping."

Eden stopped. Took a breath. She seemed totally calm now. Totally focused.

Quinn couldn't say she disagreed with her thinking.

"If you're determined to stay, there are some things you're going to have to do to ensure your safety. Tomorrow, first thing. Do you understand?"

She said she did, and Quinn resumed. "You have internet here, correct?" When Riley answered in the affirmative, she continued. "You buy a security system with cameras. I recommend two cameras. One for outside your door, and one for inside. You want to pay for the recording service. If you don't know how to set it up, get a Geek. If none are available, call me."

"Is that it?"

"If you don't already have pepper spray, get some. When you're out and about you're going to have to be hyper-vigilant. Especially at night. Just because they attacked you here this time, doesn't mean they won't choose a different approach next time."

Quinn saw the fear creeping back into her eyes. A good thing, she thought. Maybe she would change her mind about staying.

"Do you have a gun?"

She shook her head.

"Do you know how to shoot one?"

"God, no."

"Do you like dogs?"

"Yes . . . why?"

"You might think about getting yourself one. A Pit Bull or German Shepherd."

"You're trying to scare me."

"You should be scared." Quinn stood. "I'm calling in a report tonight, so there's a record of the incident.

"Just in case, huh?"

Quinn knew what she meant. In case he came after her again. In case he intensified his attack.

She wasn't going to lie to her. "Yes."

"What do I do now?"

"What do you mean?"

"I don't know if I can . . . Should I go to a hotel until I can get a camera installed?"

Quinn knew she should say yes, get a hotel room. There were plenty of 'em in this city; who cared that it was the middle of the night?

Quinn didn't say that. Instead, she offered her guest room. When she did, Quinn had the feeling that was exactly what Eden Riley had planned on her doing.

THIRTY-SIX

7:05 A.M. *Tuesday*.

Quinn awakened to the smell of coffee. She breathed in the aroma, smiled sleepily and snuggled deeper under the covers. *Rick*. She loved how he did this, awoke first and brought her a cup to sip in bed, so she could wake up slowly. Loved how he would watch her while she sipped, as if her every movement and expression were somehow magical.

She pictured him there, in her tiny kitchen, wearing his jeans and nothing else, imagined slipping out of bed, only to draw him back to it and making slow, intoxicating love.

In that instant, reality broke through the last remnants of sleep. Quinn opened her eyes, fully awake. Not Rick. Not ever again.

Longing took her breath. A sharp, sudden ache of loneliness.

Get over it, Quinn. You didn't want the same things as he did.

Annoyed with herself, she tossed the covers aside and climbed out of bed. She stepped into her jeans and, using one of the scrunchies she kept in her nightstand drawer, piled her hair into a messy pineapple.

After a quick stop in the bathroom, she headed to the kitchen. Eden stood at the sink, looking out the window above it.

"Did you sleep okay?" Quinn asked.

She turned. The dark circles under her eyes answered the question before she did. "As well as could be expected, I guess."

"Have you had a change of heart about staying?"

"No."

Quinn hadn't expected a different answer but decided to take another stab at sanity. "I'd reconsider that. Your physical safety has to be your first priority."

"No."

She turned back to the window. Quinn shook her head and crossed to the coffeepot. She poured a cup. "You've got guts, I'll give you that. Good sense, not so much."

"Thanks for the vote of confidence."

"I'm being honest. If you don't do what they ask, they'll come after you."

Eden looked at her. "They?"

"Whoever is behind this." She added some cream to her coffee, took a sip. "Personally, I think the man in your apartment was hired help. I won't be able to stop them, Eden. I won't be there."

Eden curved her arms around herself. "Thank you for caring about what happens to me."

"That's what cops do."

A smile touched her mouth. "I thought they busted the bad guys?"

"They do. Because they care." She went to the pantry. "I'm going to make toast. You want a slice?"

"Yes, please. I'm starving."

Quinn got to it: dropping the slices of bread into the toaster, getting out the butter and nut butter, jelly and utensils.

"I met your cat."

"Beignet."

"He was at the door, so I let him in. He's sort of a tough guy, huh?"

Quinn tore off two paper towels to use as napkins. "He's been known to be, but we have an understanding."

"I gave him a can of food and he calmed down."

"I'll bet he did." Quinn handed her a plate with two crunchy slices.

"Thanks." She slathered some of the peanut butter on and took a big bite. "Are you dating anyone?"

Quinn stopped, looked at her. "Where did *that* come from?"

"I'm not hitting on you. In my mind, if we're going to be working together, we should get to know each other better."

"We're not working together."

"Are you? Dating anyone?"

"No."

"Why not?"

"Seriously?"

"Yeah," she said around the toast.

Quinn carried her plate to the table and sat. "Too busy. Too tired. Maybe I don't think relationships are all they're cracked up to be." She took a bite. "Take your pick."

"You had your heart broken."

"You're sort of a pest, you know that?"

She grinned. "I've been told that before."

"Big surprise."

Of course, it wasn't, but Eden didn't seem to take offense.

"Writers are nosy. It's part of the gig. Are you gay?"

Quinn almost spit out her coffee. "No, but it's none of your business if I was. None of this is any of your business."

Eden ignored that and started on her second piece of toast. "I was recently dating someone. A fellow instructor at the college."

"What happened?" she asked, curious despite herself.

"Mom. Her murder. I'm not sure if I went off the rails, as he said, or if he didn't have the guts to hold me up."

She liked the honesty, Quinn decided. "What was his name?"

"Brandon. Brandon Benjamin Burch." She polished off her toast. "Being a total word nerd, I liked the alliteration."

Quinn relented. "I was seeing someone until very recently."

"Why'd it end?"

She offered Eden the same line she'd offered Rick. "Cops suck at relationships."

"That sounds convenient."

"Excuse me?"

"My guess is, you're scared of commitment. Either because you're afraid they'll let you down or you're afraid you'll let them down." She stood, grabbed a spoon and the jar of peanut butter. "You mind?"

"As long as you don't double dip, no."

"What about girlfriends?" Eden asked. "You have a BFF?"

"Am I fifteen? No, I don't."

She scooped out a heaping spoon of the nut butter, then screwed the lid back on the jar. "I bet you consider your partner your closest friend."

She did and was sort of annoyed. "What makes you say that? About Dobby being my closest friend?"

"First, if cops really do stink at relationships, I'd bet that carries over to friendships, as well. Second, from what I can assess about the job and its dangers, there's a high level of trust between partners, which in turn leads to a high level of intimacy and co-dependency."

She was right. About all of it. Uncomfortable with the direction of the conversation, Quinn changed it. "Who else have you told what you told me? About your mom?"

Eden finished the peanut butter and carried her plate and spoon to the sink. "No one. To everyone else, I'm writing a book. Period."

"You didn't go to Lieutenant Tillerson, as I suggested?"

She shook her head. "No."

"Who have you personally made contact with?"

"Charles and Bill Hudson. Their long-time attorney, Daniel

Shaw, and his son, Logan. I talked to your dad's old partner Mike Bruzeau, and I understand Cynthia had a maternal aunt in the area, I plan to track her down this week."

"Dad always called Shaw the Hudson's 'fixer.'" Quinn frowned, searched her memory. "Why the son? He was really young at the time of the crime. Eight, if I remember correctly."

"Not only has he known the family all these years, he works for The Hudson Group. He must have heard things."

Quinn stood, went to the coffeepot, thoughts whirling. Mentally sorting through the pieces of this puzzle. Her dad's suicide. Angela Riley's series of receipts and the picture they painted. Eden's attacker, warning her to go home. The flyer left on her windshield.

She stopped on that. *Your father didn't kill himself.*

Not a bad joke by a pissed-off colleague. An anonymous invitation. A provocation.

There was something important here. Important enough that somebody wanted to keep it secret. Wanted it desperately, evidenced by the event of last night.

Suddenly, Quinn couldn't catch her breath. Her heart thumped heavily against the wall of her chest, and her hands began to shake.

"Excuse me," she managed. "I'll be right back."

She went into the bathroom, shutting and locking the door behind her. Slumping against it. *Don't do this Quinn. You can't be thinking what you're thinking.*

Of taking up her father's cause. Picking up where he left off, risking her job and professional reputation to do it.

Maybe even her life, judging by the attack on Eden.

She brought the heels of her hands to her eyes. Why would she risk all that? For Eden? She barely knew the woman. For justice for Cynthia and Grace Hudson? That wasn't her job.

She dropped her hands, the truth reverberating through her. To clear her dad's name and to prove he *hadn't* killed himself.

That's why she would risk everything. Whoever left the flyer on her windshield had bet that's exactly how she'd feel.

Her thoughts spiraled back to the last time she'd spoken to her dad. He'd called, excited. He'd uncovered something big, something that was going to break the case wide open.

He'd said that before and each time, the big thing had turned out to be nothing.

What if he really had uncovered the one piece that tied all the others together and been killed for it?

No, Quinn. He took his own life. You inspected the scene yourself.

She pictured it, him. The gun on the floor, directly under his dangling hand. The location and the angle of the blood spatter. Gunshot residue on his hand; his prints and no others on the gun. It checked out. All of it.

She lifted her gaze to the ceiling. Why do it then? That day? He'd been so excited and positive.

Their argument. Her hanging up on him. She'd blamed herself. Carried that secret guilt these past five years.

That explanation didn't work. It never had. Her father had been as pig-headed and stubborn as they came. A good Irishman, through and through. He would have seen his discovery through to the bitter end, not only had it been that important to him, it was the way he was built.

Stand up for what's right, Quinnie. Stand up for those who can't stand up for themselves.

He'd been drinking. A lot, judging by the empty bottle, his slurring words. Which was the reason she'd hung up.

He drank all the time. Why kill himself that night?

She heard her father's voice in her head. *"What are you going to do, Quinnie? Are you a Conners, or not?"*

She was, God help her. Through and through.

THIRTY-SEVEN

Quinn stuck her head into Captain Franks office. "Warrant arrived. Detective Dobson and I are on our way to Russell's place. A patrol unit is meeting us there."

He looked up, nodded. "Keep me posted."

"We will." She started to duck out, then stopped. "Captain, a friend of mine was broken into last night. She was threatened but left unharmed. I'd like to ask a few questions, chase down a lead or two?"

"Where'd this crime occur?"

"Right here in the Second. It shouldn't take much time."

He nodded curtly. "As long as you don't let it get in the way of your active investigations."

"Yes, sir. Thank you."

As they started downstairs, Dobby looked at her. "What the hell was *that*?"

"The friend thing?"

"Yeah, that thing."

"Middle of the night, Eden Riley called me, scared out her mind, and I went over."

They fell into step together. "The writer? She's a friend now?"

"I used the term loosely. Figured calling her an acquaintance wouldn't fly."

"Details. Now."

"Someone broke into her place while she was sleeping. Pinned her to the bed and told her to go back home. Or else."

"She called you? Not 911?"

"Yes."

"Why? She hardly knows you."

"They told her not to call 911. Besides, you know how it is, you know a cop, you call 'em when there's a problem. Human nature."

He didn't look convinced; she pressed on. "I'm thinking she's stepped on some pretty sensitive toes. Maybe powerful ones."

"The Hudsons?" He looked incredulous. "That seems a little farfetched. They're not thugs."

"They don't want a book to be written, so they hire someone to scare her into going home."

"Why not stonewall her?"

"She's insistent, I know that from experience. They don't want it all brought back up. It's not the kind of attention they want."

"How'd you leave it with her?"

"Told her if she insisted on staying—"

"Which she did, right?"

"Right. I told her to invest in a couple cameras, get pepper spray and to be careful. He laid hands on her once, he would do it again."

"Stupid for her to stay."

"Agreed." They reached their desks, collected their things and headed out. Rain threatened, and Quinn glanced up at the heavy, dark clouds. They looked ready to unleash buckets at any moment.

"I don't like this," he said.

"What?" She looked at him. "The weather?"

"You interacting with Riley. I thought you weren't interested in getting involved?"

"I wasn't interested in helping her with her book. This is different. Someone wants her gone pretty badly and I want to know why."

"Just promise me something, okay?"

"Sure. Anything."

They reached her vehicle. She unlocked the doors and they climbed in. He met her eyes.

"Promise me this doesn't have anything to do with your dad."

"Why would it?"

"Come on, Quinn. Your dad. The Hudsons. The case he killed himself over."

For a moment she couldn't breathe. Like a giant fist had grabbed ahold of her lungs and squeezed. She fought it off, filled her lungs. "Arguably killed himself over, and I can't believe what you're suggesting."

"Seriously? You're human, Quinn. No way this couldn't be a little bit personal."

"It's not. Okay?" The words came out sharper than she'd intended. Defensive.

He looked hurt. "Fine. It's your party. If it goes south, it's your ass on the line."

THIRTY-EIGHT

3:10 P.M.

"At least we got the planner," Dobby said, trying to strike a positive note.

But no gun. No bullets, gun case, receipts from the range—nothing that would tie Russell to ownership of a weapon.

He had followed them around, watching them go through his and Karlee's things, strangers shuffling through his life. He'd talked to Karlee's mother, her sister, then his lawyer. After the conversation with the attorney, Russell had begun videoing their search on his phone.

"Russell's no dummy," Quinn said, not taking her eyes from the road. "He kills Karlee, the first thing he does is get rid of any evidence that could incriminate him. The gun is the one thing that would absolutely marry him to her murder."

"*If* he killed Karlee." She felt his gaze on her. "Maybe he's innocent?"

She hated to admit it, but she was having doubts. His impassioned plea of innocence today had sounded sincere. The way he had choked up had rung authentic, his devastated expression as he'd followed them around.

She sighed, glanced quickly at Dobby. "Then why lie about the gun? If he's innocent, ballistics would prove it. He would know that, right?"

"He's a gun guy so, yeah, he has to know that."

They fell silent. Quinn navigated traffic, turning her thoughts to the attack on Eden, and to her next step. Charles and Bill Hudson.

Ahead on her right loomed the Hancock Whitney Center, the tallest building in New Orleans and home to The Hudson Group's corporate headquarters.

You really want to do this, Quinn? It's not too late to back out.

Yes, she thought, spying a parking spot and navigating her vehicle into it. "Quick stop," she said, cutting the engine and unclipping her safety belt.

"What are we—" Dobby bit the question back, realization coming into his expression. "You don't intend to question the Hudsons about the assault on Riley?"

"Of course, I do."

He groaned. "Are you out of your mind?"

"How do I *not* talk to them? Somebody pinned Eden to her bed and told her to leave New Orleans, or else. Who do you think could have been behind that?"

For a long moment, he was quiet. "You do this, you're on your own."

"You're that scared of them?"

"You said this wasn't personal."

"It's not."

"Bullshit. You're—" He made a sound of frustration. "Do whatever you want. It's your career."

"Thanks, I will." She dropped the keys onto the center console. "Back in fifteen."

The Hudson Group's headquarters took up three floors of the building. She alighted the elevator on the first of the three.

The reception area smelled of fresh flowers; the colors were muted, the furnishings sleek. As was the young woman manning the desk. "Good afternoon," she said, her accent distinctly British. "How can I help you?"

"I'm Detective Conners." Quinn held up her shield. "I'm here to speak to Mr. Hudson."

"Charles Hudson or Bill Hudson?"

"Both."

"May I tell them what this is in reference to?"

"Eden Riley."

Recognition crossed her features. "One moment, I'll see if either Mr. Hudson is available."

She made the call. Several minutes later, a woman in a taupe suit and impossibly high heels stepped off the elevator and crossed to Quinn, hand out. "Hello, Detective. I'm Leslie, Mr. Hudson Senior's personal assistant. Follow me."

They took the elevator up to the executive floor, passed through another reception area to a set of double doors, their dark, glossy wood fitted with shiny brass fittings. A nameplate on the door announced Charles Hudson, CEO.

Quinn had seen pictures of Charles Hudson, but those hadn't done the man justice. He was certainly in his seventies by now, but he exuded strength. What was it? she wondered. The sharp gaze that seemed to miss nothing? Or the way he held himself, as if he not only understood he commanded attention, but that he demanded it?

Another man was with him. Bill Hudson, she realized. She remembered him from pictures as being Hollywood handsome. No longer. Today he looked victim of too many cocktails and late nights, too much self-indulgence and not enough self-reflection. Losing his wife and child that way, who could blame him? Self-reflection was not always what it was cracked up to be.

Quinn shifted her gaze once again to Hudson senior. He, on the other hand, despised loss of control. He would see self-indulgence as weakness, and weakness as defeat. Of course, he would.

Perhaps the younger Hudson's physical state was the one area of his life where he could defy his father's will? Grab power where he had none?

"Gentleman," she said, "thank you for seeing me."

Hudson senior stepped forward. He motioned them towards the seating area: a small, leather sofa and two chairs. "Please, have a seat."

They all sat. He looked her in the eyes. "Hearing your name was like a ghost coming up from the past. How is your father?"

She stiffened slightly. "He's dead, Mr. Hudson. Something I'm sure you knew."

His eyebrows lifted ever-so-slightly. "Why would I, Detective?"

"Why? Because my father was the lead detective investigating your daughter-in-law's murder and your grandchild's kidnapping. And because he never gave up, even after everyone else had. I suspect that meant something to you and your family. Any other questions, Mr. Hudson?"

She thought she saw a gleam of admiration in his eyes. "Apparently, the apple didn't fall far from the tree."

"Just promise me this isn't about your dad. That it isn't personal."

It was, dammit. She'd hadn't realized how personal until this moment.

"I'm here today about a woman named Eden Riley. I understand she's contacted you."

"The writer? She has."

That was the way this was going to go: she would ask a question, he would give her the bare minimum of an answer.

She might as well cut to the chase.

"Ms. Riley was attacked in her home last night."

"How awful," he said, nothing in his tone expressing shock or dismay. "I'm sorry to hear that."

"Are you?"

"Excuse me?"

"Her attacker warned her there would be serious consequences if she didn't leave New Orleans."

"What could that have to do with us?" That came from Hudson junior, speaking up for the first time, opening the door for her—and in the process earning a sharp glance from his father.

"Thank you for asking." She smiled slightly; Bill Hudson flushed. "I know this is a sensitive subject, and I apologize in advance. As you know, she's writing a book about your family's tragedy, and it seems someone doesn't want her to do that."

"You have a point, I presume?"

Junior again, not masking his animosity; Quinn imagined Charles Hudson wanting to strangle his son.

"Did you encourage her to pursue the book?" she asked.

Charles stepped in before his son could respond. "Hardly."

"May I ask why not?"

"The incident happened a long time ago, Detective. We've managed to put it behind us as best we could and go on. Do we want to be reminded? No, we do not. Do we want the entire episode dredged back up in a book? Obviously not. Would you, Detective?"

She wouldn't. Exactly why she had originally refused to cooperate with Riley herself.

"You call the murders of two members of your family an incident?"

Charles Hudson stood. She'd crossed a line, angering him, she saw. "You remind me of your father. Unfortunately, it seems as if you've followed a little too closely in his footsteps."

She stiffened. "That's unfortunate, why?"

"We're out of time, Detective. Please send my regards to Ms. Riley. New Orleans, as beautiful as it is, can be a dangerous place. A young woman alone needs to be careful."

The words, their tone, were innocent enough. Almost grandfatherly. A man from a previous generation, offering his fearful outlook on life.

This was no kindly grandfather. "If it was my family," she said, "I'd want justice. No matter the cost."

"As you're aware, the cost can be quite high. Are you certain you want to go there?"

"Are you certain you do, Mr. Hudson?"

He tapped the intercom. "Leslie, please see Detective Conners out."

The woman collected her and escorted her to the elevator.

While they were waiting for a car, a man joined them. Thirty-something. Dark hair and eyes. Impeccably groomed. Too-good-to-be-true handsome.

"Leslie," he said, voice deep and smooth with a hint of amusement at the edges. "I'll see the detective down."

The unflappable PA seemed suddenly ruffled. "Thanks, Logan. If you're sure?"

"I'm positive," he said, smiling. "In fact, I'm happy to help. Charles works you too hard."

Logan Shaw, she realized. Of course.

The car arrived; he held the door. "After you."

Quinn stepped on; as the door slid shut behind them, he handed her his business card.

"Logan Shaw," he said. "At your service."

"Vice-president of hotel operations," she read aloud. "Daniel Shaw's son." He wanted something from her, she might as well cut to the chase and find out what. "How can I help you, Mr. Shaw?"

"Call me Logan," he said, lips curving. "Considering we're going to be friends, it's more appropriate."

Handsome and charming, she thought. Too bad that crap didn't work on her. "Not at all appropriate, and no, we're not going to be friends."

The car reached the first floor. Again, he held the door for her. All this ladies-first crap made her itch. She carried a gun, was trained in hand-to-hand combat, and he was treating her like a wilting southern flower.

They stepped into the lobby; he touched her elbow, steering her away from a group of executive types. When they had passed them, he leaned closer.

"To answer your earlier question, take it easy on Charles and Bill. They've been through hell."

"I hardly think a few questions from me is going to rock their world."

The expression in his eyes chided her. "They don't need to have the entire nightmare churned back up. I don't know if they can handle it."

"Oh, please. Those two?"

"I was there. I saw what they went through first-hand. It almost destroyed them."

"Not to be unsympathetic, but I don't believe an atomic bomb could destroy Charles Hudson."

Logan laughed. "I can see how you would feel that way, he is a tough SOB. Except when it comes to his family."

"You seem pretty protective of them."

"They're family. Not by blood, but in every other way. I all but grew up at the St. Charles Avenue home."

"I'm doing my job, Mr. Shaw."

"The way your father was doing his?"

Quinn narrowed her eyes. "I understand you've spoken with Ms. Riley?"

"I have."

They reached the bank of glass doors leading outside. He opened the closest; she stepped through. Although the late afternoon sun had lost the intensity of an hour before, it was still hot. She could see the waves of heat emanating from the concrete beyond the doors.

"Did you try to convince her to drop her book idea and go home?" Quinn asked.

"I did. She refused."

"Are you angry about that?"

"Why would I be?"

"Because you're so determined to protect--as you call them--your family. How far would you go to do that?"

He searched her gaze. "Why did you come here today?"

"Someone wants Eden Riley to return to Illinois." She paused then added, "Quite badly."

His brow furrowed. "What does that mean?"

"Ask your bosses."

"You don't know them at all. You're barking up the wrong tree."

"I won't take any more of your time, Mr. Shaw."

She made a move to go; he caught her elbow. Strong emotion shone in his eyes, vibrated in his voice. "I was there, the murders devastated them."

"What about you? Were you devastated?"

His grip on her elbow tightened. "You have no idea."

"Please take your hand off of me, Mr. Shaw."

He did but was undeterred. "They'll squash you like a bug, and I'd hate to see that happen."

"Are you threatening me?"

"Of course not, Detective. I know these people; I know how they operate."

"I get it. They're the kind of people who get other people to do their dirty work for them. Am I right?"

"No. They're the kind of people who have layers of lawyers. They know everyone who's anyone, and they won't hesitate to use those connections."

"Maybe they're the kind of people who threaten and frighten young women?

"They're not the mob, Detective Conners. They're the kings and queens of carnival; they throw parties and fundraisers and contribute to political campaigns. Pushing them is more likely to cost you your job than your life."

"My dad lost his life; did you know that?"

"I heard he killed himself. I can't imagine being so hopeless."

Logan Shaw knew how to strike a blow, she acknowledged. With one short sentence, he'd eviscerated her.

She stepped off the curb, he stopped her again. "If you have any questions or need anything, call. I'll help you if I can." He smiled. "It was good to meet you, Quinn Conners."

He didn't call after her a third time, and she headed for her car. Quinn slid behind the wheel and saw her hands were shaking. She willed them to stop, annoyed at herself for letting one well-placed comment get to her.

Dobby tapped his watch. "Forty minutes. I had to lower the windows."

"Sorry about that. Time flies when you're having fun." She started the vehicle, checked her rearview and pulled away from the curb.

"Who was the movie star?"

She frowned. "The movie . . . you mean the guy I was talking to?"

"Yeah, him."

"Logan Shaw. The fixer's kid."

"Missed his calling, if you ask me. How'd it go?"

Quinn glanced at him. "How do you think it went?"

He groaned. "Am I going to be looking for a new partner?"

"They'll squash you like a bug."

"Not as bad as all that. I rattled their cages a little bit, they brought up my dad, we parted as friends."

"That's it?"

"Pretty much." She slowed as the light ahead turned red. "Nothing you have to be worried about."

Even as the reassurance passed her lips, a queasy sensation settled in the pit of her gut. Accompanying it was the image of a bug, flattened under the heel of a very expensive shoe.

THIRTY-NINE

9:00 A.M. *Wednesday,*

The moment Quinn learned she and Dobby were being summoned to the Captain's office, she knew it was bad news. When she saw that Captain Franks wasn't alone, she knew where the bad news was coming from.

The Hudsons.

She recognized the man standing with Franks from the photos her father used to pour over. Daniel Shaw. Older. Maybe sicker, judging by the fit of his suit, as if he had recently and suddenly lost weight, and by his pale complexion. Healthy or not, Shaw wielded as much power as ever.

Bug. Check. Heel. Check. About to get squished?

It sure looked that way.

"You wanted to see us, Captain?" she said.

He waved them in, expression thunderous. "Take a seat. Both of you."

She dared a glance at Dobby. He didn't look happy. So much for her reassurance he had nothing to worry about.

"Conners, Dobson, this is Mr. Shaw. He represents the Hudson family." The man inclined his head in greeting. "Mr. Shaw tells me you paid a visit to Charles and Bill Hudson yesterday. Is that true?"

"I did," she said. "Dobby did not. He's not part of this."

Franks continued as if she hadn't spoken. "Am I to understand you claimed to be acting under the auspices of the NOPD and at my direction?"

Quinn shifted in her seat. "If you'll remember, Captain, you gave me permission to follow up on an attack perpetrated against a friend of mine."

He glowered at her. "Ask a few questions, follow a few leads? That one?"

She tried not to squirm under his I-call-bullshit stare. "Yes, sir."

Shaw stepped in; voice slippery as silk. "May I, Captain Franks?"

"Of course."

"You must understand, Detectives, that my clients take any visit from the NOPD very seriously and will react to the full extent of their ability according to the law. I'm sure you didn't mean to suggest my clients were involved in the attack on that poor girl?"

He paused, the question hung in the air between them, demanding an answer. With the captain's gaze on her, she felt every bit the mouse cornered by the cat. One exceptionally good at hunting.

She cleared her throat. She couldn't lie, it wasn't in her. She hedged instead. "I acted hastily, no doubt. I regret that."

For a long moment, Shaw held her gaze. Then he inclined his head. "I'm glad we've cleared that up," he said and turned to Franks. "Thank you for your time this morning. I appreciate it."

Franks walked him to the door. As it snapped shut behind Shaw, he turned to face them, expression thunderous. "Do you know who these people are? Do you realize how bad that little prank made me look? Like an idiot."

"With all due respect, Captain, prank? I hardly think—"

"You weren't thinking this time, were you?"

"I was polite. I didn't accuse them of anything—"

"Don't test me, Detective. You being there and questioning them that way implied complicity. Don't pretend otherwise, not with me."

Quinn had never seen him so angry. "I'm sorry, Captain. I didn't consider who they were. I didn't think it mattered, considering the seriousness of—"

"Then you thought wrong."

"I see, the rich and powerful are immune to police scrutiny."

The words, the challenge behind them, popped out of her mouth before she could stop them. It was the wrong thing to say. His face turned from simply flushed to ready-to-explode red.

"Not legitimate scrutiny," he snapped. "Not warranted questioning. What was this, some sort of personal vendetta?"

"Absolutely not, Captain. I explained about my friend—"

"Friend?" He made air quotes. "Is that what you're calling this writer?"

"An acquaintance. A citizen in need."

"Don't remind of my duty to the citizens of this community. I know full well what my responsibilities to this badge are. I'm not certain you do."

He turned his angry glare on Dobby. "What about you, Dobson? You were in on this?"

Dobby didn't glance her way, but she felt accusation rolling off him in waves.

He responded stiffly. "The first time I heard about the incident in question was when Conners spoke with you about it. At that point I had no idea who the 'friend' was or her intention to involve the Hudsons."

"You did before she walked through that door?"

"Yes, sir."

"Where were you at the time?"

"Waiting in the car."

"Waiting in the car," he repeated, eyebrows arching in exaggerated disbelief. "Which makes you complicit in her behavior."

Quinn jumped in. "He tried to talk me out of it, Captain. I refused to listen."

"You *tried* to talk her out of it?" Franks thundered. "In other words, you went against your best instincts . . . why? To appease your partner? You knew her intention, you knew it was the wrong thing to do, but you allowed it."

"I'm sorry, sir. It won't happen again."

"Look, Captain," Quinn said, "Eden Riley obviously stepped on toes. Powerful toes. Why else would someone be motivated to—"

"Maybe she made the whole thing up? We don't know!"

"I know. I was there. She was terrified."

"Am I supposed to trust your instincts right now? *Your* judgement?"

Her face heated. "There's more to her story. If you'll just listen—"

He held up a hand. "Don't make it worse."

"Captain—"

"You're done. Any permission I granted regarding this incident is revoked. You go anywhere near Charles or Bill Hudson, you contact them in any way, I'll suspend you. Now get out. Close the door behind you."

They stood, filed out. Quinn let out long breath when they cleared the door. "For a moment there, I thought his head was going to explode."

Dobby stopped, looked at her, his anger palpable. "Don't ever do that to me again. Don't ever put me in a position where I have to choose between you and my job."

Before she could respond, he walked away.

FORTY

6:10 P.M. *Friday.*

Beignet met her at the front door. Quinn set down the bag of groceries she carried—a can of soup, a loaf of bread, and a package of cheese slices—and scooped up the cat. He purred and rubbed his head against her shoulder.

"Hey buddy," she said, "you're the friendliest face I've seen all day."

His purr deepened and she scratched the place at the back of his head that always sent him into spasms of delight.

Rick had teased her more than once about her ability to make *him* purr. A memory of the two of them popped into her head, tangled up in the sheets and each other, sleepy and satisfied.

Beignet took that opportunity to leap out of her arms. Traitor, Quinn thought, collecting the bag of groceries and following the cat to the kitchen. She fed him, then went about putting together her own meal. She opened the can of tomato soup and dumped it in the saucepan then realizing she'd forgotten to buy milk, added a can of water.

Dobby had barely spoken to her for the entire week. They'd interacted enough to do their jobs, but no more. She'd attempted an apology several times, each time he'd shut her down.

It had been awkward and uncomfortable.

It didn't help that everyone else in their unit knew what had happened—either because they'd heard Captain Franks dressing them down, or they'd heard about it from someone who had.

She shrugged out of her jacket, hung it on the back of a kitchen chair. She retrieved the whiskey from the pantry, poured herself two fingers, then instead of returning the bottle to the pantry, she plunked it down next to the glass.

What the hell, she thought. After all, it *was* Friday night.

She realized the soup was boiling and snatched it off the heat. After assembling the bread and cheese for her sandwich, she stuck it in the toaster oven. Grilled cheese, toasted cheese, whatever. She was only eating because she knew the effect the whiskey would have on an empty stomach, and that was her dad, not her.

Her phone went off. Not Dobby, she saw, disappointed. Eden. She'd called earlier, left a message saying all was well and was touching base. Sighing, Quinn rejected the call. Eden was the last person she felt like chatting with right now and typed a text instead: Shitty day on top of a crappy week. Call you tomorrow?

After laying the phone on the counter, she carried her meal to the table. She'd scorched the soup, under-toasted the sandwich, and alienated her partner—who also happened to be her best friend.

Strike three, Conners. You're out!

She ate a few spoonfuls of the soup and took a couple bites of the sandwich, then pushed them away and turned to the whiskey.

She missed Rick. She missed the way, on a night like tonight, he'd show up with a pizza and bottle of wine and just let her talk, no judgement or advice. No pandering either, just quietly support her. Not many people did that, at least in her experience.

A couple weeks, that's all it had been since he ended it, but it felt lots longer than that. She'd abided by his wishes. He'd asked her not to contact him, and she hadn't, all the while secretly hoping he'd call her.

Quinn finished the first whiskey and poured another. Maybe pride was keeping him from calling? After all, he was the one who'd drawn the line in the sand. If she reached out, maybe he'd relent? Maybe he was missing her as much as she missed him?

Quinn glanced at the phone, a knot of longing settling in the pit of her gut. She could call him now, break the ice. If he answered at least she would know he was willing to talk to her.

She started to retrieve the device, then sat back. What if he didn't pick up? She didn't know if she could handle that, not tonight. She brought the glass to her lips, sipped, thoughts racing. At least she could open the door by leaving a message.

She got to her feet, crossed to the counter and reached for the phone. She hesitated, hand hovering over it. He'd told her not to call. Not to come see him.

Tears pricked her eyes, and she blinked them away. Crying wasn't her style. She wasn't a girly-girl. She was tough, the way her dad had taught her to be. Decisive. Hardened by life and the job.

That was okay, right? Without armor, she wouldn't survive. Maybe she could make him understand?

Dammit. If she was so decisive, why was she standing here like a total weenie, afraid to make a move?

Quinn snatched up the phone, accessed his cell number and punched send. It rang. Once. Twice. A third time. Then—

"This is Rick."

"Rick, hey. It's me. Quinn."

"Hey."

Ice. Broken. She released a pent-up breath. "I wondered . . . How's it going?"

"I'm working." He paused. "Why are you calling me, Quinn?"

"I . . . wanted, wondered—"

He wasn't going to make this easy for her; she didn't blame him. *Crack open the armor, Quinn. Do it.*

She forced the words out. "Wasn't what we had good?"

His silence stole her ability to breathe. Her head went light. She found a kitchen chair, sat down hard.

"Yeah," he said softly. "It was."

The breath filled her lungs. Relief. Hope. "So . . . why this?"

"You know why."

She pressed the phone closer to her ear. "I don't."

"Because it isn't enough."

A lump formed in her throat. She forced the words past it. "I miss you."

For a long, breathless moment he said nothing. She thought maybe, just maybe he missed her too.

"I've got to go."

He hung up, and for a long moment she sat unmoving, phone still to her ear. Finally, she lowered it, tucked the device into her pocket.

This was what she'd wanted. Wasn't it? She'd forced his hand. He wanted something she knew she couldn't give. Why pretend? Why even try?

It was over.

Tears flooded her eyes and she blinked furiously against them. Screw 'em all, she thought, grabbing the bottle of whiskey and her glass. Rick and his unreasonable demands. Dobby and Captain Franks. The Hudsons and their toady fixer Daniel Shaw.

She plunked the bottle down onto the coffee table, then held up her glass. "Here's to you and me, Pops. Same as always."

FORTY-ONE

9:10 A.M. *Saturday.*

Quinn became aware of a thundering in her head. Wincing, she cracked open her eyes. The television was on, sunlight streamed through the blinds, stinging her eyes. She brought a hand to her forehead. Pain. Her mouth felt like she'd eaten a bowl of dirt.

The pounding came again. Not in her head. At the door. Moaning, she unwound herself. She'd fallen asleep on the couch, curled into some god-awful, yoga-style position. She hadn't even removed her firearm, the spot where it had been pressed into her side was numb.

"I'm coming," she called, the words more a croak than a call. She limped to the door; peered out the peephole. Eden Riley, looking as fresh as a spring day, balancing a coffee caddy and a white take-out bag.

Quinn opened the door, reached for a coffee. "You saved my life. C'mon in."

"Are you okay?" Eden asked, crossing to the coffee table. "You look—"

She stopped at the elephant in the middle of the room—the whiskey bottle and empty glass.

Quinn took a sip of the brew. It was only lukewarm, but at that moment nothing could have tasted better. "Let's just say yesterday was *not* a good day. Correction—last week was the worst."

"I'm sorry."

"Not your fault." She took another sip. "What are you doing here?"

"Wanted to say thanks for all your help. Tried to call and couldn't reach you . . . so I took a chance you'd be here, it being Saturday and all."

"I need an Advil. I'll be right back."

"How about I get us both a glass of water? You should rehydrate."

Eden's familiarity felt a little weird, but at the same time it felt kind of right. "Yeah, whatever."

Quinn decided to wash her face and brush her teeth at the same time. She emerged from the bathroom a couple minutes later, necessaries taken care of, hair piled on top of her head in a riotous red mass, and feeling a whole lot less gross.

As she headed back to the living room, she passed under the attic hatch and as she glanced up, her dad's voice popped into her head. *"I'm missing something, Quinnie. It's right here, I know it."*

Quinn blinked, gave her head a shake. Hadn't she learned anything from the past week? The Hudson case was poison. If she didn't leave it alone, she'd end up like her dad—with an empty bottle at her side and her brains splattered across a wall.

"You okay?"

Eden stood in the opening between the living room and hallway, a glass of water in each hand.

"I am. In fact," she forced a small smile, "I feel one hundred percent better."

She joined Eden, who handed her the water. "I set us up in the kitchen. Is that cool?"

"If the food and coffee are there, it is very cool."

The moment she sat down, Quinn went for the take-out bag. It rustled as she peeked inside. Breakfast sandwiches. "This smells amazing. I didn't eat much last night."

"Too busy drinking? No judgement. Been there, made the same mistakes."

"Appreciate that." Quinn took a bite; it was so delicious she immediately took another. "This is really good."

Eden smiled, looking pleased. "It's from Mojo, the place right across the street."

"Convenient. For both of us, apparently."

Eden sipped her coffee, then asked, "You want to talk about it?"

"About what?"

"The day that drove you to drink yourself into oblivion?"

"Nope. We're not that good of friends."

"You've seen me at my worst, and I'm thinking I've seen you at yours, but okay."

She had a point. Eden showing up with coffee and food was the adult equivalent of a girlfriend holding your hair while you puked up a night's worth of sloe gin fizzes.

"I got chewed out by my captain, my partner's not speaking to me, and my ex-boyfriend made it clear we're staying exes."

"In other words, you were feeling sorry for yourself."

"Ouch. But yeah, something like that." She paused. "I questioned Charles and Bill Hudson. It didn't sit well."

"You spoke with them about what happened to me?"

"I did."

"It got you in trouble, I'm so sorry."

"I got myself in trouble. It'll blow over."

Eden shifted in her seat, looking suddenly anxious. "What did the Hudsons say?"

"That they had nothing to do with it, of course. Then they sent their Goons-R-Us attorney to talk to my boss."

When Eden opened her mouth, Quinn held up a hand to stop her. "Don't say you're sorry again."

"But I am." Eden clasped her hands in front of her and leaned forward. "What do you think I should do next?"

"I don't know. Maybe don't get on anyone's bad side?"

"Sounds like you might have that market cornered."

Quinn grimaced. "Seems like it. At least I carry a gun."

Eden's smile faded. "I know there's something, some connection, between my mom, her murder, and the Hudsons. Where should I look? I don't know."

"I'm missing something, Quinnie. It's right here. I know it."

Quinn pushed the memory away. "I tried. I'm sorry we came up empty."

She let out a disappointed breath. "It's okay. I'll figure something out."

They finished the sandwiches, and Quinn walked her to the door. "Thanks for breakfast."

"Anytime. If something comes up, you know, about the case, can I call you?"

She thought of Dobby, and the threat to their partnership; her captain and his promise of a suspension, and she pictured her father, slumped in his chair, bloodied and quite dead.

"I can't help you, Eden. Literally, my hands are tied. Your best route to success is Lieutenant Tillerson, he'll hook you up with one of the cold case detectives who work under him."

Eden looked crushed. "Sure, I get it." She let out a disappointed sounding breath. "I guess I'll see you around."

Quinn watched her go, resisting the urge to call her back. As much as she'd idolized her father, she acknowledged his faults. One of them, maybe the biggest, had been giving into the urges that had ruined him. She was not going to make the same mistake.

FORTY-TWO

12:40 *P.M.*

Quinn stood in the doorway to what had been her father's office, the smallest bedroom of the three-bedroom home. After inheriting the house from him, she'd painted these walls, replaced the carpet, bought new furniture, and added fresh window treatments. She rarely stepped foot inside it.

Too many memories, including the last: of finding him slumped over the desk, his lifeblood sprayed across its cluttered top.

No wonder she steered clear of the room.

"I'm missing something, Quinnie. It's right here. I know it."

It was the third time today that snippet of conversation had popped into her head. Now, standing here, the rest of the memory took shape.

She'd found him here in his office, standing in front of a wall which overnight had gone from blank to a maze of notations, photos, and lines that connected them.

"We're out of cereal, Dad." She held up the box. *"What should I have for breakfast?"*

He didn't look at her. "Make some toast, baby."

"We're out of bread, too."

"Ask Gran, she'll know what to do."

"You're hopeless, Dad, you know that?" She said it with equal parts exasperation and affection.

"Sure, baby, whatever you want."

She rolled her eyes. "I'm ten, you've got to stop calling me 'baby'. It's not cool."

He glanced over her shoulder at her, brow furrowed. "You're ten?"

"Yes, Dad." Her voice rose slightly. "And you better know that!"

A slow smile spread across his face. "Of course I do." His smile widened and he waved her to his side. "Come take a look at this."

She crossed to stand beside him and stared at the maze of photos and notes and lines. "What is it?"

"The Hudson case, all in one place. Basically, a diagram of it."

"Okay . . ." She drew the word out in a question.

"Detectives use them as a way to study a crime, all the pieces right out where you can see them."

"Like a puzzle," she said.

"Right. Because all—"

"—crimes are a kind of puzzle," she finished for him, repeating what he'd drummed into her head for years. "Some, with only a few pieces, are easy to solve, and some have lots of pieces and are super-difficult to solve. Like this one."

"Smarty pants." He smiled down at her. "And sometimes all it takes is a fresh pair of eyes to find the piece you're looking for."

The tips of her fingers tingled. "Am I the fresh pair of eyes?"

"If you're up to the challenge?"

"You're being dumb, Dad." She squared her shoulders. "I'm a Conners, so of course I'm up to it."

Quinn smiled at the memory and crossed the room, stopping in front of the wall he'd used, now blank, its expanse not even broken by a framed print or plaque. After she had taken everything down, it'd been a mess, she remembered. Riddled with thumbtack holes and tape tears.

"I'm missing something, Quinnie, a piece, a connection point, something—

The realization hit her like a thunderbolt. Right here. His scene board had been the window into his thought process. Every piece of evidence he'd accumulated, his questions about every aspect of the case, his suspicions. His theories. He'd worked on it until his very last day alive.

The night he died, she hadn't wanted any of his colleagues to see it, a visual of the dark depths to which he had sunk— as if his bloody, shattered skull and lifeless body hadn't been enough of a visual. She'd taken it down, saved every thread, every post-it and notecard.

She drew her eyebrows together. None of it had been in the bins with his other materials. *Think, Quinn, what did you do with them?*

She pictured that night, the scene. A used mailer, there on his desk. Pre-printed. Fed-Ex or USPS.

She'd grabbed it because it was handy, tucked all the items inside. She'd been in a hurry.

Her heart thundered, same as it had that night. She'd called 911 and she already heard the sirens in the distance. The coat closet, she remembered, the top shelf.

She shook her head. She'd emptied the house, had it cleaned and painted before she moved in. Every square inch but the . . . attic. Yes. The bins had ended up in the attic, so it made sense that the mailer had also.

Only one way to find out.

A couple minutes later, she stood in the attic. Unlike her dad, she wasn't known for her organizational skills. She did a slow circle. Stacked boxes. A sad-looking wreath laid on top of one. Christmas garlands in a heap. Sports equipment. A couple old suitcases parked near the top of the stairs.

She began opening the unsealed boxes, peeking inside. Books, some of her childhood mementoes. Still, no mailer.

Hands on hips, she made a last, visual sweep of the room, stopping on the two suitcases. The corner of something white peeked out from between them, as if it had slipped between.

She picked her way around to it, bent and eased the suitcases apart—and there it was. In her mad dash to get the house ready for the painters, she'd come across the Tyvek mailer in the coat closet and sort of propped it against the suitcases with plans to add it to the bins later.

Quinn acknowledged excitement and worked to manage it. Did she really believe she'd find the proverbial smoking gun in it?

Maybe not that kind of slam dunk, but something. The thing that he had missed? Or the one he told her about the night he died?

"I found it . . . This time it's for real, baby. I promise you."

Five minutes later, back in the office, she began removing the items from the envelope. The sheer number of them brought to bear the magnitude of the job she'd set out to accomplish.

Quinn narrowed her eyes, her lips curving up at the challenge. She was a Conners, of course she was up to the challenge.

After collecting the items she'd need—push pins, tape, scissors, and a water-based ink marker—she set to work. It was like being with her dad, working together on a challenging puzzle without benefit of a photo reference.

Quinn began sifting through the items, creating clusters, starting with the pebble in the still pond: the murder of Cynthia Hudson and kidnapping of her infant daughter, Grace Hudson.

Next came the subjects closest to Cynthia and Grace: the Hudson family, the staff at the mansion, Daniel and Logan Shaw.

Quinn stopped on the photo of eight-year-old Logan, recalling more of that morning she was ten and standing before her first crime scene board.

"That's my girl," her dad said. *"I'll be reading the paper, call me if you need me."*

"Fat chance of that," she muttered and turned back to the wall, her *thoughts racing. Her dad had discussed aspects of the Hudson case*

with her, but here it was, every detail. And he was asking for her help. She couldn't let him down.

She breathed deeply, in her nose and out her mouth, willing herself to be calm and focus. To begin at the beginning, the scene of the crime. Cynthia Hudson on the bathroom floor, her head bashed in. Baby Grace's empty crib.

She progressed from there, skipping from one notation, one image, to another. Absorbing. Analyzing.

About halfway through the material, she heard her father come back into the room, sensed him watching her, but she didn't pause or hurry because, as he always said, a good detective didn't rush. Rushing cheated the victim of the attention they deserved.

Finally, she stopped, looked over her shoulder at him. "This is everything?"

"Everything so far." He joined her. "Any ideas?"

She pointed to a picture of the boy, Logan Shaw. "Him. Did you question him?"

"Of course. He had very little to share and nothing consequential to offer."

"Maybe you should try again?"

"Why do you think that? He was a child, Quinn. He wasn't home when the crime occurred."

"Kids see and hear things, lots more things than adults think they do."

He'd pursed his lips, tipped his head in thought. "I'd agree if he'd been on the property at the time, but he wasn't."

He was probably right, but she wasn't ready to give up. "I still think it's worth a try. For one thing, crimes like this are hardly ever committed by complete strangers. You've said so about a billion times."

His eyebrows shot up. "You really listen to me, don't you?"

She sent him her cockiest look. "Damn straight. You gonna do it?"

He'd said he would, but from what she could tell by the items spread out before her, he hadn't. Nor had she read an account of a second interview with Logan in his notebooks.

She tapped her index finger on the photo of eight-year-old Logan Shaw. Maybe she should do it now? Her ten-year-old, fresh and untainted view of the case had zeroed in on Logan Shaw for a reason, maybe she had been onto something.

He'd given her his business card, told her to call if she needed anything. She'd tucked it in her blazer pocket; the navy one, she remembered.

Quinn stood and headed for her closet and the row of blazers in varying shades of navy; she flipped through them, found the one she'd been wearing that day, and collected the card. She turned it over in her hand. She wouldn't necessarily be crossing the captain's— or Dobby's—red line. Sure, her thinking might be a little convenient, but she figured she could defend it.

She pulled out her phone and punched in his number. He answered almost immediately.

"This is Shaw."

"Mr. Shaw, this is Quinn Conners."

"Detective Conners, this is a surprise."

"You said I could call if I needed anything. I hope I haven't chosen an inconvenient time?"

"Not at all. What can I do for you?"

"I was hoping we could get together for a chat? You call the place and time."

"How about now? I'm at The Hudson. Why don't you meet me here?"

"The hotel on St. Charles Avenue?"

"Yes. Ask for me at the front desk, they'll direct you."

FORTY-THREE

5:45 P.M.

Quinn didn't know a lot about The Hudson Hotel other than it was on the National Register of Historic Places, catered to folks with a lot more money than she had and was, oddly, home to one of the city's most sought after clubs, the rooftop H-Factor. Tonight, would be the first time she'd set foot in the place, and she had to admit she was curious.

She pulled up in front of the iconic St. Charles Avenue building, with its ornate brick facade, ruby red awnings and matching porte cochere, *The Hudson* emblazoned on it in startling white letters. The facade was flanked by two magnificent live oaks, their twisted limbs creating a dramatic contrast to the building's linear brickwork.

A valet hurried to meet her and opened her door. As she stepped out, a streetcar rumbled past.

"Detective Conners?"

"Yes?"

"Welcome to the Hudson." He smiled. "Mr. Shaw asked me to watch for you."

She wasn't sure how she felt about that and handed him her keys. "Could you keep it close? I won't be long."

"Of course, Detective. Whatever you need."

As she approached the double glass doors, both etched with an ornate 'H,' the doorman swung one open with a flourish. "Welcome to the Hudson. Check in is straight ahead."

Returning his smile, she made her way inside. The lobby ceiling was barreled, the decoration on it looked to be gold leaf. The floors were marble, inlaid with a large medallion. A huge spray of exotic flowers adorned an entryway table; the chandeliers sparkled like diamonds.

The woman manning the front desk sparkled too, in a magazine layout kind of way. Perfect makeup, perfect hair, perfect smile. Quinn wanted to ask where she'd learned to apply eyeshadow that way because . . . *damn.*

"Good evening, Detective Conners." She handed her a key card. "Mr. Shaw is expecting you. Take the main elevator to the thirteenth floor, then transfer to the Penthouse elevator."

The penthouse elevator? "What is this for?" she asked, indicating the key card.

"To operate the elevator. Mr. Shaw will be waiting for you there."

Logan Shaw was, indeed, waiting for her when she alighted the penthouse elevator. Unlike their meeting at the Hudson corporate headquarters, tonight he was dressed casually in khakis and a Polo shirt.

"Hello, Detective," he said with a smile.

"You live here? At the hotel?"

"I do."

"You didn't think to mention that?"

"I didn't think it mattered." Again, he shot her his movie star smile. "You wanted to talk, let's talk. Come in."

She stepped inside. Modern furnishings. Clean lines, muted tones. The star of the show, she saw, was the amazing view of the city.

She looked at him and realized he was watching her. "It's one of the perks of my position."

"Your position in the company? Or the family?"

"Both." He motioned toward the bar. "Can I get you a cocktail? A glass of wine? I have something open."

"I'm sure you do, Mr. Shaw. It's not that kind of visit."

"That's right, you're working."

She should let him know she wasn't on the clock or here on official business, but she liked having the power of her shield between them.

"You don't mind if I have one?" he asked.

"It's your home, your time."

"Take a look around. I suggest checking out the patio. From up here, the view of the city is quite something."

Quinn took his suggestion. She stood at the rail, admiring the New Orleans skyline, a wonderland of lights.

Shaw joined her. He'd made a highball. Whiskey. The smell was familiar, like a favorite old sweater.

She stiffened herself against its pull. "The city looks so different from up here."

"Like a jewel box," he said, the ice clicking against the glass as he brought it to his lips.

"Interesting," she said softly. "I was thinking it more like a midway at night. Chaotic and dirty, but exciting and addictive as well."

He leaned against the rail and studied her. "During the day, what's the city then?"

"Dangerous," she said simply. "That's the world I live in."

"That's why you carry the gun everywhere?"

"Yes."

"Like now?"

"A cop doesn't stop being a cop, even when they're off duty."

"In other words, you're never off duty?"

She smiled slightly. "Everybody has to sleep."

"A redhead with a gun. I'm not sure if I should be concerned or intrigued."

She flicked her gaze over him. "I'd suggest concerned."

His lips curved in appreciation. "That's your schtick, isn't it?"

"I don't know what you mean."

"The total bad-ass, tough chick thing."

"I don't know about a 'schtick,' but it keeps me alive."

He laughed low. "Never out of character. I'm impressed."

"How about you? Are you ever off duty? Ever done being a cheer-leader for the Hudsons?"

"If that day ever comes, I won't be standing here."

"They've given you a lot, haven't they?"

"Given? No. I'm not family, I'm *like* family. There's a difference and there always will be." He sipped the whiskey, never taking his gaze from hers. "Why are you here, Detective?"

"Because I'm curious about you."

"Me?" His eyebrows shot up. "Why's that?"

"You were eight at the time of the murder and kidnapping. Too young to truly be a part of the unfolding events, but old enough to be profoundly affected by them."

"Your point, Detective Conners?"

"When my father interviewed you, you told him you loved Grace and you pleaded for him to bring her back. Do you remember that?"

"I've forgotten nothing about that day." The faceted glass of his tumbler caught the light as he lowered it. "I did beg him to bring her back to me. Do you know how he replied? He promised he would. *Promised.*" Logan paused, as if to let the words sink in. "For a long time, I believed him."

Quinn didn't respond. Her dad, a seasoned detective, wouldn't have made a promise like that, not when he didn't know he could keep it. Nothing she could say would change Logan's mind, so she kept her thoughts to herself.

"Tell me about that day," she said instead. "Your perspective."

"Why?"

"Because I'm interested. Your perspective would be very different from anyone else's that day. Kids are often the most ignored piece of the crime puzzle."

He seemed to like her answer because the corners of his mouth tipped slightly up. "I was in school when it happened. Just after lunch, I was called to the principal's office. He said my dad needed me home and was sending a car for me."

"I imagine that was frightening."

"Actually, I thought it must have something to do with my mother."

"Why your mother?"

"She wasn't well." He brought the drink to his lips. "It was Charles' driver who picked me up. Nice guy, usually cracked jokes with me. He didn't say much that day."

Tony Mariano, Quinn knew. He still worked for the Hudsons.

"It wasn't unusual for me to go to the mansion after school. Dad was always working and since he had custody, he'd have to park me somewhere. More times than not, it was the Hudson mansion. There was an army of adults to help keep an eye on me, and enough space so I wouldn't be bothering any of them."

He turned his gaze to the skyline, his tone taking on a faraway quality. "When I arrived, Dad was waiting for me. He ushered me into Charles office and told me what had happened."

"He straight out told you?"

"He did. Sat me down, looked me in the eyes and said Cynthia had been murdered and Grace kidnapped. I remember how flat his voice sounded. It was so . . . odd."

"That seems a rather merciless way to tell a young boy something so horrifying."

"He had no idea how much I loved her."

"Grace? Or Cynthia?"

He rocked the glass gently back and forth. Quinn found herself mesmerized by the swoosh of the amber liquid. "Cynthia was very kind to me, but yes, Grace."

Quinn absorbed that. "It must have been a terrible shock."

He looked at her then. "Have you met my father?"

"I have."

"Then you know, he's not a warm and fuzzy guy. Don't get me wrong, he's a good dad, he taught me a lot. He wasn't—and isn't—one given to coddling or shows of emotion."

She smiled slightly. "We have something in common then. My dad was all business too. Just a very different kind of business."

His gaze seemed to warm. "Tell me about your mother?"

"She died when I was two."

"That's tough."

She lifted a shoulder. "I hardly remember her."

He leaned closer. "Can I tell you a secret?"

Something about his gaze was magnetic; she couldn't look away. "Sure."

"For a long time, I imagined Grace hidden away in the house. In a secret room or something, and I'd hunt for her. My little, lost girl."

Quinn pictured him as a young boy, searching for his missing girl. She shuddered slightly at the macabre image. "The house was searched at the time, top to bottom."

He laughed softly. "You're such a cop."

She ignored the comment. "Interesting, how you used the possessive when you referred to her."

"You mean weird, don't you?" He gave his head a small shake. "I can see how it might seem that way to you, but she was the closest to a sister I ever had. Ms. Praxton let me help care for her. Feed her and dress her, keep her occupied while she did other things."

Quinn jumped on that. "What other things?"

"I don't know, actually." He thought for a moment. "Sometimes I would hear her talking on the phone. A boyfriend mostly, I think. One time I could tell she'd been crying. Another time she was arguing with him."

The breeze shifted slightly; the smell of the whiskey stirred her senses. "What about?"

"No recollection."

She dropped her gaze to his glass, caught herself and jerked it back to his face. "During those times, she would leave you alone with Grace?"

He inclined his head. "In retrospect her behavior was quite unprofessional. Charles would have had her fired if he'd known."

"Charles? Not Bill or Cynthia?"

He held her gaze. "Charles ruled all their lives with an iron fist. He still does."

"Not yours?"

"No, not mine."

"What of your father's?"

His mouth tightened. "My father is his own man. He made his choices and he has to live with that."

"What kind of choices?"

The breeze ruffled her hair, sending curls across her face. He reached out and gently pushed them back.

She jerked her head away. "Don't do that."

"Sorry, it's a habit."

"I'll bet it is."

"Do you know the Hudson family history? Beyond Cynthia and Grace?"

"No," she said, "but I'd love to."

"Charles had two brothers. One died in Vietnam; the other was on the Pan Am flight that went down in Kenner back in 1982. His pregnant wife was with him.

"Charles' wife had no less than five miscarriages. Bill was their miracle baby, their hope for the future."

The way he said the other man's name left no doubt he had little respect for the Hudson heir.

"Tragedy befell the generation before, as well. His father had four siblings. Three of them died before their prime."

"And the fourth?"

"They had a falling out and stopped speaking. They're a cursed family, Detective."

Hypnotic, she thought. His voice. The provocative way he looked at her. She didn't doubt many a woman had fallen for his brand of magic.

Too bad for him she wouldn't be one of them.

"That would be a sad story," she said. "Except for the money and power and the ruthless way they wield it."

He leaned closer, expression amused. "Money is power, that's a fact of life no matter what your address is."

"But it doesn't buy happiness, is that what you're saying? That perhaps I should pity them?"

"I thought you should know. I thought it might help you understand why they want nothing to do with Eden Riley or the book she's writing. Or with any book about the tragedy."

She met his gaze evenly. "What's your theory? As part of the inner circle, who do you think killed Cynthia and kidnapped Grace?"

"I have no idea."

"No theory? It's human nature to want answers and closure."

"Then what does it say about me that I don't?"

"You must wonder."

"Of course, I do, but wondering is not a theory."

He reached out again, this time wrapping one of her red coils around his finger. "Do you have the temper to go with this hair, Detective?"

If he thought he might seduce her, he would be disappointed. She caught his hand. "I asked you not to do that."

He let go, took a step back. "My apologies. I'm drawn to beautiful things and have a difficult time resisting them."

"Maybe you should try harder." She took a step back from the rail. "Our chat's over, Mr. Shaw. Thank you for your time and the family history lesson. I can let myself out."

He stopped her. "Do you think she's alive?"

Quinn looked back at him. "Why do you ask?"

"Your father did. Isn't that right?"

She answered with a question of her own. "What do you think, Mr. Shaw? Is she alive?"

"I like to image her that way, grown and lovely. Happy."

"You think she's dead?"

"It's more likely." He looked away, then back at her, expression hard. "I want whoever took her to suffer, Detective. I want them to know the pain of loss, of real heartbreak. The way I know it."

He meant every word; she couldn't blame him. Too bad life didn't always work that way.

As she walked away, she noticed a puddle of blue and white silk beside the chaise lounge, most probably left behind by a pretty friend. She didn't doubt Mr. Logan Shaw had plenty of those and was thankful she was unaffected by his skilled magnetism.

FORTY-FOUR

8:20 A.M. *Monday,*

Quinn slipped behind her desk, set down her travel mug and flipped on her computer. "Morning," she said to Dobby, who was already at his desk, staring intently at his monitor.

He glanced her way. "Hey. You have a good weekend?"

She thought of her conversation with Logan Shaw. "Interesting."

He reached for his coffee. "Maybe you want to share some details?"

Her cell phone went off and she held up a finger, then answered. "This is Conners."

"Detective Quinn Conners?"

A male voice. Hushed. "That's right," she said. "How can I help you?"

"I saw you on TV. You're the one who's investigating Karlee Painter's death, right?"

"I am." Excited, Quinn motioned toward Dobby. He joined her, bent his head close to her phone. "Who is this?"

"A friend of Karlee's."

"You have a name?"

"This was a mistake." His voice shook. "I shouldn't have—"

"Wait! If you want to stay anonymous, that's cool. Just don't hang up. You called me for a reason, right?" She took his silence as agreement. "You have information about her murder, that's why, isn't it?"

"Yes."

His reply came out as a husky whisper. Dobby gave her a thumbs-up.

"Calling me was the right thing to do. I can help, I promise."

She heard him breathing on the other end, and tried another approach. "It's wrong that she's dead. She didn't deserve to die."

"No, she didn't."

He started to cry, and she realized what she'd only suspected—she was talking to Karlee's lover. "You cared about her."

"Yes," he whispered.

"I want the person who killed her to pay for his crime," Quinn said. "I want that more than anything." She paused so her words could sink in. "That's what you want, too, isn't it?"

"Yes."

"Do you know who killed her?"

"Ray did it. She told him she was breaking it off and he killed her. I know it."

WITH A BIT of coaxing and a lot of assurances, Karlee's lover turned out to be a wealth of information, the most consequential piece, the fact that he and Karlee communicated via burner phones and that she hid hers in her gym bag.

In a matter of hours, the judge granted a search warrant. They'd served it, collected Karlee's gym bag, and struck evidentiary gold: the burner phone, tucked into her right running shoe.

Not yet sundown, Quinn sat across the interview table from Ray Russell and his attorney. She folded her hands on the brown paper mailer on the table in front of her and smiled serenely. "Hello, Mr. Russell, thank you for joining us this afternoon."

Attorney Dicks spoke up. "This is harassment, plain and simple."

Quinn ignored him. "Mr. Russell, have you ever heard the term burner phone?"

"Sure. Who hasn't?"

"You must know then, the advantage of having a burner over say, a regular plan through a carrier like Verizon or AT&T?"

He looked annoyed. "It's pre-paid with no contracts. Big deal."

"They're often used by criminals, correct?"

"Again, everybody knows that."

"And why do criminals use them?"

He looked at his lawyer. The man shrugged and indicated he should go ahead and answer. "To hide what they're doing, so they're not tracked."

"Or spied on," she said.

Russell frowned. "What are you getting at?"

"What kind of cell phone did Karlee have?"

"An iPhone."

"Did you routinely scroll through it to check up on her?"

Dicks stepped in. "Detective, where is this line of questioning going?"

She ignored him. "Did you, Mr. Russell?"

"Of course not." He folded his arms across his chest. "I trusted her."

"Detective, I have to insist you—"

"Karlee had two cell phones, Mr. Russell. Her iPhone and a burner phone." She opened the mailer, retrieved a clear evidence bag and laid it on the table between them. "This Cricket Phone."

"That's a lie."

"She used it to hide what she was doing from you. She knew you were suspicious and checking up on her." She tapped the bag. "How do I know this? Because it's recorded here in both texts and voice messages between her and her lover."

He launched to his feet, face crimson, hands curled into fists. "This is bullshit!"

Hand going automatically to her weapon, Quinn stood. "Sit back down, Mr. Russell!"

Dicks looked alarmed. "Ray! Calm down. Let me handle this."

Russell hesitated a moment, then conceded. He sat stiffly, as tense as a rattler, ready to strike.

"Detective, my client vehemently denies that Ms. Painter was having an affair. If that phone is incontrovertible proof she was, we will accept it, but, obviously, my client was in the dark about her infidelity."

Quinn looked at Russell, going for a sympathetic demeanor. "You really knew nothing about it?"

"Nothing."

He blinked either against tears or in the attempt to manufacture them. No surprise, she was going with the latter.

"She didn't confess to you the day of the crawfish boil?"

"No, of course not."

"You didn't become enraged when she told you she was leaving you?"

"She never told me that. It would have destroyed me. I loved her."

"The day of the party, she didn't try to give you back your ring?"

Something flickered behind his eyes. "No."

"You didn't threaten her?"

A muscle jumped in his jaw. "Of course not! If I had done that, why would she have gone with me to the party?"

"I don't know. Maybe she was scared not to?"

The lawyer made a sound of disapproval. "You're fishing, Detective. I think we're done here." He touched Russell's arm. "Let's go, Ray—"

"Not so fast, Mr. Dicks. We still have things to discuss." She slid a print-out from the brown mailer. "This is a print-out of Karlee's texts to her lover. I'll read you a sample. "I know he suspects. I caught him snooping in my iPhone. I pretended I didn't see him."

She let the words sink in, then read another. "He accused me of cheating today. I wanted to tell him the truth, but I was so scared. He threatened to kill me if he found out it was true. I think he would."

Russell's face pinched with fury. "I can't help what she was thinking. Maybe she was crazy. Playing on that guy's sympathies to make herself look like less of a slut."

"A slut, Mr. Russell? Is that how you refer to the woman you loved?"

"She was fucking another guy. What would you call her?"

Russell stared hard at her. Hatred burned from his eyes. It wasn't the first time some guilty-as-hell perp looked at her that way, it wouldn't be the last. Far from intimidating, it fueled her to push harder.

"This one's interesting," she said. "He found the test stick. He knows I'm pregnant."

"You're enjoying this, you sick bitch."

"Not at all, Mr. Russell. I'm just doing my job." She leaned toward him. "You lied about owning a gun. Then you lied about why you got rid of the gun. You lied about knowing about the pregnancy and now, you've lied about knowledge of Karlee's affair. What else have you lied about, Mr. Russell?"

He didn't respond and she proceeded. "The morning of the crawfish boil, Karlee tried to break it off with you. She called her lover. She was hysterical. He'll testify that you threatened to kill her if she tried to leave you. Terrified, she begged you to forgive her and went to the party, pretending nothing had happened."

"This is bullshit."

"Maybe she had a plan you didn't know about?"

She had his attention then. "Mr. Russell, Karlee's lover was waiting for her outside the party. She was leaving you right then, that was their plan. She was going to tell you everything, right there at the party and walk out. She figured with all those witnesses, she'd be safe."

Quinn tapped the evidence bag. "It's all here, Mr. Russell. What could you do to stop her, right there in front of everybody? Nothing. She was going to walk away."

Her words were having an effect. The muscle in his jaw twitched; sweat glistened on his upper lip.

She continued. "She didn't anticipate gunfire breaking out. How could she have? What perfect timing, you didn't even have to look her in the eyes. You shot her in the back. Twice."

He wiped away the sweat. His eyes darted from her to the evidence bag, then back.

"Detective, I need a word with my client."

No way was she about to give Russell a breather, not now. She was too close to breaking him. "What pushed you over the edge, Ray? Was it when she told you the baby wasn't yours? That's on the phone, too. At the party, she was going to tell you it wasn't yours. She knew the last thing you'd want was somebody else's kid."

He'd started to shake. "You don't know that. It could have been mine."

"I do know it. Her lover told me. That week you went fishing, they fucked liked bunnies. While she was ovulating, without protection. Whose baby do you think it was?"

His control was disintegrating right before her eyes. Quinn went in for the kill. "I actually understand. If it had been me, I'd have been consumed with anger and resentment. How could she betray you that way? You gave her everything she wanted, and she repaid you this way?

"Shots broke out and in that moment, you saw your chance. Amid the screams and chaos, you shot her. Two times. Didn't you? In that moment, you hated her, and you wanted her dead. You pulled the trigger once, then again, didn't you, Ray? Didn't you?"

"Yes!" He jumped to his feet, shaking with the force of his fury. "Yes, I wanted her dead! She was fucking someone else! It was his baby in her belly, not mine! I pulled out my gun and I shot her!"

FORTY-FIVE

2:40 *P.M.*

Quinn emerged from the interview room, adrenaline coursing through her veins. They'd done it. Gotten a signed statement from Russell, a full confession to Karlee Painter and her unborn child's murder. The attorney had been quick to point out that his client's action had been unplanned, a crime of passion. Quinn could live with that. Despite Russell thinking her a merciless bitch, she got it. The human animal was both predictable and highly volatile.

Her head filled with the interrogation. Her questions and Russell's confession, the powerful mix of emotions that had propelled him to his feet, the truth spewing from his lips.

Then, as if realizing what he'd done, his face had gone slack and he'd sunk back to his chair and sobbed. In that moment, she'd pitied him.

"Detective Conners?"

She looked up and smiled at Captain Franks's secretary. "What's up, Sharon?"

"Captain Franks would like to see you."

"He would want every detail of Russell's confession; and she would be happy to share them. "Of course. As soon as Detective Dobson finishes up with the suspect—"

"He only wants to see you, Detective."

"Only see . . ." Her words trailed off. She noticed how Sharon didn't meet her eyes, and het stomach sank.

Her visit with Logan Shaw. It must be.

"I'll let my partner know—"

"I'll do that. Captain Franks said now."

Not good, Quinn acknowledged, heading for Franks's office, dread replacing the exhilaration of moments before. She would take a drubbing, but she could explain. She could convince him she hadn't crossed his red line.

She tapped on his partially open door.

He looked up, waved her in. "Close the door behind you."

She did, stopping three feet from his desk. He didn't ask her to sit. "We got a full confession from Russell," she said.

"I heard. Congratulations." He folded his hands on the desk in front of him. "That's not why I wanted to see you."

"No?" She put on her best I-can't-imagine-why face.

Clearly not buying the bullshit she was selling, he got right to it. "Did you or did you not, go to The Hudson Hotel last night to question Logan Shaw?"

"Yes sir."

"Did you or did you not indicate you were there under the auspices of this department?"

"No sir, I did not."

"You're saying it was a personal visit?"

That wasn't exactly right, but it was personal to her. "Yes."

"Am I to understand that you and Logan Shaw are friends?"

"No, but I did not claim to be under your direction, the direction of the NOPD, or that I was there in a professional capacity."

"When you arrived at the hotel, did you or did you not introduce yourself as a NOPD detective?"

She started to say no and realized she'd never introduced herself at all. Each member of the staff she encountered had referred to her as such. "I did not. Mr. Shaw had told his staff to expect Detective Conners; they referred to me as such. I didn't think I needed to correct them."

"Were you wearing your sidearm?"

"I was."

"What of your shield?"

"On my person. I never offered it."

"Why were you there, Detective?"

"I simply wanted to talk to Mr. Shaw."

"About the Hudson case?"

She tried not to squirm under his glare. "Yes."

"You know me well, do you not, Detective Conners?"

"Yes, Captain, I do."

"You know, above all, I'm a man of my word?"

Here it comes. She could all but hear the bullets loading into the chambers.

She nodded; he continued. "Do you remember I promised that if you bothered the Hudson family, if you came anywhere near them, I would suspend you?"

She felt sick. "Yes, sir. But—"

He didn't give her a chance to utter her next lame excuse. "You're hereby suspended, Detective Conners. One week without pay and clearance from the department shrink before you return." He pushed away from the desk and stood. "I take no pleasure in doing this, Detective."

Quinn tipped up her chin. "Then don't."

"You left me no choice. Your gun and badge."

She removed her shield, handed it to him. The gun came next; she laid it on his desk.

"One week without pay and reinstatement only after a visit with the shrink." She turned to go; he stopped her. "I understand you're in possession of materials from the Hudson case file."

"Copies. They were my father's."

"No, Detective, they were always ours. I want them all, understood?"

"Yes, Captain."

"I'll send Humphries and Nolan to collect them this afternoon."

Dobby was the only one who'd known about those files. He wouldn't betray her that way.

Or would he?

She caught her breath, feeling as if she'd been cut off at the knees.

Dobby was waiting for her at her desk. "Sharon told me what was going down. You promised you wouldn't cross that line."

His accusatory tone made her cringe. "What about you?"

"Me?"

"Did you tell Captain Franks about my Dad's files on the Hudson case?"

He looked as if she'd struck him. "You're asking me that? Like I'm the bad guy? You made me a promise, and you broke it."

"Those files were my dad's. You had no right."

"Screw you, Quinn. I'm not going to play along with this . . . fixation of yours. Or whatever it is. Get your head straight, or I'm asking for a new partner."

FORTY-SIX

Quinn paced from one side of her house to the other. She raged. At Dobby's betrayal and Captain Franks's unwillingness to bend. At Eden Riley for dragging her into this mess, and at herself for allowing it to happen.

Was this how her father had felt? Angry? At himself and everyone else? Abandoned and betrayed? Completely alone?

She decided to take a run, pound out the energy roiling inside her. She changed into her running gear and hit the street, pushing herself, the action as much a physical punishment as an emotional release. One foot in front of the other, breath in, breath out.

She would get through this, she reasoned. The week would pass, and she'd be back on the job. She would patch things up with Dobby, re-earn Captain Franks trust and before she knew it, this whole thing would be nothing more than a bad memory.

She slowed, a semblance of calm coming over her. The first order of business was getting the bins ready for Humphries and Nolan to pick up. Good riddance to them. They were poison. That case was poison. It had infected her father and had started to infect her.

Her house came into view and her steps faltered. While she was gone, someone had deposited a large floral arrangement at her door. Certain it was a mistake, she crossed to it.

Funeral flowers, she realized. White lilies, white roses and mums. She remembered the combination--and the cloying smell of the lilies —from both her grandparents' and father's funerals.

She plucked out the card.

> *You gave me the ammunition; I had to take the shot.*
> *Enjoy your week off.*

Logan Shaw. The blood rushed to her head and all that hard-earned calm evaporated. That son-of-a-bitch. She dug her phone from pocket, found his number and punched it in.

"Detective," he answered, "you got the flowers. I hope you like them?"

"You prick. You set me up."

"Hardly." He sounded amused. "You called me, remember?"

She did, which pissed her off even more. "Screw you."

"Don't be ugly about it. I was upfront about where my allegiance lies, wasn't I?"

He had been. One hundred percent. She'd known she was flirting with Captain Franks's red line when she called him, but she'd done it anyway. Whose fault was her suspension, really?

She'd been thinking like a victim. Mad at everyone for doing this *to* her. She was no victim. Her choice, all of it. And frankly, given a do-over, she doubted she would change a thing.

The realization was an epiphany. "You're right," she said, smiling. "I was foolish to expect a snake to be anything but a snake. You know what? You actually did me a favor. Thank you."

He laughed. "I find that hard to believe."

"Believe it anyway." She smiled, feeling almost giddy. "Have yourself a great day, Mr. Shaw."

She ended the call, scooped up the flowers and carried them

across the street to the neighbor who had been so kind when her dad passed, and making up a story about being allergic, handed them over.

From there, she headed to the living room and the plastic bins. She began putting files back inside, carefully placing them in the proper order—a waste of time and energy since the department was going to shred them—in a show of respect for her father.

She snapped the lids onto the first three bins and carried them one by one to the foyer and set them by the front door. The fourth bin —the one stacked full of her dad's crime scene notebooks—she carried to the office and tucked it into the closet there. They were his personal records. Filled with *his* thoughts, *his* observations. They belonged to her, not the department.

No sooner had she deposited them than the doorbell sounded. Humphries and Nolan, she saw, looking uncomfortable. As she opened the door, Beignet darted between them and inside, causing Humphries to nearly fall off the front step. They collected the bins and were gone.

Quinn stood at the door a moment, collecting her thoughts. She had one week to reconstruct her dad's crime scene board, study it as a seasoned detective—not a child—and see if she saw anything worth investigating.

She drew in a deep, focusing breath. She recalled the words he'd said to her the night he died, could hear his whiskey-soaked voice in her head.

"Quinnie . . . I found it . . . This time it's for real, baby. I promise you."

"Okay, Dad," she said softly, pushing away from the door. "This is your chance. Show me."

FORTY-SEVEN

8:45 P.M.

For the next several hours, her memory still fresh from having recently read the file, Quinn worked feverishly. She began with the clusters of major subjects she had created Saturday, then moved on to gathering together the events of the first twenty-four hours after the crimes had occurred, sorting, pinning items to the wall, stretching the colored string between subjects and witnesses. All the stuff she knew.

The first twenty-four hours progressed to the first week, then to the first month of the investigation. She took a different tact than her father had; her creation looked more like a bullseye or a spider's web —the crime at the center, orbiting around it: the family, their staff, then friends and associates.

She stepped away from the wall, cocking her head, she admired her progress. She'd made a dent. A big one. Her web was taking shape.

Quinn glanced at the window and the dark street beyond. As she did, her closest neighbor's porch light popped on. Her stomach rumbled and she checked her watch. She hadn't eaten anything since the half of a ham sandwich at noon. No wonder she was hungry.

She rolled her shoulders, then stretched. The bathroom. Feed Beignet. Then a protein bar and glass of water. Maybe a cup of coffee after.

She headed that direction, reaching for her phone to check for messages.

It wasn't in her pocket.

She'd left it in the kitchen, she saw moments later. On the counter beside the coffeepot. The brew was burnt; she dumped it and started another pot. While she waited, she checked her phone and saw that Mikey had called. Twice.

She dialed him back. "Uncle Mikey," she said when he answered, "it's me."

"Hey Kiddo. I was getting worried when I couldn't get you."

"Sorry. Didn't have my phone with me." She grabbed a Cliff bar from the pantry. "What's up?"

"I heard about the suspension. I'm sorry."

She'd figured he would have. "Yeah, me too."

"Do you have a plan for the next week?"

She pictured the office wall with its emerging web, and promptly told him what he wanted to hear. "Yeah, get my shit together so I can get back to work."

"That's my girl." He paused. "Heard about why you were suspended, too. I thought you were going to leave the Hudson case alone?"

"I was, but I got sucked in, probably because I have so much history with it."

"The hold it had on him was unhealthy, Quinn. Remember that."

"Why couldn't he let it go, Uncle Mikey? He even let it come between your friendship."

For a long moment, Mikey was quiet. When he finally spoke, she heard something in his tone she hadn't before. "You probably don't know this, but the Hudson murder and kidnapping . . . that case was his first back on the job after your mom's death."

Her breath caught. "I didn't know that."

"He wasn't ready, he shouldn't have been there. The crime, a young mother, cut down in her prime, an infant daughter . . . it was all too close to home."

A lump formed in her throat. Way too close. It made her hurt for him.

"I should have done something, but he insisted he was fine. That he needed to be on the job. That it was good for him to be working."

"As the weeks and months passed, I saw him unraveling." Mikey cleared his throat. "I figured I could hold him together, you know? Support him. Cover for him. It was the wrong thing to do and I . . . I regret that decision every day."

"Then you gave up on him?" She heard the condemnation in her voice and wished she didn't. "You could have stepped back in—"

"And what? By then it was too late. The case had gotten inside him." His voice thickened. "He couldn't accept its outcome and let go. Just like he couldn't accept—"

He stopped before he finished the thought, but she knew what he'd been about to say. "My mom's outcome."

"Yes," he said softly. "In the end, I had to protect myself. My job. My family. At some point you have to get off a sinking ship or you go down with it."

How could she blame him? Towards the end she had gotten off, too.

She thought of Dobby, what he'd done. She'd called it a betrayal —her dad would have to, if it'd been him and Mikey. It wasn't a betrayal, she acknowledged.

You see your partner about to drive off a cliff, you do whatever necessary to stop them.

"He used to say that the Hudsons were covering for someone or hiding something. What made him think that?"

Mikey didn't hesitate. "Because they were, just not what he thought. People like that, they don't like their lives exposed. They don't want the Lifetime Movie treatment. Once they believed Grace was gone forever, they closed ranks. They wanted it over, and they wanted their privacy back."

Which was why they were so adamant about stopping Eden from writing about the crime. Logan Shaw had said pretty much the same thing.

"I get that, Uncle Mikey, but what about justice? Didn't they want justice for their family? Wouldn't they still?"

"They wanted it, of course they did. What they didn't want was false hope or wild theories, which was what your dad kept bringing them. I tried to talk to him but everything I said fell on deaf ears."

"He accused you of selling out."

"Yeah, he did. After everything we'd been through, and everything I'd done to try to protect him, it broke my heart."

She swallowed past the lump in her throat. Her dad hadn't shielded her from his thoughts about Mikey. That he didn't trust him. That he believed him a traitor. She remembered being so sad about it. Angry and disappointed that her Uncle Mikey could do that to her dad.

"It's okay," Mikey said softly, as if reading her silence. "You were a kid."

"That doesn't excuse me from—"

"Yeah, it does. He was your everything, and I knew that."

Her father *and* mother, her mentor, her hero. Best friend. "Thanks for talking to me about this, Uncle Mikey. I'm glad you're still in my life."

"I'm glad too, kiddo. My only regret is not stepping in and trying to save him sooner. I loved him like a brother, all the way to the end."

They talked a few moments more, then hung up. Quinn pocketed the phone and returned to her dad's office.

She stood in front of the recreation, studying her progress, feeling its pull and imagining her dad, his grief a fresh, oozing wound. Her gaze settled on a photo of Cynthia Hudson.

Young and beautiful. A new mother. The way his Maggie had been. Cut down too soon.

He'd wanted justice. If not for justice, what was life worth?

It had colored the rest of his life. His choices. Their relationship.

She dragged the desk chair across the room, positioning it dead center in front of the emerging web. She peeled the wrapper from the protein bar, took a bite, thoughts on her dad.

What happened the night he died? Did he give up the search for justice? When that happened, had he decided life was no longer worth living? Did it all turn black? No justice. No hope. Not even his only child to cling to?

Her thoughts hurt so bad they took her breath away. Tears pricked her eyes. She hadn't been there for him, not at the end. Maybe ever. How could she have if she'd never completely understood the depth of his grief or the demons that drove him?

To say she understood now would be arrogant, but she did have a deeper glimpse into the psyche of the man she had worshipped.

Quinn cleared her throat of the tears strangling her and swept her watery gaze over the wall with its photos and notes and string; over the floor with the unplaced pieces of this puzzle.

She owed him this. A last hoorah. A deep dive into the case that had meant everything to the man who had meant everything to her.

FORTY-EIGHT

7:40 A.M. *Tuesday*.

Bleary-eyed, Quinn shuffled toward the office, over-sized coffee cup clutched between her hands. She'd worked into the night. The later it had become, the more confusing the bits and scraps of notations became. The three whiskeys hadn't helped and around midnight she'd fallen into bed.

Yawning, Quinn crossed to the wall and the chair in front of it. She brought the coffee to her lips, sipped, then sipped again. Instant ambition, she mused. Just the taste of it made her more alert.

She studied the pieces spread out on the floor. The beginning of the web had been easy, with many items that obviously went together and lots of movement in the investigation, all of it clear-eyed and orderly.

As time passed, that movement slowed, became scattershot, then non-existent. What was left appeared to be outliers. Or maybe the false hopes and wild theories Uncle Mikey had mentioned. Cup in one hand, she stood and crossed to a neon orange Post-it that she had stared stupidly at last night. In bold, black marker her dad had penned WILLOW STREET, followed by a series of questions marks.

"Willow Street," she murmured to herself. "Why is that ringing a . . ."

She stopped, sucked in a sharp breath.

A sound passed her lips. Of surprised disbelief. She pictured Eden's baby book, all its blanks filled with her mother's precise handwriting. One, in particular, filled her head: *Baby's First Home*.

Willow Street.

Quinn found the chair, sat back down. Her dad had done it. Found the puzzle piece everyone else had missed.

Quinn realized her hands were shaking and set her cup on the floor. She wanted to dance. To jump up and down and pump her fist. Shout it from the rooftops.

She brought a hand to her mouth, to the smile splitting her face. *Way to go, Dad. You did it!*

With a laugh, she jumped to her feet and pumped her fist. "Yes!" she shouted. "Yes, yes, yes!"

After another victory lap, she gathered herself together, slightly winded but raring to go. She crossed to the wall and thumbtacked the Post-it to the web.

Where to take this information was the question. Normally, she would call Dobby. She couldn't trust him with this, not now. She couldn't trust he wouldn't go to Captain Franks—which wouldn't bode well for her career.

She thought of Mikey, then eliminated him. Same problem, different spin. Eden was a possibility. She would be beyond excited, no doubt.

And crushed if it came to nothing.

Quinn nodded her head, coming to a decision. Until she had thoroughly investigated this lead, she would keep it to herself.

An hour later, showered and dressed respectably, Quinn stood in front of a turquoise-colored, shotgun-style cottage at the beginning of Willow Street. This was a pretty block, green and well-tended, lined with residences ranging in architectural style from double gallery classical to the shotgun and creole cottages Uptown was known for.

This house was small, maybe eighteen-hundred square feet of living space, but big on charm. It had a covered porch, wide enough and deep enough to comfortably accommodate the porch swing that hung at one end. On the Craftsman-style front door hung a brilliantly colored wreath.

The door opened and a woman stepped out, a young child clinging to her hand. The woman saw her and stopped, relaxed expression becoming wary. "May I help you?" she asked.

Quinn crossed to the front gate and smiled. "I'm doing some research on this neighborhood. Have you lived here long?"

The woman scooped the child up, obviously uncomfortable with the conversation. "We've only been here a couple of years, so I don't think I can help you."

"You still may be able to help." She smiled again. "I'm actually a detective, and I'm looking into a cold case."

The woman's eyes widened. "I know that case! You have the wrong house."

"I do?"

She shifted her daughter from her right hip to her left. "The little yellow bungalow up the block, that's where they lived. The one that's for sale."

Quinn looked the way she indicated. "Where they lived?"

"Yes. The child who was run down in the street. I hope you catch whoever did it. If that happened to my baby, I think I'd go crazy."

Quinn didn't correct her about the case. "You know of anyone here on the block who's been around a long time?"

"If you're looking for information, you want to talk to Jonah. He's lived here forever."

"Which house?"

"The blue one, it's looking a little overgrown." The child on her hip squirmed and she quieted her. "He's a sweet old guy. Lost his wife about a year ago."

Quinn thanked her and headed to the house the woman had indicated. She went through the front gate and up the walk. The front door opened before she reached it and a wizened man stepped out onto the porch, his dark skin deeply lined from age and life in the deep south.

"Afternoon, ma'am," he said. "Just so you know, I'm on a fixed income and I'm not going to buy anything."

She smiled. "I'm not selling anything, I promise. I'm researching this neighborhood and the lady down the street directed me to you. Said you know everything there is to know about it."

He smiled. "Yes, ma'am, I do." He waved her onto the porch. "It's a pretty day. How about I get us both an iced tea, and we'll have us a chat?"

"I'd like that, thank you."

A few minutes later he returned with the two glasses and handed her one, then sat.

Quinn broke the ice. "I hear you lost your wife not that long ago. I'm so sorry."

He inclined his head. "My Gertie. We were married sixty-eight years. How can I complain about that? We were so blessed. Six kids, ten grands. Besides, I know she's waiting for me up there."

He pointed a gnarled finger toward the sky. "You can't rush God's timing, and that's a fact."

"Yes sir, it is." She decided she might as well get to the point and mentally crossed her fingers. "I wanted to ask you about an old neighbor of yours. Angela Riley."

"I wondered if that might be why you were here." He sipped his tea, the ice clinked against the glass. "She was a nice lady. A nurse."

Although itching to fire questions at him, Quinn sat back, sipped her tea, giving him time. She'd learned that oftentimes the important information didn't follow a question but instead came out in between them.

"It near broke my heart. Gertie's too." He paused. "I was right here on this porch when it happened. Gertie was inside, thank

God." He squinted up at the blue sky a moment, then looked back at her. "Some folks pointed fingers at Miss Angela, but that's not the way it went down. I saw, and I set them straight every chance I got."

Quinn made a sympathetic sound, and he went on. "Little angel was with her mama; she had her hand . . . until they reached the mailbox. Miss Angela let go for a second; the little one saw a cat and toddled right into the street and—"

He stopped. Quinn saw the horror of that moment on his face, as fresh as if it had happened yesterday.

"The driver mowed her down. I can still hear her screams."

"The child's?"

"No, Miss Angela's."

The power of those simply spoken words gave her goosebumps. Quinn rubbed her arms, wanting to speak but having nothing to say.

"Sweet little thing was dead on impact, so at least she didn't suffer." He sighed, a deep sound from an old, tired man. "There are some things you can't unsee, no matter how long you live."

He lowered his gaze to his glass. Condensation dripped from it. "I ran inside, shouted for Gertie to call 911 and made her promise not to come outside until I told her she could. I didn't want her . . . it's better that only I had to live with that."

She felt his pain. She understood it. She reached across and squeezed his hand. "How old was the little girl?"

"Don't remember exactly. Not quite a year yet. She was a precocious little thing, walked real early. Always giggling."

"I can tell you're a good man, Jonah. Your Gertie was a lucky lady."

Tears glistened in his eyes. "I always thought I was the lucky one."

What did this have to do with The Hudsons? Something important. The Willow Street address being a notation on her dad's evidence board couldn't be a coincidence.

"You remind me of someone," he said. "Someone who came

'round a few years back. Young fella. He was asking questions about Miss Angela, too."

Could it have been her dad? Except for her hair and eye color, she looked so much like him, people used to comment on it all the time.

"We sat right here, where you and I are now. That day we had cookies, Gertie's butter cookies. They would melt in your mouth. Wish I could offer you one."

"You must miss her very much."

"Yes, ma'am. Our oldest makes them for me sometimes, but they don't taste the same."

She was losing him, Quinn thought. "One last question, Jonah. Whatever happened to Angela Riley?"

"She up and left one night. No goodbye; left most of her stuff behind. Grief does strange things to people."

Her road trip from New Orleans to Grand Forks, North Dakota. "That it does."

He fell silent. She waited. When he didn't offer up anything more, she asked, "After she and her daughter up and left, you never heard from them again?"

He sent her an odd glance. "No, ma'am, like I said, her daughter died that day."

"I meant her other daughter."

"She only had one child. Little Eden, the one she buried."

FORTY-NINE

1:30 PM.

Quinn stood in front of the tomb, with its marble front and small vase of wilted flowers. She hadn't believed him. She'd thought him confused. An old man, mixing up names and families, which child belonged with whom.

He had been adamant. He had attended the funeral, he said. Little Eden was entombed at Greenwood Cemetery, in the memorial garden.

Quinn reached out, traced a finger over chiseled letters, forming the name as she did.

Beloved Child
Eden Rose Riley
March 10, 1993-April 2, 1994

WHO WAS the woman who called herself Eden Riley? She knew, of course she did.

Eden Riley was baby Grace Hudson, all grown up.

FIFTY

3:30 *P.M.*

Quinn shut her laptop. The news story had been easy enough to find, once she knew what she was looking for—a toddler run down on a quiet Uptown street. Newsworthy but quickly overshadowed and forgotten.

She stood, stretched, then crossed to the window and gazed out at the perfect spring day. The birds were singing, and puffy white clouds drifted across a brilliant blue sky. A day fitting of this moment, she thought.

You did it, Dad. I'm so damn proud of you.

A lump formed in her throat, and she turned away from the window. He'd never given up on finding Grace, even when everyone else had not only given up on her, but on him as well. She didn't yet know how he'd made the connection between Angela Riley and Grace Hudson, but that would come. Maybe she would find it here, in the bits and pieces yet to be placed on her web. Or the Cold Case Unit would connect those dots, for surely Captain Franks and the Chief would insist on the case being turned over to them.

Which, surprisingly, she felt okay about. Just not yet.

Quinn took in the study, the recreated story board, picturing her dad as she did. His dark head bent over his work, looking up at her and smiling.

She drew in a deep breath, then let it out slowly, feeling as if an oppressive weight was lifting from her being.

She crossed to the desk, to her phone there. She'd turned it off, a kind of reprieve, something an active duty cop never did. She picked it up, thinking of Dobby and longing to share the news with him.

Eden first. For this discovery impacted no one as much as it did her.

Quinn acknowledged it an understatement in the extreme. How did she tell her that her whole life had been a lie? How did she tell her that if what she strongly suspected was true, the mother she'd adored was either a kidnapper and murderer . . . or an accomplice to both?

She restarted the device and called up the other woman's number. It rang once, twice, on the third Eden answered.

"It's Quinn." Quinn heard the other woman's sharp exhalation of breath and pressed on. "Where are you?"

"Running errands. Why?"

"Come to my place. I found something. It's big."

FIFTY-ONE

4:20 P.M.

Eden stared at her; eyebrows drawn together in confusion. She shook her head. "I don't understand what you're telling me."

"I'm saying that I found the connection between your mom and the Hudsons. It's you, Eden. You're Grace Hudson."

Eden started to laugh; the look on Quinn's face stopped her. She lowered her gaze to the orange Post-it with its bold WILLOW STREET. "That's . . . crazy."

"The woman you called mom, Angela Riley, lost her own child in a tragic accident. She replaced her with Grace Hudson."

For a heartbeat she simply stared at Quinn. Then, as if the full meaning of the words hit her, she recoiled. "That's not true. It's not!"

"Eden, please listen. I know this is really difficult—"

"Difficult," she repeated acidly. "You're saying my mom . . . *kidnapped* me? That she *murdered* Cynthia Hudson to get me?"

"Or was an accomplice to the acts. Yes."

She took a step backward, "You didn't know her! If you did, you'd realize what you're suggesting is impossible!"

"Let me walk you through what I uncovered. How it happened."

Quinn kept her voice low, soothing. "Then you can make your own decision. Could you try?"

She folded her arms across her chest. "I'm listening."

"The night my dad died, he said he had found 'it.' The thing that would break the Hudson case wide open. He'd said things like that before, he'd always been wrong. I didn't believe him and hung up."

She indicated the wall with its photos and notes and string connecting them all. "What you're looking at is my recreation of his investigation board. He would spend hours in front of it, drinking whiskey and studying it.

"I didn't want anyone to see it, because I knew what they would think, how they'd judge him, so I took it down before I even called 911. I forgot about it until yesterday and went searching for the envelope I'd stuffed all the items in."

She glanced at Eden. The other woman was staring at the wall, expression heartbreakingly sad. "I know I said I had reached a dead end and couldn't help you anymore, but I remembered something my dad said about Logan Shaw and—"

"What does he have to do with this?"

"Nothing really, except he got me suspended."

"You got suspended!"

"That doesn't matter right now . . . the point is I found the mailer and had the time and . . . I thought I owed it to my dad to give his theory one last shot."

"That's where you found the Post-it," Eden said softly.

"Yes. I remembered you said your mom lived on Willow Street, and knew it was the connection between your mom and the Hudson case that we'd been looking for."

Quinn told her about the young mother directing her to Jonah, and Jonah reciting the tragic death of Eden Riley, then directing her to Greenwood cemetery.

"Before I called you, I researched what he told me. The hit and run that killed Angela Riley's daughter happened exactly as Jonah described. According to city records, Angela Riley had one daughter, and we already knew Grace Hudson had been born at what was then Mercy-Baptist Hospital, where your mother was a nurse."

Eden crossed to the small couch and sank onto it. She dropped her head into hands and sobbed, her shoulders shaking with the force of her tears. Although warm and fuzzy wasn't her strong suit, Quinn sat beside her and awkwardly rubbed her back.

Eden leaned into her, the way a child would a parent. Surprised, Quinn found herself gently rocking, murmuring that it was going to be okay. Minutes passed. The force of Eden's tears lessened; her quaking body stilled. She eased away, wiping the wet from her cheeks.

"I'm a mess."

Quinn went for the tissues, handed her the box.

"Thanks," she whispered, then blew her nose.

"What are you thinking?" Quinn asked.

"I don't know," she said, expression stricken. "It's like my mind's so full it's . . . blank."

"That's shock, it's normal."

They fell silent. After several moments, Eden stood. "Do you mind if I go wash my face?"

"Go ahead. There are clean washcloths in the bathroom linen closet."

She thanked her and went that direction, returning a couple minutes later. Although her eyes were red and puffy from crying, she looked refreshed. And resolute. "You asked me what I was thinking."

Quinn nodded. "I did."

She took an audible breath, let it out. "I want to see little Eden"s grave."

FIFTY-TWO

6:10 P.M.

Eden didn't cry as she stood silently, almost stoically, in front of the marble marker. The minutes ticked past. Five. Ten. Fifteen. Finally, she turned to Quinn.

"I'm ready to go."

Quinn nodded and they fell into step together. They reached the car and Quinn unlocked the doors; they both slipped inside. Eden buckled her belt, then met Quinn's eyes.

"I don't know what to do. What comes next?"

"The next steps are mine," Quinn said. "I need to inform the department, share my findings. They'll evaluate what I give them, and if it passes scrutiny—"

"If?" She sounded shocked. "It might not?"

"I don't have a shadow of a doubt that it will, but it's protocol. The department, including the chief of police, will have to be as confident as I am before he brings this information to the Hudson family. In addition, they're going to want to question you."

She twisted her fingers together. "Me?"

"They'll need to hear everything you told me directly from you. You'll need to share the receipts, the call history from your mom's phone, the envelope and breadcrumbs—all of it."

She swallowed hard. "How long until I have to face all that?"

"My best guess is a few days, but it could be less. You need to be ready for what's coming."

She paled. "What do you mean?"

"Once the news gets out, it's going to be a media circus. The scrutiny will be intense." Quinn turned in her seat. "This is a *big* story, Eden. It'll be national news. Expect every outlet, print and broadcast, to be after you for an interview."

Her chin quivered. "Can't we keep it quiet?"

Her heart went out to the other woman. "It doesn't work that way. I know it sounds overwhelming, and I'm really sorry."

"I don't know if I can handle all that."

"You can, and you will. You're a strong person, Eden. If you weren't, you wouldn't have gotten this far."

Eden blinked against tears. "I feel so alone."

"You're not alone." Quinn held out her hand. Eden took it, gripped it tightly. "I'll be with you every step of the way. I promise."

EDEN HAD REFUSED Quinn's offer of her guest room. She needed time alone to process, she said. Quinn understood. She also needed time alone to do what she needed to do. At the top of her list was calling Dobby. Despite recent events, he was her partner; she wanted and needed him by her side.

Next, she wanted to let Uncle Mikey know. He'd been through so much with her dad; the case had become personal to him, too. He'd be happy about this. For her, sure. But mostly for her dad.

Stomach growling, she made herself a peanut butter sandwich and poured herself a whiskey. After wolfing down the first half, she wiped her fingers on a paper towel, then picked up her phone. It rang in her hand.

Dobby. Calling her.

She took a fortifying sip of the whiskey and answered. "Hey, you."

"Hey." He sounded uncomfortable. "How're you doing?"

An easy opening. She took it. "Good, actually. How about you?"

"All right. They partnered me with Manelli. Except for his garlic burps, he's okay."

Manelli was famous for those burps. The joke around the Second went that if you needed a confession, lock the perp in an interrogation room with Sammy Manelli when he was on a roll, and the deal was as good as done. "Tough to be in a closed vehicle with him."

"Luckily, the weather's been good." He fell silent a moment, then said, "What you accused me of the other day, telling Captain Franks about your dad's files, it wasn't me. If I had done it, I would have owned it. That you don't know that about me, it cuts deep, Quinn."

"I do know that about you, Dobby. I wasn't thinking clearly and I lashed out." She cleared her throat. "I shouldn't have. I'm sorry."

"Going to Logan Shaw that way, you shouldn't have done it. You knew it was questionable, but you did it anyway."

"You're right, and I acknowledge it was a shitty move." She paused, drew a hopeful breath. "I don't want to lose you, Dobbs."

He went quiet for a moment. "And I don't want to work with anybody else. You're my partner."

"I'm really glad to hear that, because there's something I have to share with you. In fact, I was dialing you when you called me. Promise you'll listen to everything I have to say. *Everything*."

"That doesn't sound like someone who's been getting their collective shit together."

"I think you'll be surprised. In a good way. Promise me."

He let out a long breath. "You're killing me, Quinn. All right, I give you my word."

"You want the whole story? Or the SparkNotes version?"

"Oh, hell." She could imagine him bringing his hand to his forehead in that way he did sometimes. "Give me the SparkNotes."

"Grace Hudson is alive. And I found her."

FIFTY-THREE

8:40 P.M.

"I need a drink," Dobby said when she opened the door.

Quinn waved him in. Over the phone she'd told him everything—how she'd remembered dismantling and packing up her dad's crime scene board, that she'd located the materials and recreated the board as best she could. She relayed about finding the Post-it note, being directed to Jonah, and standing in front of Eden Riley's grave.

When she'd finished, he'd insisted on coming over. He needed to see it all for himself.

He followed her to the kitchen. She poured him a stiff whiskey, then another for herself. He held up his glass. "If this is for real, Chief Thompson is going to lose his mind."

She tapped her glass against his. "It's for real, all right. Come see."

While she'd waited for him to arrive, she'd laid everything out for him on the desk—the Post-it, copies of the items Eden had left with her: the map, the receipts, all of it; she had printed out the news stories about the hit and run of toddler Eden Riley, and a photograph she'd taken of Eden Riley's grave marker.

They entered the room; he stopped short, eyes on the far wall, its web of photos and notes and connective string. "Damn."

"I know, and it's not even finished. Once I found the Willow Street address and made the connection, I didn't see the need."

"You're going to have to repaint that wall."

He said it deadpan and she laughed. "Yes, I am, and I'll be happy to do it."

Quinn guided him to the desk. He sat. She sipped her whiskey and watched as he absorbed the material. He was meticulous in the way he approached evidence, always careful not to rush to judgement, the way her dad had tried to teach her to be.

Dobby set aside the last piece of evidence then looked up at her. "You did it, Quinn. You fucking did it."

A smile split her face. "I did, didn't I?"

He jumped to his feet, gave her quick, hard hug, then stepped away, searching her expression. "This is huge. You get that, right?"

She couldn't stop smiling. "I do."

He downed the whiskey, shook his head. "You know what this means?"

"That you need another drink?"

"Hell, yes I do. But that's not what it means."

He followed her to the kitchen. She fixed them both another; he lifted his glass again. "It means you're a hero. A big-deal hero."

She shook her head. "You're tipsy."

"Nope." He shook his head. "You, partner, are going to get an award. The Badge of Honor, I'll bet."

"You know me, in it for the awards." She tapped her glass to his, then realizing they could both use something to soak up the booze, got a bag of popcorn out of the pantry and stuck it in the microwave. As the smell of the popping corn filled the room, her mouth started to water.

The popping slowed, then stopped; Quinn removed the bag and dumped the contents into a bowl, setting it on the table between them.

They both dug in. It was the best tasting thing she'd eaten in weeks. Maybe years.

"You know I don't care about awards and stuff, right?" she said.

"Yeah, You should, though. That stuff matters." He munched on the crunchy snack, expression growing thoughtful. "Have you told Riley?"

"I told her first."

He nodded, acknowledging it had been the right call. "How'd she react?"

"Like someone whose world had been turned upside down and inside out."

"I have a confession to make."

"Yeah?"

"I wasn't sure about her."

"What do you mean?" Quinn helped herself to another handful of the popcorn.

"I figured she was full of shit."

"In what way?"

"That she was lying to you. Making it all up."

"Why? She had documentation of her facts. I talked to the detective in Dekalb."

"I'm sort of embarrassed to say."

Dobby embarrassed? Now he had her attention.

"Looking back, I think I was jealous."

Quinn laughed, earning a scowl from him. "Sorry. In God's name, why?"

"After you got involved with her, you started to change. We started to change. I didn't like it."

She'd noticed the change in them too. Only she had blamed him.

"Quinn?"

"Yeah?"

"I owe you an apology."

"No, you don't."

"You were right, but I didn't trust your instincts."

"If the roles had been reversed, I don't know if I would have trusted yours."

"You would have."

"It's water under the bridge."

"Is it?"

She looked him dead in the eyes. "It is. You were right. If you see your partner about to go off a cliff, you try to stop them."

He stood. "I should go before I have to call Cherie to come pick me up."

"You sure you're good?"

"I am."

"I need you to do something for me," she said. "Tomorrow."

"Name it."

"Take everything I uncovered to Captain Franks. Get me my badge back."

He grinned. "You can get your own damn badge back."

"Since I'm suspended, I figured you should do it."

"Well you figured wrong. You do it, I'll ride shotgun."

FIFTY-FOUR

6:00 P.M. *Friday.*

Less than seventy-two hours Quinn arrived at The Hudson Group headquarters, Dobby by her side. Captain Franks had reviewed the evidence, given her a resounding "atta-girl" and called Chief Thompson. Once the departmental due diligence had been done, including bringing Lieutenant Tillerson and his team onboard, the chief arranged this after-hours meeting with Charles and Bill Hudson.

Quinn stepped onto the elevator and squared her shoulders, mentally preparing herself. Would the two men be appreciative and hopeful at the possibility that Grace had been found? Or would they be surly and suspicious? She had a pretty good idea it'd be the latter—after all, tigers didn't change their stripes.

"You look confident," Dobby murmured.

"Fake it until you make it, baby."

He laughed. The car stopped; the doors slid open. Captain Franks, Lieutenant Tillerson and Chief Thompson were waiting; was with him.

The chief smiled broadly. "Good work, Detective Conners." He held out his hand. She took it and he clasped it with his other as well. "This is a proud day for this department. Damn proud day."

"Just doing my job, Chief."

The executive assistant she remembered from her last visit signaled that the Hudsons were ready for them. She led them to the conference room; Charles and Bill Hudson were waiting, Daniel Shaw with them.

"Charles, Bill, thank you both for agreeing to meet with us so quickly," the chief said. "Do you know everyone here?"

They did and everyone took their seat. Charles folded his hands in front of him. "You indicated you've had a break in the case. A suspect, I hope?"

The chief glanced at her, then back at Hudson. "Yes, but not only a suspect. We believe we've found your granddaughter."

Bill went white. "Grace? Dear God."

Charles glanced at Shaw, then back at Chief Thompson. Quinn noticed that his hands shook.

"Where did you . . . find them?"

"Them?"

"Her remains."

The chief's face went momentarily slack, then tightened in distress. "Charles, forgive me, I misspoke. We believe we've found Grace. She's alive."

The room went graveyard-at-midnight silent. The men's expressions gradually went from thunderstruck to disbelieving.

Shaw cleared his throat, but even so, when he spoke his voice shook. "I'm sure you understand the emotional magnitude of what you're suggesting. To come in here and announce to my clients that the child, their precious daughter and granddaughter, who has been lost to them for more than a quarter century—"

Charles cut him off, expression tight. "You'd better have proof, Chief."

The Chief didn't waver. "We do. If you'll allow me to lay it out for you?"

When the men agreed, Chief Thompson began and Quinn listened as he shared both the evidence she'd assembled and how it had come about, careful to refer to Angela Riley anonymously—a nurse who worked in the hospital where Grace had been born. She listened for the inconsistency, the gaping hole that could cost both her and Chief Thompson their jobs.

She didn't hear either. Yes, there were questions yet to be answered: Did Angela Riley actually know Cynthia Hudson? What made Riley choose to kidnap Grace Hudson? Did she have an accomplice? If so, who?

"We owe this discovery to Detective Conners's dedication and determination, even in the face of suspension."

Quinn felt all the eyes in the room settle on her. When she didn't respond, Dobby elbowed her.

"Thank you, Chief," she said stiffly, uncomfortable with the praise. It felt wrong, like she didn't deserve it.

Because she didn't, Quinn realized. Her father did. This was the result of his work, not hers. His sacrifice, not hers.

She cleared her throat. "Before we move on, I want to note that if there's a hero here, it's my father. If not for his tireless search for the truth, this could have stayed buried forever."

"Indeed," Charles said softly, "if this proves accurate and my granddaughter is alive, we will be eternally grateful. Won't we son?"

"Absolutely, Dad."

"The woman," Charles continued, returning his attention to Chief Thompson, "this nurse, what's her name? Is she in custody?"

"Her name was Angela Riley. Unfortunately, she's dead. She was murdered a few months back."

Shaw spoke up. "Do you think her murder had anything to do with—"

"Not at this point, no."

"The girl who claims to be Grace, where is she?"

"Right here in New Orleans. I believe you've met her already."

Hudson senior looked blank for a moment, then made the connection. "You can't mean that writer—" he looked at Shaw "— what was her name?"

"Eden Riley," Quinn said sharply. "Yes, we do mean her, Mr. Hudson,"

He shook his head. "You've been scammed, Detective."

The chief sent her a sharp glance, then stepped in smoothly. "What we have, the information Detective Conners amassed, is highly credible. If it wasn't, I wouldn't be here."

"I'm not saying it isn't a good con. I'm not even saying there aren't elements of truth there, but that young woman is *not* my grand-daughter."

Quinn stiffened. "What makes you so certain?"

He leaned forward, expression hard. "Do you think she's the first? Over the years a half dozen young women have showed up at our door, claiming to be our Grace. It's not surprising. Who wouldn't want to be Grace Hudson?"

"Someone who would prefer not to have her entire life proved a lie," Quinn shot back. "Someone who loved the woman she called mom and being the missing Grace Hudson would make that woman both a kidnapper and a murderer. That's who wouldn't want to be Grace Hudson."

"Detective—"

The warning came from the chief, she forged ahead anyway. "For some of us, life is about more than money and power."

Charles smiled slightly. "That's so sweet, Detective. Surprisingly naive for someone in your line of work, but sweet."

Shaw stepped in. "Let us privately review and authenticate the material. Once we've verified—"

Charles held up his hand, stopping the attorney. "I have a better idea, and a quicker way to end this. Give her a choice, Detective Conners. She can either take a DNA test or accept a check for fifty thousand dollars and disappear."

"Charles," Chief Thompson said, "this is in play for us, there's no turning back."

Hudson continued as if the chief hadn't even spoken; his gaze never wavered from hers. "Do it, Detective. I think you're in for a surprise."

She narrowed her eyes. "Actually, Mr. Hudson, I think you are."

FIFTY-FIVE

5:35 P.M. *Thursday.*

Quinn realized she was humming. No particular song, just an upbeat melody running through her head. She smiled to herself, unlocked her car and slipped behind the wheel. She'd been doing that a lot lately, so much that Dobby had commented on it. Very un-Quinn-like, he'd said.

She rather liked this new Quinn Conners, this new world where everything, and everyone in it, appeared a little rosier.

She started the engine and kicked on the AC. Who could blame her for the skip in her step? After twenty-eight years, the Hudson case was all but solved and her dad's good name was on the road to restoration. Details had yet to be worked out—the how and why—but they would come. The most important piece of the puzzle had been found; baby Grace would be reunited with her family.

Not everyone was as openly optimistic. Until DNA proved beyond a shadow of a doubt that Eden was Grace Hudson, Captain Franks had ordered complete secrecy. Likewise, Chief Thompson remained hopeful but cautious. A team from the cold case unit had

had already begun digging into Angela Riley's past; Quinn had no doubt they'd have the rest of the story pieced together soon.

As far as Quinn was concerned, Eden was the missing Grace Hudson and the DNA confirmation would prove it. Then the cat could be let out of the bag, and she would be able to celebrate in earnest.

A few more days and the test results would be in. Eden hadn't considered Charles Hudson's offer of fifty grand, not even for a moment. In fact, she'd been offended. Not a great way for Charles to have begun his relationship with his long-lost granddaughter.

Quinn navigated the neighborhood streets, working her way towards Carrollton Avenue. Up ahead, a kid walked along the side of the road, head bent, hands stuffed into his front pockets. As she passed him, he looked up and over. Their eyes briefly met, and she was hit by a shock of recognition.

The kid from the surveillance video, the one who had tucked the flyer under her windshield wiper, the one with a note on the back saying her dad didn't kill himself.

Quinn pulled to the side of the road, opened the console and withdrew the print-out from the video. Yup, it was definitely him.

She did a U-turn, then tapped her siren. The kid froze and looked back, eyes wide and expression worried. Wearing a New Orleans Pelicans T-shirt and a pair of ill-fitting khaki shorts, he appeared to be about twelve or thirteen.

She rolled up alongside him and lowered the passenger side window. "Hey," she said, "how's it going?"

"I didn't do anything wrong."

"I'm not saying you did. I have a question, that's all."

He seemed to relax a little. "Okay. What?"

She reached across the seat with the flyer. "You ever see this before?"

He crossed to the car, reached through the window and took it. One look and his apprehension reappeared. "I don't think so, Officer."

"You sure about that?"

He shifted from one foot to the other. "Pretty sure."

"This might help jog your memory." She held out the photo print-out. "You ever see him before?"

He stared at it a moment, looking sick. "It's a piece of paper, I didn't think I could get in any trouble!"

"Somebody paid you to do it?"

"Yeah, some lady. She paid me twenty bucks."

Quinn jumped on the pronoun. "She? A woman asked you to do this?"

He nodded.

"You have a name?"

He shook his head. "She was just some lady . . . she seemed nice enough and I thought it was a joke."

"What'd she look like?"

He squinted his eyes in thought. "She was white. Brown hair, I guess. 'bout your age maybe. I don't know."

A thought planted; one she didn't want to be true.

"Let me show you a photo." Quinn grabbed her phone and accessed Eden's Facebook page. She held out the device; he leaned in, studied the image. "I think so . . . yeah, that's her."

She scrolled to another photo, held it out. "You're sure?"

"Yeah." He nodded vigorously. "Can I go now?"

After warning him about the dangers of easy money, she sent him on his way and went hers, thoughts reeling.

She replayed her and Eden's interactions, starting with that very first phone call, mentally ticking through each piece of "evidence" Eden had presented, each of her responses, alternately telling herself it didn't mean anything and knowing that one lie almost always led to another.

Home, she fed Beignet, poured herself a whiskey and heated a frozen dinner. The chicken and pasta dish tasted like cardboard, but Quinn forced herself to eat most of it before she pushed it away.

Eden paid a kid to put that flyer on her windshield. Why? She answered her own question: to manipulate her into thinking about her father, his death, and the case that had brought him to it.

Quinn recalled her first impressions of Eden. Naive and too trusting. Out of her depth. Quinn remembered suggesting she run back to her safe little community.

Then she had presented her "evidence." The receipts and map. The phone calls. The breadcrumbs. She recalled finding it all compelling but had refused her plea to get involved.

Now look where she was: waiting for the results of the DNA test proving Eden was the kidnapped Grace Hudson.

How'd Eden do it? Quinn wondered, bringing the rocks glass to her lips. She'd gone from wanting nothing to do with Eden or the Hudson case to jumping in with both feet.

The attack. It had changed everything.

Did it even happen? Quinn stood, crossed to the window and gazed out at the dark. What proof did she have? Some tears? Appearing shaken, frantic? Dobby had even asked her why Eden had called her instead of 911. He had seen a red flag, but she had been blind to it.

Because she'd secretly *wanted* to get involved. To solve the case and restore her father's reputation.

Eden had accurately predicted it all.

Quinn downed the last of the whiskey and stood. Quite simply, she'd been had. And she wasn't the kind who could let that stand.

Fifteen minutes later, Quinn pulled up alongside Eden's building and looked up at her brightly lit windows. Good, it looked like she was home. Quinn plucked her phone from the console and tapped in Eden's number; the woman answered on the first ring.

"It's me," Quinn said, opening the car door. "Can I come up?"

"Oh my God, did the test results come in?"

"Not yet. This is about something else."

"Sure, I'm on my way down."

A couple minutes later, Eden let her in, and they headed up the stairs to her apartment. She closed and locked the door behind them. "I have wine if you'd like a—"

"No thanks."

At her clipped tone, Eden's forehead wrinkled. "What's going on?"

"I've got a question for you. What's your game?"

"My game?" Her smile faded. "I don't know what you're talking about."

"Really? Maybe this will help." Quinn retrieved the folded flyer from her purse and held it out.

Eden unfolded it and frowned. "What is this?"

"An anonymous message that was left tucked under my windshield wiper."

"Tonight?"

"No. Right before we met."

She looked at it once more. "Your dad didn't kill himself? I don't understand. Why are you showing this to me?"

"Let's see if I can help clarify it for you." Quinn handed her the copy of the surveillance image.

She took it, and as she had with the other, took a moment to study it. "A kid stuck it on your windshield?"

She was the picture of confused innocence. *Unbelievable.* "I ran into him today. He told me a woman paid him twenty bucks to leave it for me."

Realization dawned on her face and she brought a hand to her chest. "You don't think *I* had anything to do with—"

"Stop the charade, Eden. I showed him your Facebook profile picture and he confirmed it was you."

"I didn't do it."

"Right." Quinn looked up at the ceiling a moment, acknowledging how disappointed she was. She'd actually started to like her.

"It was your opening gambit. A way to get me thinking about my dad and the Hudson case."

"That's crazy."

"Is it? He looked at your photo and *confirmed* it was you."

"Then he was lying." Her eyes welled with tears. "Why would I even do that?"

"You knew about my Dad's suicide. You knew he was obsessed with the case and, no doubt, you'd learned how close he and I were. You used it all to manipulate me into helping you."

"Just . . . go." She swiped at a tear that escaped and rolled down her cheek. "Sleep it off or whatever—"

Quinn held her gaze, unmoved by the tears and quiver in her voice. "Here's what I'm wondering, did you stop at the flyer? Or, when I refused to help, did you up the ante?"

"I don't what you're talking about."

"The attack. Did it even happen?"

"Yes! Someone broke in and threatened me. Just the way I said. It was terrifying."

"What about the breadcrumbs? That was a clever twist, one you, the writer, quickly pointed out."

She lifted her chin. "I didn't do any of this, but I'm not going to beg you to believe me."

Quinn started for the door, then hesitated, a thread of doubt pulling at her. What if the kid had lied to get her off his back? Or he'd simply been wrong?

She turned back to Eden. As she did, her gaze caught on a cornflower blue and white silk, draped over the arm of a chair. She'd seen that scarf before. Recently.

The image filled her head. At Logan Shaw's penthouse, on his patio, at the foot of the chaise.

She shifted her gaze to Eden's. "Are you seeing him?"

"Who?"

Eden knew who she meant—her demeanor had become that of a cornered rabbit. Quinn shook her head in disbelief. "Logan Shaw is a snake, Eden."

"Not to me. He's really sweet."

Quinn made a sound of disbelief. "There are a lot of words I would use to describe Logan Shaw, but never in a million years would 'sweet' be one of them."

"Because you don't know him the way I do."

"Because I'm not *fucking* him the way you are?"

"You don't understand—

"Oh, I think I do. How long has this been going on?"

Her throat worked. She twisted her fingers together. "Awhile. He's one of the first people who agreed to talk to me about the case and we hit it off. He invited me to dinner."

"Did you ask yourself why?"

"I knew why. Because we immediately clicked."

Could she really be that clueless? "Maybe he was *instructed* to 'click' with you? Did you even consider that?"

"Instructed? By who?"

"His bosses, Charles and Bill Hudson. His dad. Haven't you heard the saying, keep your friends close but your enemies closer?"

"That's not what happened."

"Were you there the night I went to see him? Hiding somewhere in the penthouse?"

Her cheeks flamed red. "I didn't know why you were there, and I was afraid you'd be—"

"Pissed off? The way I am now?"

"Yes," she whispered. "I'm so sorry. I wish I'd had the guts to come clean then, I should have."

Eden had known that Captain Franks warned her not to approach the Hudsons again or risk suspension. She'd told Logan, and he'd used that information against her. What other information could Eden have shared with him?

Her dad's files, of course. She thought of Dobby, of how she'd accused him of betraying her. Regret rose like bile in her throat, shame with it. She had betrayed *him*, not the other way around.

"You told him about my dad's files, didn't you?"

"I didn't think it was a big deal." She brought a hand to her chest. "I trust him, Quinn. We really care for each other."

"What, do you think he's in *love* with you?"

At the sarcasm in her voice, Eden jerked her chin up. "I know he is. He told me so."

Quinn rolled her eyes. "He's using you, Eden. His loyalty is to the Hudsons, which he made perfectly clear to me. In fact, he reminded me of that when he had me suspended—"

Quinn bit the words back. "You know what? I called him a snake, but I'm thinking you are, too. In fact, you probably did hit it off— because you're as double-dealing as he is. I'd tell you to have a nice life, but I really don't care that much. Goodbye, Eden."

FIFTY-SIX

7:50 A.M. *Friday.*

Quinn's doorbell sounded as she was filling her travel mug with what would be her third cup of coffee of the morning. She hadn't slept well, her rest stolen by nightmares she couldn't recall but even so, still felt unnervingly real.

She snapped the lid on the cup, dropped an apple into her tote bag and hurried to answer it.

A smile died on her lips as she saw Daniel Shaw standing on her doorstep. The morning sun washed out his already pale face, giving him a bit of a zombie vibe.

"Good morning, Detective," he said, his smile thin. "I see I've caught you on your way out."

Quinn stiffened with dislike. "What can I do for you, Mr. Shaw?"

"May I come in?"

She glanced at the time, then stepped aside. "I only have a minute."

"Of course." He moved his gaze over the interior. "You've really changed the place."

Uneasiness settled in the pit of her gut. "Excuse me?"

"I was here, back when the house was your dad's."

"That's odd, considering. Just as it's odd you're here today."

"Then, like now, I was delivering news."

She folded her arms across her chest and waited.

"I had a lot of respect for your dad."

"Bullshit."

"It's true. He was a fighter, smart and determined. Like I am." He smiled slightly. "Like you are."

She didn't respond, but maybe he didn't expect her to. "Shame about the drinking. It clouded his judgement and made him less of a man than he was meant to be."

She didn't bite although she longed to. She crossed her arms. "You said you had news?"

"I thought you'd want to know first, before your superior officers. I felt certain you'd want to prepare yourself."

Her stomach sank. He could only be talking about one thing—the results of the DNA test.

He held out an envelope. She took it, slid the report out—and read it three times before lifting her gaze to his once more. "This can't be right."

"It is. Eden Riley's DNA is not a match with Bill Hudson's."

Her mouth went dry. For a moment she couldn't speak. "How did you manage this?"

Even as she asked the question, she saw no way he or the Hudsons could have manipulated the results. The genetics lab they'd chosen was beyond reproach—and beyond the reach of even the Hudson's wealth and influence.

He shook his head, expression infuriatingly smug. "Such a shame that you staked your reputation on the word of this . . . con artist. I don't know who Eden Riley is, but she's not Grace Hudson. Sorry to ruin your day."

He wasn't sorry. Of course, he wasn't. Quinn shut the door behind him, then rested her forehead against it. This couldn't be happening. She'd been so certain. The evidence, although circum-stantial, had seemed so strong.

Just another dead end in a case that had been littered with them. She thought of her dad, pictured him, and her eyes burned.

She blinked furiously against the tears. *I'm sorry, Dad. I tried. It's not going to happen.*

In her pocket, her cell phone vibrated. She checked the display and her heart sank. Captain Franks. Calling her before 8:30 this morning.

Not good.

She cleared her throat. "Captain Franks, good morning."

"I just got off the phone with Chief Thompson—"

"Before you say anything more, I know about the DNA test results. Daniel Shaw came by with them."

"How the hell did this happen?"

"No one's more surprised than I am."

"The Chief found out from Charles Hudson. Apparently, their conversation was tense."

Of course it was. Dammit. "What we had was good, Captain. Good enough that everyone on the team voted to move forward, including the chief."

"If you want to point that out to him, I welcome you to do it." He waited a moment, then delivered a bombshell. "Charles Hudson has a demand."

She squeezed her eyes shut, knowing in her gut what it was going to be. Wishing for it to be anything but.

An instant later, her intuition proved correct.

"He wants a personal, face-to-face apology from you."

Angry heat flooded her cheeks and she counted to five before replying. "For what? Chasing every lead in an effort to find his missing granddaughter? They should be thanking me for all my hard work."

He sighed. "Look, I'm not happy about it either, but I'm not the one in charge."

"If I refuse?"

"Don't do that, Quinn. You're a good detective, and I don't want you to do something today that you'll regret tomorrow."

In other words, she didn't have a choice. Do it or suffer the consequences. A stalled career. A transfer to a shitty detail, a demotion down the road for perfectly "justified" reasons.

"You championed this, Detective. You have to take the fallout."

She imagined groveling before Charles and Bill. She knew a simple apology wasn't what he was looking for. He wanted to pair it with heavy dose of humiliation. "I don't know if I can do it, Captain." She tightened her grip on her phone. "I shouldn't have to."

She heard his quick intake of breath; he had expected her to be a good soldier and acquiesce.

"In a perfect world you wouldn't, and this world ain't even close to perfect. Take a personal day, Detective. Blow off some steam, get your head straight. I know you'll do the smart thing."

She hung up and called Dobby. He'd hardly finished uttering "good morning" when she let loose. "You are not going to believe this! It's fucking bullshit!"

"Hold up, partner. What's going on?"

"Shaw came by my place this morning and—"

"Daniel Shaw?"

"Yes. To personally let me know the results of the DNA test. It was negative."

"Whoa, wait— are you saying Eden Riley is *not* Grace Hudson?"

"That's exactly what I'm saying."

"Take a deep breath. This isn't end of the world. It didn't go the way you thought it would, that happens sometimes."

"Says the man whose ass isn't on the line."

"That's not fair, Quinn. You're my partner, what affects you effects me."

"This would have cleared my dad, I was so—" Happy, she thought bitterly. Excited and proud. "Dammit!"

"It didn't clear him, so today is really no different than yesterday or last week, for that matter. C'mon, you know that."

She didn't want logic from him; she didn't want to be pacified. "The chief wants me to apologize to the Hudsons. Can you believe that shit? Apologize *in person*. For what? I did nothing wrong!"

"Saying you're sorry costs you nothing. A little pride. Big deal."

"Again, from the one not being forced to grovel in front of an arrogant, amoral asshole!"

"True, and it sucks, no doubt. When are you going to do it?"

"I haven't decided if I am."

For a long, painful moment, he said nothing. When he finally spoke, he sounded weary, the way Uncle Mikey used to sound with her Dad.

"Don't be crazy, Quinn. Just do it."

"I don't know if I can."

"I'm really sorry it turned out this way, I know how certain you were that the results would be different. Have you spoken with Eden yet?"

"No, but I'm certain her lawyer has received a copy of the report. He'll call her."

"You don't think you need to talk to her yourself?" he said, sounding surprised.

"Oh yeah, you don't know this yet because I was going to fill you in this morning. Yesterday I discovered that Eden was the one who left that flyer on my windshield."

"What the hell!"

"Yeah, she was the one who paid the kid to do it. He said so himself, ID-ed her from her Facebook cover photo. When I confronted her, she tearfully denied it and, patsy that I am, I almost believed her. Then I discovered that she and Logan Shaw are an item."

"As in they are *together* together?"

"Exactly like that. Apparently, it's been going on since she first arrived in New Orleans. If I don't feel compelled to call her, I think I'm justified."

"I get it." Again he let silence overtake them, then, quietly, he said, "If she isn't Grace Hudson, who is she?"

His question startled her. In the shock and disappointment of the moment, she hadn't even considered it.

"The receipts, how do you explain them?"

"Maybe she manufactured them? It's possible."

"The grave marker? Jonah's testimony?"

"I don't know. Maybe Angela adopted a child and gave her the same name?"

"And used the same birth certificate?"

She didn't want his logic. She wanted to be pissed off, to lash out. "Maybe Eden's a brilliant, fucking con artist! It's not my problem. Not anymore."

She heard the sound of his car door slamming; the greeting of another officer arriving for their shift; Dobby responding before refocusing on his conversation with her. "You've always been a hard ass, Quinn, and that was okay. Because at the same time you had a good heart and a strong sense of right and wrong. Maybe you should think about that while you figure out what you're going to do next."

In the next instant, he hung up.

FIFTY-SEVEN

9:05 P.M.

Hours later, Quinn pulled into her driveway, shifted into park but didn't make a move to cut the engine or climb out. She was exhausted, physically and mentally. She'd packed the day full, with anything and everything she thought might distract her from her own thoughts. A punishing run on the levee. Hours on the gun range. A drive north, across Lake Pontchartrain, to visit a former colleague who had left the NOPD to join a rural force there. A movie she'd been longing to see.

The attempts to quell her own thoughts had been only partially successful and had left her emotionally spent as well. She couldn't bear the thought of subjugating herself to Charles Hudson, but she loved her job. It was as much a part of her as she was of it.

Was this how her dad felt each time he had been reprimanded? Is it why he'd finally thrown in the towel?

Quinn cut the engine and climbed out of the car. As she reached the front stoop, Beignet appeared from under the bushes beside the porch and meowed plaintively at her. She unlocked the front door and went to scoop him up, but he squirmed free and darted inside.

"Et tu, Beignet?" she muttered, locking the door behind her. She dropped her keys on the entryway table and headed to the kitchen. After giving him one of the salmon treats he loved—earning her his signature cross between a meow and a purr—she went to the pantry to scrounge up a treat for herself.

Her gaze landed on a bag of Pepperidge Farms chocolate chip cookies, and she smiled. Nothing was better than the first cookies out of a brand-new bag. She grabbed it and the Jameson and carried them both to the living room. Whiskey and cookies, a match made in heaven. She might even binge-eat the whole, freakin' bag.

She'd turned her phone off, in no mood to field a call from anyone. Especially Dobby. She wouldn't like what he'd have to say or the way those words would make her feel—like she was being unreasonable, like she was in the wrong.

Checking it now, she saw she had several messages, one was from Rick. A lump in her throat, she hit play.

"Quinn, it's Rick. I wanted to let you know . . . Bebe died."

His neighbor. A sweet octogenarian who used to bring them baked goods and who had taken a surprising shine to Quinn. Tears pricked her eyes.

"She, um . . . passed in her sleep a couple nights ago. The service was this afternoon . . . I should have called sooner but I—"

He stopped, choked up. After a moment, he began again. *"She always asked about you. Why you didn't come around anymore. I—"*

Quinn squeezed her eyes shut and waited. Hoping, praying, for an opening. An invitation back into his life.

"I told her you couldn't love me."

Not that she didn't love him. That she *couldn't*. She pressed her lips together to hold back a sound she feared would be a whimper.

"Be well. Goodbye, Quinn."

That was it, then. Another chapter in her life ended. Just like so many other chapters, so many relationships before this one.

She sat, phone to her ear, the sound of emptiness resounding in her head. What was wrong with her? Why did she push away everyone in her life? Why couldn't she compromise?

Fear of loss? Is that why she'd adopted her tough I-don't-need-anybody persona? To push people away? Keep them at a safe distance? After all, it was hard to get hurt if no one got close.

Is it why she'd pushed Rick away?

She felt weird. Like her every nerve ending was humming and all five senses were set on hyper-alert. Like she was awaking from a long, deep sleep.

She jumped to her feet and ran to the bathroom. There, she washed her face and brushed her teeth, splashed water in her pits, rolled on deodorant, then did her best to tame her wild hair. From there, she headed to the bedroom, changed into a fresh button up shirt and her favorite jeans.

Grabbing her purse and phone, she exited the house and ran to her car, feeling as if she had wings on her feet.

She didn't want to feel that old way anymore. She didn't want to be alone.

She wanted Rick.

FIFTY-EIGHT

10:30 P.M.

Rick lived Uptown on a shady side street in a renovated camelback painted egg-yolk yellow. The porch was wide and shaded; it smelled of the nearby neighbor's wisteria bush. When Quinn rang the bell, Moxie, Rick's ninety-pound Golden Retriever, began to bark.

The barking seemed to go forever, then she heard him hush her—or try to—and Quinn's heart performed a funny, little acrobatic move in her chest.

No backing out now.

Not that she wanted to. She'd never wanted to be anywhere as much as she wanted to be standing here now.

He opened the door. She'd awakened him. His hair was a mess and his jeans and shirt were rumpled, as if he had grabbed them from the floor, chair or wherever he had dropped them before climbing into bed. His feet were bare, and he was wearing his emergency glasses, the funny ones with the clunky frames.

In the next instant, Moxie pushed her way past him and nearly knocked her down in excitement.

Quinn dropped to her knees and hugged her. "Sweet, sweet girl, I missed you!" The dog immediately rolled onto her back for belly rubs. Quinn complied and Moxie went spastic with delight.

Quinn glanced up and caught Rick looking at her with so much regret it hurt. She gave the dog a couple last pets and stood back up.

"Hello, Rick," she managed around her wildly beating heart.

Wariness came over his expression. "Hey."

"I got your message about Bebe. I'm so sorry."

"Yeah, me too."

She realized her hands were shaking and slipped them in in her pockets. "I know I could have texted, but I . . . I wanted—"

She stopped. He didn't help her out, only lifted his eyebrows slightly, expression otherwise impassive.

He wasn't going to make this easy for her. She didn't blame him. "Some things have happened recently, to me, and I need . . . wanted, to share them with you."

He waited, refusing to reveal even a hint of his thoughts. Did he hate her now? Had he met someone else? Or had he decided that she wasn't worth the trouble?

"What I've realized, through these things that happened—" Quinn stopped. Why hadn't she prepared what she was going to say? She wouldn't be standing here stammering like a crazy person.

Instead, she opened her mouth and the words spilled out, raw and unfiltered. "I'm so lost, Rick. I pushed you away, hell, I push everyone away, and I don't know why." With the words came tears. "I don't want to be that person, Rick. I want to be happy . . . why won't I let myself be happy?"

She swiped at the tears. "I miss you. I miss us. The truth is . . . *you* make me happy, Rick. In a way no one else does. That's all I've got . . ." She searched his gaze. "Is it enough?"

One second became two. Not even a glimmer of emotion crossed his face. She wondered if she would ever breathe again. Then he held out his hand and smiled. "What do you think?"

She took it and he led her inside and to his bed. There, they made love. Quinn clung to him. Each stroke, each kiss or caress, she wanted to take deeper and last forever.

His body, against and in hers, fit perfectly. As if they had been made for each other, or were a lost part of the other, joined again at long last.

The final piece of a puzzle snapping into place.

Had she ever before been all in? She was now, she acknowledged, arching up, crying out in a shattering orgasm.

He caught her cry with his mouth, meeting her release with his own until they both stilled save for their ragged breath and wildly beating hearts.

Moments of silence ticked past, becoming minutes.

She curled up next to him, loving the feel of his naked body against hers. "I missed this," she said softly, propping herself up on an elbow to look at him. "More than I even realized."

"I missed *you*."

She drank him in. How could she have let him go? Now she'd fight to keep him.

"What?" he asked, trying to stifle a yawn and failing miserably.

"I'm sorry I woke you up."

His lips lifted. "I'm not."

"Are you sure you want to do this?'

His eyes creased at the corners. "This? Seriously?"

She laughed. "Not *this*. Me. I'm the same hot mess I was before."

"Hot for sure."

She pinched him. "I'm being serious here."

"Me, too." He eased onto his side, so they lay face-to-face. "What's been going on with you?"

"What do you mean?"

"You obviously had some sort of epiphany. You said, and I quote —some things had happened recently—as if those things had propelled you to my front door."

Quinn liked the way he traced lazy figure eights on her hip, not even aware he was doing it. "It's a long story."

"I have all night."

Her stomach growled and he grinned. "How about you tell me over a snack?"

He threw on a pair of sweatpants and tossed her one of his old workout jerseys. "I'll go see what I can scrounge up."

A couple minutes later, she joined him in the kitchen. He stood in front of the refrigerator, freezer door open and looked over his shoulder at her when she entered the room. "How about leftover pizza and ice cream?"

"What kind do you have?"

"The pizza or ice cream?"

"Both."

"Pepperoni and either—" He held up the two pints. "—Ben & Jerry's Cookies and Cream or Peanut Butter Cup."

"Yes."

He laughed. "All three then. Good choice."

Quinn knew his kitchen well and helped him gather the things they'd need. They sat across from each other at his reclaimed cypress table, reheated pizza and two pints of ice cream between them. Quinn reached around the pizza to snag the pint of the Peanut Butter Cup, sticking a spoon into it, then making an "Mmm" sound as the rich, sweet concoction melted on her tongue.

"Typical Quinn," he said, "going for the sweets first."

"I'm eating the whole pint," she said. "Don't try to stop me."

"Fat chance of that." He got a spoon and reached for the other flavor. "I'd rather join you." He took a spoonful. "Damn, that's good."

"I know, right?" She helped herself again, then nudged her carton his way. "Try this one."

He did, made a sound of approval, then slid the Cookies & Cream across. "Talk to me," he said, licking his spoon.

She began, starting with finding the flyer tucked under her windshield wiper and Mikey's call to tell her about the writer who had approached him about the Hudson case, and finishing with Eden's

DNA test coming back negative and Charles Hudson's demand for a face-to-face apology.

Through it all, he simply listened, nodding occasionally, stopping her only once, for clarification. When she stopped, he laid down his spoon. "What are you most upset about?"

She thought a moment. There were several items on that list: Eden's betrayal, the Chief's pandering to wealth and influence, her captain's refusal to stand up for her, Dobby's failure to fully have her back. Herself for being drawn into the whole damn thing. None of those accurately answered his question.

"Not restoring my dad's reputation. I wanted everyone to know . . . no, I wanted it to go on record, that he was right not to let the case go."

A knot of tears caught in her throat, and she swallowed hard. "That would have been his happy ending. He deserved it."

"It still could be."

"I'm done. With Eden Riley, the Hudson case and if I don't plead forgiveness from King Hudson, my career as well."

The bitterness in her voice made her cringe but Rick seemed unaffected by it. He looked her square in the eyes. "It takes two, Quinn."

Her brow furrowed. "What does that mean?"

"The most obvious thing of all." He leaned slightly forward. "Maybe Grace wasn't Bill Hudson's child?"

Quinn sat back, shook her head. "Cynthia wasn't having an affair."

"How do you know?"

"Because during the investigation her every move prior to her murder underwent intense scrutiny, and there wasn't even a whisper of her being unfaithful. Bill, yes. Not her."

He lifted a shoulder. "You say the thing that's most important to you is restoring your dad's good name, so maybe taking another look at that is worth a try?"

She gazed at him, dumbfounded. Awed, and completely head-over-heels infatuated. She stood, went around the table and held out her hand. He took it and she pulled him up and against her chest. Cupping his face in her hands, she gave him a long, deep, sticky kiss.

She ended it but didn't drop her hands. "Do you have any idea how sexy you are to me right now?"

A smile touched his mouth. "I'm not sure I do. Maybe you better show me?"

FIFTY-NINE

7:50 A.M. *Saturday*

Quinn stood in Rick's bedroom doorway, watching him sleep, cup of coffee cradled between her palms. She'd awakened early, mind racing with what her next steps would be, and lounging away the day in bed with Rick wasn't one of them.

"I smell your coffee," he mumbled, not bothering to open his eyes.

He had one of the Nespresso machines that took those fancy-ass, saucer-shaped pods. She brought the velvety dark brew to her lips. "God, I missed this."

At that, he cracked open his eyes. "I always knew you liked that coffee more than me."

"You were always the main attraction, but this coffee is a pretty great perk. You want a sip?"

He yawned and sat up, the sheet falling away to reveal his chest. "Sure."

She sat on the edge of his bed and handed him the cup.

"Why are you dressed?" he asked around sips. "It's Saturday."

"I have work to do. Before you say anything, it's your fault."

"My fault?" He handed the mug back. "How so?"

"What you said last night. About my dad being worth me checking out the theory that Cynthia was unfaithful."

"Since you're hightailing it out of here, I'm guessing you have a plan."

"I do. Cynthia had a maternal aunt who lived in the area, I'm going to see if I can track her down. It seems to me if Cynthia had confided in anyone, it would be with her only close family member."

"Just like that, the party's over."

She knew he was teasing, but bent, kissed him and whispered. "It's only just begun."

HOME, Quinn went right to work. The files were gone, but she had the evidence web and her dad's notebooks. Pinned to the wall was a photograph of a woman with a strong resemblance to Cynthia Hudson and beside it the notation: L. Green, maternal aunt.

Quinn collected the appropriate spiral, flipped through until she found her dad's notes about Lynette Green. As she scanned them, she remembered that day. She'd ridden along with him to the interview, to a trailer park someplace on the other side of the Mississippi River Bridge. After the interview, he'd been excited. He'd called what she'd given him a strong lead.

Terrytown, she saw as she turned the page. He'd penned both the woman's address and phone number. Could the number be the same all these years later?

No, Quinn discovered a moment later as the irritated man on the other end of her call told her she had the wrong number. Disappointing but not surprising, she admitted.

What of her address? It was less likely to have changed but still, it had been a long time. She went to her laptop, called up the internet and typed 'Lynette Green Terrytown' into the search bar.

Up she popped, current address the same as the one in her dad's notes. Grabbing her purse, Quinn headed for the door. Being it was

Saturday morning, she was likely to be home. If she wasn't, she would wait.

Twenty-five minutes later, Quinn turned into Paradise Pines mobile home park. It had changed very little and memories of that day—and of her dad—washed over her. The crunch of the gravel beneath the vehicle's wheels, the tall, skinny pines that lined the entryway; her dad's deep voice directing her to keep the doors locked and to lay on the horn if she needed him.

She stopped in front of Green's residence—it, too, appeared unchanged by the intervening years—cut the engine and climbed out of her vehicle. A moment later she knocked on the screen door.

The woman answered, peering through the screen, dishtowel in her hands. "Can I help you?"

Quinn held up her shield. "Lynette Green?"

She frowned. "Yes?"

"I'm Detective Quinn Conners, I wonder if I could have a few minutes of your time?"

At the name, Quinn saw a flicker of recognition cross her features. "What's this about?"

"Your niece, Cynthia Hudson."

She hesitated. Twisted the towel between her hands. "What about her?"

Quinn knew that sometimes you held your cards close, sometimes you laid them all out. This was a time for the latter. "I think her daughter Grace is alive, and I'm hoping you'll agree to help me prove it."

Her stunned expression turned achingly vulnerable. "Is this some sort of a joke?"

"I assure you it is not. May I come in?"

Green nodded, unlocked the door and pushed it open. Quinn stepped inside. The interior was worn but tidy; a vase of fading daisies sat on in the middle of the coffee table.

Green motioned towards the seating area. "You want tea or anything?"

Quinn took the chair. "I'm good, thanks."

Green sat across from her, then realizing she still clutched the dishtowel, self-consciously laid it aside. She cleared her throat. "Are you kin to Rourke Conners?"

"I am. He was my dad."

"Oh." She paused a moment, throat working. "I'm sorry about what I did back then. To him, I mean."

"Recanting?"

"Yes."

"I was here that day," Quinn said, "waiting in the car. He thought the information you shared might be the break he was searching for."

"I'm sorry," she said again.

"Were you lying, the way you said later?"

She twisted her fingers together. "No. Everything I told him was true. Especially the part about Bill being a cheating pig."

"Why'd you recant?"

She shook her head, looked away.

"The Hudsons made you an offer you couldn't refuse, didn't they?"

She pressed her lips together, expression anguished. "I can't say."

"You don't have to." Quinn leaned forward slightly. "I'm not here today to get you into any kind of trouble, and I'm not going to take what you tell me back to my Captain. This is between you and me."

The woman's tired blue eyes met Quinn's. "After I talked to your dad, Charles Hudson's henchman paid me a visit."

"Daniel Shaw?"

She nodded. "He told me if I insisted on 'lying' about Bill, I would regret it. He said Charles had a very long memory. He never forgot and he never forgave, and that he could make my life a living nightmare. Then he offered me five thousand dollars.

"Cynthia was gone, Grace was gone, and I was in a bad place." Tears filled her eyes and her chin wobbled. "I've never forgiven myself."

Quinn thought of her dad, and was unmoved by her tears. Words were cheap. The time had come for the woman to stop feeling sorry for herself and do the right thing.

"In your original statement to my dad, you described Bill as a habitual adulterer. Did Cynthia consider leaving him?"

"Oh, yes. Many times."

"Why didn't she?"

"Because of Grace. She knew he would take her away from him. In fact, he threatened her with it. He said she'd be lucky to get a visit on Mother's Day."

"She believed that?"

"Of course! You know who they are! There's nothing they can't do."

The resignation in her voice firmed Quinn's resolve. Power over the powerless was alive and well, here in Louisiana, but everywhere else as well. The Hudsons were proof of that.

"Lynette, I have to ask this, and I need you to be truthful. It's really important. Was Cynthia having an affair?"

"An affair?" she repeated. "Why would you think that?"

"Because I have good reason to. Was she?"

Her gaze shifted slightly. "She was a good girl, Detective. She wanted to make her marriage work."

"It wasn't working, was it? He was an adulterer and from what I know of him, his character goes downhill from there. She was unhappy in her marriage, she'd thought of leaving him but stayed out of fear of losing custody of her daughter, so the idea of her looking for affection elsewhere isn't a stretch. In fact, I'd be surprised if she hadn't turned to another man."

Green started to cry. "Bill was awful, gone all the time, running around. She was so lonely."

"I'll take that as a yes."

"It wasn't just an affair. She was in love with someone else."

Quinn though of Karlee Painter. "Who was he? What was his name?"

"She never told me."

"Give me a break, Lynette. I don't believe that. She trusted you, her only close relative. She told you everything else, why not his name?"

"It's true! She was so afraid Bill and Charles would somehow find out!"

Which meant Cynthia hadn't fully trusted her aunt to keep her secret. "Was it someone from the Hudson household?"

"No. I asked her that myself. She was adamant it wasn't anyone associated with the Hudsons, not friends, employees or associates."

Quinn doubted that. It would eliminate nearly everyone she came into in contact with on a daily basis. If she had been adamant, perhaps she was trying to protect someone?

"I think it was somebody she knew before Bill. An old friend or even a former flame."

"Do you have any reason to believe that?"

"Because I knew her. That high and mighty life didn't sit with her. She was never comfortable in that house or with those people. She was so unhappy!"

"There wasn't a whisper of her being unfaithful that emerged during the investigation? I'm wondering how that could be."

"I was frightened for her and Grace, but she assured me she was being careful, that she had a fool-proof plan that let her slip away for hours at a time. She would call her personal shopper at Saks or Macy's and have them pick out several outfits for her, charge them on her card and have them waiting. That way, she would come home from an afternoon of shopping with proof that's where she had been. That's all I know, I swear!"

"Why didn't you come forward with this at the time of the murder?"

"I didn't have any proof she was having an affair—I didn't even know his name. Besides, they would have turned her into a slut, somehow made this *her* fault. I wasn't about to let that happen."

"You didn't consider that maybe Cynthia's lover was the one who killed her?"

"I knew he wasn't." Her voice struck a whiny tone. "By the way she talked about him. He was a good guy, really decent, kind to her."

Quinn mentally shook her head at the blind naiveté of it. This "good" and "decent" man had been knowingly sleeping with a married woman.

She'd gotten the first part of what she'd come for—confirmation that Cynthia was having an affair—now she needed to land the second.

"Did you love your niece, Lynette?"

"Of course, I did." Her eyes teared up once more. "Very much."

"And it sounds like she loved her baby, Grace."

"More than anything."

"Then I hope you'll help me, because there's something that only you can do."

She nodded. "Name it."

"I don't only think Cynthia's daughter is alive, I believe I've found her. I need your DNA to prove it."

SIXTY

10:20 A.M.

Quinn exited I-10 at Florida Blvd, which dumped her into her Lakeview neighborhood. Green had agreed to the DNA test. Considering the woman's history, Quinn wasn't going to celebrate until the blood had been drawn and was on route to the lab—but she'd be lying to herself if she denied being excited.

This time, she wouldn't go off half-cocked. Until the DNA confirmed Eden was Cynthia's daughter, she kept this to herself. No Captain. No Dobby. She couldn't have the Hudson's learn what she was up to and scuttle the whole thing.

One step at a time, Quinnie. Methodical. Decisive.

First step, contact Eden.

Unfortunately, she didn't trust her.

The light ahead turned red and she stopped, flexing her fingers on the steering wheel as she waited for the green. Eden had manipulated and lied to her. She was in a relationship with Logan Shaw, whose alliance was with the Hudsons.

But she couldn't do this without Eden's blood.

That wasn't her only conundrum. Captain Franks was awaiting

her decision regarding her apology to Charles Hudson, and she wasn't certain what her decision would be.

Quinn turned onto her street and saw Eden's moss green Scion sitting in front of her house. An interesting turn, she thought, a smile touching her mouth. Convenient as well.

Quinn turned into her drive, cut the engine and stepped out of her vehicle. In concert, Eden stood and crossed to meet her.

As she neared, Quinn realized how angry she still was at the other woman. Need her or not, she wasn't about to let her off the hook. "This is a surprise," she said, folding her arms across her chest.

Eden met her gaze defiantly. "I figured you wouldn't agree to meet, so I took matters into my own hands."

"You're right, I wouldn't have. What do you want, Eden?"

"To apologize," she said, then quickly added, "but not for what you think. What you accused me of doing, I did not do. I'm not a snake, Quinn."

"The kid identified you."

"I *didn't* do it. He was confused or lying. I don't know which or why, it doesn't matter. I'm telling the truth."

"That said," she continued, "I *do* need to apologize, because I haven't been completely candid with you. I kept back information, important information."

Eden was trying to reel her back in, the way she had before; little did she know she was already in— but for a different reason. "Such as?"

"My mom's relationship with Daniel Shaw."

Quinn did not expect that. Her surprise must have shown, because Eden made a face.

"You see why I didn't want you to know? How could she be anything but complicit? At the same time, I feel so guilty because—" She stopped, took a breath. "—it's my fault she's dead."

A car full of teenagers rolled past, music blaring from the open car windows; somewhere on the block a lawnmower roared to life; in the yard next door a group of children laughed and squealed.

Even so, Eden's softly uttered words resounded in her head. "Okay, you've got me. C'mon inside."

Moments later, they faced each other across the coffee table. Eden jumped right into her story, sounding relieved, like she had been holding onto it for a long time.

"I always had a feeling my mom was looking over her shoulder. I don't remember how old I was the first time I consciously acknowledged that feeling, but once I did, it never left me.

"As I got older, I began to question things about her and our lives. Things like how often we moved and the fact she never made friends. I noticed that all the other kids had extended family, aunts and uncles, cousins or grandparents, and I had none."

She paused, running her hand over the nubby sofa cushion. "Every time I questioned my mom, she explained it all away. She grew up in foster care; being a traveling nurse paid so much more; she was a private person and liked keeping to herself."

"She had no other family?"

"None. Except me. She said that's all she ever wanted and all she needed. A child of her own to love and give a happy life."

"Because it was what she never had."

Eden nodded. "You have to understand . . . she was a good person, a great mom. I couldn't have asked for better." She folded her hands in her lap. "But like I said, I had this feeling something wasn't right. I started snooping around, going through closets and stored boxes."

"How old were you?"

"Sixth grade."

"Tough age."

"Particularly tough when you were the new kid in school. Which I always was." She leaned slightly forward. "It was also the age she agreed to no more after-care at school or babysitters to watch over me for the hour and a half until she got home. Which provided me with the time and opportunity to dig around in places I wasn't supposed to."

Quinn understood. She'd done a bit of that herself as a kid.

"The first thing I found was the baby book. Of course, I thought it was mine. After all, it was my name written in the book. I learned I was born in New Orleans, something I didn't know before. Our address, the name of the OBGYN who delivered me, all sorts of details I didn't know. There was even a newborn picture of me, all squinty-faced and red."

She tucked her hair behind her ear. "I couldn't figure out why she had it packed away. Why not share it with me?"

"Where did you find it?"

"Hidden in a blanket on the top shelf of her closet."

"No way you could ask her about it without exposing yourself."

"Exactly. I have to admit, I tried to come up with a reasonable explanation for finding it."

"How about you were cold and needed a blanket?"

"Perfect if not for the fact we had plenty of other blankets in much easier to access places. I knew if she found out what I was doing, she'd find a way to stop me from doing more of it.

"My next major find was a sealed moving box in the attic. It contained photographs, some framed, others in a small album, and others stuffed into a drugstore photo processing envelope. There was also a stuffed bunny with satin ears, a lovey blanket, soft little onesies and bibs, a binky, and a monogrammed bath towel."

As she recounted the items, her eyes filled with tears. "I didn't understand why she had packed it all away. Especially the photos. Why not display them? The pictures she did display were ones of me when I was older. I asked her once why there were no baby pictures of me, and she said they were lost in a move."

"I almost shared the find with her, because at the time I didn't think she'd lie to me. I thought she'd be excited they weren't lost."

"Why didn't you? Besides the fact that she would know you'd been rooting around in the attic?"

"This might sound weird, but I had my . . . fantasies." She looked away for a long moment, expression achingly vulnerable. "Childishly romantic ones about my dad. Who he might be. Was he dangerous? A criminal or maybe someone rich and famous who wanted to take me away from my mother."

Common fantasies of parentless or adopted children. "When did you find the receipts and newspaper clipping about Grace Hudson's kidnapping?"

"That same year. Truthfully, at the time neither meant much to me. I remember being drawn to the kidnapping story because it was so shocking and wondering if mom had known the lady who got killed."

Eden cleared her throat. "High school came along and we planted in Dekalb. Mom did it for me, so I could have a more normal life with friends and dates, the whole high school experience."

"Did you?"

"Yes." She twisted her fingers together. "I loved it. For the first time I felt a part of something. A community, other families, the whole bit."

"You forgot about your suspicions and fantasies."

"I packed them away," she corrected. "I told myself they were silly and childish . . . I guess on some level I didn't need them anymore. I was . . . happy.

"When it came time for college, I chose N.I.U., right there in Dekalb." She laughed to herself. "After moving so much when I was young, I never wanted to leave.

"Fast forward to February of this year. Mom and I would do movie nights together once a week. She'd pop popcorn and I'd bring M&Ms or Twizzlers and we'd have an old fashioned girl's night."

"Sounds really nice," Quinn said, acknowledging the pinch of longing in her chest.

"It was." Her eyes turned glassy with tears, and she blinked against them. This particular night, she was working on the popcorn and I was channel surfing. I happened upon this show about infamous unsolved crimes—"

"The Hudson case?"

"Yes. I remembered finding the clipping and I was . . . transfixed. When mom came out of the kitchen and saw what I was watching, she was so freaked out she dropped the bowl of popcorn. It went everywhere, made a huge mess. She claimed clumsiness, but I saw utter panic in her eyes, and instead of cleaning up the popcorn, she grabbed the remote and switched off the show. But not before I saw him."

"Him?"

"Daniel Shaw. They introduced him and called him the family's spokesperson." She met Quinn's gaze. "The thing was, I recognized him. We'd met."

"You'd met Daniel Shaw?" Quinn heard the stunned disbelief in her own voice. "How? When?"

"I came home from school one day and there was a car I didn't recognize parked in front of the house. There was some guy waiting in the front passenger seat, he didn't see me because he had his head back and eyes closed. He had headphones on, so I figured he was listening to music. I didn't think too much of it and went inside. That's when I saw him."

"Daniel?"

"Yes, but Mom didn't introduce him to me. She was acting weird and told me to go to my room and get started on my homework. She never did that."

Eden took a moment, then began again. "At the time I thought there was something sort of creepy about him, the way he looked at me and my mom. It made me uncomfortable."

"How old were you?"

"It was right after we moved to Dekalb, so around fifteen. I tried to eavesdrop, but they went out on the back porch."

"After he left, I asked her if he was my dad. She acted shocked by the question and denied it vehemently. I could tell he was someone she didn't like, and I asked her why. She responded that she'd thought he was a good guy but he wasn't. Then she changed the subject."

"Did that hold water?"

She shook her head. "All my life, anytime I asked about my dad, she'd told me he was bad guy. Now she was saying it about *this* guy who obviously made her uncomfortable and came off super creepy to me."

"What'd you do?"

"Dropped it. I was sure she was lying to me about him not being my father, but he sort of scared me, so I gave her a pass, you know?"

Quinn did, and Eden pressed forward with her story. "When I saw him on the TV, I realized my mother knew something about the kidnapping, and that Daniel Shaw was involved in it. That's why we were constantly on the move for all those years. It's the reason Mom was so shaken the day he came to our house. She was afraid of him."

"Did you think you were Grace Hudson?"

"I'd seen my birth certificate, my baby things, so no. Besides, really, how could I seriously consider it?"

"What do you mean?"

"I *adored* my mother. She was everything to me. I believed to my very core that the woman I called mom could *never* have anything to do with a murder or kidnapping."

"Until I—" Her throat closed over the words. She forced them out, choked and anguished sounding. "—was standing in front of my own grave and I had to accept that Mom had no right to me, that she was a criminal."

Quinn acknowledged sympathy for the other woman. She didn't want to soften toward Eden, but felt it happening anyway. "After recognizing Shaw on the TV, what did you say?"

"Something like 'Mom, isn't that the friend who came to see you that day?' She denied it was him. Was adamant, actually. We ended up having a fight, something we almost never did. I accused her of lying." Eden sighed. "She lied again by denying that, as well. Which only firmed my resolve to ferret out the truth."

Eden's hands had begun to shake, she clasped them tightly in her lap. "It took me a couple of weeks to make a plan and then screw up my courage. I got my hands on Mom's phone and called him."

Quinn's heart began to thump heavily against the wall of her chest. "You called Daniel Shaw? Ballsy move."

"It was a stupid move. It—" She bit back what she was about to say and drew in a deep breath, then let it out slowly. "I pretended I was Angela and told him I was having second thoughts about keeping silent. I told him Eden suspected something and that she deserved the truth. I figured he'd either confirm what I was saying or think I'd lost my mind."

"He didn't think you were crazy, did he?"

She shook her head. "No. In fact he told me what I was thinking was dangerous. Very dangerous. That the position of the people he'd warned me about hadn't changed; they were still a threat. He said if she told me the truth, she'd be risking my life. Then he asked me how I was doing financially, and if I needed anything."

"He was trying to buy your mom's silence without actually offering you money. Just in case you were recording the call."

"I wish I had been! I never even thought to do that."

"How did you leave it with him?"

"I got scared and I hung up." Her chin wobbled. "I couldn't think, couldn't process . . . Everything I'd thought about myself, who I was, my mother . . . I wondered if it was all a lie."

"You didn't go to your mother and tell her what you'd done and what you knew, did you?"

Eden shook her head. "I'd immediately deleted the call so she wouldn't see it. I didn't know what to do . . . and didn't think that taking time to decide the right course of action would . . ." She let the words trail off, but they hung in the air between them:

Get her killed.

"How long between when you called Shaw and she received that 504 call?"

"Twenty-four hours, give or take."

Quinn visualized the timeline, putting herself in both Shaw's and Angela's shoes. "It sounds to me like Shaw called 'her' back, covering his tracks by using a burner phone. According to the call data, she didn't pick up. My guess is after a couple days, her curiosity got the best of her and she returned his call. You said the call was short . . . five minutes?"

"Four." Eden looked stricken. "He must have brought up that call I made to him and what I said. That means she knew what I did! It explains her call to the NOPD and The Hudson Hotel. The message she left me the day she died, she wanted to talk to me about something. I'm sure that's what it was."

Eden curved her arms protectively around her middle. "You know how I said that when I found my mom shot, she kept trying to tell me something?"

Quinn nodded. "I remember."

"She did, but—" Eden bit the words back and looked guiltily away.

"It wasn't that he had 'found' the two of you," Quinn said softly. "Because he already knew where you lived."

"Yes." Eden met Quinn's eyes again, hers brimming with tears. "She kept trying to tell me *she* was sorry. It was I who should have asked her forgiveness. She was dying because of me. Because I couldn't leave well enough alone!"

"You don't know she was killed by Shaw. Her death could have happened exactly as Detective Rhea believes. None of this is your fault, Eden."

"Then why does it feel like it is?" Tears spilled over and rolled down her cheeks; she brushed them impatiently away. "I miss her. I miss the life we had together."

Quinn reached her hand across the coffee table; Eden clasped it. In that moment, she realized her anger had evaporated, and although she didn't want to feel sympathy for Eden, she did.

They sat that way a moment more, then simultaneously let go.

"I have one more question, Eden. Why didn't you tell the police the true story?"

"What proof did I have? Of any of it? He would have thought I was unstable or a liar."

"Instead, you came to New Orleans to uncover the truth yourself?"

"Yes."

"You never planned to write a book about the Hudson case, did you?"

She shook her head. "Although I've always wanted to write a book, it was a ruse. A way to get people close to the case to talk to me."

"Do you still want to uncover the truth?"

"More than ever."

"Good. Because I have a plan, and it's already in motion."

SIXTY-ONE

"You have a plan? I thought you'd washed your hands of me and this case."

At Eden's flabbergasted expression, a smile tugged at Quinn's mouth. "I do, and I had." She let that sink in, then explained. "This isn't about you or the case, it's about my dad and his legacy. He wasn't wrong and I'm going to prove it, even if it costs me my job."

"How can I help?"

"I made contact with Cynthia's aunt; she's agreed to give a DNA sample."

"Lynette Green? That aunt?" Quinn agreed and Eden shook her head in disbelief. "When I called she hung up on me, so I tracked her down and she slammed the door in my face. Before she did, she told me she didn't want anything to do with the case or the Hudsons."

"She doesn't, but she really loved Cynthia." Quinn paused a moment. "She confirmed what I suspected, Cynthia was having an affair, Eden. It had been going on quite some time."

"An affair?"

"That's why your DNA wasn't a match for Bill Hudson's. He's not your father."

"Oh, my God." She sat back, expression thunderstruck. "Then . . . who is my father?"

Quinn shook her head. "She swears she doesn't know. I'm sorry."

Eden looked crestfallen; Quinn understood why. After wondering all her life who her father was and to have possibility dart so close but prove illusive, must be devastating.

"She said Cynthia was too afraid to say more and that Bill had threatened to take Grace away from her if she left him."

"Then he knew about the affair?"

"We don't know that, but if he did—"

It would have changed the entire course of the investigation. Bill would have become the prime suspect. Everything he and Charles said or did would have been put under a microscope.

Charles and Bill would have moved mountains to keep the secret of Cynthia's infidelity.

"What are you thinking?" Eden asked.

Quinn didn't answer, thoughts whirling, seeing the crime scene as her father had seen it, mentally shuffling through the pieces. She stopped on one. A minor detail from the crime scene, explained away by the fact that Cynthia had been packing for a weekend away with her husband.

The suitcase.

"Oh my God." Heart pounding, she turned, hurried for the study. She heard Eden behind her, calling her name, asking what was wrong. She went to the wall, the spider's web of deceit, unpinned the photo of the suitcase. Turned it over.

Penned neatly on the back: Samsonite, black. 18.5" X 28"

Quinn crossed to her laptop, accessed the internet, googled suitcase sizes. A chart popped up: a case that size was recommended for a two-week trip.

Two weeks.

Quinn turned, met Eden's eyes. "Cynthia was leaving him."

"I don't understand. What—"

"That day. She was leaving him. She wasn't packing for a weekend away with her husband. The truth was here all along, right under everybody's nose."

"You're scaring me."

"I know what happened. Bill came home unexpectedly and caught her packing . . . He realized what she was doing, flew into a rage and killed her."

"Charles said—"

"He lied, Eden. About everything. "Picture this, Bill Hudson, out of breath, stunned and bloodied. Bill realizes what he's done and panics. He knows the consequences of what he's done. What would he do next? He's weak and self-indulgent; he's been catered to his entire life?"

"Run to Daddy," Eden said. "The way he always has."

"Exactly."

Eden swayed slightly. She crossed to the chair and sank onto it. "What do we do now?"

"I don't know. Let me think a minute."

Quinn crossed to the window above the desk, gazed blankly out at the morning. If she went to Captain Franks with this, he'd be more than skeptical. He would insist on passing the information to Tillerson and his team. Lynette Green would most likely deny they'd spoken and refuse the DNA test. Without her, the size of the suitcase would earn nothing more than a 'What woman doesn't overpack?' and a shrug.

She could call Dobby? He would be sympathetic, maybe even positive . . . but he would insist she inform Captain Franks.

Those were her other options and they sucked. Quinn turned away from the window, met Eden's eyes. "We need something besides conjecture, a big suitcase, and the word of a woman with a history of being unreliable."

"Okay. What do we do?"

"We move forward with my original plan."

"Which is?"

"A Matrilineal DNA test to definitively prove you are Cynthia Hudson's daughter. We get that by comparing your blood to that of your maternal aunt, Lynette Green. There are local outfits that can handle getting the samples and sending them to a lab, and I say we do it first thing Monday morning."

Eden let out a pent-up breath. "Okay. Just tell me where to go and what time."

"I'll set it up with Lynette as well. One more thing, Eden, you can't tell anyone what we're doing." She paused for emphasis. "Especially Logan."

Quinn saw resistance creep into her eyes. "He's not who you think he is."

"He's exactly who I think he is. I know you believe you're in love with him, but his allegiance is to his dad and the Hudsons. I promise you, the first thing he'd do is go to Charles or Bill, and the Hudsons successfully bought off Lynette Green before and I have no doubt they could do it again."

Eden lifted her chin ever-so-slightly. "You're wrong about Logan, but if it's secrecy you want, I'll give it to you."

"No word to him or anyone else until the samples are taken and on their way to the lab?"

"Complete secrecy."

Quinn still didn't trust her, but she had little choice but to accept her promise. "I'll set everything up for Monday morning and let you know the details when that's done."

SIXTY-TWO

The waiting was hell. Quinn paced from one end of her small house to the other. She'd called in sick. To avoid talking to Dobby, she text him that she felt like crap and wouldn't be in. Not a lie—that's what happened when you didn't sleep because you were risking your career on a move that was anything but a slam dunk.

She couldn't stop worrying that Lynette Green would get cold feet and back out at the last moment. If that happened, she wasn't certain what her next move would be. Beg maybe.

She blinked and realized she was standing in the doorway to the office, staring blankly at the evidence web. She blinked again and it came into focus, the way a puzzle would after time away from it.

The emerging picture. What was missing? What didn't jibe?

Quinn moved closer. A piece of the puzzle jumped out at her. One that she hadn't placed.

A second photograph of Daniel Shaw.

She tipped her head. Since Shaw was already represented on the board, she had stuck the photo off to the side, outside the confines of the web.

Quinn looked from it to the web, then back, eyebrows drawn together. Why did her dad include a second photo of Daniel Shaw?

It hit her like a shock of cold air.

Because Shaw had played a second part in the story.

She unpinned the photo of Shaw, moved it to the very bottom edge of the web. There, she attached a string to its pushpin and stretched it straight to the center, to original photo of Shaw.

Her gaze jumped to the bright orange post-it. She stared at it, heart thumping uncomfortably against the wall of her chest.

Willow Street.

She was such an idiot. She had realized the importance of the address because of Eden, but her dad would have needed a connection to something here, on this wall.

Someone here on the wall. Someone, maybe, represented not once, but twice.

Daniel Shaw.

She knew of only one person who might be able to confirm her suspicion.

AN HOUR LATER, Quinn parked across Willow Street from Jonah's cottage. He was sitting on his porch, almost as if he'd expected her. She climbed out of the car, and the light breeze ruffled her hair, sending curling tendrils across her face. She tucked them behind her ear and crossed the street.

She'd come armed with a photo of Daniel Shaw, one from around the time of the murder and kidnapping. It was tucked in her purse, and she hiked the bag's strap higher on her shoulder, mentally crossing her fingers that Jonah recognized him.

"Good morning, Jonah!" she called when she reached his gate. "Do you have a few moments to chat?"

Jonah waved her in, his face creasing in a broad smile. "I have nothing but time. Come and sit a bit."

Quinn returned his smile and made her way through the gate and up to the porch. "I hope you remember me," she said when she reached it.

"Of course, I do. We had a chat about Miss Angela and the accident that took her sweet little girl."

She smiled and took the rocker beside his. "That's right."

He lifted his gaze to the heavens. "I thank the Almighty every day that my mind's still good."

"My grandma used to tell me, if I gave thanks where thanks were due, I'd always have enough." She paused. "My mom died when I was a baby and Grandma helped my dad raise me."

"You see, God provides." He smiled serenely. "Have you followed your grandma's good advice?"

She hadn't, Quinn realized. She'd gotten too caught up in her disappointment and grief, too caught up in the day-to-day dark grind of police work. "Not always. Sitting here with you is a reminder that I should."

He rested his head against the chair's high back, rhythmically rocking. "To what do I owe your visit this beautiful morning?"

She retrieved the photo of Shaw and handed it to him. "I was wondering if you recognize this man?"

"Danny," he said, squinting at the image. "I don't recall his last name . . . He lived up the street. Had a handsome little boy."

"He definitely lived on this block?"

"That he did." He motioned to his right. "Up that way."

She said a silent thank-you for the answered prayer. "Do you recall, were he and Angela friendly?"

"We were all friendly on this block. It was different times." He grew quiet as he rocked, as if remembering those days. "I do believe he and Angela were close. He worked a lot and she watched his boy sometimes."

"Do you recall which house was his?"

"Don't know the number, but I can show you."

He got slowly to feet and made his way to the edge of the porch. He pointed. "It's that one there, the turquoise."

"On this side of the street? With the arbor in front?"

He inclined his head. "The arbor wasn't there back then."

"You're certain that was his house?"

His gaze chided and she smiled. "You're right, that was silly of me. Thank you so much. Once again you've been so helpful." She walked him back to his chair. "I enjoy visiting with you, Jonah. May I come back another time?"

He smiled up at her. "I'm looking forward to it already."

With a final wave, Quinn returned to her car.

The question of how Grace had ended up with Angela had been answered— Daniel Shaw—but so many remained.

Quinn thrummed her fingers on the steering wheel. Had Daniel Shaw been the mastermind of the kidnapping? Or a pawn in it? What roll had Cynthia's affair played in her death? And what of her original hypothesis that Bill discovered his wife leaving him and killed her?

Her phone vibrated. Eden, she saw and answered. "Hey. How'd it go?"

"It's done," Eden said. "I'm with Lynette now."

"You're with her?"

"Yes. We're having coffee."

She sounded near tears and Quinn frowned. "You sound upset. Are you okay?"

"Fine." She sniffled. "I've never had any family besides Mom and now . . . I have an aunt and cousins. It's surreal."

She wanted to caution her—that there was a chance it wouldn't prove true, that until they had the DNA confirmation in their hands, it was dangerous to become too attached—but she didn't. To burst her bubble seemed incredibly mean. The future, and any bad news that might come, could take care of itself.

Quinn released a soul-deep, pent-up breath. "That's fantastic, Eden. I'm happy for you."

SIXTY-THREE

8:30 *P.M.*

Quinn rested her head on Rick's shoulder. They sat, curled-up together on his old whicker settee, enjoying the mild night and the star-sprinkled sky. Moxie laid on the patio at their feet and every so often released a soft 'woof' at some creature scurrying up a tree or in the bushes.

"I missed our Monday nights," she murmured. Since he worked weekends, and unless there was something big going on in the city, he took Mondays and Tuesdays off. It had become their time.

"Me too." He drew lazy figure eights on her upper arm. "Tomorrow's going to be a big day for you."

It was. Back to work. Forced to take a stand one way or another.

"Have you decided whether you're going to apologize?"

Her stomach tightened; the peace of the moment shattered. "I haven't."

He tipped his head to look at her. "You love your job, Quinn. You know what could happen if you refuse."

"I do know." She imagined those consequences and shuddered.

He tightened his arm around her. "I shouldn't have brought it up."

"No, it's good you did. I'm so torn. Yes, I love my job and I've worked hard to get where I am, but Charles and Bill, they're bad people. They're guilty, Rick. At the very least, of impeding an investigation and lying to police officers and at worst, of murder and kidnapping. I don't know if I could force the words past my lips without choking on them."

He curled his fingers around hers. "I'm sorry you're in this position."

"What do you think I should do?"

He hesitated, then began, tone cautious. "I can't tell you what you should do, but I can say what I believe the Quinn I know wants and needs."

"Okay." She inclined her head. "Tell me, I really want to know."

"That Quinn wants to live to fight another day, no matter what it costs her."

She blinked, surprised by his acuity. He was right. She'd been focusing on her resentment and wounded pride. She needed to take her emotions out of the equation. Apologizing to Charles Hudson was nothing more than a strategic play in a game she intended to win.

She smiled up at him. "How did you get to be so smart?"

"Spending every night behind a bar you learn some stuff."

"Sounds sexy," she teased as her phone went off. Rolling her eyes at the interruption, she answered, "This is Conners."

"Detective Conners, this is Daniel Shaw."

She sat a little straighter. "Mr. Shaw, this is a surprise."

"I suppose it would be." He coughed; the sound raw. "I apologize, I've been under the weather."

"Nothing serious, I hope."

"Quite serious, actually. Lung cancer." He coughed again. "Hold the fake sympathy, Detective, I didn't call you to talk about my health."

"What did you call me about, Mr. Shaw?"

"I'd like for us to meet as soon as possible. Perhaps first thing tomorrow morning? My home."

Odd. Very. "May I ask why?"

"I have a story I'd like to share with you."

The hair on her arms stood up. She got to her feet, too excited to sit. "A story about what?"

"I think you know."

Cynthia Hudson's murder. Baby Grace's kidnapping. "It'll have to be early, I clock in at 8:30."

"Oh yes, tomorrow's a big day for you."

"Excuse me?"

"You have an apology to deliver."

"I'm not sure that's going to happen, Mr. Shaw."

He laughed, the sound thick and wet. "You are so much like your father. Let's say 7:30."

After giving her his address, he hung up, sounding exhausted. Quinn turned and looked at Rick. "Shocker."

"Who was that?"

"The Hudson family fixer. He wants to meet." She heard the anticipation in her voice. "This is it, the break we've been waiting for. I feel it in my bones."

He cocked his head, forehead creasing. "We've?"

Only then did she realize what she'd said and who she'd meant. "Me and Dad," she said simply. "It's been a long time coming."

SIXTY-FOUR

7:25 A.M. *Tuesday*.

Daniel Shaw lived in a lovely Georgian style home in the posh, Old Metairie neighborhood. The first real suburb of New Orleans, Old Metairie had become so popular in the nineties that wealthy city dwellers had begun snapping up the small brick homes, bulldozing them and building McMansions on the tiny lots.

This was one of those.

Quinn parked in front, cut the engine. She took a deep, steadying breath. Dobby first. Not that long ago he'd warned her to never make him choose between her and his job, and she wouldn't However, she needed to let him know where she was and why. Hopefully he wouldn't need that information, but only a fool journeyed into enemy territory without cluing in the cavalry.

She was admittedly impulsive and sometimes intemperate, but she wasn't stupid.

She accessed her messages and began to type:

Meeting with Daniel Shaw now. His place. He requested the meet. Love ya like a brother.

She sent the message, then took another deep breath and

swung open the car door. She had cuffs and her sidearm in case things went sideways. She was, after all, heading solo into the lion's den. The lion may be old and sick, but he was still dangerously clever.

Quinn alighted her vehicle and headed towards his flower-lined walkway. At the sound of another car door slamming, she stopped and looked back to find Logan Shaw striding toward her, expression thunderous.

"You couldn't leave him alone for one day?"

"Mr. Shaw, your father and I have an appointment."

He reached her, hostility radiating from him. "The man's dying, for God's sake!"

"He called me," she said calmly. "Not the other way around."

He leaned closer. "Bullshit. He was released from the hospital yesterday."

Quinn held her ground despite his being in her face. "He requested I meet him here this morning."

"I spoke with him last night and he didn't mention it."

"Maybe that's because it had nothing to do with you?"

"I want you to leave." He pointed towards her car. "Now."

She didn't budge. "I'm sorry to hear that, but I'm not leaving until I speak with your father."

"Then I'm to understand you're here in an official capacity?"

"No," she said carefully, "Your father called me last night and personally requested I come see him this morning. It was not in reference to any case; he simply said he had a story he wanted to share with me. Why don't we settle this by asking him?"

He flushed. "Fine, let's do that."

He brushed past her and started up the walk. She followed and moments later, he opened the door and stepped into the silent foyer.

"Dad!" he called. "It's me. Detective Conners is here to see you."

The elder Shaw didn't answer, and Logan crossed to the bottom of staircase and tried again. When he still didn't get a response, Logan started up the stairs.

Quinn shifted her gaze left. A library. Books strewn across the floor, paintings hanging lopsided, lamps toppled.

"Logan, wait!" He stopped, looked back in question. "The library," she said.

He turned, saw it too. His face went blank, then tightened with alarm. In the next instant he bolted up the stairs, shouting for his father.

"Logan! It's not safe—"

Knowing she was wasting her breath, she bit the words back and went after him. She found him exiting the master bedroom and caught his arm.

"The intruder could still be here. Let me do a search—"

"Fuck that." He shook off her hand. "If you're so worried about me, keep up."

He pushed past her, going from room-to-room, then back downstairs, growing more panicked by the moment.

She followed, weapon out, covering him. He charged into the empty study. Quinn spotted the blood first, then Shaw, sprawled on the floor, half-hidden by the desk and chair.

Logan caught sight of him at the same moment, a sound of anguish ripping past his lips. Before she could stop him, he was on his knees beside the body.

"Logan," she said sharply, "look at me."

He did, his eyes wet with tears. She gentled her tone. "I'm so very sorry, but I you need to move away from the body."

He blinked. "But Dad, he—"

"This is a crime scene. The only thing you can do for him now is help me preserve it."

He nodded and stood. She took his arm and led him out of the room. "My next step is calling this in. Once done, it's going to get pretty crazy around here and you don't want to be in the middle of all that. After a complete search, I'll need to question you. Is there somewhere you would be comfortable waiting?"

His throat worked. "The patio." He motioned vaguely toward the back of the house.

She steered him in that direction, passing through a large, bright kitchen. From there, the patio beckoned, sunny and green. She opened the door to the bright morning.

"Can I call someone?" he asked, suddenly looking young and lost. "To come sit with me?"

He meant Eden; she knew he did. After telling him he could and that she'd be sending an officer this way as well, she headed back inside, phone already to her ear.

Forty minutes later, Quinn squatted beside the body of Daniel Shaw, Dobby beside her. They had done a complete search of the house; the perp had been highly organized, focused and thorough. Either he had known Shaw had a safe, or had figured there was a good chance of it and had systematically searched for one.

Quinn studied Shaw's wounds. Two shots. Close range. She moved her gaze from Shaw upward to the wall safe. It had been hidden behind a painting of a Louisiana swamp—considering who Shaw worked for that seemed appropriate—and stood open.

They stood. The safe was empty but for three items: a Sig Sauer 9mm pistol, a plastic, zip closure bag containing a clutch of micro-cassette tapes, and beside the bag a device to play them on.

Quinn drew her eyebrows together, looked at Dobby. "Why didn't he take the gun? Thieves love guns."

"My guess is he used it to kill Shaw, it'd be no good to him after."

"That works." She nodded. "He wiped it and left it."

"I'm thinking he found the safe and got Shaw to open it, then killed him."

"Would Shaw have willingly gone along with that?"

"What choice did he have?"

"True." She massaged the back of her neck. "The perp had to have had a gun, so why use Shaw's? If that's in fact what happened."

"He uses Shaw's, his is still clean. Easy."

She frowned. "I don't know. Something doesn't feel right about this."

"Question, Quinn, what were you doing here this morning?"

"Shaw contacted me last night. He wanted to meet ASAP, and we set it up for today at 7:30."

"Why?"

"He said he had a story to tell me, one that I'd really want to hear."

He held her gaze; she saw the condemnation in them. "When you hung up with him, you should have immediately called me."

"I sent a text."

"A weak, cover-your-ass text."

She couldn't deny it and didn't try. "If I'd told you, you would have insisted I talk to Captain Franks, and I knew I wouldn't like what he had to say."

"You have anyone who can corroborate your version of events?"

She couldn't believe he would ask her that. "Really, Dobby?"

"You don't think Franks is going to ask? When you act outside of chain of command, shit happens. You know that."

She did. "Yeah, Rick can back me up. I was with him when I took the call. He heard my side of the conversation and asked me about it after. Satisfied?"

"Rick?" A slow smile spread across his face. "You guys are back together?"

"We are."

"When were you going to tell me?"

"It happened this weekend, and until Mr. Shaw here got in the way, I was going to tell you first thing today."

He pursed his lips a moment, then nodded. "I consider this good news."

"I do, too." She grinned. "Obviously."

Simultaneously, they returned their attention to Shaw's murder.

Dobby indicated the cassette tapes and player. "90s technology at its finest."

"The question is, what did he record that's so important he kept it in his safe?" Capturing the bag by a corner, Quinn eased it out of the safe. Make that four items, she saw as a key that had been hidden under the bag dropped to the floor.

Dobby picked it up, held it out. Attached to the key was a tag engraved with #107. "A safety deposit box key maybe?"

"That'd be my guess." She made a note to ask Logan if he knew about a safety deposit box, then turned back to the bag of tapes. The cassettes were labeled, and she squinted to make out the tiny print. They came into focus and her knees went weak.

"Oh my God."

Dobby looked at her. "What?"

"This tape. It's labeled Timeline/Praxton."

SIXTY-FIVE

1:45 P.M.

"And you disposed of the child?"

Charles Hudson's voice filled the room, unmistakably his. Quinn had listened to him utter those words twice before already, but they still sent a sickening chill down her spine.

"Just as you requested."

Daniel Shaw's voice was just as clear.

"Dear God . . . How?"

That voice was Bill's, tremulous, a man on the verge of falling apart.

"I think the less you both know, the better. Both of you."

"Tell me she didn't suffer . . tell me—"

"For God's sake, Son, pull yourself together! You're the reason we're in this mess—"

"I didn't mean to do it! It wasn't my fault!" He started to cry. *" She was leaving me. For another man . . . and Grace . . . she said Grace wasn't even mine . . . I couldn't . . . I lost it—"*

His voice went from broken to garbled, but he painted a clear picture of what had happened. As Quinn had hypothesized, Bill had come home, found Cynthia packing and they'd fought. Most likely he had threatened her by dangling custody of Grace over her head, and Cynthia had responded by throwing Grace's true parentage in his face. Enraged, he'd killed her.

Quinn moved her gaze over at the group assembled around the table—besides her and Dobby, the chief, Captains Franks and Tillerson and the District Attorney. Their expressions ranged from disbelief to disgust.

"Are you quite done with the melodramatics? You're pathetic. You have so little self-control, sitting there and blubbering like a baby. Do you realize what you've done? Put us, the family, our business, every-thing in jeopardy. We could lose it all."

No words of regret at his son taking not only the life of his wife, but the life of a precious baby he had thought his own blood.

Quinn wasn't surprised. In his notebooks, her father had called Charles Hudson 'the coldest son-of-a-bitch he'd ever met.' Ice cold, she thought. Beyond despicable.

"A thank you would be nice."

A hushed, simultaneous sound of shock and revulsion moved around the table.

"I'm sorry, Dad. You're right." His voice strengthened. *"Thank you for helping me."*

As she had surmised, Bill had run to his father for help. Weak and spoiled; she doubted Bill Hudson had ever faced real conse-quences for his actions. No way Charles would have had him face these, the worst of consequences.

"Toughen the fuck up, son. It's over. Move on."

Shaw spoke up. *"You two dragged me into your mess, you begged me to make this right. Maybe you can stop squabbling and listen to what I have to say? The timeline is everything. Rourke Conners is a top-notch investigator and he's going to hammer us on it, over and over. He's already suspicious. One slip up and we all go to prison. Got that?"*

As they moved through the recordings, a knot formed in Quinn's throat at each mention of her dad, although her pride swelled as the tapes revealed how suspicious he had been and how hard he'd made them squirm.

As she listened, Quinn had to give props to Shaw. From go he'd realized that the two men wouldn't hesitate to throw him under a bus and had planned for that eventuality. In each recorded conversation he had been careful to call both Charles and Bill by name, he worded his every comment deliberately, making it clear who had been in charge and who had been following orders.

Just following orders? Committing murder, tampering with and destroying evidence, lying to investigators. Daniel Shaw had been one hell of a foot soldier.

The last recording ended, and Captain Franks hit the Stop button. A heavy silence fell over the group.

Chief Thompson broke it with one word.

"Unfathomable," he said.

The word rankled. Unfathomable to him maybe. Not to her dad. He had 'fathomed' quite well, and as the tapes had made clear, been punished for it. Sidelined. Stripped of his rank and later, his badge.

Anger rose in her throat, hot and bitter. He'd never given up. Never stopped following his gut instinct about the Hudsons.

Chief Thompson and the administration before him had pandered to Charles Hudson, tip-toed around him because of his position in society and his wealth.

Sickening. The chief should be ashamed. They all should.

Quinn curved her hands into fists, fighting the urge to stand up and give them a history lesson, remind them of their own behavior. Career be damned, she wouldn't be silenced by power, not anymore.

As if he read her thoughts, Dobby touched her arm. A reminder. A gentle warning. He was here for her. He had her back.

His words from the other day filled her head. *"I don't want to do this job with anyone else."*

Sending him a look of gratitude, she relaxed her fists and breathed deeply. Time to keep her eyes on the prize: snapping handcuffs on Charles and Bill Hudson's wrists and making them pay for their crimes.

Her attention jumped back to the table. The Chief was speaking. " . . . keep the full story from the media as long as possible. If you're pressed for a statement, you're authorized to acknowledge Shaw's murder, nothing more. The Hudson family will not respond well to scrutiny, ours or the media's—"

"You're still protecting them?" The accusation passed her lips before she could stop it.

His eyebrows shot up. "I'm protecting the NOPD, Detective. I want to be armed to the hilt with evidence when we confront Charles Hudson. With his army of lawyers and limitless funds, it'd be a fool's mission not to be."

Captain Franks stepped in to her defense. "Detective Conners is concerned that the Hudsons will learn of their coconspirator's death and make preparations that will shield them from arrest."

The D.A. spoke up. "We have enough to charge now, more than probable cause. My inclination is to aggressively move forward."

The chief turned to Quinn. "Detective Conners, what do we know about the key found in Shaw's safe?"

"His son, Logan, confirmed the existence of a safety deposit box. It's located at his father's longtime bank, the Hancock Whitney downtown. The younger Mr. Shaw has no idea what, if anything, is in it."

"Why wait?" the D.A. asked. "The warrant to access will take time and I want this to happen today."

"What do you think, Detective Conners? This is your baby."

Damn right it was. Her baby. Her dad's before her. "We've got the key and the son's permission to access the box, and he has a durable power of attorney over his father's affairs. Draw up the arrest warrant while Detective Dobson and I see to the contents of the box."

"I can live with that," the D.A. said, looking at the chief for confirmation.

He nodded in agreement. "I'll contact the bank president and let him know we're coming and that we'll have the proper paperwork. You're in charge, Conners. Assemble a team, including an evidence tech. I want video documentation of your every move. Let's not give Hudson's legal team anything to latch onto. Are we clear?"

They were and the group dispersed. Captain Franks caught her at the door, took her aside. "A moment, Detective."

She met his gaze. "Of course."

"Is there anything else I don't know?"

"About what, Captain?"

"The solo investigation you've been conducting."

She feigned surprise. "I thought we'd covered all that?"

"I thought we had, too."

Quinn tried not to fidget under his laser focused stare. "As I explained earlier, Shaw called me out of the blue and asked for a meeting."

"And you thought it was wise to take the meeting?"

"Yes, sir. I thought it was important."

"Anything else?

"Only . . . Eden Riley's awaiting new DNA results comparing her genetic code to that of Cynthia's Hudson's maternal aunt, Lynette Green."

"Did you have anything to do with that?"

"A bit, sir."

"That's it? Nothing else you need to share with me?"

"Not quite." At the deep flush that started at his collar and moved up his face, she added, "I did learn, but haven't officially confirmed it via property records, that Daniel Shaw and Angela Riley were neighbors on Willow Street."

He released a long, careful sounding breath. "When this is put to bed, Detective, you and I need to have a long talk."

SIXTY-SIX

The bank manager was waiting for them. Quinn arrived with Dobby, a crime scene tech, and two uniformed officers. The safety deposit box was rigged with a tandem key system and the bank manager assisted her without question.

"If you need anything else, Detective Conners, I'll be right out front."

Quinn thanked him and removed the army green metal box and set it on the center island. She fitted on gloves and looked at the crime scene tech. "Ready?"

He gave her a thumbs-up and activated his video camera. She unlatched and lifted the lid. The first item was large and wrapped in white, butcher-style paper. She removed it from the box, surprised by its weight. Carefully peeling the paper away revealed an ornate, crystal vase.

She immediately knew the significance of the vase. "Looks like we've got ourselves the murder weapon."

Dobby whistled. "Hot damn, jackpot."

Quinn cautiously tilted the vase to reveal what was clearly a partial, bloody handprint, marveling at Shaw's duplicity. Not thirty minutes ago, they had listened to Shaw promising Hudson he had destroyed it.

Dobby obviously remembered the same thing because he quipped, "You can't trust anyone anymore. How disappointing for them."

Quinn snorted, set the vase aside and returned to the only other item in the box—a plastic bag containing a single micro-cassette. She held the bag up by a corner. "Interesting, this one being here and the others in his home safe." She turned the bag to read the label. The blood rushed to her head when she did.

'Plausible Deniability/Conners suicide.'

She knew what that label meant; the truth tore through her. Her knees went weak and with her free hand she grabbed the counter for support.

"What?" Dobby asked.

When she didn't respond, he took the bag from her. He released his breath in a whoosh.

"You don't know for sure—"

"I do know," she said, voice anguished. The camera was rolling; she could not cry, she would not.

She felt like she was dying inside.

"I need some air. Take over."

SIXTY-SEVEN

Rourke Conners
2016

1:10 A.M.

Rourke groaned and cracked open his eyes. The world spun sickeningly, and he squeezed them back shut. A noise. The creak of the loose floorboard in the hall.

Quinnie? He moved his mouth, calling out to her, but no sound passed his lips. Or had it? He didn't know. The tornado in his head drowned all else out.

He groaned again, forced his lids to lift. At his desk, he realized. Head on a photo . . . who?

A shadow fell over him. A sound penetrated his drunken stupor.

Breathing.

"Hello, Rourke."

Not Quinn. No . . . Who? He tried to lift his head but only managed to roll it slightly to the left. A face came into view.

Daniel Shaw.

His blood thundered as adrenaline coursed through him.

Shaw clucked his tongue and shook his head. "Look at you, Rourke. I'm so disappointed at what you've done to yourself."

He bent closer so they were face-to-face. "I always respected you, I want you to know that. Your dedication and perseverance. You're like me, you do what you have to do, no matter the obstacle in your way."

Rourke shouted a denial—it came out of his mouth a garbled collection of sounds.

"What were you thinking tonight? Calling me? Tipping your hand? What kind of cop does that?"

Shaw laughed softly and straightened, moving out of Rourke's field of vision. "You weren't thinking. The booze was."

His gun on the desk. Inches away from his hand.

Move, Rourke. You can do it.

His body responded. His head lifted slightly as his fingers wrapped around the gun's grip.

"Oh, no you don't."

Shaw's gloved hand came down over his, cementing his to the grip. With his other hand, he jerked Rourke's head upright.

"I have to kill you," he said, bringing the gun, clasped in their joined hands, to his temple. "I have way too much to live for and have sacrificed too much to go to jail now."

As the bullet exploded from the barrel, Rourke saw his beautiful Maggie. She extended her arms in welcome and the blinding pain transformed into a brilliant, all-consuming light.

SIXTY-EIGHT

Quinn Connors
Present day

4:10 P.M.

Quinn sat alone in the interrogation room, the micro cassette player on the table in front of her. After listening to the damning recording, she had asked Dobby and Captain Franks for a moment alone to process.

She struggled to breathe evenly, to center herself. Hearing Shaw describe how he'd killed her incapacitated father had been agony. Hearing how her dad, drunk, loose-lipped and overconfident, had recklessly called and threatened Shaw, tipping him to how dangerously close he was to exposing his crimes, had ripped her wide with guilt.

I wasn't there for you, Dad. I'm so sorry.

She choked back a whimper. She would not fall apart. She meant to be a part of what came next, and she wouldn't be unless she convinced Franks she had her shit one hundred percent together.

She had to shift her focus. Push back guilt and pain, focus and direct her outrage: at Bill and Charles Hudson, who had literally gotten away with murder; at Shaw, who took her Dad's life, preying on him when he was most vulnerable. Like the absolute coward he was.

On the tape he'd said her dad had "forced his hand." She heard him in her head, heard Charles congratulating him.

Congratulating? The bastard. And Bill's self-satisfied "Good riddance" made her blood boil. The sons-of-bitches weren't getting away with it. She was taking them down.

Dobby tapped on the door, poked his head in. "She's here."

Eden. Quinn had her picked up and brought in because what was going down affected her. It wouldn't be right for her to hear it over the airwaves or from a reporter at her door.

Quinn nodded and stood. "Where?"

"Interview number one."

She thanked him and made her way there. Eden looked up when she stepped into the room, her eyes wide and face pale.

"Hello, Eden."

"Quinn, thank God!" She jumped to her feet. "What am I doing here? Officers came to my door, said I had to come with them, but they wouldn't tell me why!"

"They were following my directions. I'm sorry you were upset, it was necessary under the circumstances."

She looked confused. "I don't understand."

Quinn crossed to the table, pulled out a chair. "Let's sit down. We need to talk."

"Is this about Logan's dad? Because I already know—"

"Please, Eden. I don't have a lot of time.."

She did. Quinn noticed her hand were shaking.

"I was there this morning." Quinn paused, let that sink in. "With Logan when he found his dad."

Eden's expression went blank. She drew her eyebrows together. "How? Why were you—"

"Daniel and I were set to meet this morning." She shifted the subject. "How's Logan doing?"

Eden blinked against tears. "He's devastated."

That devastation was about go deeper, for both of them.

"I'm sorry for his loss."

A tear rolled down Eden's cheek, she brushed it away. "He's been trying to get more information, but nobody will talk to him. They keep telling him it's an active investigation."

"I believe they're talking to him now." Quinn refocused on what she needed to say, how she would say it. "We uncovered some troubling things at the scene of Daniel's murder. Ones that, if your DNA test comes back a match to Lynette Green's—"

"It will, I know it."

"These things we uncovered, they're going to affect you."

She frowned. "Me?"

"Hear me out, okay?" Eden nodded, and Quinn began again. "We found proof that Bill did, indeed, murder Cynthia. As we surmised, Bill came home unexpectedly, discovered she was leaving him for another man, and killed her."

Eden brought a hand to her mouth. "Oh, my God."

"Charles came up with the kidnapping scheme to send the police looking in another direction. Which was brilliant, after all, who would kidnap their own child?

"Charles knew he couldn't pull it off without help, so he turned to his right-hand man."

Eden opened her mouth, then shut it, as if what she had been about to say no longer worked. "You don't mean . . . You're not saying that Logan's dad was part of it?"

"I'm sorry, Eden."

She drew in a sharp breath. "No."

"Charles brought Daniel in to implement the plan for him. He was supposed to 'get rid' of baby Grace, and to do that he had to kill Lucy Praxton." Her throat tightened, and forced the next words out. "I also learned today that . . . he murdered my father."

Hands clenched into fists, Eden shook her head. "This can't be true. What kind of proof do you have?"

"Incontrovertible, Eden."

Those tight fists began to shake; she lifted her chin in defiant denial. "Tell me or I won't believe you. You're talking about Logan's father."

"I can't share the details yet, but the evidence is rock solid. We're making arrests this afternoon."

"Arrests?" she whispered, her defiance dissolving, eyes flooding with tears.

"Yes."

Eden broke down, her entire body shaking with the force of her sobs. Quinn stood, went around the table and drew her into her arms. She held her while she cried, understanding her devastation. If she could break down, she would. Cry out in grief and despair, for her father, for herself.

But she had a job to do.

Dobby poked his head into the room. "We have the warrants."

Quinn nodded. "I'll be right there. Could you get Ms. Riley a box of tissues?"

A minute later, Quinn handed Eden a tissue, waiting while she wiped her eyes, then blew her nose.

"Are you going to be okay?" Quinn asked.

"Define okay."

"Good point. I'm really sorry."

"That warrant, you're going to arrest them, the Hudsons, aren't you?"

"Yes."

She plucked another tissue from the box. "Does Logan know?"

"My guess is, he does now."

"Can I go to him?"

"I'll get an officer to take you wherever you want to go. Give me a few minutes to arrange that."

She nodded, swallowed hard, looking on the verge of crumbling again.

Dobby stuck his head into the room. "Quinn? We're waiting."

She gave him a thumb's up, then turned back to Eden. "I've got to go, but I'll be in touch."

"Quinn?"

She stopped, looked over her shoulder.

"I hope I'm not her. I don't want to be Grace, her own family cared so little . . . They wanted her dead, Quinn. An innocent, little baby."

Quinn didn't know what to say, so she said nothing. She joined Dobby in the hallway.

He touched her arm, murmured, "You don't have to do this, Quinn. No one would blame you if you took a pass on it."

"Are you kidding?" She looked him square in the eyes. "I wouldn't miss this for the world."

SIXTY-NINE

5:05 P.M.

Quinn and her team met at the main entrance of the Hancock Whitney Center, the two uniformed officers falling in step behind her and Dobby. They entered the building, presented their credentials at the front desk, then accessed a waiting elevator.

Quinn pressed the button for the executive level, then lifted her gaze, watching the numbers climb, thinking of her dad. Wishing she could share this moment with him.

A smile tugged at her mouth. *We did it, Dad. You and me.*

She glanced at Dobby. "You called ahead, let Charles know I was on my way?"

"I did. Spoke with his assistant, Leslie."

"Perfect."

"You're sure you want to play it this way? He's going to think you're coming to apologize."

"Are you kidding? It's exactly the way I want to play it."

The car stopped; they stepped off. At the sight of them, the woman behind the sleek counter looked alarmed. She stood. "I think you have the wrong floor."

"We don't," Quinn said, crossing to her. She held up her shield. "We're here for Charles and Bill Hudson."

"I'm sorry, but without an appointment—"

"We have an appointment."

"You do?" Flustered, the woman looked down at her computer screen. "I don't see—"

"Tell him Detective Conners is here to see him. He's been expecting me."

She looked unconvinced but reached for her phone. "Leslie, there are police officers here insisting on seeing Charles and Bill." She paused, then continued. "Yes, it is Detective Conners. Shall I send them—oh, of course. I'll let her know."

She hung up and turned back to Quinn. "Charles and Bill will be out in a moment. If you'd like to have a seat—"

Quinn folded her arms across her chest. "No thank you."

They only had to wait a couple of minutes. Both Charles and Bill appeared, briefcases in hands, obviously heading home for the day. Or so they thought.

They stopped in front of her; their smug smiles were the icing on the cake of her day.

Charles spoke first. "You finally made it in for your apology. I don't know whether I'm surprised it took this long or that you're here at all."

He was going to be surprised all right. "Maybe you want us to go to your office for this?"

"Not at all. I have no problem with this being a public display. In fact, the more the merrier."

From the corners of her eyes she saw a group of employees stop to see what was going on. "You're sure about that?"

"Absolutely." He looked from her to Dobby, then the two uniformed officers behind them. "I see Chief Thompson sent witnesses along. I appreciate that."

"I'm sure you will. Make certain to tell him when you see him." She paused a heartbeat, then resumed. "I'm sorry for your recent loss. I know how important Daniel Shaw's service was to you."

"Really?" His eyebrows lifted. "I heard you were there. A fact I find highly suspicious."

"Are you accusing me of something unethical, Mr. Hudson?"

"Maybe that depends on your apology," Bill said with a smirk.

She ignored him, kept her focus on Charles. "Did you know that Mr. Shaw had a wall safe?"

He lifted a shoulder. "Why would I?"

"People keep so many . . . unusual things in safes." She looked at Dobby. "Isn't that so?"

"Eye-opening even," he replied.

Something uncomfortable flickered behind Charles' eyes. "What are you getting at?"

She ignored the question. "He had a safety deposit box as well."

"Many people do."

"For their most precious—sometimes most secret—valuables."

He folded his arms across his chest. "What my former attorney stored in his home safe or at his bank has nothing to do with me."

"Are you sure about that?"

He shifted his gaze to the two uniformed officers. "I hope you're taking notes, because Detective Conners seems to be playing games." He looked back at her. "Which I don't appreciate."

"That's right," she said, "you expected an apology. One where I admit the error of my ways and bow down to the mighty Charles Hudson."

"I certainly didn't expect more of your disrespectful behavior. You dishonor your badge, Detective."

A smile touched her mouth. "You know nothing of honor or what it takes to uphold this badge."

He flushed, turned to assistant. "Leslie, get me Chief Thompson."

"Save yourself the trouble, it's not going to do him any good. Not this time."

"Leslie, make the—"

"You see, Leslie," Quinn said, turning to face Charles once more, "—I have warrants for the arrests of your boss, Mr. Charles William Hudson, and his son, Mr. William Beauregard Hudson."

"How dare you!"

Quinn took the warrants from her jacket pocket. "I dare quite well, thank you."

The elder Hudson radiated indignation. "This is ridiculous. On what charges?"

"Murder. Accessory to murder. Conspiracy to commit murder. Kidnapping. You want me to continue?"

Hudson junior moaned. His father shot him a sharp look. "Don't say a word, not one word until our lawyer arrives. This is nonsense."

"Would you like to take a look at our nonsense?" Quinn held out the document.

Not only did he refuse to take it, he wouldn't even look at it. "I'll have your badge before this is over."

Quinn motioned to the uninformed officers. "Cuff 'em."

She shifted her gaze to the clutch of employees looking on, some gaping with disbelief, some with a hand to their mouth, a few others with something akin to satisfaction in their expressions.

Charles Hudson became aware of them, too. A subtle flush crept up his cheeks. "This is all a misunderstanding." With forced nonchalance, he motioned them in the direction of the elevators. "Head on home. Monday will be business as usual."

They didn't move. Quinn could see his stature shrinking in their eyes. He saw it too. With the realization came a whiff of fear, a hint of panic. The world as he knew it had begun to crumble.

A smile pulled at her mouth. He wouldn't be able to buy or bluster his way out of this. Not this time.

"Charles William Hudson," she said as the uniformed officer snapped the cuffs on his wrists, "you have the right to remain silent . . ."

SEVENTY

5:55 P.M. *Thursday.*

Quinn angled her SUV into a parking spot alongside Pour. She cut the engine but didn't make a move to get out of the vehicle. She breathed deeply, once then again. The past forty-eight hours had passed in a disconcerting blur, like a weird, out-of-body experience. She had been in the midst of the fray but separate from it. Untouched. Even the news that her dad would receive a posthumous commendation from the department had elicited no emotional response.

She'd gone through the motions, said the right things but felt . . . nothing.

Dobby had noticed, commented that she seemed off. As had Rick. She'd assured both she was fine. Tired, that was all.

Then why were her hands shaking? She looked down at them curious. Too much coffee, she thought. Not enough rest.

Charles Hudson had retained the top legal defense firm in the south, but even so, both Charles and Bill had been denied bail. The judge cited the seriousness of the crimes, the amount of evidence against the two, and flight risk concerns. Press conferences had led to interview requests and mics being shoved in her face at every turn.

As she had warned Eden, interest from the press had been rabid. Local and regional of course, but the national outlets as well. Quinn expected the attention to become even more intense when they learned that Eden's DNA results had arrived and proved that Eden Riley was, indeed, the missing heiress Grace Hudson.

The test results had arrived that afternoon. Eden had been nearly hysterical—on the one hand overjoyed to know the truth, but on the other, overwhelmed by the weight of the truth, the emotional and spiritual ramifications of it.

When she'd set off from Dekalb, determined to find the father she'd never known and prove he murdered her mother, she'd been armed with pieces of a puzzle that seemed to fit together the way she imagined. Instead, the true picture turned out to be something she'd never imagined—and never would have wished for. To discover her life had been a lie? That the mother she adored had been a kidnapper? Her birth family amoral monsters? With all that, she still didn't know who killed the woman she had called mother, or who her father was.

Wasn't that human nature? Expecting life to reflect our own picture-perfect vision?

Quinn leaned her head against the seat back. She'd hadn't been able to shake thoughts of Daniel Shaw, his death or what he meant to tell her that day.

The need to fill in the blanks and complete the picture was driving her quietly mad. How had he convinced a grieving Angela Riley to take Grace and run? And what of Angela's murder?

Just today, in the hopes of answering that question, she'd contacted Detective Rhea at the Dekalb P.D., sent him ballistics from the weapon in Shaw's safe and Shaw's prints.

It was a long shot—after all, why would Shaw keep a weapon he'd used in the commission of a crime—but this entire case had been a long shot.

Taking one last, centering breath, Quinn climbed out of her vehicle and started toward the bar's entrance. Rick had suggested dinner out. An evening for the two of them, good food, a bottle of fine wine. Initially she'd resisted, then acquiesced, thinking maybe he was right. Maybe that was what she needed—

"Surprise!"

She stopped short. Familiar faces, wreathed in smiles. Balloons. A banner. Everyone was here. Dobby and Cherie. Captain Franks. Mikey and Betsy. Her fellow detectives, folks from the D.A.'s office.

A whiskey was shoved into her hand. Rick kissed her, whispered in her ear. "Dobby's idea," and drew her into the sea of well-wishers.

One drink became two, became three. Quinn made the rounds of backslaps and "Atta girls," hugs and handshakes, toasts, and roasts.

Through it all she held her breath. At least, that's the way it felt. Like she was holding something in, so tightly she couldn't breathe. Her cheeks hurt and she wondered if she stopped smiling, would she shatter into a million frozen pieces?

She didn't know who said it—a comment to the effect that she must be ecstatic to know her father hadn't killed himself—but when they did something shifted inside her, creating a fissure.

Her head filled with images of her dad, one after another: His quick smile, the way he would cock one eyebrow in question or amusement; his voice, the love in it, the rumble of his laughter.

The fissure widened, deepened, threatening to split her wide open. Mumbling something, she started blindly for Rick's office. Inside, with the door locked behind her, the dam broke and all the emotion she'd been holding in came flooding out. A tsunami of grief and guilt.

She sank to her knees, doubling over in anguish. The sound that passed her lips came from the very center of her being. She'd hung up on him. That night . . . she refused to listen . . . and he'd called Shaw. It was her fault . . .

Her dad was dead because of her.

SEVENTY-ONE

10:45 A.M. *Five days later.*

From somewhere in the house, Quinn's cell phone screamed at her. She groaned and crushed the bed pillow over her ear in an attempt to drown out the device. It didn't and she counted the now-muffled rings—

Four . . . five . . . six . . .

Silence.

She eased the grip on the pillow, rolled onto her back and stared blankly up at the ceiling. The night of the party, Rick had found her on his office floor, curled into a fetal position and unable to stop crying. He and Dobby snuck her out through the service entrance and brought her home.

She hadn't left since.

She turned her face toward the window. Judging by the sunlight pouring in and around the edges of the blinds, it was late morning. She wondered what day it was and tried counting backwards, but the days all fused into a fog of whiskey and tears, guilt, grief and self-condemnation.

Her doorbell sounded. Once, then again.

Muttering an oath, Quinn dragged herself out of bed and made her way to the front of the house. Halfway there, a vigorous thumping replaced the bell.

"Open up, Quinn!"

Dobby. It figured. "Go. Away."

He thumped on the door again, the sound mirroring the thunder in her head.

"Either you let me in, or I'll kick the door in."

"You will not. Leave me alone!"

"Test me, Quinn. I dare you."

She rested her forehead against the door. "Please, Dobby . . . go away."

"Can't do it, partner." His voice gentled. "Talk to me, Quinn."

"I can't." She pressed her palm flat against the door. "It hurts too —" Her throat closed over the inadequate words. Hurt too much? It was agony.

"I know this is about your dad," he said softly, tone coaxing. "I get it, I do. You never really grieved his loss. You are now and that's okay, but please don't shut everyone out."

She thought of everyone who'd called over the past days, reaching out, concerned. Especially Rick. He'd called every morning and every night, left food and flowers on her doorstep. His kindness, all of their kindnesses, had made her want to weep. She didn't deserve it. Any of it.

"Talk to me," he coaxed again. "C'mon, Quinn. I've got your back, you know I do."

Tears leaked from the corners of her eyes. "I know you do. It's just . . ."

"What, partner? Tell me. I'm here."

She brought a hand to her mouth to hold the words back. She couldn't bear to say them aloud. Couldn't bear to share her shame.

They spilled out anyway, anguished. "It's . . . my . . . fault . . . he's

. . . dead . . . because of me. I . . . I can't bear . . ." The rest was swallowed by sobs.

"Open the door, Quinn." He rattled the knob. "Please, let me help you."

"I don't deserve you. I'm not worthy of—"

"Goddammit, Quinn!" He shook the knob, then pounded with his fist. "Open this door or I swear to God I'm kicking it in!"

She fumbled with the deadbolt then twisted, the door opened, and she fell into his arms.

"I hung up on him," she sobbed. "It's my fault . . . he was my . . . everything . . . and I—"

He held her tightly, letting her cry, patting her back, murmuring over and over again that it was going to be okay. Little by little, the rhythmic sound of his voice calmed her.

When her weeping quieted, he led her to her couch and they sat, his arm around her and her head on his shoulder. The moments ticked past, turning into minutes.

Finally, she straightened, shifting away from him, mustering the hard-ass persona she relied on day in and out. "Pretty damn rude of you, interrupting my vacation this way."

He laughed softly and handed her a tissue. "Some vacation. You look like hell and smell like whiskey."

"And you look as fresh as a new cadet. Suck up."

He laughed again. "At least I did, until you blubbered all over me."

She grabbed another tissue, blew her nose. "Did Rick call you?"

"More than once. He's crazy worried but didn't want to push you too hard."

Because she would have pushed back, done something she would have regretted. The men in her life knew her pretty well.

She cleared her throat. "Something you, apparently, had no problem with."

"The way I figure, I've earned that right."

He had. One hundred percent. She swallowed hard, not liking how exposed she felt. So much for the tough-girl schtick.

He looked her in the eyes. "It's not true, Quinn. What you said about it being your fault, it's not."

"The timeline proves otherwise." She wanted to look away, to hide even from him, but couldn't. "Dad called Shaw *after* I hung up on him. If I'd listened to him . . . gone over . . ."

"You'd set boundaries with him about his drinking. He was killing himself and you knew the only way to help him was to stop enabling him."

"That didn't work out too well, did it?"

"You were being a good daughter."

"I abandoned him." She shredded the tissue. "What kind of daughter does that?"

"When he called you, he was drunk, and when he called Shaw he was even drunker."

"You don't know that."

"Yeah, I do. Because your dad was a good cop and a really smart investigator. *That* detective would never have done something so stupid, and you know it."

He *was* a good, smart cop. Until the booze owned him. His failing didn't release her from her responsibility.

She hung her head. "I should have been there for him."

"What're you going to do? Drink *yourself* to death? Lay down and die? Is that what your dad would want you to do?"

"Screw you."

He stood. "The truth is, your father killed himself long before Shaw put that bullet in his head. Isn't that why you set those boundaries?"

"Get out of my house." She got to her feet, indicated the door. "Just get the fuck out!"

Clearly unfazed, he made his way to the door, stopping and looking back at her when he reached it. "By the way, I talked to

Detective Rhea this morning; your hunch paid off. Shaw's gun was the same gun used to killed Angela Riley. Yeah, another murder solved because of action *you* took."

He paused to let his words sink in. "Maybe it's time for this pity party bullshit to end and for you to get back to work?"

SEVENTY-TWO

11:50 A.M.

Quinn stood frozen for a full fifteen seconds before she propelled herself to the door and yanked it open—only to see Dobby driving off.

Spitting mad, she ran to collect her phone from the arm of the couch. She punched in his number; he answered almost immediately.

"Pity party?" she all but spat into the phone. "How would you feel if some evil bastard put a gun to one of your parent's heads? Huh? What if you realized you could have done something to stop it? How would you feel?"

"Pretty damn shitty, I imagine."

"You're damn right you would!" She took a breath. "And you know what? You're supposed to be my best friend. You're supposed to understand me and support me. Pity party?" she said again. "You son of a bitch!"

"You're not crying anymore, are you?"

She wasn't, she realized at the same moment she realized he sounded way too pleased with himself. "You were *manipulating* me?"

"Manipulating? That's an ugly word, Quinn. No, I was being honest. Unsparingly honest. The same as you would be with me."

She opened her mouth to argue; he didn't give her the opportunity. "In fact, I doubt you would have waited five full days to let me know I needed to get a grip. Am I right?"

She held tightly to her temper, being fighting mad was so much better than the agony of the past days.

"You there, Quinn?"

"Yeah, I'm here."

"Would you have? Waited five days?"

"Twenty-four hours," she forced out, her grip on temper slipping. "Forty-eight, absolute max."

She could almost feel his relief through the phone. "That doesn't change the fact that I'm super-pissed at you."

They both knew that was a lie—she wasn't pissed, she was thankful.

She couldn't tell him that, not now anyway, because she didn't want to cry. She was done crying. "Was it true," she asked instead, "about the ballistics match?"

"Of course."

"What about a print match?"

"Nada. I think we're good without one."

They were, but it wasn't as neat. "True," she said drawing the word out.

"I hear the 'but' in your voice. What's bothering you?"

"The gun linked Shaw to the murder, why would he keep it? It doesn't make any sense to me. The man wasn't stupid."

Dobby was quiet for a moment. "Maybe he didn't think there'd be any way he'd be linked to a murder in Dekalb, Illinois."

"It's sloppy and he didn't strike me as sloppy guy."

"You're looking for problems, Quinn. Even really smart guys make mistakes. We see it all the time."

He was right, but something still gnawed at her. The tapes, she realized. "Answer me this. Why did Shaw have all but one of the tapes in his home safe? Wouldn't he have kept them together?"

"Easy. That day he meant to tell you everything—except that.

Think about it, he killed your dad, he probably worried you'd shoot him."

"I might have," she admitted. "Still, that doesn't explain the vase."

"How so?"

"Why share tapes with me but not the murder weapon?"

"Maybe an ace-in-the-hole, final bargaining chip he planned to use as leverage to get a lighter sentence? I think you're making this more complicated than it is."

Tension settled across her shoulders and she rolled them. She recalled puzzle building with her dad and trying to jam a piece into an ill-fitting spot, remembered her annoyance and his calm direction.

It's the wrong piece, Quinnie. No matter how hard you try to make it the right one, it will always be wrong.

The tension in her shoulders eased, and she drew a determined breath. "Let's recap: crafty bastard that Shaw was, he keeps a weapon that links him directly to a murder he committed in his home safe, but keeps the one that proves a murder someone else committed in a bank box? We're good with that?"

"Here's what I think," Dobby said. "Shaw wanted to meet with you that morning because he was going to rat out Charles and Bill. He was going to convince you he was telling the truth by playing you the recordings."

"Implicating himself in the process. Why do that? He had everything to live for, why confess?"

"Did he? He was sick, maybe dying. People do selfless things when they think it's the end."

"He wanted to unburden his soul?" She made a face. "I'm not sure he had one."

"This is really bothering you, isn't it?"

"Yeah, it's not reasonable, not for me."

"What are you going to do about it?"

She made a sound of frustration. "What can I do? He's dead and the answers to my questions went with him." She paused, thinking of

Eden, how this news would affect her. "Have you let Eden know, about the ballistics match?"

"It came in this morning, figured you'd want to do it."

Want? No. Feel compelled? Yes. "Thanks, Dobbs. I'll call her now."

"Will I see you in the morning?"

"Monday," she said. "I'm cleared for two more days of vacation and I've got some clean-up to take care of."

"Clean up?"

"Besides returning five days of phone calls and making up with my guy, I've got an office wall in desperate need of spackle and paint."

He laughed. "Have a good time with that. See you Monday."

"See you then."

"Quinn?"

"Yeah?"

"I'm glad you're back. I missed you."

SEVENTY-THREE

12:05 P.M.

Even after Dobby ended the call, Quinn stood with the phone to her ear, his final words replaying in her head.

He was glad she was back. He'd missed her.

Gratitude swelled inside her. Thankfulness. For as good a friend as Dobby. Someone who cared enough, knew her well enough, to drag her back from the abyss.

She released a long, deep breath, one that felt as if it came from her very core. She was glad to be back, too. Not absolved of guilt, but willing, no, *able* to fight against it.

The darkness wouldn't have her. Not today.

She tucked her phone into her back pocket and made her way to the office, to the wall strung with evidence. It started here, by taking down the web, putting the Hudson case to bed.

She hadn't solved the case, but her actions had led to it being solved—and to her dad's reputation being restored.

Thinking of him, pride swelled in her chest. Without his perseverance and hard work there would have been no trail for her to follow. She moved her gaze over the web, taking in all the pieces of what had been a very complex puzzle. She stopped on the very center, the picture of Cynthia Hudson, battered, bloodied and quite dead.

Bill Hudson was in jail, accused of her murder; Charles Hudson was also jailed, accused of being, among other things, his accomplice. She shook her head. Evil, soulless sons of bitches.

You were right, Dad. Your instincts about it all.

Quinn unpinned the photo of Cynthia, laid it on the desk and dropped the pushpin into a container of them. Returning to the wall, her gaze settled on the photos of baby Grace and the empty crib. No longer missing, more justice served.

She removed the photos, carried them to the desk.

The photos of Daniel Shaw were next. His part in this puzzle had been the most profound. He had been tasked with cleaning up the Hudson family's muck. He'd killed Miss Praxton in order to get his hands on Grace. For a reason they may never know, instead of killing Grace he'd given her to Angela Riley to raise, then years later killed Angela to protect their secret.

For the same reason he'd killed her father.

It hurt. She breathed past the pain to move on and forward. If she didn't, she'd end up like her dad, her only companions bitterness and a bottle.

She removed all those photos and more. One's of suspects interviewed and released, leads chased to dead ends, evidence, addresses, names, and corresponding notes about each. With every new hole in the wall exposed, she felt an invisible weight being lifted from her.

Finally, she stood in front of the naked, scarred wall. Done. Mystery solved. The guilty would be punished, justice served. Some justice, anyway. Daniel Shaw would never have to face the consequences of his actions. Her dad could not be brought back to life. Neither could Angela Riley.

She had to call Eden. Had to tell her this latest piece of news.

It would hurt. Terribly. She knew from experience.

Eden had been right about so many things. That her mother had been keeping secrets, that she'd been somehow involved with the Hudson kidnapping, and that she had not been murdered in a botched robbery.

Was Eden responsible for her mother's death? No more than she was—and wasn't—responsible for her dad's. It didn't make it hurt less, but it lessened the guilt.

Her phone pinged a text coming in. Rick, she saw.

Just checking on you.

She experienced a pinch in her chest, realizing how much she had worried him. And how much she missed him. Instead of texting back, she called him.

He picked up right away. "Is it really you?"

"It is. How are you?"

"Better now. You?"

"Same."

"Moxie's missed you."

"I've missed her, too. A lot."

She knew he wasn't really talking about the dog, but neither was she. "I'm sorry I shut you out. I was, am, struggling with some things."

"You ready to talk about it?"

"Almost." She paused. "Just give me a little longer, okay?"

"I can do that. I'm here for you, Quinn. I hope you know that."

"I do and it . . . means a lot to me." She sounded borderline sappy and gave her head a small shake. "Are you at Pour tonight?"

He said he was, and she told him she'd stop by, then ended that call and made another.

"Eden," she said when the woman answered, "it's Quinn."

"Quinn! Are you all right? I've tried to reach you . . . I was getting really worried."

"I'm okay. Getting there anyway. How are you?"

"It's been really hard." She lowered her voice. "For Logan, too. We're working through it together."

Quinn hated to make things more difficult for Eden, but she couldn't keep this information secret. "I have some news."

"From your tone, I'm betting it's not good news?"

"I sent ballistics from Daniel Shaw's gun to Detective Rhea and—"

"Oh my God."

"They were a match to the gun used to kill your—"

"No, please, Quinn—"

"Both bullets came from the same gun, Eden. I'm so sorry."

For long moments, Eden was quiet. When she finally spoke, her voice came out tight. "What do I do with this? Where do I put it?"

"I don't know. I'm sorry," she said again, feeling helpless.

"You're certain? I mean . . . there's no doubt?"

"None."

She whimpered. "I need to go."

"Eden, wait! How can I help you?"

"I . . . I can't talk right now. I'll call you . . . later."

Quinn lowered the phone, hurting for the other woman. It was a totally screwed up situation, but knowing that didn't make it any easier to deal with it. She started to call her back, thought better of it and sent a text instead. She typed, simply:

I'm here if you need to talk.

Taking one last look at the naked wall, she retrieved the plastic bin marked *Notebooks* and carted it out to the living room. She collected the spirals and tucked them into the bin chronologically, the way her dad would have wanted her to.

She stopped on the last, partially filled and dated almost exactly three months before he died. She hadn't even opened it as the proceeding one had devolved into a cross between a personal journal and the ramblings of an angry drunk.

Curiosity got the better of her and she flipped it open. The very first line sucked her straight in.

Quinn asked me to do this. She said I have to. She's right, I know she is.

Quinn realized the conversation he was referring to. She'd told him he had to quit drinking. She'd told him it was killing him—and destroying their relationship.

She read on even though she knew how this story proceeded—with every day the same as the proceeding one. He'd awaken full of regret and recriminations, promise himself he was finally done with the booze, then succumb to the booze, only to hate himself all over again the next day.

The action never changed, but the narrative did. Some days he cursed himself, and his weakness; sometimes he blamed the whiskey, the PD for firing him, Mikey for abandoning him, her for the ultimatum, God.

Sometimes he cried out to his beloved.

Mags, I miss you so much! I don't think I can do this without you. I need you Mags. Why did you leave me!

No matter who he blamed or how he pleaded, the alcohol always won the battle. One drink, he'd rationalize, to take the edge off. That drink would lead to many. She could only guess how many.

Those entries were the most difficult to read. As she read, she could hear his disjointed, slurred speech in her head.

I've los'her, Mags . . . Like I a'ways feared . . . like I d'serve. I'm not worthy t'be her father . . . never'as . . .

G'damn cancer . . . why . . . 'ou, . . . wh—

Quinn swiped the tears from her cheeks, angry at herself. This wasn't the way she wanted to remember her dad, so why was she torturing herself this way? Did she feel she deserved to be punished? Or to be alone and unloved, because that's how he felt?

She didn't deserve that. It wasn't her fault he turned to booze instead of her. Like it wasn't her mother's fault she got cancer and died. It was life, and shitty, goddamned things happened! She needed to get the fuck over it.

She launched to her feet and flung the notebook, Frisbee style, at the wall. Instead of hitting the wall, it hit a partially empty water bottle, toppling it and sending the liquid cascading onto the floor.

"Dammit!"

Feeling like a complete idiot for her temper tantrum, she darted to the kitchen for a dishtowel to mop up the mess. Good thing she was a better aim with a gun than a make-shift Frisbee, she thought moments later, as she carried the wet towel to the laundry room. She dropped it on top of the washing machine, then went to retrieve the offending notebook.

It had fallen open to the last page with writing on it; she noticed scraps of paper left in the metal spiral. A page had been torn out. No, not a page, she realized, looking closer, two pages.

She ran her fingers over the ruffled paper edges, then over the blank page that followed. She could feel the indentations from her dad's handwriting and frowned. Her father had taught her a detective never removed a page from his notebook; that instead, if a mistake was made, he marked through it.

Her mind tumbled back to that day, that lesson.

"Here's the thing, Quinnie, if your actions are called into question, your notes become a form of back up for you. If a page is missing, it can look like you're trying to hide something."

"How would they know a page is missing?"

He'd grinned and tapped the end of her nose with his index finger. *"That's why I always note both date and time on every page."*

Not all detectives lived by rules as strict as his, but he had. She flipped back a couple pages and saw that, sure enough, every new entry listed both the date and time. Even his drunken ones.

Which meant that someone else had ripped out those two pages.

Shaw. Of course, Shaw. Silencing her father had been only part of his mission that night. The other part? Finding and eliminating evidence.

Quinn pictured that night, finding her dad. There at his desk. The empty Jameson bottle, his glass. There'd been a file, open. His head on it, lots of blood. Quinn dug deeper into her memory, trying to recall every corner of the desk.

One of his spirals, yes, also on the desk. Off to the side, out of the path of the blood spray.

Or had it been? She examined the spiral's cover, its sides and back. Sure enough, a few, almost microscopic spatters. She'd missed them before because she hadn't been looking. Neither had anyone else.

Whatever her dad found, he would have noted in this spiral. Shaw would have been rushed, his adrenaline pumping, he wouldn't have taken the time to read every page. Maybe there was more here.

Quinn backtracked and began the notebook again, reading for the thing that didn't belong with his drunken musings.

A name, in the margin. With it a phone number.

Mrs. Marian Thompson.

Quinn recognized the name. From where? She stood, started to pace, thoughts racing.

The Hudson case. On the timeline.

She stopped, squeezed her eyes shut, picturing the web. Early on in the case, yes. With her mind's eye, she sifted through the pieces—names, photos, notes on each.

Mrs. Thompson. Marian. The crime scene, no. Not the bedroom. Nor the nursery. She visualized her dad, descending the staircase. Hudson senior. His staff.

Her eyes flew open. Marian Thompson had been the Hudson's housekeeper.

As quickly at her heart rate had accelerated, it slowed. Quinn closed the spiral and tucked it into its designated spot in the bin. If she had seen the notation and noticed the torn pages the night of his death, it might have made a difference. She might have wondered about it, even followed up.

Useless, old news. The guilty parties were either dead or in jail.

She snapped the lid on the bin. *Move on, Quinn. Time to live in the present, not the past.*

SEVENTY-FOUR

8:35 P.M.

At her first glimpse of Rick, Quinn's heart skipped a beat. He stood behind the bar, chatting with a couple she recognized as regulars. From across the room, she heard his voice and it lured her forward like a siren's song.

This was living in the moment. This was moving on.

She'd gone the whole nine yards for this outing, hair and full make up, skinniest jeans and the V-neck shirt he called "sexy as hell." He caught sight of her, and she saw by his expression that it had been worth it.

She slid onto a barstool and he leaned across and kissed her.

"It's damn good to see you," he said.

"Same."

"Whiskey?"

"Nah. I think I've had enough whiskey to last me awhile. How about a glass of red?"

His eyebrows shot up in mock horror. "Quinn Conners, drinking wine?"

"And a water chaser. With lemon."

He laughed at her request; she at his expression. The night passed like that, the two of them teasing one another, laughing and visiting with bar patrons, sneaking kisses between customers.

Still, every so often, when Rick left to tend to a customer, her thoughts would turn back to her dad's notebook or the gun and tapes in the safe. When she caught herself, she forcibly returned them to the moment at hand, assuring herself it was normal to have difficulty letting go of a big project, and that she wasn't obsessive, the way her dad had become. She reminded herself that he had been searching for answers, and she had found them. Circle complete.

Everyday would get easier, she promised herself.

If only she believed it.

SEVENTY-FIVE

1:55 A.M. *Sunday.*

Quinn's eyes popped open. Instantly alert, she took stock of her surroundings. Dark. No glimmer of early morning light through the blinds. Other than Rick's rhythmic breathing and Moxie's gentle snore, the house was silent.

Same as she had the past three nights, she slid carefully out of bed, grabbing her cell phone from the night table and her Glock from under the mattress. She tiptoed out of the bedroom, earning a single thump of Moxie's tail on the wooden floor.

She closed the door behind her, being as quiet as she could be, not wanting to wake Rick.

Out of habit and an abundance of caution, Quinn did a quick search of the house, found it clear and went to the kitchen. Her mouth was dry, and she poured herself a glass of water, then deciding water wasn't going to cut it, grabbed a spoon and went for the ice cream. A fresh pint of Ben & Jerry's Peanut Butter Cup.

She carried it and her gun to the table, sat and dug in. It was the *whys* that kept waking her. Why did Shaw keep a gun he knew could incriminate him? Why did her dad, two days before he died, write

Marian Thompson's name in his notebook? Why did Shaw keep some evidentiary items in his home safe and others in a safety deposit box?

There were *whats* tormenting her as well. What had her dad written on those missing pages from his notebook? What had Shaw intended to tell her that morning?

She dug out another spoonful of the dessert

For the love of God, Quinn, let it go. It's over, case closed

"You've resorted to ice cream. It must be bad."

Rick. Looking sleepy and more than a little concerned.

"Maybe I just like ice cream?"

He yawned and crossed to the table. "You're up, middle of the night, three nights in row? I don't think so. Talk to me."

She rolled her shoulders. "I need to get back to work. That's all."

He cocked an eyebrow, reached for the ice cream. "Liar. Something's eating at you. Is it us?"

"No," she said quickly. "We're good. In fact, we're great."

He took her spoon. "Then what?"

"It's ridiculous." She stood and crossed to the sink, stared out the window above it a moment, then turned to face him. "I can't let go of the damn case, and it's driving me crazy. I feel like an idiot."

He helped himself to the ice cream. "Which damn case?"

She looked at him, exasperated. "The Hudson case. Of course."

"What's the problem?"

"It's closed. Mystery solved. Puzzle complete."

"Then why can't you let it go?"

"It's a good thing I don't have my gun, because I might just shoot you."

He smiled, took another bite. "I'm being serious. Why can't you let it go?"

"There are a couple things that I'm having trouble reconciling."

"Like what?"

She went on to explain about the gun in the safe, how it defied logic for Shaw to have kept it. She told him about the tapes and the vase, the problem—as she saw it—with the location of the items.

"The man was organized and highly strategic. I don't get it."

"You've shared all this with Dobby?"

"Yes."

"What does he say?"

"To let it go."

"But you can't?"

She glared at him "I think we established that."

"No need for sarcasm."

She pinched the bridge of her nose. "Dobby's right. Even really smart, well thought-out criminals make mistakes, and some questions will never be answered. Like why Marian Thompson's name shows up in Dad's notebook two days before Shaw kills him. It doesn't matter."

He looked confused. "Whoa, back up. Who's Marian Thompson and what notebook?"

Quinn returned to the table. She explained about her dad's notebooks and the things she'd read. When she choked up, he reached across the table and caught her hand. She curled her fingers around his and pressed on, sharing how she found the housekeeper's name and realized two pages had been torn from the spiral bound notebook.

"The spiral was on the desk that night, but I never even looked at it." She cleared her throat. "Nobody did."

"Don't you want to know what was written on those two missing pages and why your dad and Marian Thompson were in contact?"

"Of course I do, but it won't make a difference. Shaw is dead. We know he killed my Dad and basically why. Nothing changes whether I track Thompson down or not."

He was a quiet a moment. "Are you certain of that? Maybe you start sleeping through the night again."

"Very funny."

"I wasn't joking." He leaned toward her; expression concerned.

"You've told me more than once that gut instinct is the best weapon in a cop's arsenal."

"This isn't the same thing."

"No? Why not?"

She made an exasperated sound. "Because there's no case! It's over. Closed. Bad guys in jail."

"One last comment, then I'll back off. We both know this isn't about the case. It's about your dad and what happened to him." He searched her gaze. "Maybe following up on this will give you more closure?"

"The woman would be in her eighties; she could be dead."

"Yeah, she could be."

She was running out of excuses, and he knew it. She tried one more. "Besides, today's Sunday."

He shrugged. "What better day than to pay someone a friendly visit?"

SEVENTY-SIX

"Mrs. Thompson, thank you for taking the time to see me."

They sat at a small bistro table in the woman's sunny little kitchen. It hadn't been difficult to locate her—she was not only still alive but living on her own in a garden home that was part of a senior living community on New Orleans' north shore. As she had explained on the phone, she'd moved there to be closer to her sister, nieces, nephews, and their children. Family, she'd said, was everything.

The woman smiled tremulously. "I've been wondering if someone from the police would come to see me."

For the moment, Quinn let her believe she was there on official business. "Why's that, Mrs. Thompson?"

She'd made them both an iced tea and the ice clinked against the glass as she took a sip. "The news about the Hudsons, of course. Like everyone, I've been completely undone by it."

"You had no inkling Charles and Bill were involved in Cynthia's murder or Grace's disappearance?"

"Oh, my Lord, no! I still can't fathom it. Cynthia was such a sweet girl, always a smile and kind word for everyone."

"I'm wondering, Mrs. Thompson—"

"Please, call me Marian."

"Marian, do you remember speaking with my father? Detective Rourke Conners."

"I knew it! I kept thinking you must be related. The name Conners, of course, but also how much you resemble him."

"Except for the hair," Quinn said with a smile. "That's what everybody says. I got my mother's hair."

"How is he? He came across as stern, but there was a twinkle in his eye that suggested a teddy bear hiding behind that badge."

For a variety of reasons, her father's murder had taken a back-seat to other parts of the story, which was fine with her. Her father wouldn't have wanted that to be the world's final image of him.

"He passed away," Quinn said. "Five years ago."

"I'm so very sorry. He was so young."

"He was." Quinn returned the conversation to the reason for her visit. "Do you recall how many times you spoke with him?"

"Many times over the years, before I retired anyway."

"When was that?"

She tapped an index finger against her lips. Quinn noticed that it was misshapen by arthritis.

"Ten years after the tragedy."

"The murder and kidnapping?"

She agreed. "That's how I mark the past, before and after that horrible day."

Quinn nodded, understanding. She marked hers before and after her dad's death.

"Did you speak to him after you retired? About five years ago?"

The woman looked suddenly uncomfortable. She shifted in her seat, averted her gaze.

"Marian? I have reason to believe you did."

She met Quinn's gaze, hers glistened with tears. "I did. I called him, and we met."

Her voice shook and Quinn gentled her tone even more. "You're not in any trouble, Marian. I'm trying piece together my father's final days. He died shortly after he met with you."

Her eyes widened and she brought a hand to her mouth. "No wonder."

"No wonder what?"

"Why I never heard back from him. That day, he seemed excited about what I told him and promised he would get back to me, but he never did."

Quinn worked to keep her breathing slow and measured, kept her own agitation from showing. This moment was harder than she had anticipated it would be. "What did you tell him that day?"

"That Cynthia and Daniel had been having an affair."

It took Quinn a moment to fully process that information. "You're telling me Daniel Shaw and Cynthia Hudson were lovers?"

She folded her crooked hands on the table in front of her. "Yes," the word came out a husky whisper. "It had been going on awhile. I caught them kissing."

"Did they know you were onto them?"

She dropped her watery gaze. "No."

"You're certain you didn't mistake what you saw?"

"Positive. After catching them that time, I started to notice how they would exchange secretive glances, how their hands would brush. How they found reasons to be alone together."

"You were spying on them."

Her cheeks bloomed an uncomfortable pink. "I'm so ashamed."

"Why didn't you say something?"

She blinked against tears. "Truthfully. I didn't blame her for being unfaithful. Bill was an unkind, selfish man. A horrible cheat." She looked away, then back. "Cynthia was starving for affection . . . and she deserved it."

"After the murder, you still said nothing?"

She tipped up her chin, though it trembled slightly. "I did. I was afraid that Danny—Mr. Shaw—maybe he was involved. I went to Charles and Bill, I told them what I'd seen and what I suspected. They thanked me and said they would take the information to the police."

"What happened next?"

"Nothing, and we never spoke of it again." Anger tinged her tone. "Now I know why. They were all in on it. If I'd taken it to the police instead of to Charles . . ."

"You did tell my dad, you called him all those years later. Why?"

"Out of the blue, it started nagging at me. I saw something in the news, some mention of the crime, and I started to worry that I'd done the wrong thing. I was afraid—" She let out a long, tired sounding breath. "I didn't want to die with that on my conscience."

The information her father had been so excited about. The information that had gotten him killed.

She sighed. "He loved that baby so much."

Her softly spoken words pulled Quinn back into the conversation. "Who? Daniel?"

"No, little Logan. He *adored* her, and Cynthia was so sweet with him. I had secretly hoped they'd all become a family someday." She suddenly sounded every one of her eighty-some years. "Afterwards, Logan was the one I felt most sorry for. Everyone else seemed to move on, but not him. He grieved Grace and Cynthia's loss for as long as I was around. It's no wonder, without a mother of his own."

"I understand she had health problems," Quinn said.

"Mental health," she corrected. "As far as I know, he didn't have any contact with her, poor little boy. Then he lost Cynthia and baby Grace. One can only imagine the emotional toll it took on him."

SEVENTY-SEVEN

1:10 P.M.

Beignet greeted Quinn at her door. He wanted out, and after allowing her to scratch behind his ears, he darted onto the porch and into the bushes. Quinn watched him go, feeling unsettled and off kilter, her jumbled thoughts like the pieces of a brand-new puzzle, dumped straight from the box.

She gave her head a shake, closed and locked the door. The Hudson case wasn't a new puzzle; it was one that had been completed. Thanks to Daniel Shaw's duplicity, they had what amounted to full confessions—the guilty parties describing their deeds in detail—as well as the murder weapon, complete with bloody prints.

Check, double check.

Except if that was true, where did she place this new information? Or didn't it belong at all? Maybe it was part of another puzzle?

Dammit! She made a sound of frustration and pressed the heels of her hands to her forehead. What was wrong with her? Why couldn't she call it done and let go?

Her father's voice popped into her head, something he'd taught her a long time ago.

"Sometimes, Quinnie, it looks like you have the answer, but you don't, not yet. A good detective doesn't cut corners and never calls a case closed just because it's convenient."

At the memory, Quinn dropped her hands. That was it, what had been waking her up at night. She couldn't let go because there were still too many dangling threads. Marian Thompson had added one more.

Another memory popped into her head.

"No picture to follow, Dad? You've got to be fucking kidding me!"

"Language, young lady!"

She rolled her eyes. "You say it all the time."

"I'm not fifteen, you are. Understood?" He waited for her to agree, then went on. "Here's the thing, someday all you're going to have is questions and a nagging certainty that you missed something. There'll be no clear picture that tells you what to do or where to go next. I'm training you for that moment."

This moment, she thought.

"Okay, Dad," she said aloud. "No threads left untied, no nagging questions or ill-fitting pieces. I'm in."

Feeling as he was by her side, Quinn headed into her office and went to work. First, she dumped the contents of the mailer onto the desk and sifted quickly through the items, retrieving the photos of Danial Shaw, Charles and Bill Hudson, baby Grace, Cynthia, young Logan, and Marian Thompson.

Next, she assembled the materials she needed to create the rest of the story: index cards and a black marker, scissors and string, the container of push pins. She rifled through the stack of newspapers she'd yet to recycle and found the one with a picture of Eden on the front page.

She cut it out, laid it with the others on the desk. Another edition of the paper had a published a small photo of both her and her dad;

she cut them out as well. Carrying them all to the wall, she pinned them up in no particular order, then stepped away to study them.

As if he was in the room with her, she heard her dad ask: *"What doesn't fit, Quinnie?"*

"Charles and Bill," she murmured. "They don't belong in this story."

Because this was a *new* story. With new protagonists.

She crossed to the wall, moved the photos of the two men to the side, then returning to the desk and working quickly, she drew a safe on one card, a gun on another. A cell phone. Four cassette tapes, the vase. A building to represent the bank. She tacked them to the wall.

Her questions—the 'whys' that had been tormenting her—came next. With her fat, black marker she wrote directly on the wall:

WHY DID A COLD-HEARTED, MERCENARY BASTARD LIKE SHAW SPARE BABY GRACE'S LIFE?

WHY DID SHAW CALL HER? WHAT DID HE PLAN TO TELL HER THAT MORNING?

WHY DID A CRIMINAL AS SHREWD AS SHAW KEEP A WEAPON THAT WOULD TIE HIM DIRECTLY TO A MURDER?

WHY STORE THREE EVIDENTIARY TAPES IN ONE PLACE, BUT THE FOURTH IN ANOTHER?

She stood back, studying, rereading the questions, *why . . . why . . . why . . .* repeating like a drumbeat in her head, thundering against her skull.

"You've got this, Quinnie. You already know why."

Marian Thompson had told her. Hands shaking, she gathered together the pictures of Daniel, Cynthia and baby Grace and pinned them together in a cluster. The center of the web, she thought. The beginning.

Quinn found the chair and sat down hard. Daniel Shaw had been the other man. The man Cynthia was having an affair with, the man she'd been leaving Bill to be with.

Most likely baby Grace's father.

Quinn stood, went to the wall and with string, connected the cluster to the picture of the housekeeper.

Her mind raced. Cynthia might not have been certain of Grace's paternity, but she would have suspected. She would have shared her suspicion with her lover.

Daniel Shaw hadn't been able to kill Grace because she was *his* child.

Eden's father—a dangling thread, one she hadn't thought mattered.

The magnitude of the discovery settled in, and Quinn's gaze jumped to the photo of Eden and then to the one of grown-up Logan. Her mouth went dry. Eden and Logan . . . brother and sister.

If she was right.

Quinn turned her back to the images. After everything Eden had already been through, how could she deliver this new blow? And although Logan wasn't her favorite person, Quinn could acknowledge his recent traumas. His father's death and learning that the man he'd called Dad was a murderer, a kidnapper, and that he had lied to Logan his entire life.

Quinn recalled her father's notes, that Logan had told him he loved Grace, that he had implored him to bring her back to him. That night at his penthouse, Logan had shared how he used to search the mansion for her.

His little, lost girl.

Goosebumps raced up her arms and she rubbed them. In a way, Logan had always been in love with Grace.

She dropped her head into her hands. How would she tell them?

A sudden realization struck her, and she lifted her hand, turned her gaze to the web, to the picture of Daniel. The moment the DNA test had come back negative, proving Eden was not Bill's blood, he would have known for certain Eden was *his* daughter.

Quinn wiggled her fingers, trying to expel the nervous energy, stay focused. Would he have told Logan? No. Unless he had known they were romantically involved.

She returned to the chair, gaze never wavering from the picture of Daniel. Had he known? According to Eden, she and Logan had been seeing each other for some time. What reason would Logan have had to keep it a secret?

At first, he would have been hesitant. Sure. Eden had been asking questions, rocking the boat. Later, especially with his father in the hospital and maybe even close to death, why wait?

Quinn imagined the moment Logan shared the happy news. Daniel would have demanded Logan stop seeing Eden. He would have made up some bullshit reason that Logan refused to accept. There would have been an ugly confrontation. Perhaps that had been the moment the entire house of lies began to crumble.

What lies could Daniel have told him that would sway his son? None. Nothing would work but the truth.

"Because she's your sister, Logan."

Quinn visualized Logan's reaction. Disbelief. Fury. Maybe even fear. At the thought he might lose Grace again.

"I used to hunt for her, my little, lost girl . . . He didn't know how much I loved her . . .

"He adored her. Called her the most beautiful thing he'd ever seen."

Quinn slid her gaze from the photo of Daniel to the one of Logan and Eden. Together.

A new story. New protagonists.

A new question.

Quinn launched to her feet, jolted forward by the truth. She grabbed the marker and crossed to the wall. On it she wrote in all caps:

WHAT WOULD LOGAN DO TO KEEP GRACE BY HIS SIDE?

SEVENTY-EIGHT

3:00 P.M.

Quinn paced, her heart thundering. What she was thinking was crazy. Wasn't it? Could Logan be so obsessed with Grace that he would kill his own father? His only family? To hold onto a woman he barely knew?

She stopped. Took a deep breath. She had occupied his thoughts and fantasies for years. What he felt for her wasn't rational, but to him it was real.

He'd thought her lost to him forever. Then suddenly, there she was, in his life again. His every imagining come true. No way he would have allowed his father to ruin it by making her aware of their biological relationship.

Quinn turned back to her list of questions; her gaze drawn to the second on the list: WHY DID SHAW CALL HER? WHAT DID HE PLAN TO TELL HER THAT MORNING?

Not, as she and Dobby had theorized, to confess to his part in Grace's kidnapping. No, he'd meant to confess to his affair with Cynthia, and to acknowledge that he was Grace's father.

Quinn nodded, feeling as if a piece of the puzzle had snapped securely into place. He had believed, rightly, that she would tell Eden and the truth would become public—and Logan and Eden's relationship would go from that of lovers to siblings.

She took a deep, centering breath, working to quell the excitement tugging at her. About now, her dad would tell her to slow down. To be methodical and think it through.

He'd be right. She didn't even know for certain that Daniel had been aware his son was dating Eden, but she could easily find out.

Quinn dug her phone out of her pocket and punched in Eden's number. "Hey," she said when the woman answered. "I wanted to check on you, see how you're doing."

For a long moment Eden said nothing. When she finally spoke, her voice was small and choked. "Dealing with everything, It's been . . . tough. How about you?"

"Same. I've been struggling with a lot of guilt." Quinn hadn't meant to go there and cleared her throat. "How about Logan? How's he handling everything?"

"It's been really hard on him, too. We—" She bit whatever she was about to say back. "Never mind."

"No, tell me. The two of you what?"

"We're . . . taking a break."

"You broke up?"

"No! We love each other. It's . . . I needed some space. To clear my head."

"That's understandable, Eden."

"I know you don't like him."

Quinn heard the hint of accusation in her voice. "That's in the past. I was being a cop and he was being loyal to people he thought deserved loyalty."

"Thank you." Her voice wobbled slightly. "I appreciate you saying that."

"I care about you and you care for him. In fact, when things quiet down and you're both up to it, let's all get together."

"I'd like that. I think Logan would, too."

Quinn wasn't so certain about that. "I look forward to it. Before I hang up, I was curious about something. Did Logan's dad know you two were dating?"

"That's sort of a weird question, considering. Why?"

"You know me, forever curious. I would think he'd want to known his son was happy, especially since he'd been sick."

"That's why Logan told him, that last time he was in the hospital. He was afraid he might die."

Shaw had called her the very day he'd been released from the hospital because he was afraid he would run out of time. Noting would have been more important to him than ending Logan and Eden's romance.

"We'd kept it a secret before that, because of his dad's connection to the Hudsons. We worried it would make it really uncomfortable for him. Of course, we had no idea . . ." Her voice trailed helplessly off.

Quinn finished for her. "His true involvement with Hudsons?"

She made a sound of agreement. "They wanted me *dead*, Quinn. It's difficult to think Logan's *dad* was a part of it all. I mean, how do I let *that* go?"

"Don't forget that although he was ordered to kill you, he didn't. Or couldn't." Quinn paused, then took a stab. "Do you wonder why?"

"Even rotten human beings draw the line somewhere?"

"How did he react to the news you and Logan were romantically involved?"

"I wasn't there, but Logan said he was happy for us."

"Considering what we know now, that surprises me."

"It is odd," she agreed, voice small. "Who knows, maybe he thought their secrets would stay hidden forever?"

Quinn glanced over at her emerging storyboard. Eden and Logan occupied the center of this narrative. Who were the other important players?

She was one, certainly. Without her involvement, would Charles and Bill have been found out? Where would Eden be on her quest to learn her true identity?

The flyer, she realized. The breadcrumbs. The attack on Eden.

"Quinn? You still there?"

"Sorry, I was thinking . . . wondering—" She paused as if gathering her thoughts. "Why did Daniel send you the breadcrumbs?"

"Excuse me?"

"The letter with the breadcrumbs, he must have sent it to you. If not, who did?"

For a long moment the other woman was silent. Quinn suspected the question had unsettled her.

Finally, she responded, "No, you're right, it must have been him."

"Why do you think he did it?"

"I don't know."

Eden sounded upset; Quinn pressed on anyway. "It's not logical, is it?"

"No, but he . . . he must have had a reason."

"Hmm," Quinn murmured, "I get the attack. I always got that. The Hudsons wanted you gone; Daniel surely wanted you gone. Why would he send breadcrumbs to lure you to—"

Eden interrupted her, voice shaking, sounding on the verge of tears. "I can't talk about this right now, Quinn. It's too fresh."

Quinn regretted upsetting Eden, but if she was right—and she was certain she was—the other woman would thank her later. "It's the cop in me. When something doesn't add up, I can't seem to leave it alone."

"It's okay, it's me. I feel ridiculous, I'm crying all the time."

Sympathy tugged at her and she backed off. "You've been through so much, I shouldn't have brought it up."

They talked a moment more before saying goodbye. Quinn pocketed her phone more convinced than ever that she was on the right track.

No way Daniel Shaw would have sent those breadcrumbs to entice Eden to New Orleans. Likewise with the flyer—he wouldn't have wanted police involvement in Eden's search. Nor would he have wanted to plant the seed of doubt in her head about her dad's suicide.

Who else could have been responsible? Eden, absolutely, but she believed her denial. Charles or Bill? Laughable. There was no one else but Logan—he'd wanted nothing more than to have his lost girl home again.

Quinn massaged the back of her neck, thoughts still racing. That didn't work unless . . . he knew she was alive and had found her.

She dropped her hand, suddenly remembering something Eden said about the first time she met Daniel Shaw, about coming home from school and seeing an unfamiliar vehicle in front of her house, that there'd been a guy waiting in the front passenger seat; he'd looked to be asleep.

What if that guy had been Logan? What if he hadn't been sleeping and had seen her? Her breath caught and she turned to her own scrawled questions.

WHY WOULD A CRIMINAL AS SMART AND ORGANIZED AS DANIEL SHAW KEEP A WEAPON THAT TIED HIM TO A MURDER IN HIS HOME SAFE?

He wouldn't. She knew it with every fiber of her being. With every bit of knowledge and experience her dad had imparted on her. That's what had been waking her at night, gnawing at her.

The safe and its contents. The gun. It was all so perfect, so obvious what had happened. No cop would seriously dispute that Shaw had been killed in a burglary gone bad.

Same as Angela Riley.

Quinn froze on the thought. A coincidence? Could be, but it didn't feel like it. It felt like something. Something important.

What she was thinking . . . could it be true? Could *Logan* have killed Angela Riley?

Her gaze darted to her scrawled questions, zeroing in on the first: WHY DID A CRIMINAL AS SMART AS DANIEL SHAW KEEP A WEAPON THAT CONNECTED HIM TO A MURDER?

It wasn't his gun.

Overwhelmed by the direction of her thoughts, she strode to the kitchen. There, she poured herself a whiskey. Took a long sip.

"Slow down, Quinnie. Consider every angle, every source."

At her dad's voice in her head, she breathed deeply. Why would Logan have killed Angela? Even as the question registered, she answered it: To set in motion his plan to bring Grace back to him. Angela would have been the only thing standing in his way.

Her thoughts ran one into another. When would he have even formulated his plan? When he learned Grace was alive? When was that? Recently? Or when Eden was fifteen and Daniel had visited her mom in Dekalb?

Whiskey in hand, Quinn crossed to the sink. There, she stared out the window, breathing deeply, consciously slowing herself down. Her dad was right, she had to consider everything. Including her own motivations. She didn't particularly like Logan Shaw. He'd gloated about getting her suspended; she didn't trust him. Could her personal feelings be influencing her?

Honestly, she couldn't deny it. She needed an impartial opinion. Dobby's opinion, she acknowledged. There was no one she trusted more.

He picked up her call right away. "Hey partner," he said. "What's up?"

"That's what I was going to ask you."

"We're on our way to Cherie's folks' house for a barbecue. It's her Dad's birthday."

He'd mentioned that but she'd forgotten. She checked the time. "It's probably going to go late, huh?"

She could all but feel his frown. "For a Sunday night. Why?"

"I wanted to bounce a few things off you."

"What sort of things?"

"I'd rather tell you in person. It's . . . complicated."

"Do I need to be concerned?"

Knowing how he was, she quickly reassured him. "Of course not. I'll be in tomorrow, we'll talk then."

"You're sure?"

By the sound of his voice, he was already worrying. "Absolutely. It was no big deal. Have fun tonight and tell Cherie I said hello."

"Will do. Talk to you in the A.M."

As she ended the call, Quinn made her way back to the office. What did she have that was chargeable? Nada. Even if he admitted to paying the kid to plant the flyer or to sending Eden an envelope containing breadcrumbs.

She'd come off looking like a vindictive cop. Or a fool.

No, she needed to prove Logan was responsible for either his father's murder or Angela's, and right now, all she had was specula-tion. Which was worth squat if she couldn't back it up with evidence.

She mentally sifted through her options. She didn't have many, short of Logan confessing. Except for one—tying Logan to the scene of Angela's murder.

She nodded at the direction of her thoughts. Maybe Logan had gotten sloppy and left a print at Angela's? That would be easy to check. All she needed was a good set of prints to send to Detective Rhea.

A determined smile tugged at her mouth. Maybe the time had come to extend the olive branch to Logan, offer to meet so they could talk it out?

SEVENTY-NINE

Logan had agreed to meet her at Pour at five o'clock. Quinn had overcome his skepticism by claiming she was wanting to put the past behind them, but only for Eden's sake.

Time to alert Rick to her plan. He was already at the bar and she dialed him.

"Pour, this is Rick."

"Hey, gorgeous."

"As provocative as that greeting is, I have to warn you, I have a girlfriend and she carries a gun."

Quinn laughed. "Yes, I do, and I wouldn't be afraid to use it."

"Where are you?"

"On my way to see you. I need your help with something."

"Sure, what's up?"

The light ahead turned from green to yellow, and she slowed to a stop. "I'm meeting Logan Shaw at the bar at five."

"Shaw? Any relation to the Shaw who was involved in the Hudson scandal?"

"Yeah, his son."

"Interesting. What do you need me for?"

"I'm hoping to lift his fingerprints from a glass."

"You need me to collect the glass and set it aside for you?"

"Yup. Will you do it?"

"For you? Of course."

"I hope to beat him there. If I do, I'll sit at the bar. I'll introduce you and order. If he doesn't order something, give him a glass of water."

"Can do."

She heard someone call his name and hurried to finish. "When you pick up the glass, the best way to ensure you don't contaminate his prints—"

"Is by using the cocktail napkin and picking up the glass from the bottom."

"How did you know that?" she asked, surprised and sort of impressed.

"Believe it or not, this isn't my first fingerprint rodeo."

She laughed again. "There's a story for another time."

"It's a thriller, for sure. I've got to go. See you in a few."

Quinn did beat Logan to Pour, but only by a couple minutes. When she saw him, she slid off the bar stool and held up a hand in greeting.

He sauntered her way, as handsome as ever, seemingly unaffected by his recent loss, and looking every bit the man accustomed to being in charge.

Sorry, Mr. Shaw. Not today.

"Thanks for meeting me," she said when he reached her. "I appreciate it."

"You said the magic words, I had no choice."

"The magic words?"

"I'd do anything for Grace, which I suspect you know." He took the stool beside hers, and met her gaze, his intent. "Why am I here, Detective Conners?"

"Please, call me Quinn."

The role reversal wasn't lost on him and he smiled slightly. "Now you want to be friends?"

"As I said on the phone, we can't move forward until we put the past behind us."

At that moment, Rick arrived and set a glass of water in front of them both. He wiped his hands on a bar rag then offered his right to Logan. "I'm Rick, a friend of Quinn's. Welcome to Pour."

Logan shook his hand. "Nice place. Is it yours?"

"It is, thanks. What can I get you?"

"I like California cabs, what do you have that's good?"

Rick suggested several and dispelling her worries that he might refuse a drink, Logan ordered one.

She followed suit, and the moment Rick was out of earshot, Logan turned back to her. "You two an item?"

"If by 'item' you mean romantically involved, yeah we are."

"He seems like good guy."

"He is. A very good guy."

Rick arrived with their wine, then moved on without comment. Logan tasted his, made a sound of approval and turned to her. "Why am I *really* here?"

Knowing 'I think you got away with murder' wouldn't work, she said, "I like Eden, we're friends and I'd like it to stay that way."

"Okay." He shrugged, took another sip of wine. "What does that have to do with you and me?"

"I know from experience that it's very difficult to maintain a friendship with someone when you don't get along with their significant other."

He cocked an eyebrow. "I got you suspended."

"You did—and were a giant jackass about it afterward."

He smiled slightly. "True."

"Here's what I know, at the time you believed your actions were justified. As I believed mine were."

"Turns out you were right. If you want to gloat, I deserve it."

"That's not why we're here. Actually, I'm sorry about your dad."

He made a sound of disbelief. "Sorry he's dead? Or that he was a scumbag?"

"I'm sorry for your loss."

For a moment, he simply looked at her, brow furrowed. When he spoke, his voice was low and vibrated with emotion. "My dad murdered yours, but you're *sorry* for my loss? I'm surprised you're not dancing on his grave. Not only is he dead and his partners in crime in jail, but you and your dad are both heroes."

"You misunderstand. I'm not shedding a single tear for that son of a bitch but that doesn't mean I can't have empathy for you. He was your father, for better or worse."

He took another drink of his wine, looked away.

Quinn leaned toward him. "You didn't know who he really was. *What* he was. None of this is your fault."

"It's hard to get past." The words were clipped, laced with bitterness. "Did Grace tell you we were taking a break?"

"She did."

"Did she tell you it was her idea?"

"Yes, but she also told me she loves you."

He cleared his throat, fighting she saw, to keep his emotions from showing. "She told you that?"

"Earlier today." She paused. "Being with her is all you ever wanted, isn't it?"

"That's a bit overwrought, Detective. Yes, I'm love with her; I haven't made a secret of that."

In her pocket her phone vibrated, announcing a call coming in. "Excuse me," she said, "I need to check this."

Eden, she saw, and slid the device back into her pocket.

"Everything okay?"

"A personal call."

"It's constant, isn't it? Being a cop, crime's steady march, always being on call."

It was the perfect opening and she took it. "Pretty much." She took a swallow of her wine. "I'm curious, we've been sitting here fifteen minutes and you haven't asked about our investigation into your dad's killing."

"No, I haven't." He held her gaze. "Is that a problem?"

"Of course not, but it's . . . surprising. Typically, the family of a murder victim is all over us until we've got a suspect."

"Maybe I'm not typical?" He leaned slightly forward. "The thing is, I don't care who did it."

She arched her eyebrows. "Surely, that's not true?"

"Detective Conners, my dad killed three people. He helped cover up a murder and a kidnapping that broke my heart. He lied to me my entire life. You tell me how I'm supposed to feel."

"I wouldn't presume to, Mr. Shaw."

"Isn't that what you're doing?"

"I apologize." In her pocket her phone vibrated again; this time she ignored it. "Your father was a calculating man."

"Apparently."

"Because of that, there's something I don't understand. Why he would keep a gun that tied him directly to a murder?"

"I'm sure I don't know." He finished his wine and motioned Rick for the bill.

"He was smarter, certainly more calculating, than that."

"You have a theory, obviously. Perhaps you could *presume* to tell me?"

She wanted to. Wanted to lay it out piece by piece, weigh his reaction to each. It would be a stupid, self-indulgent move.

She shook her head. "No theory. Just questions. Lots of questions."

"I'll bite, Detective," he said, sounding bored. "I would hate if this little fishing expedition of yours yielded nothing. What are your other questions?"

"You must have known he had a home safe."

"We never talked about it, but I'm not surprised."

"What of the gun? Did you know he owned one?"

"Again, he never spoke of one, but why would he have?"

"You were father and son, purchasing a firearm seems a natural topic of conversation."

"Maybe for most fathers and sons." Rick deposited the check; Logan reached for his wallet. "Not for us. As I recently learned, he kept a lot from me—like the person he really was."

"You're right, of course. Forgive my bull-in-china-shop techniques."

He laid a twenty-dollar bill on the bar and stood. "See you around, detective."

"Before you go, do you remember Marian Thompson?"

He stopped, turned. "The Hudson's housekeeper, of course. Why?"

"I looked her up. She has such vivid memories of you from that time. Of your father and Cynthia, their relationship." Quinn forced a nonchalant smile. "You know how detectives can be, always following the trail of breadcrumbs."

Something ugly crossed his handsome face and she knew she had pushed too hard. If he was, indeed, guilty of the crimes she suspected, she would have to watch her back. Starting now.

EIGHTY

When she was certain Logan would be long gone, Quinn retrieved her print kit from her car. Rick was waiting for her in his office, glass in hand.

"What the hell was that?" he asked, voice low.

She set the utility box on his desk. "What do you mean?'

"You all but announced you had something on him."

"Just making him sweat, that's all."

"Isn't that dangerous?"

She recalled the animus that crossed Logan's features. "It's the way cop's do it."

"You didn't answer my question. Is it dangerous?"

"I'm not worried."

"I am." Making a sound of frustration, he dragged a hand through his hair. "What do you think he did?"

"It's complicated."

"Fuck that, Quinn. What'd he do?"

"I suspect he killed his father to keep him quiet. Maybe Eden's mother, too."

He stared at her a moment, red creeping up his jawline. "Son of a bitch, Quinn. You don't wave a red flag in front of a bull."

"You do if you're a cop. You want to make them squirm."

"When you have back-up. Not when you're pulling some bull-shit, one-man operation!"

"I had back-up." She patted her side. "Conceal and carry style."

"Although I think your belly band holster is super hot, it's no substitute for Dobby, and you know it."

She did. "I'm bringing Dobby onboard first thing tomorrow."

"Bring him in now."

"He's celebrating his father-in-law's birthday. Besides, Shaw's not going to come after me."

"How can you be so sure?"

"Because right now, he's wracking his brain, reliving his every move to determine his exposure. He's going to realize, as I did, that it's very low. He won't do anything to jeopardize his relationship with 'his' Grace." She cupped his face in her hands. "Trust me on this."

He didn't want to, she saw it in his eyes. She also saw resignation. "You're sleeping at my place. Got it?"

"I do." She kissed him. "You go take care of your customers and I'll see if we got a clean print."

As the door clicked shut behind him, she sat and thinking of her dad, reached for her print kit. Every sworn officer in the department knew how to lift prints from a scene. It'd cost a fortune in manpower to send a crime tech to every two-bit break-in or burglary. Besides, sometimes a situation called for PR prints—ones collected from a crime that wouldn't go anywhere, investigation-wise, but made victims feel good about both the job you were doing and the NOPD as a whole.

She ran her hand almost reverently across the top of the box. It was a plain utility box, beat up from years of use, nothing special about it—other than it'd been a gift from her dad on her fifteenth birthday. That made it special, the most special.

She hadn't thought of that day in ages, but she did now. The memory bloomed in her head in such detail it could have happened yesterday instead of nearly fifteen years ago.

She'd been ready for bed when he'd finally gotten home, looking completely exhausted.

"Sorry I'm late, Quinnie."

"It's okay, Dad." She flipped off the TV, the latest episode of Forensic Files, her favorite show.

"No, it's not. It's your birthday and we had a date."

She shrugged. "Grandma and grandpa took me for pizza. She made a cake. Chocolate, our favorite."

He kissed the top of her head. "I totally suck as dad, don't I?"

"Are you kidding? You're the best dad ever."

"I think your grandma would disagree."

Quinn arched an eyebrow, a mannerism of his she'd adopted. "Then it's a good thing she's your mom not your daughter."

"Yeah, I guess it is." He grinned. "Got any of that cake left?"

"Of course."

While she got out the cake, plates and forks, he poured a whiskey.

"Wait," he said, "where are the candles?"

"I blew them out earlier."

"Too damn bad, you're doing it again. Sit."

She shook her head and took a seat at the table, watching as he placed the used candles on what was left of the cake. One part of her was secretly pleased with the gesture, but the other was mortified. She was fifteen, not a baby who needed a big fuss made over her.

He lit the candles and set the cake in front of her. "Make a wish."

She rolled her eyes but did it, wishing for the same thing she did every year— that someday her dad would be truly and completely happy. Maybe this was the year, she thought, and blew them out.

"Good job," he said, handing her a fork. "Gonna tell me what you wished for?"

"Hell no."

He laughed and took a big forkful of the cake, not bothering with a slice or plate. She followed suit, smiling at how scandalized her grandma would be.

"How was today?"

"Great." She paused to lick some chocolate icing from the corner of her mouth. "Except for school. Complete bullshit. When will I ever need Algebra?"

"You never know. And watch your language."

"Please." She took another big bite of cake. "Besides, I'm going to be a cop like you. Do you ever use algebra?"

He laughed, reached for his whiskey. "Nope."

She indicated the Jack. "Can I try some?"

"How old are you?"

She angled up her chin. "Fifteen."

He hesitated a moment, then nodded. "Okay. Just a sip." He nudged the glass her way. She brought it to her mouth and took a tentative sip. It tasted like battery acid, or what she imagined battery acid tasted like. "Not bad," she lied and took another bite of cake to get the taste of it out her mouth.

"Good girl. No self-respecting Conners doesn't like whiskey. But no more until you're twenty-one." He added a splash more to his glass, then carried the bottle to the pantry. "You ready for your present?"

"Duh. I was ready for it this morning."

He disappeared to the back of the house, then returned a few moments later, grinning from ear-to-ear and carrying a large, sloppily wrapped box. He set it in front of her with a thud. "Sorry the wrapping's such a mess. That was your mom's area."

He said that every time. She had to admit, for a man who was so precise in his investigative technique, he was the absolute worst at things like wrapping gifts or decorating for the holidays. An absolute disaster.

"Go on, open it."

She ripped away the paper—nothing dainty about her—to find a khaki grey utility box. She lifted her gaze to his in question and saw *anticipation in his. Whatever he'd decided was an appropriate gift for his teenage daughter, he was super excited to see her reaction.*

She unfastened the latches and carefully opened the box. She recognized the contents right away. "A fingerprint retrieval kit! No way!"

"It's all professional quality," he said proudly. "The same equipment I use. I thought you were ready."

Heart beating double-time, she reverently removed each item from the box. Two brushes, one fiberglass, the other feather, three different lifting tapes, standard lifting powder, magnetic powder and an aerosol powder, a magnetic powder applicator, fingerprint cards, and even a portable UV light.

"Do you like it?"

Tears stung her eyes and she blinked against them. "Are you kidding? I love it!"

"Good. Because I figured I'd give you your first lesson tonight."

The memory dissipated and she reached for Logan's wine glass and carefully held it up to the light. It looked promising, but the proof was in the finished transfer.

She set the glass back on the desk and opened her kit. In it, she kept everything she'd need to lift prints from a variety of surfaces. For this, she chose the aerosol powder, fiberglass brush, and the polyethylene stretchable lifting tape, best for the curved surface of the wine glass.

After fitting on nitrile gloves, she applied the powder, spun the brush ever-so-lightly over the surface to remove any excess and held the glass to the light.

"Gotcha," she murmured, smiling at the perfect set of prints revealed by the powder.

She lifted the thumb first and transferred it to a backing card; then collected the first through third finger and the partial pinkie in a separate lift. After transferring that lift, she marked each card with the date, Logan Shaw's name, where the print was collected and sat back to admire her work.

They were good, clear prints. Every cop's best-case scenario. All she needed was for lightning to strike with a match on Detective Rhea's end. It was better to have a long shot than no shot at all.

Quinn packed up the prints and her tools, thanked Rick, promised she would see him later and headed to her car. Next stop was the Second to upload the prints and send them to Rhea.

Buckled in, print kit stashed in the trunk, she checked her phone. She had three calls, one from Dobby and two from Eden—with messages waiting. She played back Dobby's message first.

"Hey partner, you sure you don't need me to come by tonight? I could make it about 9:00. Let me know."

Quinn shook her head. He was worrying, of course he was. Knowing he would prefer a text, she answered: *Tomorrow morning is perfect. I'll see you then. Enjoy your evening.*

Next, she listened to Eden's messages.

"It's me. Your call this afternoon, since then I—" She drew in a deep, wobbly-sounding breath. *"—I haven't been able to stop thinking about what you said."*

She paused, sniffling. *"The breadcrumbs . . . I can't think of a single reason Daniel would have sent them. He didn't want me here! Why would he, considering what he'd done—"*

The message clicked off. Quinn's phone automatically skipped to the next message. Eden tear-soaked voice filled the car.

"There's something else . . . When we first met, why didn't Logan recognize my name? After you uncovered everything . . . I asked him . . . he said he didn't. How could he not?"

Eden's shaky voice took on a hysterical edge. *"Logan wouldn't lie . . . I keep telling myself to trust but—"*

She stopped on a sob. *"How could he have forgotten a little girl he knew getting run over . . . how do you block out something like that? He wasn't a baby, he was eight-years—"*

The message timed out and cut her off; she didn't call back again. Quinn checked the time of the calls and messages.

Forty-five minutes ago.

She had to tell Eden everything, proof or not. She was obviously already troubled about Logan's behavior; by staying silent, she was protecting Eden from nothing. She might even be endangering her— she didn't know how Logan would react if Eden confronted him.

Quinn started the engine, backed out of her parking space, then returned Eden's call. It rang six times, then her recording picked up.

"Hi, this is Grace Hudson, leave a message and I'll get back to you. Thanks for calling!"

Momentarily surprised by Eden's use of her original given name, Quinn stumbled over the beginning of her message. "Umm, Eden . . . I mean, Grace, it's me. I . . . sorry I couldn't pick up earlier, I was in the middle of something. I'm available now. Call me back."

Traffic was light and she navigated the city streets with ease. In less than fifteen minutes she reached the Second, thoughts on her next move: Photograph the prints and send the digital files to Rhea at the Dekalb P.D.

She climbed out of her car and hurried into the building. Prints recovered from crime scenes would normally go to the Latent Print Unit for comparison and identification by trained latent print examiners. As these prints were neither recovered from a crime scene nor part of an official investigation, she was going DIY.

Using the unit's high resolution scanner, she scanned the prints, uploaded the file to her Dropbox, then emailed Rhea the link to retrieve them along with a note that read:

Compare to prints from the Riley scene. Daniel Shaw may not have been the shooter.

She started to hit send, then stopped, gaze on the *Cc* address line. Deciding an insurance policy might be in order, she added Dobby's email address then hit send.

Five minutes later, Quinn was back in her car. She checked her phone; Eden still hadn't responded. It hadn't been *that* long since she'd left a message—thirty, thirty-five minutes—but she frowned, suddenly uneasy. Eden had been so upset, so anxious to connect, wouldn't she have called back by now?

She recalled Logan's expression as he left Pour, the naked animosity in his eyes. A troubling thought wormed its way it her head. He'd wanted to lash out at her—what if Eden contacted him? How would he react if Eden shared her doubts with him?

Not well, she had no doubt.

Quinn tried calling again—and again got Eden's voice mailbox. Instead of leaving a message she decided to text.

I'm on my way over. If you're not home, I'll wait. It's urgent.

EIGHTY-ONE

6:50 P.M.

Eden buzzed her up; Quinn found her surrounded by piles of clothes, open suitcases and moving boxes.

Eden stopped what she was doing and looked at Quinn. "I'm sorry I didn't return your calls. It's been sort of nuts here."

Judging by her appearance—hair half up and half down, mascara circles under her eyes, clothes that looked like she had randomly plucked them from a hamper—Quinn believed it.

"Are you okay?"

She blinked, as if startled by the question. "What do you mean?"

Quinn frowned. She seemed completely off. "You called, sounding hysterical . . . twice. Now seeing you—" she motioned the room around them— "and all this, I think it's understandable that I'm concerned."

"Everything's good now."

"I'm glad to hear it. What happened?"

"Logan and I talked. He reminded me about our promise, that we'd never lie to each other." She held up a shirt, examined it then set it on one of the stacks. "That's why I was so upset when you suggested he did."

"I didn't suggest that, Eden."

She stopped what she was doing and looked blankly at Quinn. "Yes, you did."

Quinn drew her eyebrows together, concerned not only at Eden's behavior, but her reasoning as well. "I didn't say Logan lied, I wondered why Daniel would have sent the breadcrumbs. Did you ask Logan what he thought?"

"I did."

"How did he respond?"

"He had a really good point." She selected another item of clothing. "He said we'll never know what was going on in his dad's sick mind."

"That wasn't an answer, Eden. It was a diversion."

"No, he's definitely right, we don't know, and we never will. I've got to let it all go. That's why I agreed with him that we needed some time away."

"From each other? I thought you were already taking a break."

Eden drew her eyebrows together. "We were, but we're back together now. We decided we needed to get away from here and everything that's happened."

Alarm bells sounded in her head, and Quinn breathed deeply, working to stay calm and focused. "Where are you going?"

"His dad owned a house in the Algarve region in Portugal and it's his now. He showed me a picture, it's so beautiful there. It'll be the perfect place for us to recenter our relationship."

Obviously, Logan had either determined his exposure was greater than she'd thought, or he suspected that she'd uncovered Grace's full parentage. He meant to get out of the country with Grace before his web of deceit collapsed around him.

Sorry, Logan, too late for that.

Quinn crossed to the other woman, took the t-shirt out of her hands, then grasped them tightly. "You can't leave the country with him, Eden. There's something you need to know, I learned who your father was."

Her expression went momentarily blank, then realization filled it. "You know who my dad is?"

There were no right words to lessen the shock of the truth, no way to massage this into being okay. "Daniel Shaw was your father. I'm sorry, Eden."

For a full ten seconds, she simply stared at Quinn, then she shook her head. "No."

"He's the one Cynthia was having an affair with—"

"No," she said again, firmly, and freed her hands. "That can't be right."

"I spoke with the Hudson's old housekeeper; she caught them together."

Eden's eyes flooded with tears. "Why are you doing this to me?"

Quinn pressed on. "I found her name in my dad's final notebook, a notation made right before his death, so I called her. Believe me I was as stunned as you are."

"I need to sit down." She cleared a space on the couch and sank onto it. After a moment, she looked back up at Quinn. "This can't be happening."

"I'm sorry."

"How long . . . have you known?"

"Just this morning."

"This morning?" Her brow furrowed. "We . . . talked this afternoon, why didn't you say anything then?"

"Say anything about what?"

At Logan's voice, Quinn turned. He stood in the doorway, keys dangling from one hand and Rock-n-Sake take-out bag in the other.

Eden launched to her feet. "Did you know?"

He stopped halfway to the kitchen. "Know what, baby?"

"About your dad and . . . Cynthia. That they were . . . that we're brother and—" She choked on the last, unable to even say it.

"What are you talking about?"

Quinn answered for her. "She's talking about the fact that your dad was the man having an affair with Cynthia. Bill didn't father Grace, your dad did."

"That's ridiculous."

"Is it?" Quinn took a step, inserting herself between them. "Your dad had constant access to the mansion, no questions asked. Cynthia was lonely, your dad was single, charming and like you, handsome. They were together a lot, weren't they?"

"It's not true, is it?" Eden's expression was heartbreakingly hopeful.

"No, baby, it's not. I was there, I would have known if they were involved." He held out his arms. "Come here, sweetheart. She's trying to tear us apart."

Eden ran to him and he enfolded her in his arms. "Why would you hurt her this way? You're sick."

"Marian Thompson, remember? I told you I spoke with her. She caught your dad and Cynthia together."

"She must be what, ninety? And you're going to take her word about something that happened almost thirty years ago? Why are you so desperate to break us up?"

Eden looked at her, expression hurt. Accusing.

She was losing her, Quinn realized. She had to plant at least one seed of doubt about Logan.

"You're right," she said evenly, "why would I take her at her word? Why should you? A simple blood test would prove definitively, one way or another, if you two are siblings." She looked directly at Eden. "Wouldn't you like that reassurance?"

Logan answered for her. "She doesn't need it. She believes in me and in us."

"Is that why you decided to whisk her out of the country at a moment's notice? Or were you afraid all your secrets were about to be revealed, and when they were you'd lose her?"

"Enough!" Eden cried. "I don't know why you hate him so much—"

"I don't hate him, I'm trying to protect you!"

Logan laughed, the sound hard. "From who, Detective? The man willing to die for her? The man who would put her before everyone and everything?"

"Before everyone," she shot back. "Even your father, right? To keep him quiet, you killed him."

"Don't listen to her," Logan said gently, turning Eden to face him. "She's pathetic and jealous of what we have. Our flight leaves in three hours, we have to go."

If she tried to physically restrain either of them, Quinn knew, she would put herself in professional and legal jeopardy. The only weapon she had was the truth . . . and her willingness to speak it.

"When you told your father about the two of you, that's when he spilled the beans, isn't it? After he'd thrown out a bunch of reasons you shouldn't see her anymore? After he'd ordered you to stop seeing her and you flatly refused, is that when he told you Eden's your sister?"

"She'll never have what we have, baby. Not with her current guy or anyone else. She's too tough to allow herself to feel, isn't that right, Detective? Or are you just scared?"

She didn't react to his words, not outwardly anyway. Inside, they cut deep, exposing a deep, gaping wound. "What did that moment feel like, Logan? All your plans and dreams crashing in around you? Like you couldn't catch your breath? Like a part of you was dying?"

"Poor Rick, he doesn't know yet that he's too nice for you. Way too nice. But you already know that, don't you?"

"This isn't about me," she said through gritted teeth. "It's about you and what an amoral scumbag you are. Just like your old man."

"Then arrest me." He stretched out his arms. "I'm here, cuff me. Take me in." When she didn't move, he made a sound of disdain. "You can't, because you've got nothing. Nada. Go, leave us alone."

Quinn looked at the other woman. "What do you want me to do, Eden?"

She bit her bottom lip, looked at Logan. "What difference would two days make? We don't want this hanging over us."

Logan grasped her hands in his, brought them to his mouth. "You're my person, Grace. And I'm yours. We're meant to be together."

He reached into his jacket pocket and pulled out a red leather box. He opened it and held it out: an amazing diamond glittered against the ivory silk lining. "I wanted to do this when we were in Portugal, away from all this, but—"

He got on one knee. "Will you marry me, Grace?"

"Oh, my God." Eden looked from the ring to Quinn, then at Logan. There were tears in her eyes. "I don't know what to say."

"Ask him why he's doing this now," Quinn said quickly, knowing the clock wasn't on her side. "Ask yourself why he's hurrying you out of the country. What doesn't he want you to find out?"

She saw a muscle jump in Logan's jaw, the sheen of sweat on his upper lip. Time to go in for the kill. "Don't you find it creepy that he adored you when you were a baby, and he still does? He even calls you 'baby.' That's obsession not love."

He got to his feet, handsome face contorting. "Shut up!"

"You sent the breadcrumbs, you're the only one who could have. Which means you knew who Eden was, you knew where she lived, and that Angela was dead. How did you know Angela was dead, Logan?"

"If you don't shut up, I swear to God I'll—"

"What? Kill me like you killed Eden's mom, Angela?"

A raw sound passed Eden's lips.

"She's lying, baby, I promise you." He had her hands, he was kissing them. "I'm not a killer."

"This afternoon, at Pour, I lifted a print from your wine glass. Before I came here, I sent it to Detective Rhea at the Dekalb P.D. Show Eden what your word is worth, change those flights. Or maybe you're not that confident anymore?"

He flinched, ever-so-slightly, but enough for Eden to feel it and free her hands, her expression one of horrified disbelief.

When she spoke, the words sounded as if from the pit of her stomach. "Did you do it? Did you kill my mother?"

Quinn prepared herself. Logan's fight-or-flight response had kicked in: elevated heart and respiratory rate, increased perspiration, flushed face and dilated pupils.

This cornered animal would fight. But she had to wait for him to make the first move.

Reassured by the weight of her gun nestled in the belly holster, she took another swing. "Of course, he did it. Look at the way he's sweating. He sent the breadcrumbs, and paid the kid to place the flyer on my windshield, he killed your mom. He did it all to get you back to New Orleans. Then, to ensure you stayed by his side, he killed his own father. Through it all he lied to you. Is that who you want to be with, Eden?"

He lunged at her, face twisted with hatred. Quinn went for her weapon but was a second too late. He slammed her against the wall, his hands around her throat.

"You couldn't stop, couldn't leave well enough alone! You've ruined everything!"

She had prepared for his attack, but his desperation gave him a bigger advantage than she had expected. She saw stars; heard Eden scream for him to stop.

She couldn't get to her sidearm, but managed to extend her arms, forcing him to loosen his grip. She gulped a lungful of air and twisted free, delivering a hammer blow to the back of his neck.

He grunted in pain, but came back after her, managing to knock her off balance. She crashed into the side table, righted herself and went for her gun.

Her hand closed over the grip. "I don't want to shoot you! Back down now!"

With a howl of rage, he rammed her, knocking her to the floor. Her gun flew from her hand, skittering across the wooden floor. In the next instant he was straddling her, hands around her throat once more.

"My old man was a lying, murderous piece of shit. Why do you care if I killed him? I did you a fucking favor!"

Ten seconds. That's all she had until he incapacitated her. Quinn fought him, managing to briefly loosen his hands and suck in air before he clamped down again.

"What're going to do now, you crazy bitch? You going to leave it alone now?"

"Get off her!" The shout came from Eden, standing over them with the gun, tears rolling down her cheeks. "I swear to God I'll shoot you!"

His grip loosened, and Quinn seized the opening, breaking his hold and sending him toppling backward with a kick to his solar plexus.

A moment later she on her feet, working to steady herself. "Give me the gun, Eden."

"No." She didn't take her gaze from Logan.

Quinn gentled her voice, held out her hand for the weapon. "You don't want to do this, Eden."

"You're wrong about that. This is *my* story."

"Grace, baby—"

"Don't call me that. Not now."

"I only wanted us to be together."

"No more lies." Her voice hardened. "That's what we promised each other. I want the truth, all of it."

Quinn noted the steadiness of her voice, the confidence of her grip on the gun, her intent gaze. Eden had transformed from an emotional wreck to a woman on a mission.

"When did you know?" she demanded. "That we were brother and sister?"

Not if, Quinn noted, but when.

"I found out right before his last stint in the hospital. I shared about us . . . that's when he told me." His voice deepened. "You can't imagine how it felt, the woman I love, who I'd moved heaven and earth to be with . . . my sister? In that moment I hated him more than I ever had."

"Actually," Eden said, voice ice cold, "I think I can imagine. Go on."

"I promised him I'd stop seeing you. That his secret was safe with me." His voice turned bitter. "His secrets had been safe with me for a long time, though he didn't know it. The first time he went into the hospital for surgery, we didn't know how it would come out. In case he died, he gave me the combination to his safe and shared the location of his safety deposit box and key. There was a letter in there for me, he said. One that would explain everything and tell me how to proceed. Then he made me promise not to use the information unless he died."

"But you were curious," Quinn murmured.

"Very. Ironically, even though he'd always been secretive about his finances and what he actually did for the Hudsons, what drove me to break my promise was the letter. I had to know what it said."

Quinn agreed. "Considering his secrets, ironic indeed."

He looked pleadingly at Eden. "I never thought of my dad as a thug. I knew he was slick, not afraid to bend the rules and test the limits of the law, but I didn't think he broke them. When I found the gun in his home safe, I was shocked. He'd never mentioned owning one, which I thought was weird, but since so many people own them, it was easy enough to explain away."

He paused, grimacing as he prepared for what came next. "It was the safety deposit box that rocked my world. I had no idea what they'd—" His voice cracked. "—done. Never even suspected. I was devastated."

"The tapes were in the box?" Eden asked, voice trembling for the first time.

"Yes."

Quinn jumped in. "All of them?"

He nodded. "I listened to every minute of each recording. That's when I started to hate him."

"Because they took Grace from you," Quinn said.

"Yes. And Cynthia. She was more a mother to me than my own. Much more. I couldn't forgive any of them. He didn't have to cover for them. He could have been a hero instead of a villain." He stretched out a hand toward Eden. "I thought you were dead. I thought Dad had followed orders."

"When did you realize I was alive?"

"When Angela called." His voice shook slightly. "I overheard him talking, and the memory of that visit we'd made to Dekalb came crashing back."

"You were the one waiting in the car."

"I was. Dad and I were in Chicago, doing a father-son thing and checking out the graduate programs at Northwestern and U Chicago. Dad sprang the side-trip to pay a visit to an old friend on me while we were there. I remembered Angela Riley, remembered how she'd lost her daughter."

"You weren't sleeping, you saw me."

"I did and I asked him about you. He said that Angela had married and had another daughter. I had no reason not to believe him."

"Until you heard him on the phone."

"He called her Angie and mentioned something about dangerous people still being a threat to Eden."

"My knees went weak. Eden was dead. I was there when it happened. That's when I began to suspect what he'd done." Hand still out, took a step towards her. "I began to believe you were alive."

"It's all been a lie." Eden said. "How we met, falling in love, all of it."

He took another step closer to her. "No, baby . . . sweetheart . . . I had to make *us* happen, but our love is real."

"How can you say that? People fall in love. They're not schemed into loving someone."

He flinched as if she had struck him.. "It's still love, and what we feel for each other is real."

"Don't come any closer." She firmed her grip on the gun. "I have one more question and you know what it is."

"We'll live in Portugal, by the beach. It'll be perfect. Just you and me."

"Did you kill my mother, Logan?"

"She didn't want us to be together. She didn't understand."

A whimper escaped her. "She was the most important person in the world to me."

"That was another life, baby. You have me now."

"You son-of-a-bitch! I hate you now, I—"

"Sweetheart, don't say that." He shook his head, expression wounded, as if he was the one who had been betrayed. "You love me, you always have. We were meant to be—"

Quinn wasn't certain which came first, Logan's advance or the bullet exploding from the barrel. It struck him in the chest, and he stopped cold, close enough he could reach his hand out and take the gun. Instead, he lurched forward and wrapped his arms around her in a bear hug.

"—together. Me and you, Grace. That's the way—"

Hysterical, she fired again. His body jerked at the impact, but he still didn't let her go. "—forever . . . you and—"

With the third shot, he finally released her. As he went down, Grace's name formed on his lips.

EIGHTY-TWO

9:45 A.M. *Three months later.*

"Ready?" Rick asked.

Quinn took one last glance in the mirror. She wore her full-dress uniform—dark jacket and trousers, crisply pressed dress shirt, authorized tie with star and crescent tack. She'd managed to tame her curls so the Garrison cap perched perfectly atop her head.

She smiled. "I am."

In a little over an hour, in a solemn ceremony attended by all the department brass as well as the Mayor, her dad was receiving two posthumous medals, one of commendation and the other a purple heart, the latter for having lost his life in the pursuit of justice.

Nothing else really mattered. None of it. Not that in the same ceremony she, too, would receive a medal of commendation. Not the continuing antics of the Hudsons' team of lawyers, not the fact that Eden's story had been optioned by Netflix for a limited series, which she was going to help write; not the media attention, or her and Rick's decision to move in together.

Today her dad's reputation would be restored. For all time,

Detective Rourke Conners would be recognized as a hero and one of the NOPD's finest.

Between her and Eden's matching statements, the crime scene and the bruises on her neck, Eden hadn't been charged in Logan's death. One of Logan's fingerprints matched one lifted from the Angela Riley scene, further confirming their version of events and sealing the deal.

Quinn joined Rick on the front porch and together they headed to his car. For several minutes they rode in silence, then he broke it.

"You're quiet," he said.

"Eden will be there."

"That's nice. Right?"

"Right." She looked out the side window, watching New Orleans roll by. "I keep thinking about that night."

"Which one?"

"The night she shot Logan. I wish I'd done things differently. I should have gotten the gun away from her. It was my weapon; I should have been in control of it."

"You're too hard on yourself. Besides, you were reprimanded for it. Let it go."

She rubbed the bridge of her nose, at the tension that settled in that spot every time she thought of that night. "I hate that along with everything else Eden's had to deal with, she has his death hanging over her head."

He reached across the seat, squeezed her hand. "And *you* don't have enough to deal with?"

"It's my job."

He didn't get it, and that was okay; she appreciated his support. Lacing her fingers with his, she let out a long, deeply held breath. "I'll never have another case like that one."

"You hope."

"I didn't say that." At his expression, she laughed. "You know me, I can't leave well enough alone."

He grinned and his eyes crinkled at the corners in the way she loved. "I guess I'm going to have to stock up on ice cream?"

The Sheraton came into view. Quinn saw that the local news stations had already arrived, and it looked as if Eden was holding court in front of the hotel. Mikey was there as well, chatting with Dobby and Cherie.

She met Rick's eyes and smiled. "Yeah, I guess you are."

ALSO BY ERICA SPINDLER

The LOOK-ALIKE

THE OTHER GIRL

THE FIRST WIFE

JUSTICE FOR SARA

WATCH ME DIE

BLOOD VINES

BREAKNECK

LAST KNOWN VICTIM

COPYCAT

SEE JANE DIE

IN SILENCE

DEAD RUN

BONE COLD

ALL FALL DOWN

CAUSE FOR ALARM

FORTUNE

FORBIDDEN FRUIT

RED

The Lightkeepers series

RANDOM ACTS (prequel)

THE FINAL SEVEN

TRIPLE SIX

FALLEN FIVE

CPSIA information can be obtained
at www.ICGtesting.com
Printed in the USA
BVHW032050200322
631960BV00011B/319/J